THE COP, THE PUPPY AND ME

BY
CARA COLTER

MILLS & BOON

First published in Great Britain 2012
by Mills & Boon, an imprint of Harlequin (UK) Limited,
Eton House, 18-24 Paradise Road, Richmond, Surrey TW9 1SR

© Cara Colter 2012

ISBN: 978 0 263 89429 5
ebook ISBN: 978 1 408 97102 4

923-0512

Harlequin (UK) policy is to use papers that are natural, renewable and recyclable products and made from wood grown in sustainable forests. The logging and manufacturing processes conform to the legal environmental regulations of the country of origin.

Printed and bound in Spain
by Blackprint CPI, Barcelona

Sarah told herself it was a hello kind of kiss—a door opening, something beginning between them.

That was what she thought she tasted on his lips: realness and strength and the utter spring freshness of new beginning. When his lips left hers she opened her eyes reluctantly.

He took a step back from her and she read a different truth entirely in his eyes. They were suddenly both shadowed and shuttered.

It hadn't been hello at all. It had been goodbye.

Then Sullivan straightened and smiled slightly— that cynical my-heart-is-made-of-stone smile.

"Sarah," he said softly, "you've got your hands full trying to save this town. Don't you even try to save me."

Then he turned and walked through his open door. He was alone, even though the puppy was with him. He was the gunfighter leaving town. Not needing anyone or anything. Not a woman and not a dog.

Dear Reader,

I am a technophobe. My six-year-old grandson shows me how to use our DVD player. Smartphones make me cringe. I finally have a cellphone, but my message says, 'Don't leave a message.' It's not because I'm unfriendly! It's because I leave the phone for days at a time, gathering dust in a corner.

I don't text or Twitter. My website became glitchy months ago, meaning I can't update it and I don't get mail from you. The designer has gone AWOL and I don't have a clue what to do next!

Imagine my surprise when I discovered I *love* Facebook. It's such an immediate, simple and lovely way of having contact with you! Readers helped me name the hero and his two nephews in this story. So please come and join the fun. You can find me at Cara Colter, Author. I can't wait to hear from you!

With warmest wishes,

Cara

Cara Colter lives on an acreage in British Columbia, with her partner Rob and eleven horses. She has three grown children and a grandson. She is a recent recipient of the *Romantic Times* Career Achievement Award in the 'Love and Laughter' category. Cara loves to hear from readers, and you can contact her or learn more about her through her website: www.cara-colter.com

To Rob (again) who loves me through it all.

CHAPTER ONE

OLIVER SULLIVAN—who had been called only Sullivan for so long he hardly remembered his first name—decided he disliked Sarah McDougall just about as much as he'd ever disliked anyone.

And he'd disliked a lot of people.

Meeting dislikable people was a hazard of choosing law enforcement as a profession, not that Ms. McDougall fell into the criminal category.

"Though I have dealt with criminals who were more charming," he muttered to himself. Of course, with criminals he had the advantage of having some authority over them.

All this naked dislike, and Sullivan had yet to even speak to her. His encounters had all been filtered through his voice mail. He'd never seen her, let alone met her, and he would have been only too happy to keep it that way.

But she'd gone to his boss.

Her voice on the phone had been enough to stir his dislike of her and her bulldog-like persistence had cemented it.

Not that her voice was *grating*. It was what she wanted from him that was the problem.

Call me back.

Please.

It's so important.

We have to talk.

Mr. Sullivan, this is urgent.

When he'd managed to totally ignore her, she'd eventually gone to his boss. Sullivan mulled that over with aggravation. Which was worse? The fact that she had gone to his boss? Or the fact that his boss had *ordered* him to comply?

At least go talk to her, the chief had said. *In case you haven't figured it out, you're not in Detroit anymore.*

Oh, Sullivan had figured that out. In about his first five minutes on his new job.

Being a cop in small-town Wisconsin was about as different from being a homicide detective in Detroit as Attila the Hun was different from being Mother Theresa.

"What moment of insanity made me choose Kettle Bend, Wisconsin?" he growled.

Of course his moment of insanity had a name, and her name was Della, his older sister, who had discovered this little pocket of American charm and chosen to come here with her orthodontist husband, Jonathon, to raise her two boys. She'd been trying to convince Sullivan to join their happy family ever since his whole life had gone sideways.

Sullivan shook that off, focused on the town instead. He took in the streets around him with a jaundiced eye.

It looked like the kind of town Walt Disney or Norman Rockwell would have imagined, wide, quiet streets, shaded by enormous trees that he, hard-bitten product of some of Detroit's worst neighborhoods, had no hope of identifying.

Still, there was no missing the newness of the leaves, unfurling in those tender and vibrant shades of spring, the sharp, tangy scent of their newness tickling his nose through his open car window.

Nestled comfortably in the leafy shade were tidy houses, wearing their age and their American flags with equal pride. The houses, for the most part, had a pleasant sameness about them. White with pale yellow trim, or pale yellow with white trim, the odd sage-green and or dove-gray thrown into the mix.

All had deep porches, white picket fences around postage-stamp yards, splashes of spring color in the flower beds lining walkways that welcomed.

But Sullivan refused to be charmed.

He disliked illusions, and he knew this particular illusion to be the most dangerous: that there were places left in the world that were entirely safe and uncomplicated, porch swings and fireflies, cold lemonade on hot summer afternoons.

That there was a place where doors and windows were unlocked, where children rode their bikes unescorted and unafraid to school, where families laughed over board games. That there were places of unsullied innocence, places that whispered the word *home*. He kept trying to warn Della all was probably not as it appeared.

No, behind the windows and doors of those perfect and pretty houses, Sullivan was willing to bet he would uncover all kinds of secrets that belied the picture he was seeing. Behind some of those closed doors were probably booze bottles hidden down toilet tanks. A kid with a crack problem. Unexplained bruises and black eyes.

It was this cynicism that was making him a poor fit for Kettle Bend.

Certainly a poor fit for Sarah McDougall's plans for him.

Her message on his voice mail chimed through his head, making him shudder. *We need a hero, Mr. Sullivan.*

He wasn't about to be anybody's hero. This wasn't how he wanted to be spending his day off. He was about to make one Sarah McDougall very, very sorry she'd gone after this bear in his den.

Checking addresses as he went, Sullivan finally pulled over, stepped out of his car and steeled himself against the sleepy appeal of the street he found himself on. On principle, he rolled up his car window and locked his door. The people of Kettle Bend might want to pretend nothing bad ever happened here, but he wasn't going to trust his new car stereo to that notion.

Then he turned to look at the house that sat at 1716 Lilac Lane.

The house differed from its neighbors very little. It was a shingle-sided, single-story bungalow, painted recently—white, naturally—the trim a deep, crisp shade of olive. Vines—he guessed ivy because that was the only name of a vine that he knew—showed signs of new growth, and would shade the wide porch completely in the heat of summer.

Sullivan passed through an outrageously squeaking gate and under an arbor that he knew would drip the color and fragrance of climbing roses in a few more weeks.

He shrugged off the relief it was not happening now, as if there was something about all this charm that was nattering away at his defenses—not like a battering ram, more like an irritating humming, like being pestered by mosquitoes. The scent of roses would have been just one more thing to add to it.

Peripherally, he made note that the concrete walkway was heaved in places, but lined with an odd variety of spring flowers—deep purple, with a starburst yellow interior.

He noticed only because that was what he did.

Sullivan noticed *everything*. Every detail. It made him a great cop. It hadn't helped him be a better human being, as far as he could tell.

He went up the wide stairs to the front door, crossed the shaded porch to it. Before he rang the bell, he studied the outdoor furnishings.

Old wicker chairs, carefully painted the same olive-green as the house trim, held impossibly cheerful plump cushions, with red and yellow and orange flowers in the pattern. Just as the town painted a picture, so did this porch.

A place of rest. Of comfort. Of safety. Of peace.

"Ha," Sullivan snorted cynically, but was aware of setting his shoulders more firmly against the buzzing of all the pesky details working at convincing him he could maybe try letting this woman down softly. He could try being a nice guy.

"Ha," he said again. So far, subtleness had not worked on her. When you phoned a person sixty-two times and they didn't return your calls that did not mean, *Go to the boss.*

It meant, *Get lost. Go away. Find yourself another hero.*

He turned deliberately away from the invitation of the porch, not prepared to admit for even one small moment, a fraction of a second, that he had imagined himself accepting the invitation.

Rest.

He shook his head, and turned to the door, found the bell—a key type that needed to be turned—and twisted it.

The exterior door was a screen door, white with elaborate carvings around the edges framing the oval of the screen in the middle. The green interior door was open, and he could hear the bell echo through the house.

No one answered, but he figured leaving a door hanging open was an invitation, plain and simple, for prying eyes.

So, unlike the invitation to rest, he took this one, peering in at the house.

The door opened directly into the living room, though a handmade rag rug designated a tiny entry area, and suggested the owner liked order—and wiped feet.

Afternoon sunlight spilled through the open door and through the picture window, slanting across wood floors that were golden with the patina of age.

Two small couches, a shade of sunshine-yellow that matched the interior of the flowers that marched up the front walk, faced each other over a scarred antique coffee table. Again, there was a sense of order: neatly stacked magazines and a vase of those flowers that had lined the walkway, dipping low on slender stems.

Sullivan had not formed a mental picture of his stalker.

Now he did. Single. No evidence—and there was always evidence—of a man in residence.

No children, because there was no sign of toys or mess, though his eyes caught on a wall of framed magazine covers, hung gallery-style, just inside that front door.

They were all covers from a magazine called *Today's Baby*.

They did nothing to change his initial impression of her. *No life.*

Sullivan was willing to bet the resident of this house was as frumpy as her house was cute. She was no doubt a few pounds too heavy, with frizzy hair and bad makeup, busy making her house look pretty as a picture while she fell into middle-aged decline.

Now that there was nothing left to do on her house—obviously it was magazine photo shoot ready—she'd turned her attention to the town.

Mr. Sullivan, Kettle Bend needs you!

Yeah, right. Kettle Bend needed Oliver Sullivan the way Oliver Sullivan needed a toothache.

He could smell something faintly, drifting through that open door. The scent was sweet. And tart. Home cooking. The sudden, sharp feeling of yearning took him totally by surprise.

He felt it again, like a whisper along his spine.

Rest.

Again, he shook it off, along with annoying yearnings. He *had* rested. For a whole year. Tying flies and wearing hip waders. It wasn't for him. Too much time for thinking.

Sullivan rang the bell again, impatiently this time.

A cat, a gray puffball with evil green eyes slid out of a hallway, plunked itself in the ray of sunshine and regarded him with slitted dislike, before dismissing him with a lift of its paw and a delicate lick. The cat fit his picture of her life *exactly*.

Still, that cat *knew* he didn't like animals.

Which was what made the whole situation that had gotten him to this front door even more irritating. A hero? He didn't even like dogs. And so he didn't want to answer the question—not from her and not from the dozens of other reporters and TV stations that were hounding him—why he had risked his life for one.

Sullivan gave the handle of the screen door a firm tug, let the door squeak open a noisy inch or two before releasing it to snap shut again.

Come on. An unlocked door?

It made him feel grim. And determined.

This cozy little world was practically begging for a healthy dose of what he had in abundance.

Cynicism.

He backed off the steps and stood regarding the house.

"She's in the back. Sarah's left that rhubarb a bit too long."

Sullivan started. See? It *had* gotten to him. His guard had been down just enough not to notice that his every move was being monitored by the next-door-neighbor. She was a wizened gnome, ensconced in a deep Adirondack chair.

From under a tuft of cotton-ball hair, her bright black marble eyes regarded him with amused curiosity rather than the deep suspicion a stranger *should* be regarded with.

"You're the new policeman," she said.

So, he wasn't a stranger. There was no anonymity in a small town. Not even on your day off, in jeans and a T-shirt.

He nodded, still a little taken aback by how trust was automatically instilled in him just because he was the new cop on the block.

In Detroit, nine times out of ten, the exact opposite had been true, at least in the hard neighborhoods where he had plied his trade.

"Nice thing you did. With that dog."

Was there one single person on the face of the earth who didn't know? Sullivan was beginning to hate the expression *gone viral* more than any other.

She wouldn't think it was so nice if she knew how often since then he just wished he'd let the damn thing go down the river, raging with spring runoff, instead of jumping in after it.

He thought of it wriggling against him as he lay on the shore of the river afterward, gasping for breath. The puppy, soaked, another layer of freezing on top of his own freezing, had curled up on his exposed skin, right on top of his heart, whimpering and licking him.

Sullivan knew he didn't really wish that he hadn't gone in after it. He just wished that he wished it. And that a person with the cell phone had not recorded his leap into the swollen Kettle River and then posted it on the internet where it seemed the whole world had seen it.

"How is the dog?" she asked.

"Still at the vet," he answered, "but he's going to be fine."

"Has anyone claimed him yet?"

"No."

"Well, I'm sure there will be a long lineup of people who want to adopt him if his owner doesn't show up."

"Oh, yeah," he agreed.

Because of the video, the Kettle Bend Police Department was fielding a dozen calls a day about that dog.

Sullivan followed the narrow concrete path where it curved around the side of the house and then led him down a passageway between houses. Then the path opened into a long, narrow backyard.

There was no word for it.

Except perhaps *enchanting*.

For a moment he stood, breathing it all in: waxy leaves; mature trees; curving flower beds whose dark mounding loam met the crisp edge of freshly cut grass.

There was a sense of having entered a grotto, deeply private.

Sacred.

Sullivan snorted at himself, but a little uneasily this time.

He saw her then.

Crouched beside a fence lined with rows of vigorously growing, elephant-eared plants.

She was totally engrossed in what she was doing,
yanking at the thin red stalks of the huge-leafed plants.

It must be the rhubarb her neighbor had mentioned.

She already had a stack of it beside her. Her face was
hidden in the shade of a broad-brimmed hat, the light
catching her mouth, where her tongue was caught between her teeth in concentration.

She was wearing a shapeless flowered tank top and
white shorts, smudged with dirt, but the long line of
strong legs, already beginning to tan, took his breath
away.

As he watched, she tugged vigorously on one of
the plants. When the stalk parted with the ground, she
nearly catapulted over backward. When she righted herself, she went very still, as if she knew, suddenly, she
was not alone.

Without getting up, she pivoted slowly on the heels
of her feet and looked at him, her head tilted quizzi-
cally, possibly aggrieved that he had caught her in a
wrestling match with the plant.

Sarah McDougall, if this was her, was certainly not
middle-aged. Or frizzy-haired. She was wearing no
makeup at all. The feeling of his breath being taken
away was complete.

Corkscrew auburn curls escaped from under the brim
of her hat and framed an elfin face. A light scattering
of freckles danced across a daintily snubbed nose. Her
cheekbones and her chin mirrored that image of deli-
cacy.

But it was her eyes that threatened to undo him. He
was good at this: at reading eyes. It was harder than
people thought. A liar could look you straight in the

face without blinking. A murderer could have eyes that looked as soft as suede, as gentle as a fawn's.

But eleven years working one of the toughest homicide squads in the world had honed Sullivan's skills to a point that his sister called him, not without a hint of admiration, scary in his ability to detect what was real about a person.

This woman's eyes were huge and hazel, and stunningly, slayingly gorgeous.

She was, obviously, the all-American girl. Wholesome. Sweet. Probably ridiculously naive.

Case in point: she left her door unlocked and wanted to make *him* a hero!

But instead of that fueling his annoyance at her, instead of remembering his fury that she had called his boss, Sullivan felt a surge of foolish protectiveness.

"You should lock your front door when you work back here," he told her gruffly. Part of him wanted to leave it at that, to turn his back and walk away from her. Because obviously what a girl like that needed to be protected from most was a guy like him.

Who had seen so much darkness it felt as if it had taken up residence inside of him. Darkness that could snuff out the radiance that surrounded her like a halo.

Still, if he left without giving her an opportunity to see that in him, she might pester him, or his boss, endlessly.

So he forced himself to cross the yard until he stood above her, until his shadow passed over the wideness of those eyes.

He rarely shook hands. Keep the barriers up. Establish authority. Don't invite familiarity. Keep your distance.

So it startled him when he wanted to extend a hand to her.

"Sarah McDougall?" he asked, and at her wide-eyed nod, "I'm Sullivan."

The aggrieved look faded from her face. She actually looked thrilled! He was glad he had shoved his hand in his pocket instead of holding it out to her.

"Mr. Sullivan," she said, and scrambled to her feet. "I'm so glad you came. May I call you Oliver?"

"No, you may not. No one calls me Oliver. And it's not Mister," he said, his voice deliberately cold. "It's Officer."

A touch of wariness tinged her gaze. Hadn't she been able to tell from her unanswered pleas that he was a man who deserved her wariness?

"No one calls you Oliver?"

What was she asking that question for? Hadn't he made it eminently clear there was going to be nothing personal between them, not even an invitation to use first names?

"No." His voice had a bit of a snap to it.

Which she clearly did not recognize, or she would have had the sense to back away from the subject.

"Not even your mother?" She raised a skeptical eyebrow. Her looking skeptical was faintly comical, like a budgie bird trying to look aggressive.

"Dead," he snapped. He could see sympathy crowding her eyes, and there was no way he was allowing all that softness to spill out and touch him. His mother had died when he was seventeen years old.

And his father.

Seventeen years ago was a place he did not revisit.

There was no sense her misconstruing his reasons for being here, and there was only one way to approach a person like this.

Brutal bluntness.

"Don't call me anymore," he said, holding her gaze, his voice deliberately low and flat. "I'm not helping you. Not if you call six million times. I'm not any kind of hero. I don't want to be your friend. I don't want to save your town. And don't call my boss again, either. Because you don't want me to be your enemy."

Sullivan saw, astonished at his failure, that his legendary people-reading skills were slightly off-kilter. Because he had thought she would be easily intimidated, that he could make her back down, just like that.

Instead he saw that cute little mouth reset itself in a line that was unmistakably stubborn and that could mean only one thing for him.

Trouble.

Sarah stared up at her unexpected visitor, caught off balance, not just by her tug-of-war with her rhubarb, but also by the fact she'd had a witness to it!

Add to that his unexpected sharpness of tone, his appearance in her yard, his appearance, period, and her feeling of being unbalanced grew.

She'd been totally engrossed in wresting the rhubarb from the ground. Which was what she needed from her house, her yard, her garden and her work.

There was always something that needed to be done, the hard work unending. But her total focus on what she'd been doing had left her vulnerable. Though Sarah suspected that even if you had been expecting this man, had laid out tea things and put on a presentable dress, the feeling you would have when you experienced the rawness of his presence would be one of vulnerability.

The grainy video she had seen—along with millions of other people—had not really prepared her for the reality of him. Though she had already figured out from her unanswered calls that he was not exactly going to be the kind of guy the heroic rescue of a drowning puppy had her wanting him to be.

From thirty seconds of film, from him ripping off his shirt and jumping into the icy water just past where the Kettle River ran under the bridge in downtown Kettle Bend, to lying on the bank after, the pup snuggled into the pebbled flesh of his naked chest, she had jumped to conclusions.

He was courageous. That much was in his eyes. A man afraid of nothing.

But she had thought—a man willing to risk his life for a dog, after all—that he would be gentle and warm.

If his message on his voice mail had been a touch abrupt, she had managed to dismiss that as part of his professional demeanor. But then the fact that he had not returned her increasingly desperate calls?

And now he had been downright rude to her.

Plus, there was nothing warm in those dark eyes. They were cool, assessing. There was a wall so high in them it would be easier to scale Everest.

Sarah felt a quiver of doubt. The reality of Oliver Sullivan versus the fantasy she had been nursing since she had first seen the clip of him did not bode well for her plan, unless he could be tamed, and from looking at him that seemed highly unlikely!

Sullivan was dressed casually, dark denims, a forest-green T-shirt that molded the fullness of his chest, the hard mounds of firm biceps. A hundred other guys in Kettle Bend were wearing the same thing today, but she bet none of them radiated the raw potency that practically shivered in the spring sunshine around him.

He looked like a warrior wearing the disguise of a more civilized man.

He was one of those men who radiated a subtle confidence in his own strength, in his ability to handle whatever came up. It was as if he was ready and waiting for all hell to break loose.

Which was so utterly at odds with the atmosphere in her garden that it might have made her smile, except there was something about the stripping intensity of his expression that made her gulp instead.

Despite astonishing good looks, he had the expression of a man unutterably world-weary, a man who expected the absolute worst from people, and was rarely disappointed.

Still, he *was* unnervingly good-looking. If she could talk him into doing some TV interviews, the camera would love his dark, chocolate hair, short and neat, slashing brows over eyes so dark brown they could have been mistaken for black. He had a strong nose, good cheekbones, wide sensual lips and a devilish little cleft in his chin.

She could not allow herself the luxury of being intimidated by him.

She just couldn't.

Kettle Bend needed him.

Not that she wanted to be thinking of him in the same sentence as the word *need*.

Because he was the kind of man who made a woman aware of things—*needs*—she was sure she had laid to rest.

He was the kind of man whose masculinity was so potent it could make a woman ache for things she had once had, and had no longer. Fevered kisses. Strong arms. Laughter in the night.

He was the kind of man who could almost make a woman entirely forget the terrible price, the pain that you could invite by looking for those things.

Sarah McDougall didn't need anyone looking out for her, thank you very much! It was one of the things she prided herself on.

Fierce independence.

Not needing anyone. Not anymore. Not ever again.

Inheriting this house, and her grandmother's business, Jelly Jeans and Jammies, had allowed her that.

She could *not* back down from him! So, with more confidence than she felt, in defiance of his hostility, she whipped the gardening glove off her hand, wiped it on her shorts just in case, and extended it to him.

Then she held her breath waiting to see if he would take it.

CHAPTER TWO

OFFICER Oliver Sullivan looked at Sarah's extended hand, clearly annoyed at her effort to make some kind of contact with him.

She knew he debated just walking away now that he had delivered his unfriendly message.

But he didn't. With palpable reluctance, he accepted her hand, and his shake was brief and hard. She kept her face impassive at the jolt that surged, instantaneously, from her fingertips to her elbow. It would be easy to think of rough whiskers scraping a soft cheek, the smell of skin out of the shower.

Easy, too, to feel the tiniest little thrill that her life had had this unexpected moment thrust into it.

Sarah reminded herself, sternly, that her life was full and rich and complete.

She had inherited her grandmother's house in this postcard-pretty town. With it had come a business that provided her a livelihood and that had pulled her back from the brink of despair when her engagement had ended.

Kettle Bend had given her something she had not thought she would ever have again, and that she now could appreciate as that rarest of commodities: contentment.

Okay, in her more honest moments, Sarah knew it was not complete contentment. Sometimes, she felt a little stir of restlessness, a longing for her old life. Not her romance with Michael Talbot. No, sir, she was so over her fiancé's betrayal of her trust, *so* over him.

No, it was elements of her old life as a writer on the popular New York–based *Today's Baby* magazine that created that nebulous longing, that called to her. She had regularly met and interviewed new celebrity moms and dads, been invited to glamorous events, been a sought-after guest at store openings and other events. She had loved being creative.

A man like the one who stood in front of her posed a danger. He could turn a small longing for *something*—excitement, fulfillment—into a complete catastrophe.

Sarah reminded herself, sternly and firmly, that she had already found a solution for her nebulous longings; she was going to chase away her restlessness with a new challenge, a huge one that would occupy her completely. Her new commitment was going to be to the little community that was fading around her.

Her newfound efforts at contentment relied on getting this town back to the way she remembered it being during her childhood summers spent here: vital, the streets overflowing with seasonal visitors, a feeling of endless summer, a hopeful vibrancy in the air.

So, handshake completed, Sarah crossed her arms over her chest, a thin defense against some dark promise—or maybe threat—that swirled like electricity in the air around him.

She wanted him to think she was not rattled.

"I have a great plan for Kettle Bend," she told him. She had interviewed some of the most sought-after people in the world. She would not be intimidated by him. "And you can help make it happen."

He regarded her long and hard, and then the tiniest of smiles tickled the corner of that sinfully sensuous mouth.

She thought she had him. Then...

"No," he said. Simple. Firm. Unshakable, the smile gone from the corner of that mouth as if it had never been.

"But you haven't even heard what I have to say!" Sarah sputtered indignantly.

He actually seemed to consider that for a moment, though his deeply weary sigh was not exactly encouraging.

"Okay," he said after a moment, those dark eyes shielded, unreadable. "Spit it out."

Spit it out? As an invitation to communication, it was somewhat lacking. On the other hand, at least he wasn't walking away. Yet. But his body language indicated the thread that held him here, in her yard, was thin.

"The rescue of the dog was incredible. So courageous."

He failed to look flattered, seemed to be leaning a little more toward the exit, so she rushed on. "I've seen it on the internet."

His expression darkened even more—if that was possible—so she didn't add that she had watched it more than a dozen times, feeling foolishly compelled to watch it again and again for reasons she didn't quite understand.

But she did understand that she was not the only one. The video had captured hearts around the world. As she saw it, the fact he was standing in her yard meant that she had an opportunity to capitalize on that magic ingredient that was drawing people by the thousands to that video.

"I know you haven't been in Kettle Bend very long," Sarah continued. "Didn't you know how cold that water was going to be?"

"If I had known how cold that water was going to be, I would have never jumped in."

That was the kind of answer that wouldn't work *at all* in the event she could talk him into being a participant in her plan to use his newfound notoriety to publicize the town.

Though that possibility seemed more unlikely by the second.

At least he was talking, and not walking.

"You must love dogs," she said, trying, with growing desperation, to find a chink in all that armor.

He didn't answer her, though his chest filled as he drew in a long breath. He ran an impatient hand through the thick, crisp silk of his dark hair.

"What do you want from me?"

Her eyes followed the movement of his hand through his hair, and for a moment the sensation of what she *really* wanted from him nearly swamped her.

Sarah shook it off, an unwanted weakness.

"Your fifteen minutes of fame could be very beneficial to this town," she said, trying, valiantly, and not entirely successfully, not to wonder how his hair would feel beneath her fingertips.

"Whether I like it or not," he commented dryly.

"What's not to like? A few interviews with carefully chosen sources. It would take just the smallest amount of your time," she pressed persuasively.

His look of impatience deepened, and now annoyance layered on top of it. Really, such a sour expression should have made him much less good-looking!

But it didn't.

Still, she tried to focus on the fact that he was still standing here, giving her a chance. Once she explained it all to him, he couldn't help but get on board!

"Do you know what Summer Fest is?" she asked him.

"No. But it sounds perfectly nauseating."

She felt her confidence falter and covered it by glaring at him. Sarah decided cynical was just his default reaction. Who could possibly have anything against summer? Or a festival?

Sarah plunged ahead. "It's a festival for the first four days of July. It starts with a parade and ends with the Fourth of July fireworks. It used to kick off the summer season here in Kettle Bend. It used to set the tone for the whole summer."

She waited for him to ask what had happened, but he only looked bored, raising an eyebrow at her.

"It was canceled, five years ago. The cancellation has been just one more thing that has contributed to Kettle Bend fading away, losing its vibrancy, like a favorite old couch that needs recovering. It's not the same place I used to visit as a child."

"Visit?" It rattled her that he seemed not to be showing the slightest interest in a single word she said, but he picked up on that immediately. "So you're not a local, either?"

Either. A bond between them. *Play it.*

"No, I grew up in New York. But my mother was from here, originally. I used to spend summers. And where are you from? What brings you to Kettle Bend?"

"Momentary insanity," he muttered.

He certainly wasn't giving anything away, but he wasn't walking away, either, so Sarah prattled on, trying to engage him. "This is my grandmother's house. She left it to me when she died. Along with her jam business. Jelly Jeans and Jammies. You might have heard of it. It's very popular around town."

Sarah was not sure she had engaged him. His expression was impossible to read. She had felt encouraged that he showed a slight interest in her. Now, she was suspicious. Sullivan was one of those men who found out things about people, all the while revealing nothing of himself.

"Look, Miss McDougall—"

She noticed he did not use her first name, and knew, despite that brief show of interest, he was keeping his distance from her in every way he could.

"—not that any of this has anything to do with me, but nothing feels or looks the same to an adult as it does to a child."

How had he managed, in a single line, to make her feel hopelessly naive, as if she was chasing something that didn't exist?

What if he was right?

Damn him. That's what these brimming-with-confidence-and-cynicism men did. Made everyone doubt themselves. Their hopes and dreams.

Well, she wasn't giving her hopes and dreams into the care of another man. Michael Talbot had already taught her that lesson, thank you very much.

When she'd first heard the rumor about Mike, her fiancé and editor in chief of *Today's Baby*, and a flirty little freelancer named Trina, Sarah had refused to believe it. But then she had seen them together in a café, something too cozy about the way they were leaning into each other to confirm what she wanted to believe, that Mike and Trina's relationship was strictly business.

Her dreams of a nice little house, filled with babies of her own, had been dashed in a flash.

No accusation, just, *I saw you and Trina today.*

The look of shame that had crossed Mike's face had said it all, without him saying a single word.

Now, Sarah had a replacement dream, so much safer. A town to revitalize.

"Yes, it does have something to do with you!"

"I don't see how."

"Because I've been put in charge of Summer Fest. I've been given one chance to bring it back, to prove how good it is for this town," she explained.

"Good luck with that."

"I've got no budget for promotion. But I bet your phone has been ringing off the hook since the clip of the rescue was shown on the national evening news." She read the answer in his face. "*The A.M. Show, Good Night, America, The Way We See It, Morning Chat with Barb*—they're all calling you, aren't they?"

His arms had now folded across the immenseness of his chest, and he was rocking back on his heels, watching her with narrowed eyes.

"They're begging you for a follow-up," she guessed. She wasn't the only one who had been able to see that this man and that dog would make good television.

"You'll be happy to know I'm not answering their calls, either," he said dryly.

"I am not happy to know that! If you could just say yes to a few interviews and mention the town and Summer Fest. If you could just say how wonderful Kettle Bend is and invite everybody to come for July 1. You could tell them that you're going to be the grand marshal of the parade!"

It had all come out in a blurt.

"The grand marshal of the parade," he repeated, stunned.

She probably should have left that part until later. But then she realized, shocked, he had not repeated his out-and-out no.

He seemed to realize it, too. "No," he said flatly.

She rushed on as if he hadn't spoken. "I don't have a hope of reaching millions of people with no publicity budget. But, Oli—Mr.—Officer Sullivan—you do. You could single-handedly bring Summer Fest back to Kettle Bend!"

"No," he said again, no hesitation this time.

"There is more to being a cop in a small town than arresting poor old Henrietta Delafield for stealing lipsticks from the Kettle Mug and Drug."

"Mug and Drug," he repeated dryly, "that sounds like my old beat in Detroit."

Despite the stoniness of his expression, Sarah allowed herself to feel the smallest stirring of hope. He had a sense of humor! And, he had finally revealed something about himself. He was starting to care for his new town, despite that hard-bitten exterior.

She beamed at him.

He backed away from her.

"Let me think about it," he said with such patent insincerity she could have wept.

Sarah saw it for what it was, an escape mechanism. He was slipping away from her. She had been so sure, all this time, when she'd hounded him with message after message, that when he actually heard her brilliant idea, when he knew how good it would be for the town, he would *want* to do it.

"There's no time to think," she said. "You're the hot topic *now*." She hesitated. "Officer Sullivan, I'm begging you."

"I don't like being impulsive." His tone made it evident he *scorned* being the hot topic and was unmoved by begging.

"But you jumped in the river after that dog. Does it get more impulsive than that?"

"A momentary lapse," he said brusquely. "I said I'll think about it."

"That means no," she said, desolately.

"Okay, then, no."

There was something about the set of his shoulders, the line around his mouth, the look in his eyes that he had made up his mind absolutely. He wasn't *ever* going to think about it, and he wasn't *ever* going to change his mind. She could talk until she was blue in the face, leave four thousand more messages on his voice mail, go to his boss again.

But his mind was made up. Like the wall in his eyes, it would be easier to climb Everest than to change it.

"Excuse me," she said tautly. She bent and picked up her rhubarb, as if it could provide some kind of shield against him, and then shoved by him. She headed for the back door of her house before she did the unthinkable.

You did not cry in front of a man as hard-hearted as that one.

Something in his face, as she glanced back, made her feel as if her disappointment was transparent to him. She was all done being vulnerable. Had she begged? She hoped she hadn't begged!

"You should try the Jelly Jeans and Jammies Crabbies Jelly," she shot over her shoulder at him. "It's made out of crab apples. My grandmother swore it was a cure for crankiness."

She opened her back screen door and let it slam behind her. The back door led into a small vestibule and then her kitchen.

She was greeted by the sharp tang of the batch of rhubarb jam she had made yesterday. Every counter and every surface in the entire kitchen was covered with the rhubarb she needed to make more jam today.

Because this was the time of year her grandmother always made her Spring Fling jam, which she had claimed brought a feeling of friskiness, cured the sourness of old heartaches and brought new hope.

But given the conversation she had just had, and looking at the sticky messes that remained from yesterday, and the mountains of rhubarb that needed to be dealt with today, hope was not exactly what Sarah felt.

And she certainly did not want to think of all the connotations friskiness could have after meeting a man like that one!

Seeing no counter space left, she dumped her rhubarb on the floor and surveyed her kitchen.

All this rhubarb had to be washed. Some of it had already gotten tough and would have to be peeled. It had to be chopped and then cooked, along with all the other top secret ingredients, in a pot so huge Sarah wondered if her grandmother could have possibly acquired it from cannibals. Then, she had to prepare the jars and the labels. Then finally deliver the finished product to all her grandmother's faithful customers.

She felt exhausted just thinking about it. An unguarded thought crept in.

Was this the life she really wanted?

Her grandmother had run this little business until she was eighty-seven years old. She had never seemed overwhelmed by it. Or tired.

Sarah realized she was just having an off moment in her new life.

That was the problem with a man like Oliver Sullivan putting in a surprise appearance in your backyard.

It made you question the kind of life you *really* wanted.

It made you wonder if there were some kinds of lonely no amount of activity—or devotion to a cause—could ever fill.

Annoyed with herself, Sarah stepped over the rhubarb to the cabinet where she kept her telephone book.

Okay. He wasn't going to help her. It was probably a good thing. She had to look at the bright side. Her life would have tangled a bit too much with his had he agreed to use his newfound fame to the good of the town.

She could do it herself.

"WGIV Radio, how can I direct your call?"

"Tally Hukas, please."

After she hung up from talking to Tally, Sarah wondered why she felt the tiniest little tickle of guilt. It was not her job to protect Officer Oliver Sullivan from his own nastiness.

"And so, folks," Sarah's voice came over the radio, in that cheerful tone, "if you can spare some time to help our resurrected Summer Fest be the best ever, give me a call. Remember, Kettle Bend needs you!"

Sullivan snapped off the radio.

He had been so right in his assessment of Sarah McDougall: she was trouble.

This time, she hadn't gone to his boss. Oh, no, she'd gone to the whole town as a special guest on the Tally Hukas radio show, locally produced here in Kettle Bend. She'd lost no time doing it, either. He'd been at her house only yesterday.

Despite that wholesome, wouldn't-hurt-a-flea look of hers, Sarah had lost no time in throwing him under the bus. Announcing to the whole town how she'd had this bright idea to promote the summer festival—namely him—and he'd said no.

Ah, well, the thing she didn't get was that he didn't care if he was the town villain. He would actually be

more comfortable in that role than the one she wanted
him to play!

The thing *he* didn't get was how he had thought about
her long after he'd left her house yesterday. Unless he
was mistaken, there had been tears, three seconds from
being shed, sparkling in her eyes when she had pushed
by him.

But this was something she should know when she
was trying to find a town hero: an unlikely choice was
a man unmoved by tears. In his line of work, he'd seen
way too many of them: following a knock on the door
in the middle of the night; following a confession, out-
pourings of remorse; following that moment when he
presented what he had, and the noose closed. He had
them. No escape.

If you didn't harden your heart to it all, you would
drown in other people's tragedy.

He'd *had* to hurt Sarah. No choice. It was the only
way to get someone like her to back off. Still, hearing
her voice over the radio, he'd tried to stir himself to annoyance.

He was reluctant to admit it was actually something
else her husky tone caused in him.

A faint longing. The same faint longing he had felt
on her porch and when the scent from her kitchen had
tickled his nose.

What *was* that?

Rest.

Sheesh, he was a cop in a teeny tiny town. How much
more restful could it get?

Besides, in his experience, relationships weren't restful. That was the last thing they were! Full of ups and downs, and ins and outs, and highs and lows.

Sullivan had been married once, briefly. It had not survived the grueling demands of his rookie year on the homicide squad. The final straw had been someone inconveniently getting themselves killed when he was supposed to be at his wife's sister's wedding.

He'd come home to an apartment emptied of all her belongings and most of his.

What had he felt at that moment?

Relief.

A sense that now, finally, he could truly give one hundred percent to the career that was more than a job. An obsession. Finding the bad guy possessed him. It wasn't a time clock and a paycheck. It was a life's mission.

He started, suddenly realizing it was that little troublemaker who had triggered these thoughts about relationships!

He was happy when his phone rang, so he didn't have to contemplate what—*if*—that meant something worrisome.

Besides, his discipline was legendary—as was his comfortably solitary lifestyle—and he was not thinking of Sarah McDougall in terms of the "R" word. He refused.

He glanced at the caller ID window.

His boss. That hadn't taken long. Sullivan debated not answering, but saw no purpose in putting off the inevitable.

He held the phone away from his ear so the volume of his chief's displeasure didn't deafen him.

"Yes, sir, I got it. I'm cleaning all the cars."

He held the phone away from his ear again. "Yeah. I got it. I'm on Henrietta Delafield duty. Every single time. Yes, sir."

He listened again. "I'm sure you will call me back if you think of anything else. I'm looking forward to it. No, sir. I'm not being sarcastic. Drunk tank duty, too. Got it."

Sullivan extricated himself from the call before the chief thought of any more ways to make his life miserable.

He got out of his car. Through the open screen door of Della's house—a house so like Sarah's it should have spooked him—he could hear his nephews, Jet, four, and Ralf, eighteen and half months, running wild. He climbed the steps, and tugged the door.

Unlocked.

He went inside and stepped over an overturned basket of laundry and a plastic tricycle. His sister had once been a total neat freak, her need for order triggered by the death of their parents, just as it had triggered his need for control.

He supposed that meant the mess was a good thing, and he was happy for her, moving on, having a normal life, despite it all.

Sullivan found his sister in her kitchen. The two boys pushed by him, first Jet at a dead run, chortling, tormenting Ralf by holding Ralf's teddy bear high out of his brother's reach. Ralf toddled after him, determined, not understanding the futility of his determination was fueling his brother's glee.

Della started when she turned from a cookie sheet,

still steaming from the oven, and saw Sullivan standing in her kitchen door well. "You scared me."

"You told me to come at five. For dinner."

"I lost track of time."

"You're lucky it was me. You should lock the door," he told her.

She gave him a look that in no way appreciated his brotherly concern for her. In fact, her look left him in no doubt that she had tuned into the Tally Hukas show for the afternoon.

"All Sarah McDougall is trying to do is help the town," Della said accusingly.

Jet raced by, cackling, toy high. Sullivan snagged it from him, and gave it to Ralf. Blessedly, the decibel level was instantly reduced to something that would not cause permanent damage to the human ear.

Sullivan's eyes caught on a neatly bagged package of chocolate chip cookies on the counter. His sister usually sent him home with a goodie bag after she provided him with a home-cooked meal.

"Are those for me?" he asked hopefully, hoping she would take the hint that he didn't want to talk about Sarah McDougall.

His sister had never been one to take hints.

"Not now, they aren't," she said sharply.

"Come on, Della. The chief is already punishing me," he groaned.

"How?" she said, skeptical, apparently, that the chief could come up with a suitable enough punishment for Sullivan refusing to do his part to revitalize the town.

"Let's just say it looks like there's a lot of puke in my future."

"Humph." She was a woman who dealt with puke on a nearly daily basis. She was not impressed. She took the bagged cookies and put them out of sight. "I'm going to donate these to the bake sale in support of Summer Fest."

"Come on, Della."

"No, *you* come on. Kettle Bend is your new home. Sarah's right. It needs *something.* People to care. Everyone's so selfish. Me. Me. Me. Indifferent to their larger world. What happened to Kennedy? *Think not what your country can do for you, but what you can do for your country?*"

"We're talking about a summer festival, not the future of our nation," he reminded her, but he felt the smallest niggle of something astonishing. Was it *guilt?*

"We're talking about an attitude! Change starts small!"

His sister was given to these rants now that she had children and she felt responsible for making good citizens of the world.

Casting a glance at Jet, who was using sweet talk to rewin his brother's trust and therefore get close to Bubba the bear, Sullivan saw it as a monumental task she had undertaken. With a crow of delight, Jet took the bear. She obviously had some way to go.

If she was going to work on Sullivan, too, her mission was definitely doomed.

"Why on earth wouldn't you do a few interviews if it would help the town out?" Della pressed him.

"I'm not convinced four days of summer merriment *will* help the town out," he said patiently. "I haven't been here long, but it seems to me what Kettle Bend needs is jobs."

"At least Summer Fest is an effort," Della said stubbornly. "It would bring in people and money."

"Temporarily."

"It's better than nothing. And one person acting on an idea might lead other people to action."

Sullivan considered his sister's words and the earnest look on her face. Had he been too quick to say no? Strangely, the chief going after him had not even begun to change his mind. But his sister looking at him with disapproval was something else.

It was also the wrong time to remember the tears sparkling behind Sarah McDougall's astonishing eyes.

But that's what he thought of.

"I don't like dealing with the press," he said finally. "They always manage to twist what you say. After the Algard case, if I never do another interview again it will be too soon."

Something shifted in his sister's face as he referred to the case that had finished him as a detective. Maybe even as a human being.

At any other time he might have taken advantage of her sympathy to get hold of those cookies. But it was suddenly there between them, the darkness that he had seen that separated him from this world of cookies and children's laughter that she inhabited.

They had faced the darkness, together, once before. Their parents had been murdered in a case of mistaken identity.

Della had been the one who had held what remained of their family—her and him—together.

She was the one who had kept him on the right track when it would have been so easy to let everything fall apart.

Only then, when she had made sure he finished school, had she chosen to flee her former life, the big city, the ugliness of human lives lost to violence.

And what had he done? Immersed himself in it.

"How could they twist what you had to say about saving a dog?" she asked, but her voice was softer.

"I don't present well," he said. "I come across as cold. Heartless."

"No, you don't." But she said it with a trace of doubtfulness.

"It's going to come out that I don't even like dogs."

"So you'll come across as a guy who cares only about himself. Self-centered," she concluded.

"Colossally," he agreed.

"One hundred percent pure guy."

They both laughed, her reluctantly, but still coming around. Not enough to take the cookies out of the cupboard, though. He made a little bet with himself that he'd have those cookies by the time he left here.

Wouldn't that surprise the troublemaker? That he could be charming if he chose to be?

There it was. He was thinking about *her* again. And he didn't like it one little bit. Not one.

"You should think about it," his sister persisted.

It occurred to him that if he dealt with the press, his life would be uncomfortable for a few minutes.

If he didn't appease his sister—and his boss—his life could be miserable for a lot longer than that.

"*I* think," Della said, having given him ten seconds or so to think about it, "that you should say yes."

"For the good of the town," he said a little sourly.

"For your own good, too."

There was something about his sister that always required him to be a better man. And then there was a truth that she, and she alone, knew.

He would do anything for her.

Yet she never took advantage of that. She rarely asked him for anything.

Sullivan sighed heavily. He had a feeling he was being pushed in a direction that he did not want to go in.

At all.

CHAPTER THREE

The phone couldn't have rung at a worse moment. Sarah was trying to shovel her latest batch of rhubarb jam into jars. How had her grandmother done this without getting jam everywhere? It was dripping down the outside of the jars, ruining the labels. She had managed to get sticky globs everywhere, including her hair!

Frisky? Sarah felt utterly exhausted.

Her phone had been ringing more than normal because of the free time on the Tally Hukas radio show yesterday, but still, she had the thought she had had every single time her phone had rung since she moved here to Kettle Bend.

She hoped it was Mike. She hoped he was phoning to beg her forgiveness. She hoped he was phoning to beg her to come back!

"I can't wait to tell him no," Sarah said, wiping goo off her hand before picking up the receiver.

Her ex-fiancé begging her forgiveness would go a long way in erasing the sourness of a heartache!

"Miss McDougall?"

It was definitely not her philandering ex-fiancé calling—Sarah would recognize that voice anywhere!

She froze, licked a tiny trace of rhubarb jam off her wrist. Her heart was pounding unreasonably.

The jam seemed a little too tart.

Just like him.

"Oliver?" she said. She used his first name deliberately, hoping to aggravate him. No doubt, he was not calling voluntarily. Forced into it by the notoriety he had come into yesterday as a result of that radio show.

She enjoyed the sensation of having the upper hand.

But she also liked the way his name sounded on her lips. She had liked his name ever since she'd seen that video on the internet, and heard his name for the first time.

And this just in, fantastic footage out of Kettle Bend, Wisconsin, of Officer Oliver Sullivan...

His silence satisfied her. Then the silence was shattered by the shriek of a baby. For a stunned moment, she allowed that Oliver Sullivan might be married. There had been no ring on his finger. But lots of men did not wear rings. Especially if their line of work might make wearing them a hazard.

Sarah considered the downward swoop of her stomach with amazement. Why would she feel *bereft* if Oliver Sullivan was married?

"I'm having an emergency," he said, after a moment. "I've tried everything. I can't stop the baby from crying."

"Wh-wh-what baby?"

He had her off balance, again. He was supposed to be caving to pressure, begging her to let him do some interviews!

"My nephew, Ralf. My sister takes pity on my bachelor state—"

Bachelor state. How silly that it felt as if the light was going back on in her world!

Her world, she reminded herself sternly, was jam and Summer Fest.

"—and has me over for dinner when I'm off. But she's had a family emergency last night. Her husband was in a car accident on his way home from work. She had to leave suddenly. I don't want to call her at the hospital and tell her the baby won't stop crying. She's got enough on her plate already."

Sarah felt a faint thrill of vindication. She had just *known* this kind of man was lurking behind that remote facade he presented. The kind of man who would rescue a dog. Who would shield his sister from more anxiety.

"How is your brother-in-law?"

"Jonathon is fine. The injury is not life-threatening. It's just a complicated fracture that needs surgery. It's serious enough that she's not leaving him."

He would be like that, too, Sarah thought with a shiver. Fiercely devoted. If he ever allowed anything or anyone to get by his guard. Which seemed unlikely. Except this phone call would have seemed unlikely, too—yet here it was.

"And here I am," he said. His voice was unreasonably sexy. "Jet, get down from there! With a four-year-old nephew who is climbing the curtains and hanging off the rod. And with a baby who won't stop crying. Not knowing who to call."

Sarah was surprised to hear, beyond the sexiness,

the faintest note of something else in his voice. Panic? Surely not?

"And why call me?" she asked, softly. Imagining he might say, *I saw something in your face I could not forget. You are the kind of woman a man dreams of having children with. Did you know you have a tender beauty in your eyes?*

"Your front door was open when I came by to see you the other day. I saw the framed magazines on your wall. I figured you must be some kind of expert on babies. Though, Ralf's not *today's* baby, exactly. He's eighteen months old."

"Oh." Again, not what she'd expected.

"Ah, also, I figured I had a bargaining chip with you."

"A bargaining chip?"

"You want me to do a few interviews. You have the credentials of a baby expert. Maybe we could work a trade."

It wasn't begging exactly, but it was a stunning capitulation.

Still, it was so far from her fantasy of what he might say that she burst out laughing. "I have to warn you, my knowledge of babies is pretty much theoretical." *Sadly.*

"You're *not* an expert on babies?"

"I worked for that magazine for four years. I was a writer. I interviewed new moms and wrote how-to articles." Now she felt like she was applying for a job. And one she was rather startled to find that she wanted, too!

She deliberately left out info about how many nursery remodels she had done features on, thinking he would dismiss that as frivolous. She also did not mention she knew at least a dozen remedies for diaper rash, thinking that would just make him hang up the phone! She was a hair away from having Oliver Sullivan on her team.

"Were any of those how-to articles on crying babies?" he asked. She had been right. That was desperation in his voice.

Sarah stifled a giggle at how easily a little scrap of humanity could bring a big man to his knees.

"Dozens," she said. "I've done dozens of articles on crying babies."

"He's been crying for two hours."

"Babies are very sensitive to tension," she said.

"Mine?" he asked, incredulously.

"Possibly just something in his mother's tone before she left, a change in routine, now her absence and his daddy not coming home. He knows something is amiss."

"You *are* an expert! Can you help a guy out, Sarah?"

Instead of gloating that it was his turn to beg, she focused on something else, entirely.

Not Miss McDougall. *Sarah.* Her heart feeling as if it were melting should at least serve as a warning that this was a very bad idea.

But he'd said he would do the interviews! For the good of the town, she had to suck it up.

"What do you want me to do?"

"Come over."

Suddenly it felt as if she was playing with fire. She was *way* too happy to be talking to him, and it wasn't just because their arrangement was going to be good for the town, either.

Don't go over there, she warned herself. She could make suggestions over the phone. She could protect herself from whatever dumb thing her heart was doing right now.

Beating in double time.

Sarah caught a glimpse of herself in the mirror over the kitchen sink. She was blushing crazily, like a pre-teen girl getting her first call from a boy. She had her new life to think about. She had the new *her* to think about—independent, not susceptible to the painful foibles of the human heart.

She, Sarah McDougall, had learned her lessons!

She heard a crash and a howl. "What was that?"

"The living room curtains just came down. My nephew Jet was attached to them."

"I'll be right there."

"Really?"

"Really."

He gave her the address.

"Bring some of that jam," he suggested, "Crabbies, right? The one your grandmother said relieved crankiness. If ever a guy needed it, it's this one."

"You or the baby?"

"Both," he said ruefully.

Sarah knew she should not be so flattered that he seemed to remember every single thing she had said to him.

"Could you hurry?"

If she didn't hurry she would have an opportunity to make a better second impression on Oliver Sullivan. She could do her hair and her makeup. She could throw on something flirty and fabulous. But the baby in the background, his little voice hoarse, hiccupping his distress, did seem to give the situation a sense of urgency.

Plus, she did not want to give in to that urge to make Sullivan find her attractive. The situation she was heading into was dangerous enough without the complication of attraction between them.

Five minutes later, she shut her door, trying very hard not to acknowledge how happy she was to be escaping from her sticky jam jars.

Moments later, Sarah arrived at the door of a charming little bungalow that was very much like hers, at least on the outside.

When Sullivan came to the door, she realized trying to halt that particular complication—attraction—would be like trying to hold back the tide.

The man was glorious.

A few days ago, he had been all icy composure. Today, the man who came to the door was every bit as compelling as the one she had seen in the video with the puppy.

His dark chocolate hair was mussed. His sculpted face was shadowed with unshaven whiskers. The remoteness of his dark eyes was layered with exhaustion, a compelling kind of vulnerability. His shirt had damp tear blotches on it.

And in his arms was a baby.

A distraught baby, to be sure, but even so, there was something breathtaking about the contrast between such a strong man, and the baby in his arms. His muscled arm curved around the baby's behind, holding him firmly into the broadness of his chest.

For all that he was exhausted, there was something

in Sullivan's stance that said it all. This baby, fragile, vulnerable, needy, was safe with him. It would come to no harm on his watch.

A little boy squeezed between Sullivan's legs and the screen door, and pushed on it. When it gave way, he gave a little whoop of freedom, which was short-lived when his uncle freed a hand, snatched his collar and pulled him back in the house. He would come to no harm on his uncle's watch, either.

The little boy, like a wind-up toy that had hit an obstacle, changed direction and darted off down a hallway.

"Come in," he invited over the howling of the baby and the screeching of his other nephew echoing from deep within the house.

She had known coming here was entering a danger zone like none she had ever known. Seeing Oliver Sullivan standing there, with that baby in his arms, confirmed it.

He still looked every inch a warrior, strong, *ready*, formidable.

But she suspected his exhaustion, his sudden immersion into a battle of a totally different sort, one he was obviously ill-prepared to deal with, had him as close to surrender as she would ever find him.

Surrender to what? she asked herself. *Being vulnerable. Attraction. Being human.*

Run, she told herself.

But running would look foolish and she didn't want to look foolish to him. Some despicably traitorous part of her wanted to look as attractive to him as he did to her.

Perhaps she could look at this as a test of her resolve.

This was a test of how deeply committed she was to a life of giving her heart only to something inanimate, that could not hurt her, like a town.

Taking a deep breath, Sarah stepped in the open door. The air had a scorched smell to it.

As if the devil had been hard at work, creating a perfect potion to tempt her away from the life she had chosen for herself.

The baby was part of that potion, adorable, radiating sweetness despite the lustiness of his howls. He twisted his head and regarded her solemnly. His face was blotchy from crying. His voice was a croak of indignation.

"Hello, sweetie," she said softly.

The baby stopped, mid caterwaul, and regarded her with both suspicion and hope.

"Mama," he whispered.

"I know, baby. You miss your Mommy, don't you?"

A thumb went into a mouth and he slurped thoughtfully, nodded, squeezed out a few additional tears, then reached out both pudgy arms for her.

Sullivan said a word under his breath that you weren't supposed to say around babies and passed the child to her.

Sarah slid her bag off her shoulder onto the floor, then took the surprising weight of the baby in her arms. As if seeing Sullivan holding the baby hadn't been bad enough, experiencing the baby's warm, cuddly body pressed against her breast increased the squishy feeling inside of her.

"His name is Ralf," Sullivan said, his voice low, un-

intentionally sensual, the voice of a man afraid to speak
in fear of getting the baby going again.

"Hello, Ralf, I'm Sarah."

"Want Mama." Sarah stepped over an overturned tricycle into a living room that had been ransacked. The
curtain bar was up on one side and ripped down on the
other. Books had been pulled off the shelves and scat-
tered. A diaper sack had fallen over and was spilling
its contents onto the floor. She cleared a jumble of toys
off the couch and sank down on it, pressing the baby
into her shoulder.

"Of course you want your mama," she said sooth-
ingly. "She'll be home as soon as she can. Does he still
take a bottle?" she asked Sullivan.

"A bottle of what?" he asked, baffled.

"Rye whiskey," she teased with a shake of her head.
"Go check the fridge and see if there are any baby bottles in there."

"There are!" he called, a moment later, with relief.
"I've just been feeding him that baby gruel stuff. I didn't
know he still took a bottle."

"Okay, heat it up in the microwave for a few seconds
and bring it here."

He galloped in with the bottle.

"Did you test it to make sure it's not too hot?"

Sullivan looked at her as if her request was unten-
able. He glanced at the bottle, grimaced, then lifted it,
a soldier prepared to do what needed to be done.

"No!" she said, just in time. "You test it on your
wrist!"

"Oh." With relief, he shook a few drops of the milk
in the bottle onto his wrist. His wrist was large, and

square and strong, making her ultra-aware of the sizzling masculine appeal of him.

He handed her the bottle a little sheepishly. "See? An expert. I knew you'd know what to do."

Shaking her head, she took the bottle from him, nestled Ralf in the crook of her arm and put the bottle to his lips.

With an aggrieved look at his uncle and a sigh, he nestled more deeply into her, wrapped his lips against the bottle and began to make the cutest little *slurp-slurp* sound. The tiny slurping sounds grew farther and farther apart.

Within seconds the baby was asleep.

Sullivan was staring at her as if she had parted the sea.

"I can't believe that."

"He was exhausted, ready to go no matter what."

"I owe you big-time."

"Yes, you do."

His gratitude was colossally short-lived. He folded his arms over his stained chest and rocked back on his heels. "Three interviews. No parade marshal."

"I see I should have driven my bargain while he was screaming," she said ruefully. But inside she savored her victory. He was going to do it! He was going to help her save Kettle Bend by making it the best Summer Fest the town had ever had.

"I have to warn you, I'm not good at interviews. I have a talent for saying exactly the wrong thing," he said ruefully.

"Luckily for you, in my past life, I've interviewed tons of people. I know the kind of questions they'll ask you. Why don't I come up with a list, and we can do a practice run?"

What did that have to do with getting away from this man as quickly as possible?

The little boy, Jet, came back in, tucked himself behind his uncle's leg and peered out at her.

"I'm Sarah," she said.

"I'm hungry."

"Hello, hungry."

"Sullivan burned supper."

"He doesn't call you Uncle Oliver?" Sarah asked, surprised.

"I told you no one calls me Oliver."

"Who's Oliver?" Jet asked with a scowl, and then repeated, a little more stridently, "I'm hungry!"

"What's your favorite thing to eat?" she asked him.

"Mac and cheese. He burned it."

"How about your second favorite thing?" A picture of her cooking dinner for them crowded her mind. It occurred to her it was way too cozy. If attraction could be complicated, what would sharing such a domestic scene be?

She pictured washing dishes with Sullivan and then felt annoyed with herself. Is this what her life had become that she could find washing dishes with a man romantic?

Of course, she thought, as she slid the man in question a look, there wasn't much she could do with him that wouldn't feel romantic.

Which was a big problem.

"My second favorite food is Hombre hamburgers!" Jet crowed.

Sarah felt a twinge of regret that was far larger than her twinge of relief. Hombre's was a favorite Kettle Bend eatery just a few blocks away. It was a plan for supper that didn't need to include her.

"That sounds like a perfect solution for supper," Sarah said brightly to Sullivan. "You can pop the baby in the stroller, and he'll sleep all the way there."

She stood, a bit clumsily with the baby in arms. "It looks like your emergency is over, Oliver."

"Who's Oliver?" Jet demanded again.

She held out the sleeping baby. Sullivan took him, reluctantly.

"Don't go," he pleaded. "He's going to wake up sometime."

"Well, I can't stay all night."

The blush moved up her cheeks like fire, as if she had propositioned him. Or he her.

He had the audacity to look amused by it.

"No, but walk down to Hombre's with us. I'll buy you a hamburger. It's the least I can do," he wheedled.

Oh, boy. Sitting across the table from him in a restaurant would be worse than doing dishes with him. A fantasy of a happy family crowded her mind.

Of course, if her own family was anything to go by, that's exactly what happy families were. A fantasy.

One she had believed in, despite her upbringing. Or maybe because of it. One that had made her so needy for love that she had fallen for the wrong person.

She could feel that neediness in her still, and knew that was the demon she needed to fight.

"The least you can do is for me is four interviews," she said.

"Three," he replied.

"Four, if I join you at Hombre's."

What was she doing? She couldn't play at happy families with this man. She couldn't. What had made her say that, when she already knew she had to get herself out that door and away from him? Her new life was wavering in front of her like a distant mirage on a scorching desert day.

The look of amusement around his eyes deepened.

It made him more attractive than ever, even though he didn't smile. Good grief, she hoped he wouldn't smile. She'd be lost.

"I have to say that's the first time anyone has ever made me bargain with them to go on a date."

She stared at him. "A date?" she squeaked, and then forced herself to regain her composure. He was just that type of man. No, he would not have to bargain with women to go on dates with him. They would throw themselves at his feet for the opportunity.

She had been weak like that, once, but she was no more.

"I don't do dates," she said crisply.

She saw way too much register in his eyes, as if she had laid out every pathetic detail of her broken engagement to him.

"I didn't mean a *date* date." Was his tone almost gentle? Somehow, from the moment she'd first seen him risk his life for the dog, she had known there was a gentle side to him. But to see it in his eyes now and know it was pity? She hated that!

Of course he hadn't asked her on a *date*. She could feel herself squirm at the very assumption she'd made.

"Four interviews if you come to Hombre's. Not on a date. How would a date be possible with these munch-kins watching our every move?" he teased.

Dumb to wonder what he would consider a date, then. Obviously it would involve something that he wouldn't want his nephews to see!

Her eyes moved involuntarily to his lips. Would he kiss on the first date? Even allowing herself to ponder the question seemed weak and juvenile. He was obvi-ously a mature man, somewhat hardened and certainly cynical. Possibly he would expect quite a bit more than a kiss on a first date.

She had to stop this, right now. The conjecture was making her feel as if she was burning up, coming down with a fever.

He could take his nephews to Hombre's by himself. *But he might need me*, a voice inside her quibbled.

No, that wasn't the truth at all. The truth was, Sarah wanted to spend more time with him.

She tried to tell herself it was because anything would be better than going back to that jam. But she knew it was more, something leaping in the air between them, that baby creating moments of vulnerability in her that were bringing barriers down that needed to be up!

Sullivan was looking at her so intently she thought she would melt.

"Uh, maybe you'd want to do something with your hair," he said after a moment. "I think it has something in it." He reached over and touched it.

His touch was so brief. But it made her aware of a

very real danger of the awareness that sizzled in the air between them.

Or maybe not. Mortified, she watched as he looked at the blob on his finger, and then sniffed it. Then he put it to his lips and tasted.

And smiled.

That smile was just as devastating as Sarah had known it would be.

She felt weak from how it changed him, the guarded look swept from his face, revealing a hint of the light that he kept well hidden inside himself.

"It's jam," he said. "Crabbies?"

"No. Crabbies is made from crab apples. This is rhubarb. My grandmother called it Spring Fling." She blushed again when she said it, as if she had said something off-color and provocative.

"So, if Crabbies can cure crankiness, what can a Spring Fling do?" he asked and raised a wicked eyebrow at her.

What could a spring fling do? Somehow Sarah didn't want to tell him abut the promised friskiness of the jam. Or of its promised properties to erase the sourness of a heartache and herald in new hope.

"It's just jam," she said, "it can't *do* anything."

"Not a bad hair pomade, though," he said seriously.

She laughed, reluctantly, and he laughed, too. If his smile had been devastating to her carefully laid plans for her new life, his laughter was downright dangerous.

It revealed something so *real* about him. It intrigued her. It made her wonder why he was so guarded, so closed off, so deliberately unapproachable.

It made her want to rescue him from himself. It occurred to her it was the first time since her breakup that she had allowed herself to feel curious about a man.

It seemed new hope had crept into her life whether she wanted it or not.

And she did want it.

Just not from this source! People—particularly *men*—were too unpredictable. Mike had already taught her that.

Even before Mike, her father had ripped apart her own family. She would forget the lessons she had learned from the men in her life at her own peril.

Hadn't Michael Talbot *seemed* totally decent? Reliable? Even a touch staid? Exactly the kind of man one could count on building a life with?

Hadn't her father seemed like that, too? A partner in a law firm, the epitome of success by any standard?

But this man who stood before her was nothing like Mike. And nothing like her father, either. Oliver Sullivan seemed full of contradictions and dark mysteries. Something in him was deeply wounded.

It would be a mistake to think you could fix something like that without getting hurt yourself.

"I can't possibly take the children to Hombre's with you," she said quickly before she could change her mind. "Not possibly. Three interviews will be just fine. More than enough. I'll call you with the details when I've set it up."

She turned and bolted from the house, aware of his curious eyes on her, but not daring to look back.

CHAPTER FOUR

So, SHE didn't date, Sullivan thought, watching Sarah scurry down his sister's sidewalk and get in her car. She drove away with haste, a quick shoulder check, and a spin of tires.

That whole incident had been very telling for a man who read people with such stripping accuracy.

Sarah McDougall didn't date.

She was as cute as a button, refreshingly natural, obviously single and in the prime of her life. She probably had guys falling at her feet. And she didn't date?

Plus, she was devoting herself to what could very well be a lost cause, the rebirth of Kettle Bend through its Summer Fest. But at least, he saw with clarity, it was a cause that couldn't hurt her.

Heartbreak, he told himself. She'd suffered a heartbreak.

And from the way she looked holding that baby? Like a Madonna, completely serene, completely fulfilled. Her heartbreak hadn't done one little thing to cure her of what she really wanted. Her longings had been written in the tender expression on her face, in the little smile, in her unconscious sigh as that baby had settled against her.

Sarah McDougall wanted a family. Babies. Security.

She'd been wise to leave.

And he'd been wise to let her. Their life goals were at cross purposes. His was to do his job and do it well. His kind of work did not lend itself to the kind of cozy life she craved. It required a hard man who was prepared to do hard things.

People, including her, wanted to believe something else because of the video of him rescuing the puppy. But Sullivan knew himself—and his limitations—extremely well.

Sarah's life goal—no matter what she had convinced herself—had been written all over her when she'd had that baby pressed to her breast.

The other thing he could tell about her was that she was one of those naive people who believed she could use the force of her will to mold a happy world. Her devotion to Summer Fest was proof of that.

He was pretty sure he could kill her illusions in about ten minutes. Not deliberately. It was just the dark cynicism he'd developed for dealing with a tough, cold, hard world. If her illusions made her happy, even if they were hopelessly naive, he should just leave her alone with them.

Their lives would tangle once more because he'd agreed to do the interviews. Then he would put her behind him. Along with this strange yearning he felt every time he saw her.

Rest.

"I don't need a rest," he said out loud, annoyed. The baby woke up with a sputter and Jet raced by, his mother's lipstick streaked across his face like war paint.

"Except from that."

* * *

The next day, Sarah called him on his cell phone. He was at work, but it was an exceptionally quiet morning, even for Kettle Bend. It would have been a good morning to start cleaning cars, but somehow he wasn't. So far, some foolish sense of pride had prevented him from telling the chief he'd agreed to do the interviews, after all.

Sullivan registered, a little uneasily, that he felt happy to hear her voice.

"How's your brother-in-law?"

She would ask that first, a tenderness in her, an ability to care and to love deeply. Busy making her own happy world, whether she would admit to it or not.

Which meant he had to put a red warning flag beside her in his mind. Oh, wait, he'd already done that! So he shouldn't be all that happy to hear from her. But he could not deny that he was.

He tried to tell himself that between Sarah and cleaning cars, she was the clear winner. It didn't *mean* anything.

"The surgery went well. No complications. He'll be in the hospital a little longer, but my sister got home late last night."

Silence. He could tell that she wanted to ask him how the baby had been, and if they'd gone for their supper at Hombre's after all.

But she didn't. Evidently all her warning flags were waving, too.

Which was a good thing. A very good thing.

He could hear her trying to keep the distance in her voice when she asked if they could meet. She had set up the interviews and, as promised, would run a few potential questions by him.

That was perfect. She was all business. It would be good to get it over with and put his very short Sarah McDougall chapter behind him.

"Do you want me to come by your place?" he asked.

"Uh, no."

He felt relieved. There was something about her place, the coziness of those yellow sofas facing each other over drooping flowers that would not lend itself to the barriers he felt were essential to keep up between them.

"I'm in a jam. Literally," Sarah said.

He heard something in her voice that gave him pause. "You don't really like making jam, do you?" he asked quietly.

He could have kicked himself. A question like that was personal! It had nothing to do with keeping barriers up. It was as if he'd said to her, *You're not fulfilled. How come? What's up? What's getting in the way of your happy fantasy?*

The question, he told himself firmly, was what was up with him, not her!

Luckily, his question actually seemed to succeed at putting a barrier up, not taking one down.

"What would make you say that?" she asked defensively. "I happen to *love* my grandmother's business. I *love* making jam."

Leave it.

But he didn't. His *uh-huh* was loaded with disbelief.

"I do!"

A woman, if there ever was one, who was made to say *I do*. To believe in forever after.

Talking about jam, he reminded himself firmly, furious that his mind had gone there.

He could tell she was fuming. Well, it wasn't his fault that he was pretty good at reading most people, and really good at reading her in particular. Besides, fuming was good. Barriers up!

"So, where do you want to meet?" he asked.

Her voice was cool. "How about Winston's Church Hill Coffee Shoppe? What's your schedule like? Could you do it in half an hour?"

Winston's was always loud. And crowded. Very public. A good choice. He wished she had picked Grady's, which had booths and better coffee.

"Winston's would be the best," she said, as if she had read his mind. "It'll be crowded. It'll go through town like wildfire that you met me there. It might undo some of the damage to your popularity the radio show caused."

Yeah, Winston's was the town rumor mill, not that Sullivan gave a fig about popularity.

He was working. He was in uniform. That might be a good thing. There was nothing like a uniform to keep his distance from people.

She was already there when he walked into the coffee shop, bent over some papers, her tongue caught between her teeth in concentration.

He hesitated for a moment, studying her.

Sarah didn't look like she had looked yesterday at his sister's, or the way she had looked in her garden, either.

She was wearing a sundress the color of her sofa, summer-afternoon yellow. It hugged the slenderness of her curves, showed off skin already faintly sun-kissed, brought his eye to a little gold heart that winked at the vulnerable hollow of her throat.

She'd done something to her hair, too. The curls had been tamed, straightened, and her hair hung in a glossy wave to the swell of shoulders that were naked save for the thin strap of the dress.

When she glanced up, he saw that she had put on makeup and that her eyes looked dazzling. But not as dazzling as her freshly glossed lips.

It worried him that all this might be for him.

But as soon as he joined her, he saw this was her barrier, as much as his uniform was his.

She was here as a professional woman.

Sarah wore that role with an ease and comfort that was very telling.

Though he'd decided he wasn't going to try and tell her anything anymore. She was a little too touchy. It was none of his business that she was trying to run from the very things that gave her the most satisfaction.

Babies.

Her career.

There was no reason the two things could not coexist, he thought.

Not that it was any of his concern.

She got down to business right away.

"You'll be happy to know we're just going to do one interview."

We're.

"I've arranged for you to do one interview, which

will be taped with the local television station. The news anchor, Bradley Moore, will do it, and then they'll send it to their national affiliates."

He was impressed. She was a professional. "Perfect."

"I think you should wear your uniform." Her eyes drifted over him, and despite his determination to untangle their lives after this task was completed, he was more than a little pleased by what he saw.

She liked a man in uniform.

"So, just pretend I'm the person interviewing you."

A waitress came by and filled his coffee cup without asking him.

"So, Officer Sullivan," Sarah said, putting on her interviewer hat, "what did you do before you came to Kettle Bend?"

"I was a homicide detective in Detroit."

"Couldn't you elaborate?" she prodded him.

"No, I couldn't."

She dropped the interviewer hat. "But it's a perfect opportunity to introduce the charms of Kettle Bend to the conversation. You could say that you tired of the coldly impersonal life in the big city and chose the warmth and friendliness of Kettle Bend instead."

"To tell you the truth I had no objection to the coldly impersonal life in Detroit. I could go get my groceries without someone telling me there was a car illegally parked on their block. Or worse, asking me about that blasted dog," he said caustically.

"You can't call him *that blasted dog*," she said, horrified. "Why did you move here if you liked your coldly impersonal life so much?"

He shocked himself by saying, "I burned out," and

then, irritated at himself for saying it, and annoyed at the warmly curious look in her expression, he changed the subject.

"I don't like dogs," he said. It might as well come out. It might as well come out as a way of keeping her at bay. He took a sip of his coffee and watched her closely over the lip of the mug to see what her response to that would be.

"You can't say you don't like dogs!" she said. "What kind of person doesn't like dogs?"

Perfect. The kind of person little Sarah McDougall should be very cautious of.

"I'm not the warm and fuzzy type," he warned her. "And that does not translate well in interviews. I'm not going to lie about liking dogs. I'm not going to lie about anything."

"I'm not asking you to lie!" she protested.

"That's good."

"Okay," she said, determined, looking at her notes. "So, you don't like dogs. I'm sure you could gloss over that without *lying*. Something like, *there are dog people and cat people. I'm a cat person.* Maybe that would make your leap into the river seem even more heroic."

"I'm getting a headache," he said. "And I don't like cats, either."

"Horses?" she said, hopefully.

"I'm not an animal person."

"Not an animal person," she repeated, faintly distressed.

"There are animal people and not animal people. I'm in the 'not' category."

"Why wouldn't you like animals?" she asked.

Don't tell her the truth. But he couldn't help himself. "I don't like neediness. I don't want anything relying on me. I don't want to become attached to anything." He didn't have to elaborate. In fact, he ordered himself not to elaborate. Then… "I don't want to love anything."

They both sat there in shocked silence.

"But why?" she finally ventured.

Don't say it. She doesn't have to know. There is no reason for her to know.

"My parents were killed when I was seventeen." He *hated* himself for saying it. Why was he admitting all this stuff to her? It felt as if she were pulling his insides out of him without really trying, just looking at him with those warm, understanding eyes.

Sullivan pulled back into damage-control mode as quickly as he could. "That had better not come out in the interview. I don't want any sympathy. From anyone."

Her mouth had opened as if she was going to say something sympathetic. She correctly interpreted his glare, and her mouth closed slowly. But she couldn't do anything about her eyes.

They had softened to a shade of gold that reminded him of the setting sun, gentle, caressing, not simply sympathetic, somehow. Sharing his pain with him.

He shrugged uncomfortably. "Don't worry. I'm not going to say in public that I don't like dogs because I don't want to get attached to anything. I'm not even sure why I said it to you."

He was already very sorry he had.

He glanced at his watch, a hint for her to move on, and was unreasonably grateful when she did.

"So what are you going to say when or if you're asked why you jumped in the river to save the dog?" she asked curiously.

"Momentary insanity?" He looked at her face, and sighed. "I'll say I thought it probably belonged to the kid I'd seen riding his bike across the bridge earlier, and that I didn't want him to lose his dog."

"Oh," she said, pleased, "that's nice."

Nice. She wasn't getting it. Oliver Sullivan was not *nice.*

"As it turned out," he said gruffly, "the puppy didn't belong to him. They still haven't found the owner. The dog's going up for adoption next week if he isn't claimed."

"That would be good to mention. That would bring a lot of attention to Kettle Bend."

"Believe me, it already has. The police station had a call from Germany last week asking about the dog."

"If you can say that, that would be wonderful! People in Germany interested in Kettle Bend! An international angle!"

"I'll try to work it in," he said. Her enthusiasm should have been annoying. Instead, it seemed as cute as her sunshine-yellow dress. She seemed to have an absolute gift for making his mind go places it did not want to go, breaking down barriers that he had thought were high and fortified.

"Now," she tapped her pencil against her lips, "how could you work in Summer Fest?"

He groaned, and not entirely because of the mention of Summer Fest. She had drawn his attention to her lips, which were full and plump.

Kissable.

"I don't understand your cynicism about it," she said, pursing those delicious lips now.

"I'm cynical about everything." He covered his fascination with her lips by taking a swig of his coffee.

"No, you're not."

Oh, Sarah, do yourself a favor and do not believe the best in me.

"Look," he said, "I think it's naive to believe a little festival can do much for a town. I don't understand exactly what you think it's going to do for Kettle Bend."

"It's going to bring back the summer visitors. It's going to revitalize things. It's going to bring in some much-needed money. It's going to put us on the map again, as a destination. All those people who come here are going to realize what a great place this would be to come live."

Let her have her illusions, Sullivan ordered himself. But he didn't. In fact, he suddenly felt as if he was done with illusions. Like the one that he would ever taste those delectable lips.

His cynicism, his dark history, could put out that light that radiated off of her in about three seconds.

"You know, Sarah, I haven't been here long, but this town is suffering because some of its major employers are gone. The factories are shut down. How can it be a great place to live if there are no jobs here? What Kettle Bend really needs is jobs. Real jobs. Permanent jobs."

"Your sister and her family moved here," she said defensively.

"Jonathon has to commute to Madison. He keeps an apartment close to work for the days he's too tired to drive home. He makes a lot of sacrifices so my sister can have her fantasy of small-town life. I think his accident probably resulted from the fatigue of the constant commuting."

"Did you tell your sister that?" she asked, clearly horrified.

"I did." Unfortunately. So he was still off the cookie list, even though he had told his sister he would do the interviews arranged by Sarah, after all.

"You shouldn't have said that to your sister."

"No practice runs about what to say in real life," he said, putting unnecessary emphasis on *real life*.

She flinched. He covered his remorse by taking a sip of coffee.

"Summer Fest is going to help Kettle Bend," she said stubbornly.

"I've done a bit of checking. It was cancelled because there was no way of measuring whether the output of money could be justified by a temporary influx of visitors."

"I'm being very careful with the budget I've been given. I'm supplementing it with several fundraisers," she said.

"I know. My sister is donating *my* cookies to the bake sale." The very thought soured him. Well, that and the fact Sarah McDougall, with her kind eyes and her sunshiny dress, had ferreted information out of him that he was in no way ready to divulge.

"You know what I think?" He knew he was about to be a little nasty.

He also knew this was more about his lapse—his confiding in her—than it was about Summer Fest. He had to get his walls back up before she crashed right through them and found herself in a land where she didn't want to be.

He needed her to know, beyond a shadow of a doubt, he didn't want or need her sympathy. He wanted to drive what remained of that gentle look out of her eyes.

The kind of look that could make a hard man soft.

A strong man weak.

The kind of look that made a man who had lost faith in any kind of goodness feel just a smidgen of doubt about his own solitary stance.

"What do you think?" But she asked tentatively, something in him making her wary. As well it should.

"You think immersing yourself in Summer Fest is going to help you get over your heartbreak," he said.

She stiffened. He was relieved to see that look—as if her heart was big enough to hold all her own troubles and his too—evaporating from her eyes.

"What heartbreak?" she said warily.

"A girl like you doesn't come to a town like this unless you're trying to outrun something."

"That's not true!" she sputtered.

He looked at her coolly. Maybe it was because she'd somehow made him blurt out his own truth that he needed to show her he could see hers. No, it wasn't that complicated.

He was trying to drive her away.

Before he became *attached*.

"You know, Summer Fest can't make you feel the way you felt when you came here as a kid. No matter how successful it is."

"How do you know what I felt as a kid?" she asked in a shrill whisper.

He snorted. "You felt as if your every dream could come true. You were full of hope and romantic illusions."

She stared at him, two little twin spots of anger growing bright on her cheeks. Then she got up abruptly. She tossed her neatly printed sheet of questions at him.

"Here. You look at these questions yourself. I'm sure you can come up with some answers that won't manage to offend every single person who watches you on television."

He'd made her very angry. He'd hurt her. In the long run that was only a good thing.

Because there was something about her that made a guy want to say way too much, reveal way too much.

There was something about her that made a man wonder what his life could have been like if he had been dealt a different deck, or chosen a different road.

He watched her through the window, walking away from the coffee shop, her hips swishing with anger, the yellow dress swirling around her slender legs.

He picked up the papers she had tossed down, pulled on his cap and pulled the brim low over his eyes.

His uniform, his job, had always been a shield that protected him. How was it she had broken right through it, without half trying?

And why was it, that even though he had succeeded in driving her off, she had succeeded in piquing his curiosity, too? He had uncovered some truth about her, but it felt like it wasn't enough.

As a former detective he had all kinds of ways of finding things out about people without their ever knowing he had....

Sarah was furious. "Of all the smug, bigheaded, supercilious, self-important jerks," she muttered to herself, walking fast away from the café, her head high. "How dare he?"

It had really started with the phone call.

You don't really like making jam, do you?

Then it had just gone all downhill from there.

You think immersing yourself in Summer Fest is going to help you get over your heartbreak.

It was humiliating that somehow he knew that she'd had a heartbreak, as if she were some pathetic cat lady whose life tragedies were apparent to all! It was particularly nasty that he'd had the bad manners to call her on it.

And telling her that she was using Summer Fest to try and recapture the dreams of her youth was mean.

Oliver Sullivan was just plain *mean*.

She hoped he blew the interviews. She hoped the whole world hated him as much as she did! At this moment, she was too angry to care if it damaged Summer Fest!

She stomped into her house, and slammed the door extra hard when the smell of cooked rhubarb hit her.

She went and ripped off the gorgeous little sundress that she had always loved, and put on old clothes that wouldn't be ruined by making jam all afternoon. She had loved putting on that dress again!

Then suddenly it hit her.

The enormity of the thought made her sink down on her bed.

With a meow of pure contentment her cat, Sushi, found her lap and settled on it.

He'd done it on purpose. Oliver Sullivan had made her mad on purpose.

And he'd done it because he'd given something to her. He had trusted her with parts of himself. He had told her things he was not accustomed to revealing. He'd come out from behind his barriers for a little while.

And then he had gone into full retreat!

He'd succeeded, though. She bet he was feeling mighty pleased with himself right now because he'd managed to drive her away.

Sitting there on her bed she contemplated the loneliness of Sullivan's world. At least she had her cat. At least she wasn't so damaged she couldn't even get attached to an animal.

And she was making a ton of friends here in her adopted town. She adored her neighbors, she was developing friendships with many of the volunteers on the Summer Fest committees.

He had chosen a world and a job that could isolate him.

"I'm going in after him," she said out loud, shocking herself. Where had that come from?

She contemplated the absolute insanity of it, and then laughed out loud. She didn't care if it felt insane.

Sarah felt alive. Something she had not felt since Mike had driven the spike of betrayal right through her heart.

It was something she had not felt when she moved

to her grandmother's house. She had certainly not felt it stirring endless pots of jam. And Summer Fest had not made her feel like this, either.

She felt *needed*.

She felt like she could put her petty need to protect herself on hold.

She felt that she had a mission, a man to save from himself, to rescue. He had shown her that brief glimpse of himself for a reason. She was not going to turn her back on him. She was not going to leave him in that dark, lonely place.

And she knew exactly how she was going to do it, too.

"I'm going to use the puppy."

Sushi gave a shrill meow of pure betrayal and jumped off her lap.

Sarah's confidence had dwindled somewhat by the time she arrived at Sullivan's house, unannounced. Obviously, if she called him to warn him of her arrival with the dog, he would just say no.

Of course, there was plenty of potential for him to just say no, regardless.

She was also beginning to understand why Sullivan did not like dogs. Sarah's experience with dogs was very limited. The charm of the adorable cuteness of the puppy—soulful eyes, huge paws, curly black hair— wore off in about five seconds.

The puppy was rambunctious. His greeting this morning when he had been let out of his kennel in his temporary quarters at the vet's office had been way too enthusiastic.

He was gigantic, the vet said, probably some

Newfoundland or Bouvier blood—and possibly a combination of both—making him so large even though he was only about four months old.

He had nearly knocked Sarah off her feet with his joy in seeing her. Her yoga pants—picked because they were both flattering and appropriate for an outing with a dog—now had a large snag running from thigh to calf.

The puppy flung himself against the leash, nearly pulling her shoulder out of the socket. Once in her car, he had found a box of tissue in the backseat and shredded it entirely on the short drive to Sullivan's house.

Sullivan had insinuated she didn't have a clue about real life.

The puppy seemed determined to prove him correct. *Real* puppies were not fun like fantasy puppies.

So, Sarah was already questioning the wisdom of the idea that had seemed so perfect in the sanctuary of her bedroom.

The puppy was reminding her that reality and fantasy were often on a collision course.

Still, she was here now, and there was no turning back. So, ignoring the beating of her heart, unwrapping the leash from around her legs for at least the twentieth time, she went up the stairs.

Sullivan's house was not like her house. And not like his sister's. There were no flowers, there was no swing on the porch.

Everything was in order, and it was immaculate, but there was nothing welcoming about his house. There were no planters, no rugs, no porch furniture, no screen door in front of the storm door.

Because he doesn't welcome anybody, she reminded herself. He pushes away. That's why she was here.

With a renewed sense of mission, she took a deep breath, ordered the dog to sit, and was ignored, and then rang Sullivan's doorbell.

He didn't answer, and she rang it again.

Just when she thought the whole idea was a bust— he wasn't home, despite her careful and clever ferreting out of his schedule—she heard a noise inside the house. He was in there. He'd probably peered out the window, seen it was her and decided not to answer his door.

She rang the bell again. And again. Then gave the door a frustrated kick. As a result, she nearly fell inside when his door was suddenly flung open.

Oliver Sullivan stood in front of her, wearing only a towel, his naked chest beaded with water, his dark hair plastered against his head like melted chocolate.

Sarah gulped as his eyes swept her, coolly, took in the dog, and then he planted his legs far apart and folded his muscled arms across the masculine magnificence of his deep, deep chest.

The whiteness of the towel, riding low and knotted at his hip, made his skin seem golden and sensuous. Steam was rising off his heated body.

That first day he had appeared in her garden, she had foolishly imagined how his skin would smell fresh out of the shower.

But again, she could see fantasy and reality were on a collision course.

Because his scent was better than anything she could have ever, ever imagined. It was heady, masculine, crisp, clean. His scent tickled her nostrils like bubbles from freshly uncorked champagne.

It occurred to her she had been very, very wrong to come here. Her reasoning had been flawed.

Because Sarah had never seen a man less in need of rescuing than this one.

He was totally self-reliant, totally strong, totally sure of himself.

And he was nearly naked.

Which made her the exact opposite of all those things! She dropped her eyes, which didn't help one little bit. Staring at the perfect cut of his water-slicked naked legs, she felt totally weak and unsure of herself.

She forced herself to look back at his face. His gaze was unyielding. She opened her mouth, and not a single sound came out.

The puppy, however, was not paralyzed. With an ecstatic yelp of recognition, it yanked free of the leash, and hurled itself at Sullivan. It jumped up on its back legs, scrabbled at his naked chest with his front paws, whining, begging for affection and attention.

One of those frantically waving paws clawed down the washboard of perfect abs and caught in the towel.

Before Sarah's horrified eyes, the dog yanked his paw free of where it had become entangled in the towel. That scrap of white terry cloth was ripped from Sullivan's waist and floated to the ground.

CHAPTER FIVE

SARAH kept her eyes glued on the puddle of white towel on the porch floor.

Sullivan said three words in a row, universal expressions of extreme masculine displeasure. Then, thankfully, his feet backed out of her line of vision. It was really the wrong time to think he had very sexy feet!

The dog's feet also left her line of vision, Sullivan using him as some sort of shield as he backed into his house.

The front door slammed closed.

Sarah dared to lift her eyes. She wanted to bolt off the porch and go home, crawl into bed and pull the covers over her head.

Rescue Oliver Sullivan? Was she crazy? She needed to get out of here before she was faced with the full repercussions of her impulsiveness!

But there was the little question of the dog she had brought. She was going to have to face the music. Tempting as it was, she couldn't just dump the dog here—at the mercy of a man who had admitted he didn't like dogs—and run home.

With nothing to sit on, she settled on the steps, chin

in hands, trying to think of anything but that startling moment when the towel had fallen.

The door swished open a few minutes later, and Sarah scrambled to her feet and turned to face him. He had put on a pair of jeans, but his chest was still bare. And so were his sexy feet.

Wordlessly, he passed her the dog's leash, folded his arms over his chest and raised an eyebrow at her.

She didn't know what had happened in the house, but Sullivan had obviously proved himself the dominant member of the pack. The dog was subdued. It sat quietly, eyes glued adoringly on him.

"What do you want?"

Was there an unfortunate emphasis on *you* as if he would have rather seen anyone else on his door—vacuum cleaner salesman, Girl Scouts with cookies, old women with religious tracts?

"Um," Sarah said, tucking a loose strand of hair behind her ear, and making a pattern on his porch with her sneaker, "the TV station asked if you could bring the dog to your interview."

"I must have missed the memo where you scheduled the interview," he said, not making this easy for her.

"It's actually scheduled for tomorrow, at 6:00 p.m. but given how you feel about dogs, I thought maybe you and the dog should bond a little first."

"Bond," he said flatly.

"I didn't want it to be obvious to the viewers during the interview that you didn't like dogs."

"Bond," he repeated. "With a dog."

"Would you?" she asked hopefully. She dared glance up at him. She was encouraged to see he had not just gone back into his house and slammed the door. "There's a dog park in Westside. I thought maybe you could go and throw a stick for him. Just so that you look like buddies for the interview."

"Look like buddies," he said, his voice still flat, his arms crossed, his body language completely uninviting, "with a dog."

She nodded, but nothing in the stern lines of his face gave her any reason to hope.

"That's nutty," he said.

Suddenly she remembered why she was here! Just because she had nearly seen him totally naked was no reason to get off track. He was desperately alone in the world! She was here to save him from himself.

"So what if it's nutty?" she said, lifting her chin. "Does everything have to be sane? Does everything have to be on a schedule? Does everything have to be under your control?"

Coming from her, who had always been the perfect one, that was quite funny. But he didn't have to know it was out of character for her. Besides, what had all her efforts to be perfect ever gotten her?

She had spent so much time and effort and energy trying to be the perfect daughter. And then the perfect fiancée. What had it made her?

Perfectly forgettable. Perfectly disposable.

"You sound like my sister," he said, not happily.

"Can't you be spontaneous?"

He glared at her. "I can be as spontaneous as the next guy."

"So prove it. For the greater good," she reminded him.

"Please don't say it. Please."

"What?"

"Kettle Bend needs you."

"I won't say it. But come to the dog park. One hour. It's really part of your agreement to participate in the interview. I've even got it down from four interviews to one. I helped you out in your moment of need. With your nephews."

She had used every argument she had. He seemed unmoved by all of them.

"I think your being the cause of my public nakedness should clear all my debts."

"Nobody saw you," she said hastily. "And I didn't look!"

His lips twitched. Something shifted, ever so slightly. Whatever it was, it was far more dangerous than his remoteness.

"Were you tempted?" he asked softly.

She stared at him. His eyes were wicked. This was the problem with deciding to rescue a man like him.

It was akin to a naive virgin boarding a pirate vessel and demanding the captain lay down his sword for her because she thought she knew what was best for him.

It was a dangerous game she was playing, and the mocking look on his face made her very aware of it.

She took a step backward. "Sorry," she said. "Obviously this was a bad idea. One of my many. According to you." She bolted to the bottom of the steps, then stopped to unwrap the leash from around her ankles.

"Oh, wait a minute."

She turned back to him. He ran a hand through his

hair, looked away from her and then looked back at her. "Okay. An hour. To bond with the dog."

Sullivan closed his bedroom door, leaned on it and drew in a deep breath. Sarah McDougall was in his living room. With a dog. Waiting for him to throw on a shirt so they could go bond.

Him and the dog, or him and her?

"You could have said no," he told himself.

But as she had pointed out, it would be unreasonable for him to say no when she had come so willingly to his rescue when Jet had been destroying his sister's house, and Ralf had put on his marathon crying jag.

Who cares if he appeared unreasonable?

She'd seen him naked. And not under the pleasant kind of circumstances that might have been normal for a gal to see a guy naked, either. That was a good enough reason to say no.

But her face when he'd asked her if she'd been tempted to peek at him had been so funny. He *liked* teasing her.

Besides, after their interview in the coffee shop, where she had left in a fit of pique, it had taken a certain amount of bravery for her to show up here.

Also, he'd since given in to that desire to probe her secrets. Not surprisingly, she was every bit as wholesome as she appeared to be. She'd never even had a traffic ticket.

Sarah wasn't a member of any social networking website, which was both disappointing in terms of a fact-finding mission and revealing in terms of the type of person she was.

But there were plenty of other ways to find out things about a person. An internet search of her name had brought up the Summer Fest website. The four-day extravaganza of small-town activity—games, picnics, bandstand events—seemed like more, way more, than one person could take on.

But he wasn't interested in her recent activities. So he'd followed the thread to articles she had written for *Today's Baby*.

He read three or four of her articles, amazed that, despite the content, they held his interest completely. As a writer, Sarah was funny, original and talented. Which meant he'd been entirely correct in assuming some personal catastrophe had made her leave her successful life in New York behind.

Knowing those little tidbits of information about her made it difficult to send her away now.

She'd had disappointments in her life. It was possible, given the unrealistic scope of Summer Fest, she was setting herself up for another one.

So, as much as Sullivan thought spending time with Sarah McDougall had all kinds of potential for catastrophe, he could not help but admire her bravery. No matter how much he wanted to keep his distance from her, he couldn't throw that bravery back in her face.

He had been aware he'd hurt her at the coffee shop, maybe said too much and too harshly.

And so when he'd come back to his door after pulling on his jeans, with every intention of repeating the first message he'd ever given her, *leave me alone*, he'd been stunned to find he couldn't do it.

Those eyes on his face, embarrassed, eager, hopeful, ultimately brave.

Trusting something in him. Something he had lost sight of in himself a long, long time ago.

"This is really dumb, Sullivan," he told himself after he'd put on a shirt and some socks and some shoes, and opened his bedroom door to rejoin her.

He came down the hallway and saw her perched on the edge of his couch. Today she was wearing some kind of stretch pants that molded her rather extraordinary legs and derriere. She had on a T-shirt—with a cause, of course, breast cancer research, because she was the kind of girl who was going to save the world. Her curly hair had been tamed again, today, pulled back into a ponytail. Once again she didn't have on any makeup. He could see a faint scattering of freckles across her nose.

She looked about twelve years old.

It reminded him again, that there was something about her, despite her heartaches, that was fresh and innocent, eager about the world.

Which was part of what made saying *yes* to an outing with her so damned dumb, even if it was fun to tease her. Even if it was hard to say no to the brave part of her that trusted him.

He should have sucked it up and done what needed to be done.

But he hadn't.

So now he might as well just give himself over to the mistake and make sure it was a glorious one.

She turned to him with a faint smile. "What's your decor inspiration? Al Capone's prison cell?"

He realized she was bringing elements of the unexpected into his carefully controlled world and it was unexpectedly refreshing. Despite himself, he wanted to see what would happen next.

How much damage could she do to his world in an hour, after all?

And how much damage could *he* do to *her* in just an hour? He'd give himself that. Like a gift, an hour with her, just enjoying her, enjoying the spontaneity of it, since she had challenged him about his ability to be spontaneous.

Who knew? He might even enjoy the dog.

Then he'd give her the gift of never doing it again.

"Al Capone had naked girl pictures in his prison cell," he told her, straight-faced.

A faint blush moved up her cheeks. He liked that. Who blushed anymore?

"You can't know that," she said firmly.

"It's an educated guess."

"I think we've had quite enough naked stuff for one day." She had a prim look on her face, like a school-teacher.

He was astonished when, this time, the blush was his. He turned quickly from her and opened the door.

"Walking or driving?" he asked.

"Walking. He's not car-trained." She did stop at her car, though, and retrieved a large handbag from it. Her car was somehow exactly what he had known it would be: a little red Bug. Evidence of the dog and the tissue box filled the backseat, though.

After watching her struggle down the sidewalk with the dog for a few minutes, Sullivan realized the dog wasn't trained in any way, shape or form. He took the leash from her.

"Let me do that."

He did not miss her smile of satisfaction. Bonding-101 taking place according to her schedule of sunshine and light.

The funny thing was, he did feel a little twinge of pure optimism. It was a beautiful day. He liked walking with her, their shoulders nearly touching, her ponytail swinging in the breeze, her scent as light and happy as the day.

"For practicality purposes, we should name the dog," she said. "Just for today."

Sullivan cast her a glance. Oh, she was trying to wiggle by his every defense. Naming the dog would be dangerously close to encouraging an attachment to it. He could see clearly, she was that kind of girl.

If you gave her an inch, she would want a mile!

"He doesn't need a name for an hour outing."

"Just something simple, like Pal or Buddy."

"No."

"It's practical. What are we going to say at the dog park after we throw him a stick? Fetch, black-dog-with-big-feet?"

"Okay," he conceded. "It."

"We're not calling him It."

We're.

"K-9, then."

"That's not very personal," she argued.

"It's more personal than It."

That earned him a little punch on his shoulder. The smallest of gestures, and yet strangely intimate, playful, an invitation to cross a bridge from acquaintances to something more.

Don't do it, he ordered himself, but he switched the dog leash to his other hand, and gave her shoulder a nudge with his own fist.

He was rewarded with a giggle as pure as a mountain brook tumbling over rocks.

There were no other dogs at the dog park, which he thought was probably a good thing given that K-9 was very badly behaved. She said she was disappointed that K-9 wasn't going to make any friends.

He wasn't at all sure dogs made friends. He could say something about her Disneyland town and her rose-colored vision of the world, remind her of his cynicism, remind her of how different they were.

But, surprised at himself, he chose not to.

One hour. He could be a nice guy for one hour.

Sarah was rummaging in the bag and came out with a bright pink Frisbee. He could object to the color, but why bother? It was only an hour.

He took the Frisbee from her when she offered it to him, waved it in front of K-9's nose and then tossed it. The dog looked after the Frisbee, then wandered off to pee on a shrub.

"No friends, and he doesn't know how to play," she said sadly.

For a moment, Sullivan was tempted to say on the scale of human tragedy, it hardly rated. It could be the story of his own life. But again, he refrained. Instead, he went after the Frisbee and tossed it back at her.

Sarah leapt in the air, clapped her hands at it, and missed catching it by a mile. But when she jumped up like that he caught a glimpse of the world's cutest belly button. He made her jump even higher for the Frisbee the next time!

She couldn't throw, and she couldn't catch, either.

But she was game. Running after the Frisbee, jumping, throwing herself on the ground after it, making wild throws back at him. Her enthusiasm for life could be contagious! And if it was only for an hour, why not?

"Has anybody ever told you, you have the athletic talent of a fence post?" he asked her solemnly.

"In different words, I'm afraid I've been told that many times." There was something about the way she said it, even though her tone was flippant, that made him think someone somewhere had either told her, or made her feel, she didn't measure up.

There was no reason for him to take that on, or to try and do something about it, except that he had promised himself that for an hour he could manage to be a good guy. And that might include teaching her to throw a Frisbee. The world changed in small ways, after all, as much as large ones.

Isn't that what his sister had tried to tell him about Summer Fest?

He brought the Frisbee over to her, and gave it to her. "No, don't throw it. Not yet."

He went and stood behind her, leaned into her, reached around her and tucked her close to him with one arm wrapped around the firmness of her tummy. Sullivan took her throwing arm with his own.

She had stiffened with surprise at his closeness, at his touch.

"Relax," he told her. She took a deep breath, tried,

but it was as if her whole body was humming with tension. Awareness.

So was his. He was not sure what he had expected, but what he felt with her back pressed into his chest was a sense of her overwhelming sweetness, her enticing femininity. She seemed small and fragile, which made him feel big and strong.

Stop it, he warned himself. He was not going to give in to the pull of age-old instincts. He thought he should have evolved past, *Me, Tarzan, you, Jane.*

"Concentrate," he said, and she thought he meant her, but he didn't.

He guided her arm with his arm. "See?" he said softly, close to her ear, "It's a flick of the wrist. Arm all the way in to your stomach, like this, then out. Release, right there."

She missed the *right there* part by a full second. He went and retrieved the Frisbee. He contemplated how he felt.

The physical contact with her made him aware of how alone he had become in the world. Aside from the occasional hug from his sister, and being climbed all over by his nephews, when was the last time he had touched someone?

There was an obvious reason why he hadn't. Once you let that particular barrier down, it would be extremely hard to get it back up. To ignore the part of him that ached for a little softness, a little closeness, a little company.

The smart thing to do would be to back off, to coach Sarah from a distance. But Sullivan reminded himself that if he was going to make a mistake he planned to make it glorious in its scope and utter wrongness.

So he went and conducted the whole exercise all over again.

He allowed himself the pure enjoyment of a man who was doing something once. He became aware of her different scents—one coming from her hair, another from her skin, both light and deliciously fragrant.

Sullivan allowed himself to savor their differences— the way she felt, like melting butter, within the circle of his arms. He could see little wisps of golden auburn hair escaping her ponytail and dancing along the nape of her slender neck. His arms around her felt so gloriously wrong, and as right as anything had ever felt in his life.

He liked *accidentally* rubbing his whiskers against the tender lobe of her ear, then watching her flub that throw hilariously.

He liked how the nervous thrumming of her body was giving way to something softer and more supple.

After a dozen or so attempts, Sarah finally managed a half-decent Frisbee toss. The pink disc sailed through the air in a perfect arc.

Neither of them noticed. She leaned back into him and sighed, finally fully relaxed. He took her weight, easily, rested his chin on the top of her head, and breathed in the moment. He folded his arms over the tiny swell of her tummy, and they just stood like that for a moment, aware of each other, comfortable with each other at the same time.

The park suddenly looked different, as if each thing in it was lit from within. He could see individual leaves trembling on branches, the richness of the loam. The sky seemed so intensely blue it made his eyes ache.

As he watched the dog, cavorting, joyous, and felt Sarah sink deeper into him, he felt as if he had been asleep for a long time and was only now awakening.

The moment had a purity, and Sullivan felt contentment. He was aware of not having felt like this for a long, long time. Maybe not ever.

The dog suddenly seemed to catch on to the game. He retrieved the Frisbee and brought it back to them, wiggled in front of them, his tail fanning the air furiously.

"Look," Sarah said softly, "he knows he's our dog."

Sullivan could point out it was not *their* dog. But she had turned and looked over her shoulder at him, and there was something shining in her face that didn't give him the heart to do it, to steal the utter purity of this moment from her.

In fact, what he wanted to do was kiss her. To touch those lips with his own, to taste her while he was in this state of heightened awareness. He wanted to deepen the sense of connection they had.

But sanity prevailed. Wouldn't that make everything way too complicated? He wanted a glorious mistake, but he didn't want to hurt her. Not her heart. Her past heartbreak was already written all over her.

Instead, amazed by the discipline it took, Oliver gently released her and backed away from her. Afraid he had become transparent, he turned quickly away.

It was time to go home.

But he had used every ounce of discipline he had to

release her. There was none left to do what needed to be done. So, he went to get the Frisbee from the dog.

Sarah watched as Sullivan broke away from her, drank in the expression on his face as if she were dying of thirst and he was a long, cool drink of water.

She contemplated what had just happened between them. Her skin was still tingling where he had stood at her back, and she felt a chill where his warmth had just been.

He had nearly kissed her. She had seen the clearness of his eyes grow smoky with longing, she had felt some minute change ripple through the muscles in his arms and chest. She had leaned toward him, feeling her raw need for him in every fiber of her being.

Was it that need, telegraphed through her own eyes, her own body language, that had made him change his mind? Had she puckered her lips in anticipation of a kiss? Oh! She hoped she had not puckered!

"Hey, give that here!"

Sarah watched, and despite her disappointment at not being kissed, she could not help but smile.

The dog had apparently decided he liked playing Frisbee, after all. Only he invented his own version of the game, darting away whenever Sullivan got close to him.

That moment of exquisite physical tension and awareness was gone. But it seemed, suddenly and de-lightfully, like a new moment awaited. With a shout of exuberance, Sarah threw herself into that moment, and joined in the chase after the dog.

Sullivan was as natural an athlete as she was not. He was also in peak physical condition.

As if chasing the dog wasn't leaving her breathless enough, watching Sullivan unleash his power almost stopped her heart beating, too.

He was a beautifully made man, totally at ease with his body, totally confident in his abilities. It was hard not to be awed by this demonstration of pure strength and agility, Sullivan chasing after the dog, stopping on a hair, turning in midair, leaping and tackling. As he played, something came alive in his face that was at least as awe-inspiring as his show of physical prowess. Some finely held tension left him, and his face relaxed into lines of boyish delight.

What haunted him? What made this the first moment that she had seen the grimness that lingered in his eyes, that sternness around the line of his mouth, disappear completely?

"Sarah, I'm herding him toward you. Grab the Frisbee as he goes by!"

She let go of wondering what was in his past and gave herself to what he was in this moment. But of course the dog leapt easily out of her grasp, earning her a fake scowl from Sullivan.

"You have to cut him off, not jump out of his way. He's a puppy, not a herd of elephants."

"Yes, sir," she said, giving him a mock salute and jumping out of the puppy's too rambunctious path as he catapulted by her again.

"I fear you are hopeless," he growled, and then he threw back his head and laughed as she made a mistimed grab at the Frisbee when the dog came by again.

Sarah found herself laughing, too, as they both took up a frenzied pursuit of the delighted dog. She realized the moment of closeness they had experienced didn't seem to evaporate just because they had physically disengaged from it. Instead, as they chased the dog, their comfort with each other seemed to grow, as did the fun and camaraderie shimmering in the air, carrying on their shouts of laughter, the dog's happy barks.

Finally, the dog collapsed and surrendered the Frisbee. Sullivan snatched it from him, and then collapsed on the ground too, his head on the puppy's back. He patted the ground beside him in invitation, and of course she could not resist. She went and lay down, her head resting on the dog alongside his, her shoulder touching Sullivan's shoulder, her breath coming in huffs and puffs.

Clouds floated in a perfect sky.

"I see a pot of gold," she said, pointing at a cloud. "Do you?" Of course, seeing that was a reflection of the way she was feeling. Abundant. Full.

He squinted at it. "You would," he said, but tolerantly.

"What do you see?"

"You don't want to know."

"Yes, I do."

"A pile of poo."

She burst out laughing. "That's awful."

"That is just one example of how differently you and I see life."

He said it carelessly, and casually. But it reminded her that they seemed to be at cross-purposes. He wanted the barriers up. She wanted them down.

But she had a feeling she had won this round. She slapped him on the shoulder. "Don't be such a grump."

He looked astounded, glanced at his shoulder where she had smacked him, and then he actually smiled. "Oh, I see a force-feeding of a full serving of Crabbies in my future."

Future.

She was determined not to ruin this perfect moment by even thinking of that!

She was getting way too used to that smile, and how it made him look so boyish and handsome, as if he had never had a care in the world. It would be way too easy to start picturing her world with him in it.

What was happening to her? She had wanted to rescue Oliver Sullivan from himself, but she had not intended to put herself at risk! She had her new world, filled with jam and Summer Fest. Rescuing him had just been part of the new do-gooder philosophy that was supposed to fill up her life.

Only something was going wrong this morning. Because it just felt too right!

So she deliberately broke the connection between them. She retrieved her bag, pulled out water bottles. She sat back down beside him, deliberately not making contact with his shoulder again. She got her pant legs soaked trying to get the dog to drink out of one.

Then she glanced at Sullivan and was transfixed by the relaxed look on his face, taking simple pleasure of a simple moment, and she realized it wasn't as easy to break connections as she'd thought.

"I haven't felt this way since I was a kid," he said.

"I know what you mean," Sarah said, finally giving

in to it, and savoring how this closed man was revealing something of himself. What would it hurt to encourage him by revealing something of herself?

"When I worked for the magazine, the girls and I would go on all these fantastic trips. We spent a weekend shopping in San Francisco. Once we went skiing in the Alps. I feel as if we were trying to manufacture the feeling that I'm feeling right now."

She stopped, embarrassed by her attempts to explain her surprise at the exhilaration that had come from something so simple as chasing a misbehaved puppy around a park.

But was this glowing feeling inside of her from the activity? Or from being with him?

He reached over and gave her shoulder a squeeze that said, *I get it. I feel the same.*

She turned her head and gazed at his face. Really, it was mission accomplished. She had set out to rescue him from darkness and she had done it.

The echoes of his laughter were still on his face. They would probably be in her heart forever.

It would be greedy—and ultimately foolish—to want more.

But she did.

The hour he had promised her had been up half an hour ago. He'd bonded with the dog. He'd no doubt do great at that interview, the dog clearly worshipped him and it would show.

It had been more than she had hoped for.

For an hour or so, laughing and playing in the sunshine, with his arms around her, and chasing that fool

dog, Sarah had seen Oliver Sullivan at his best, unguarded. He had been carefree. Happy.

"How come you haven't felt this way since you
were a boy?" she asked, not wanting to know, *having*
to know.

He hesitated, and then he said, "I entered law enforcement really young. I had the intensity of focus,
the drive, the motivation, that made me a perfect fit for
homicide. But dealing with violence on a daily basis is
a really, really tough thing. Dealing with what people
are capable of doing to each other is soul-shattering."

Sarah thought of the grimness in his eyes, the lines
around his mouth, and was so glad she had been part
of making that go away, even if it was just for a little
while. Even if it cost her some peace of mind of her
own.

He continued softly, "If people tell you they get used
to it? They're either lying or terrible at their jobs. You
never get used to it."

"Is that why you came here, to Kettle Bend, instead?"

He was silent for a very long time. He moved his
hand off her shoulder. "I caught a really bad case. The
worst of my career. When it was done, I just couldn't
do it anymore."

"Do you need to talk about it?" she asked softly.

He snorted derisively, leapt to his feet. "No, I don't
need to talk about it. And if I did, I wouldn't pick you."

For a moment, she felt wounded. But then she saw
something else in his face, and his stance.

It wasn't that he was not trusting her. It was that he
was protecting her from what he had seen and done.

"I took a year off," he said. "That's good enough."

She had a feeling it wasn't. That he carried some dark burden inside himself that it would do him nothing but good to unload. But his face was now as closed as it had been open a few minutes ago.

"So, what did you do for a year?" she asked him, pulling the dog's head into her lap, scratching his ears, not wanting those moments of closeness between them to disappear, hoping she could get him talking again. Even if somehow it was opening her up in ways that would cost her.

"I rented a cabin outside of Missoula, Montana, and went fishing."

"Did it help?"

"As an experiment, I would say it failed. Miserably."

"Why?" she asked.

"I'd say I had too much me time. Hour after hour, day after day, with only my own dreary company. It was time to get back to work. Della had moved here. She wanted me to come, too. I thought something different would be good."

"And has it been?"

"I miss the intensity of working as a detective in Detroit. I miss the anonymity. I miss using skills I spent a lot of years developing. On the other hand, I sleep at night. I get to watch my nephews grow up. And small towns have a certain hokey charm that I'm finding hard to resist."

But she had a feeling, from the way his eyes rested on her, he wasn't just talking about small towns having a certain charm that was hard to resist.

Though she hoped hers wasn't hokey!

Still, she could not help but feel thrilled. Sarah knew

that today had been a part of that. Today, he had shared his life with someone outside of the small, safe circle of Della and her family. It had allowed him to get out of himself. To engage. To feel a reprieve from the yawning abyss of apartness that separated him from his fellow man. And she'd been part of that!

The problem with that? It was hard to let go of.

"I have to meet with the Summer Fest committees this afternoon," she said, not looking at him. She ordered herself to let go.

To say to herself, *Do-gooder, mission accomplished. Go back to your life.*

That was the problem with messing with this kind of power. Regaining control was not that simple.

Because she heard herself saying, her tone deliberately casual, "You know, in terms of the interview tomorrow, maybe you should come. It would give you a real feeling for the community spirit that is building. It might give you some ideas how to work Summer Fest into the discussion at the television station."

After his lecture to her about all the things Summer Fest was not going to do for her, she was nervous even bringing it up. She felt the potential for rejection, braced herself for it. Sullivan was probably way better at exercising control than she was.

He stared at her as if he couldn't believe she was going to try for another hour of his time.

She saw the battle on his face.

And then she saw him lose, just as she had done.

Because he ran a hand through the thick crispness of his hair and gave in, just a little.

"I have to admit I've been just a little curious about

how you are going to pull off the whole Summer Fest thing. It seems like a rather large and ambitious undertaking for a woman who can't even throw a Frisbee."

She looked at him now, stunned. "You'll come?"

"Sure," he said with a shrug, as if it meant nothing at all, as if he had not just conceded a major battle to her. "I wouldn't mind seeing what you're up to, Sarah McDougall."

CHAPTER SIX

"I can't believe you talked him into coming," Mabel Winston, chair of the Summer Fest Market Place committee, said.

Sarah let her eyes drift to where Sullivan was in deep discussion with Fred Henry, head of the Fourth of July fireworks team, and Barry Bushnell, head of organizing the opening day parade. She felt a little shiver of pure appreciation.

"He's even better in real life than he was on the video," Maryanne Swarinsky, who was in charge of the Fourth of July Picnic Committee, said in a hushed tone.

The whispered comment echoed Sarah's thoughts exactly. Oliver Sullivan was simply a man who had a commanding presence. It was more than his physical stature, and it was more than the fact he was a policeman.

He radiated a confidence in his ability to handle whatever life threw at him. He was *that* man, the one you wanted with you when the ship went down, or the building burst into flames. The one who would be coolly composed if bullets were flying in the air around him, if he had his back against the wall and the barbarians were rushing at him with their swords drawn.

But he had shared with her that he did not feel he had handled something life had thrown at him. Sarah shivered again, thinking how truly terrible it must be. *Wishing* she had been able to relieve him of some of that burden.

But she had noticed, as soon as he had entered the room, there had been a sudden stillness. Then all the men had gravitated to him and all the women had nearly swooned.

"Just look at the way that dog is glued to him," Candy McPherson, who was running the old-fashioned games day, said. "You know, maybe we should have a dog show. Just a few categories. Cutest dog. Cutest owner. That sort of thing."

There was no doubt, from her tone, that Candy had already picked the cutest owner.

"We already have six events planned over the four days," Sarah said. "That's more than enough. Maybe we'll look at some kind of dog event for next year."

Candy looked stubborn. "I could fit it into the games day, somehow."

"Is he going to take the dog?" Maryanne asked her.

Sarah glanced over at Sullivan again. The dog, worn out from his morning activities, or just plain worn out from adoring his hero, snoozed contentedly, his head on Sullivan's feet.

Sarah was amazed by what she was seeing in Sullivan. She wasn't sure what she had expected when he met the committee members. Cynicism, possibly. Remoteness, certainly.

But the playful morning with the dog seemed to have lightened him up. Sullivan looked relaxed and open.

Or maybe it was just hard to keep yourself at a distance when you were surrounded by people like these: open, friendly, giving by nature.

Unaware how intently he was being watched, Sullivan reached down and gave the dog's belly a little tickle.

"In terms of the free publicity we're getting from him and the dog," Sarah said thoughtfully, "wouldn't that be a fantastic outcome? If he kept the dog? A feel-good story with a great ending like that would bring nothing but positive to Kettle Bend."

"Talk him into it," Candy said.

Sarah smiled a little wryly. "If ever there was a man you couldn't talk into anything, it's that one, right there."

"I don't know," Mabel said. "You talked him into coming here."

Suddenly, all the women were looking at her so intently, considering her influence over that powerful man. She could tell there was curiosity and conjecture about the nature of her relationship with the handsome policeman.

Feeling herself blushing, Sarah said, "Let's get back to business, shall we?"

An hour later, she was trying to pry Sullivan away from them.

Finally, they were back out on the street, the dog padding along beside them as if it was the most natural thing in the world for the three of them to be together as a unit.

"I have to admit, Sarah," Sullivan said, "I thought you were being way too ambitious with this whole Summer Fest thing. But those people in there are really committed to you. You've built a solid team. I think, maybe, you're going to pull this off."

"Maybe?" she chided him. She stopped, planted her hands on her hips, and glared at him. Of course, it was all a ruse to hide how much she enjoyed his praise.

"Don't hit my shoulder," he begged, covering it up in mock fear with his hand. "I'll already be sporting bruises from you."

"Take it back, then," she said. "Say, *Sarah McDougall's Summer Fest is going to be an unmitigated success.*"

He laughed then. "Sarah McDougall, there is something infectious about your enthusiasm. You're even starting to get to me."

"Yippee!" she said.

His laughter deepened and made things so easy between them. She was astonished that this side of him, easygoing, relaxed, so easy to be around, was lasting. She loved how his laughter made her feel. Like the world was a good place, full to the brim with excitement and potential.

"I'm starving," he said.

She realized the hour she had promised him he would be away had now stretched late into the day. It was time to let him go.

"You want to go grab a bite to eat?"

Could it be possible he didn't want to let her go, either? Amazed at the joy in her heart, Sarah said, "I'd like that."

Like chasing the dog around the park, sitting at an outdoor table with him was really just the most ordinary of things. A guy and a gal and their dog enjoying a warm spring afternoon by having lunch on main street.

Except it wasn't *their* dog.

And they weren't really a guy and a gal in the way it probably looked like they were.

Although it felt like they were.

How could such an ordinary thing—sitting outside under an umbrella, eating French fries, feeding morsels of their hamburgers to the dog—make her feel so tingly? So wonderful and alive and happy?

Probably because the man sharing the table with her was about as far from ordinary as you could get.

They talked of small things. The ideas for Summer Fest, the weather, his brother-in-law Jonathon's recovery.

Then, out of the blue, he said, "Tell me about your job in New York."

"Oh," she said, uncomfortably, "that's in the past."

"That seems like a shame."

"What does that mean?"

"I went on the internet and read a couple of your stories for the magazine."

"You read stories by me?" she asked, astounded.

He shrugged. "Slow night for hockey."

"You read stories about babies?" she said skeptically, but something was hammering in her heart. She was flattered. Who had ever showed that much interest in anything she did?

"Don't read too much into it," he said. "Once a detective, always a snoop."

"Why would you go to the trouble?"

"Curiosity."

Oliver Sullivan was curious about her?

He took a sip of his coffee and looked at her intently. "You are really a very good writer."

"I was okay at it."

"No, actually, you were better than okay. Tell me why you decided to leave that world."

"I already did tell you that. My grandmother left me a house and a business. It was time for a change."

"That's the part that interests me."

"It's not interesting," she said evasively. But now she could see the detective in him. He was trying to find out something, and she had a feeling he would not be content until he did.

He was trying to confirm the heartbreak part of the scenario he had guessed at, when he had made her so angry and she had stormed away from the café. Now, Sarah would just as soon end the day on the bright note that they had sustained so far.

"Let me be the judge of whether it's interesting or not," he said silkily. "Why did you leave the magazine and New York? Aside from the convenient fact you were left a house and a business. If you were perfectly happy, you could have just sold them both and stayed where you were."

Her flattery was quickly being replaced by a feeling of being trapped. "Were you good at interrogations?" she demanded.

"Excellent," he said, not with any kind of ego, simply stating a fact.

"Curiosity killed the cat," she told him snippily.

"I'll take my chances."

"Why do you care?" she asked, her voice a little shrill.

"It's a mystery. That's what I do. Solve mysteries. Indulge me. I'm compulsive."

"I don't see anything mysterious about it."

"Beautiful, extremely talented young woman leaves the excitement of a big city and a flourishing career. She leaves behind shopping trips in San Francisco, and skiing in Switzerland. And for what? To live the life of a nun in Kettle Bend, Wisconsin, devoting herself to unlikely causes, such as saving the town."

She could argue she had already told him she had more fun today than skiing in Switzerland. She could argue her cause was *not* unlikely.

Instead her mind focused, with outrage, on only one part of his statement.

"A nun?" she squeaked.

"A guess. I didn't mean a nun as in saying the rosary and walking the stations of the cross. I meant, like, er, celibate."

"Huh. That shows what you know. I happened to see a naked man just this morning."

He choked on his coffee. "Touché," he said, lifting the mug to her.

"I had no idea I was appearing pathetic."

"Anything but. Which is why I'm so curious. The boyfriends should be coming out of the woodwork."

"What makes you think they aren't?"

"You don't have the look of a woman who's been kissed. And often. And by someone who knows how." He smiled and sipped his coffee.

Sarah stared at him. "How can you argue with a man who can paraphrase Rhett Butler from *Gone with the Wind*?" she asked.

"Besides, you've already told me on more than one occasion. No dating. You're obviously aiming for cynicism in the love department."

She was simply unused to a man who paid such close attention to everything she said!

"Okay, here is the pathetic truth. I was engaged to be married. While I was picking venues, pricing flowers, shopping for wedding dresses, and daydreaming about babies in bassinettes, my fiancé was having a fling with a freelancer."

"The dog," he said quietly, and then to *their* dog, "Sorry, no offense."

Really, she had said quite enough. But something about the steadiness of his gaze encouraged her to go on, to spill it all.

"He was an editor at the magazine. I caught the occasional rumor about him and Trina."

"Which you chose to ignore," Sullivan guessed.

"It seemed like the noble thing to do! To ignore malicious office gossip. I actually put it down to jealousy, as if certain people could not stand my happiness."

He shook his head. "An optimist thinks that light at the end of the tunnel is the sun," he said. "A cynic knows it's a train."

"It was a train," she agreed sadly. "I saw them together having coffee. It could have been business. I wanted to believe it was business, but there was just something about it. They just seemed a little too cozy, leaning in toward each other, so intent they never even saw me walking by the window. So I confronted him. Right until the moment I saw his face, I held out hope there would be an explanation for it. It was really just too awkward after that. I couldn't stay on the magazine and see him every day."

He was quiet, watching her intently.

"There? You wanted to know about my tawdry past, and now you do. You were right. I moved here to lick my wounds. I moved here because I felt I couldn't hold my head up in the office anymore. Are you happy?"

"Actually, I'd be happy if I could meet him, just once."

"And do what?" she asked, wide-eyed.

He shrugged, but there was something so fierce and so protective in his glance at her that a shiver went up and down her spine.

After a moment, Sullivan said, "You know what really bugs me? It's that you felt you couldn't hold your head up. As if *you'd* done something wrong."

"I was naive!"

"That's not a criminal offense."

"From the expert on criminal offenses," she said, trying to maintain some sense of humor, some sense of dignity now that she'd laid herself bare before him.

"You understand that it's entirely about him, right? It has nothing to do with you?"

"It has everything to do with me. My whole life went down the drain!"

"The career you chose to let go of, apparently, probably not your best decision ever. But him? You were lucky you saw them together. You were saved from making a horrible mistake."

That was true. If she had not found out, would he have carried on, married her anyway?

It occurred to her, if she had married Mike, she might not be sitting here.

Even leaving her career—which Sullivan said was not her best decision—if she had not done that, she would not be sitting here.

Across from him.

Falling in love with the way the sun looked on his hair, and the way his hands closed around a coffee cup, and the way his eyes were so intent on her.

"I'm going to guess you started telling yourself all kinds of lies after it happened," he said. "Like that you weren't pretty enough. Or interesting enough. Somehow, you made it your fault, didn't you?"

Falling in love with the way he had of saying things, of making things that had been foggy suddenly very, very clear.

"It's one hundred percent about him, Sarah. He's a snake. You didn't deserve that."

"Well, whether I deserved it or not, it made me cynical. Confirmed my cynicism about love and happy ever after."

He laughed softly. "You may think you are cynical, and you may want to be cynical, but, Sarah, take it from one who has that particular flaw of human nature down to an art form, you aren't."

"Well, about matters of the heart I am cynical."

"You didn't come from one of those postcard families, did you?"

Falling in love with the way he *saw* her, and stripped her of the secrets that held her prisoner.

"What makes you say that?"

"Something you said when we were playing Frisbee.
I got the impression you'd been told once too often you
didn't measure up."

Sarah gulped. He really did see way, way too much.
He read people and situations with an almost terrifying accuracy.

Yet there was something very freeing about being
seen.

"If you'd had proper support through your breakup,
you'd probably still be in New York writing. You probably wouldn't have decided to love a town instead of a
man quite so quickly."

She stared at him, but then sighed, resigned to the
fact he could read her so clearly.

"I actually did think I had a perfect family," she con-
fessed, and confession felt good, even though she had
already said more than enough for one day! "Except for
the fact my father seemed to want a boy, it was a fairly
happy childhood."

"Personally, I think that's a pretty big fact," he said,
"but go on."

"When I was eleven, my mother discovered my father was having an affair. They tried to patch it up, but
the trust was gone. There were two bitter years of fighting and sniping and accusations."

"And you'd come spend summers at Grandma's
house, and dream of the perfect family," he guessed
softly.

"I'd plot how to fix the one I had," she admitted
with a reluctant smile. "It didn't work. When my dad
finally did leave, he never looked back. He remarried

and his new family—two little boys—was everything to him. You wouldn't have even known he had a daughter from a previous relationship. His idea of parenting was support cheques and a card on my birthday. Despite his neglect, according to my mother, I started looking to replace him the minute he left. Then I did find one just like him—and nearly married him, too. Amazing, huh?"

"Not so amazing," he said softly.

She was suddenly embarrassed that she had said so much, revealed so much about herself, even if it did feel good to be so transparent. "It's a good thing I never committed any crimes," she said. "You'd have a full signed confession in front of you!"

The talk turned to lighter things, and finally Sullivan called for the bill, giving her *a look* when she offered to pay half of it.

As they walked back to his house, he charmed her with a funny story about his nephew Jet.

As grateful as she was for the change of subject, Sarah was aware of feeling dissatisfied.

He had uncovered her deepest secrets with ease, made her feel backed into a corner until she had no choice but to spit it out. Well, maybe that wasn't so surprising. That's what detectives did, right?

But now, after hinting this morning at the dissatisfactions that had brought him to Kettle Bend, he was giving nothing in return. In a way, he was keeping his distance just as effectively with the small talk as he had been with his remoteness.

Sarah bet he'd used charm plenty of times to avoid any intimacy in his life!

So, now they stood on his front porch, and Sarah was stunned by what time it was. "Shoot. I missed the vet's office. They're closed in a few minutes. I won't be able to get the dog back there in time."

She hadn't done it on purpose, but maybe the dog could wheedle by the defenses that she could not.

"Could you take him?" she asked. "Just for tonight? You have to pick him up for the interview tomorrow, anyway."

He shrugged. "Sure. No big deal."

Somehow she could not bear to say goodbye. Not like this. Not with him knowing everything there was to know about her in all its humiliating detail, and her knowing close to nothing about him.

"Are you from one of those good families?" she asked. "Or were you, before your parents died?"

He stared off into the distance for a minute. "Yeah," he finally said, slowly, "I was. I mean, it wasn't the Cleavers. We were a working-class family in a tough Detroit neighborhood. There was never enough money. Sometimes we didn't even have enough food. But there was always enough love."

He suddenly looked so sad.

"How did your mom and dad die?"

She blurted it out. Maybe because a dog getting by his defenses was not really a rescue at all.

Sarah watched him. She could tell he was blindsided by the question. It was taking a chance.

But it just felt as if she had to move deeper.

Now he looked as if he might not answer. As if giving himself over to the simple intimacies of sharing a sun-filled morning with her and the dog had been enough of a stress on his system for one day. As if his peek into her life by going to the meetings and probing into her history at the outdoor café had been more than enough for one day.

But how was it any kind of intimacy if it was not shared? If it was a one-way street?

She held her breath, pleading inwardly for this break-through. For his trust. To offer him the kind of freedom from his past that he had just offered her.

"They were murdered," he said, finally, reluctantly, quietly.

She felt the shock of it ripple along her spine, felt the dark violence of it overlay the beauty of the day.

Then she realized that this dark violence must over-lay him every single day of his life.

All day she had been watching him change, sensing his barriers go down. She had watched as he became more engaged, more spontaneous, more open. She had seen him reach out, take her secrets from her, expose them to the light of day, their power evaporated as the sun hit them.

But her secrets suddenly seemed petty, so tiny and tawdry in comparison to his tragic revelation.

The look on his face now reminded Sarah that the bond between them was tenuous, that he might, in fact, still be looking for an excuse to break it.

So even though she wanted to say something, to ask questions, or to say she was sorry, some deep, deep in-stinct warned her not to.

Instead, she laid her hand across the strength of his wrist, lightly, tenderly, inviting him to trust.

After a long moment, he said, "It was a case of being

in the wrong place at the wrong time. Mistaken identity. A gang shooting gone terribly wrong."

Her hand remained on his wrist, unmoving. Her eyes on his face, drinking in his pain, feeling as if she could take it from him, as if she could share his burden.

Suddenly he yanked his wrist out from under her hand, muttering, "It happened a long time ago."

It might be a long time ago, but it was the answer to everything. Why he had chosen the profession he chose—and more. It was the key to why he chose to walk alone.

She knew he had just given her an incredible gift by trusting her with this part of himself.

"Thank you for telling me," she said quietly.

He looked annoyed. Not with her. But with himself. As if he had shown an unacceptable lack of judgment for sharing this. A weakness.

But she saw something else entirely. She saw a man who was incredibly courageous. Oliver Sullivan had tried to take on something—or maybe everything—that was terribly wrong in the world.

But he had sacrificed some part of himself in his relentless pursuit of right. He had immersed himself so totally in the darkness of the human heart that he really did believe every light at the end of a tunnel was a train.

She had been right to come after him.

But now she could see if she had thought finding out about him would create closeness, the exact opposite was true.

He fitted his key in his door, shoved the dog inside without looking back at her. "I have to go."

Retreating. Saying no to the day and to what her hand on his wrist had offered. Saying he could carry his burdens by himself.

Even if it killed him.

Just when she thought he was going to leave without even saying goodbye, he turned back to her suddenly, took a step toward her and then stood above her, looked down at her with dark eyes, smoky with longing. He took his finger and tilted her chin up. And dropped his head over hers and kissed her.

His lips touching her lips were incredible. He tasted of things that were real—rain and raging rivers—and things that were strong and unbreakable—mountain peaks and granite canyons.

He tasted not of heaven, as she had thought he would, but of something so much better. Earth: magnificent, abundant, mysterious, life-giving, *attainable to mere mortals*.

She could feel a fire stirring to life in her belly. She thought she had doused that particular flame, but now she could see that wasn't quite right.

No, that wasn't right at all.

It was as if every kiss and every passionate moment Sarah had experienced before this one had been the cheapest of imitations. Not real at all.

She told herself it was a hello kind of kiss, a door opening, something beginning between them. That's what she thought she tasted on his lips: realness, and strength and the utter spring freshness of new beginning.

But when his lips left hers, she opened her eyes, reluctantly. He took a step back from her and she read a different truth entirely in his eyes.

His eyes were suddenly both shadowed and shuttered.

It hadn't been hello at all. It had been goodbye.

Then he straightened and smiled slightly, that cynical my-heart-is-made-of-stone smile.

"Sarah," he said softly, "you've got your hands full trying to save this town. Don't you even try to save me."

Then he turned and walked through his open door. He was alone, even though the dog was with him. He was the gunfighter leaving town.

Not needing anyone or anything. Not a woman and not a dog.

She was humiliated that she had been so transparent.

But then she realized, buried in there somewhere, in those soft words, had been an admission.

He hadn't said he didn't need saving.

He had just warned her not to try.

It seemed to her, suddenly, that in her whole life she had never been spontaneous, she had never done what her heart wanted her to do.

She'd always backed down from the desires of her heart, so afraid of being let down, of being disappointed, that she had not even spoken them, let alone acted on them.

Sarah had always chosen the safe way, the conservative way, the don't-rock-the-boat way. She had never broken the rules. She had worked hard at being the proverbial good girl.

Where had that gotten her? Had it ever earned her the love and approval she had been so desperate for?

No.

Except this morning, for once in her life, Sarah had done what she wanted to do, not what she *should* do. Because she *should* have obeyed his boundaries. But instead, she had marched up the steps of Oliver Sullivan's house with that dog, an act of instinct, as brave as she had ever been.

And today she had *lived*.

Somehow, after that, after having *lived* so completely, having experienced exhilaration in such simplicity, life was never going to be the same.

Taking a deep breath, even though she was quivering inside, Sarah decided she wasn't backing down now. With every ounce of courage she possessed, she crossed the threshold into his house, where Sullivan stood by his open door, just getting ready to shut it.

Tentatively, she reached out, touched his face. She felt the roughness of a new growth of whiskers under the tenderness of her palm. She touched the stern line of his mouth with her fingertips.

Something shifted in his face. She could clearly see the struggle there.

When she saw that struggle, she sighed, and pulled herself in close to him. She wrapped her arms around the solidness of his neck and pressed herself against the length of him.

She could feel the absolute strength of him, the soft heat radiating off his body. She could hear the beat of his heart quickening beneath his shirt. She could smell the rich, seductive aroma of him.

She held on tight, waiting to see if he would recoil from her, reject her as she had been rejected by her father. As she had been rejected when a man she'd thought she had loved, whom she had planned her future with, had cavalierly given himself to another.

Would Oliver Sullivan reject her?

Or would he surrender?

She was terrified of finding out.

But she was even more terrified of walking away without having the courage to explore what might have been.

CHAPTER SEVEN

SULLIVAN felt the delicious curve of Sarah's body pressed against the length of him. If there was a word that was not in his vocabulary, it was this one.

Rest.

From the moment he had first met her, everything about her had told him she would offer him this.

A place in the world where he could rest.

Where he could lay down his shield, and share his burdens, and rest his weary, weary heart. Where he could find peace.

He had tried to send her away, he had tried to save her from himself. And instead of going, she had seen right through him, to what he needed most of all.

He was taken by her bravery all over again. And by his own lack of it. Because he should have refused what she was offering him and he could not.

Instead, he kissed the top of her head and pulled her in close to him. She stirred against him and looked up at him, and there were tears shining in her eyes.

So, instead of doing what he needed to do—putting her away from him and shutting the door on her—he touched his fingers to her tears and then touched those fingers to his lips.

"Don't cry, sweet Sarah," he said softly. "Please don't cry."

He realized he wasn't nearly as hardened to tears as he had thought he was. Because he wanted never to be the reason for her tears.

"What do you want?" he asked, into her hair.

"I want this day to never end," she said.

He thought maybe he couldn't give her everything she wanted. In fact, he knew he could not give her the dreams that shone in her eyes: a perfect family, behind a white picket fence.

She was a nice girl who deserved a nice life. He did not perceive himself as any kind of nice person. Giving someone a nice life, given the darkness of his own soul, was probably out of the question.

But he could probably give her this one thing: a day that never ended. When he had first met her, he had thought he could spare ten minutes for her. Then this morning, he'd thought an hour with her would not pose any kind of threat to either of them.

Now, he considered. He could give her himself for the rest of the day.

He stood back from his door, inviting her in. "I hope you like hockey, then."

"Adore it," she said.

"Sure you do," he said skeptically. "Who's playing tonight?"

"The Canucks and the Red Wings, Game Two of the Stanley Cup Final."

He stared at her. Oh, boy. She was going to be a girl to contend with.

"Hey," she said, "you're looking at the girl who tried desperately to be the boy her father wanted."

"Do you know how to make popcorn, too?"

At her nod, he muttered, "I'm lost," and was rewarded with the lightness of her laughter filling up a house that had never been anything but empty.

And threatening to fill up a man who had never been anything but that, either.

The question *Where is this all going?* tried to claw by his lowered defenses. The question *How can this end well?* tried to force its way past the loveliness of her laughter.

He ignored them both. It was only the rest of the day, a few hours out of his life and hers.

What was so wrong with just living one moment at a time, anyway? Perhaps, one moment leading into another could get out of hand. Maybe it was a little out of hand already.

But it was nothing he could not bring back under his control the minute he chose to.

So they learned together that feeding popcorn to a large dog in a small room was a bad idea. He learned she knew more about hockey than anyone else of his acquaintance. She insisted on staying until one minute past midnight, so she could say their day together had never ended. And he learned a woman falling asleep against your chest was one of the sweetest things that could happen to you.

Bringing things back under his control was obviously not as simple as choosing to do it. Because as he watched her putting on her shoes, giving the dog a last pet, he heard himself say, "Do you want to come to the TV station with me tomorrow?"

She beamed at him as if he'd offered her dinner for two at the fanciest restaurant in the area.

He watched her little red Bug drive away into the night and some form of sanity tried to return. One day was clearly becoming two.

After that he would extricate himself from this whole mess he'd gotten himself into.

The next day, the interview for television went extremely well. The dog behaved, the questions were easy to answer and he managed to mention Kettle Bend and Summer Fest at nearly every turn.

Sarah was waiting in the wings, her face aglow with approval. It was a light that a man could warm himself in for a long, long time.

"I thought you said you weren't good at interviews," she teased.

"I guess it's different when you don't have a whole city howling for a crime to be solved, eager for someone to throw under the bus if an investigation isn't moving fast enough or moves in the wrong direction."

She wasn't just listening, she was drinking him in.

"Do you want to come to my place?" she asked. "We could order a pizza and watch Game Three together."

She wouldn't meet his eyes, so shy and fearful of asking him, that he did not have the heart to say no.

Besides, one day had already become two, so why not just give himself over to it?

The living room of her house was as he remembered it. A sweet, tart aroma permeated the whole place.

Sullivan remembered smelling it that first day.

And it reminded him of things gone from his life: cooking, warm kitchens, good smells. Home.

Rest.

Thankfully, before he could get too caught up in that, the dog spotted her cat and went on a rampage, under the coffee table, over the couch and through the door to her kitchen.

He finally cornered the dog in the kitchen, where he was howling his dismay that the cat had disappeared out the cat door. Sullivan stopped and surveyed Sarah's kitchen, astounded. *Could anything be further from rest than this?*

He went back into the living room. Sarah was bent over, picking up flowers that had been knocked off the coffee table out of the puddles on the floor. Her delectable little derriere pointed in the air was somewhat of a distraction.

"Um, what's with the kitchen?"

She turned and looked at him, blushed red. Because she knew he'd been sneaking a peek at her backside or because Little Susie Homemaker did not like getting caught with a mess in her perfect life?

"It's my new decorating theme," she said, a touch defensively. "I call it Titanic, After the Sinking."

"It's more like Bomb Goes Off in the Rhubarb Patch." He turned back and looked at the kitchen. Every counter was covered in rhubarb, some of it wilted. There were pots stacked in the sink and overflowing it. In an apparent attempt to prolong its life, some of the rhubarb was stuck, stalks down, in buckets full of water.

"Just shut the door," she pleaded.

"Is that rhubarb on the *ceiling*?"

She came and stood beside him with her rescued flowers. "I had a little accident with the pressure cooker."

"People can be killed by those things!" he said, his tone a little more strident than he wanted.

"I just thought I could expedite the jam-making process. As you can see, I'm a little behind."

He turned and looked at her. He saw by the slump of her shoulders that she *hated* making jam. And he also saw that this was, at least in part, his fault. She'd been out with him when she clearly should have been making her jam.

So he closed the kitchen door, partly to protect the cat and partly to protect her from whatever it was she hated so much. They ordered a pizza and watched hockey—and learned you shouldn't feed all-dressed pizza to a large dog in a small room.

After the game, he really knew it was time for him to go.

But in a way, whether he wanted it or not, she had rescued him from his life. Only for a few days, it was going to be over soon, he told himself firmly, but he wanted to do something for her.

"Let's tackle that rhubarb together," he said.

Her mouth fell open. "Oliver, that's not necessary. I can manage."

Oliver. Why did she insist on calling him that? And why did it feel so right off her lips? Part of this sensation of homecoming.

Yes, he owed her something.

"Sure, you can manage," he said. "Just fit in a few thousand jars of rhubarb jam between saving the town, and—" And what? *Saving me.* "—and everything else," he finished lamely.

"I only have a couple of dozen orders left to fill," she said. "And then I hoped to have some ready for the Market Place at Summer Fest, but if that doesn't happen it's okay."

But it wasn't really okay.

She was putting her livelihood on hold for the town. And for him.

He could help her with this. Repay his depts. Then *adiós, amiga.* He would have given her—and himself— two days, one hour and ten minutes.

"Show me to your recipe," he said.

"No, I—"

"Don't argue with me."

She looked at him stubbornly. It occurred to him he actually *liked* arguing with her.

She folded her arms over her chest. "I can argue with you if I want."

"Yes," he said, "you can. But I have to warn you, there will be repercussions."

"Such as?" she said, unintimidated.

"Such as my tea-towel snapping is world class."

"Your what?"

"Let me demonstrate." He took a tea towel from where it hung over her oven handle. He spun it, and then flicked it. The air cracked with the sound. He spun it again, moved toward her, then snapped it in the general direction of that delectable little backside.

"Hey!"

But she was running, and then they were darting around her kitchen island, and in and out of the buckets of rhubarb. They'd forgotten to shut the door, so the puppy joined in, not sure what he was chasing, but thrilled to be part of the game.

On her way by the stove, she grabbed her own tea towel, spinning while running. Then she turned and faced him, got off a pretty good crack at him. Laughing, he swiveled around, and they reversed their wild chase through her kitchen.

Finally, gasping for breath, choking on laughter, they stopped. She surrendered.

She showed him her grandmother's recipe.

"'Spring Fling,'" he read. Then he read the rest, and looked up at her with a wry smile. "You think this works?"

"Of course not!"

He looked back at the recipe. "No wonder you hate making jam," he said. "Sixty-two cups of rhubarb, finely chopped? You'd have to eat a couple of jars of the stuff first. You know, so you felt good and frisky."

"I don't hate making jam," she said stubbornly. "And I used up all my frisky being chased around the kitchen."

"Yes, you *do* hate making jam." He was willing to bet he could coax the frisky part out of her, too.

But he wasn't going to. He was going to be a Boy Scout doing his good deed for the day.

Whether or not she hated making jam, another truth was soon apparent to him. He really did like the playful interactions with her. Friskiness aside, it was fun bantering. Bugging her. Chasing her around the kitchen until the dog was wild and she was helpless with laughter.

He really did like arguing with her about what was finely chopped and what was not. About training dogs. About whether or not to try the pressure cooker again.

It was two o'clock in the morning when he stood at her front door, putting on his coat and shoes. He doubted he would ever feel free of the smell of cooking rhubarb.

"Do you have to work tomorrow?" she asked, concerned.

"Yeah, I start really early. Five-thirty. It's okay. I'm used to rough hours."

"I can't believe it! All that jam, done. And the most fun I've ever had doing it, too."

Then she blushed.

And he realized he had never left a woman's house at two in the morning with *nothing* happening.

Except thirty-two pint jars of jam sitting neatly on a counter, glowing like jewels. Except chasing her around the kitchen, snapping a tea towel at her behind. Except standing shoulder to shoulder, washing and drying that mountain of pots.

Oh, something *was* happening, all right. It felt like he was being cured of the sourness of old heartaches. It felt as if he was feeling new hope.

Dangerous ways to feel.

He hadn't even eaten any of that blasted jam! Unless the taste test off the shared spoon counted. Unless licking that little splotch off the inside of her wrist counted. It was the best damned jam he'd ever tasted, but he was well aware that what he was feeling didn't have a thing to do with the jam.

It was the circumstances that had made it so sweet and so tart. If coming home had a taste, that would be it.

He straightened, looked at her, and just could not resist.

He beckoned her into the circle of his arms, tilted her chin up and touched his lips to hers. Then he deepened the kiss.

And found out he had been wrong about the taste of coming home.

It was not in her jam.

It was in her lips.

She took a step back from him. He could see the question in her eyes.

She bent and took the dog's ears in both her hands, and planted a kiss right on the tip of his black nose.

When she straightened, she looked Sullivan right in the eye.

"I think it's time to give the dog a real name," she said.

It jolted him. Because it wasn't really about giving the dog a name. It was about whether or not he could commit.

It was about his phobia to attachment.

It was about where this was all going.

He didn't answer her, and he could see the disappointment in her face.

He'd always known he was bound to disappoint her. The truth? Sarah McDougall didn't really know the first thing about him.

Now might be the time to tell her. He was damaged.

He had failed at a relationship before. She'd made a poor choice in a man before, and he would be a worse choice.

But even telling her the details of his life and of his past implied this was all going somewhere, and he was determined that it wasn't.

So when Sarah said, "Do you want to meet after work tomorrow? We can walk the dog-without-the-name."

He knew he had to say no. He *knew* it. But he didn't. The new hope that had sprung up in him, unbidden, wouldn't let him.

"Why don't you meet me at my place around four?" he said. "Don't come earlier. I don't want to get caught in the shower again." And he realized he liked to make her blush nearly as much as he liked to argue with her.

But she wasn't letting him have the upper hand completely. She smiled sweetly and said, "I'm going to make a list of names for the dog."

As he walked away from her, Sullivan realized two days were becoming three. His legendary discipline was failing him at every turn. No, not at every turn. Maybe it was to convince himself he was still in control that he decided right then and there that he was never going to name that dog.

"Trey, Timothy, Taurus, Towanda…"

"Towanda?"

"I just threw that in to see if you were paying attention. I'm already at T and I find it hard to believe you haven't liked one single name for the dog," she commented.

"Sarah, I'm not keeping him. It doesn't make sense to name him. That will be up to the people who get him."

He said he wasn't keeping the dog, but Sarah didn't believe him.

The three of them had spent lots of time together over the last week. That dog belonged with Oliver Sullivan and he knew it! He was just being stubborn.

And he was certainly that. Stubborn. Strong.

But what most people would not know was that he was also funny. Unexpectedly tender. Gentle. Intelligent. Playful.

Sarah slid a look at him. They were walking the dog by the river, Oliver's idea, to get the dog over his fear of water.

She watched him throw a stick into the water, and felt her heart soar at the look on his face when the dog refused to fetch. Determined. Curious. Open. Tender.

What was happening to her? And then, just like that, she knew.

She wasn't just in love with things about him: the way his hair fell over his eye, the way his smile could light up her whole world, the way he could make making a walk along the river or making jam an adventure in being alive.

She was falling in love with Oliver Sullivan.

She contemplated that thought and waited for a feeling of terror to overtake her. Instead a feeling of exuberance filled her.

Life had never been better. Ever since the interview that he had done, reservations for accommodations during Summer Fest were pouring into the town. The committees were going full steam ahead, and final details were in place for most of the activities and events.

Every booth was sold out for Market Place.

In the last week, Sarah had seen Oliver every day. They had walked the dog. One day they rented bikes and rode the entire river path, the dog bounding along beside them, a reflection of the joy in the air. The most ordinary of things—making popcorn and watching hockey—became infused with the most extraordinary light.

They had exchanged tentative kisses that were growing deeper and more passionate with each passing day.

They held hands openly.

When they watched TV he put his arm over her shoulder, pulled her in tight to him. Sometimes he would take her hand, kiss it, blow on where the kiss had been, and laugh when she tried to shake off the shivers that went up and down her spine.

But that had nothing on the quivers she felt every single time she saw him. Her first glimpse of him in a day always felt as if her heart had been closed, like a fist, and now it opened, waiting, expecting to be filled.

And he never disappointed.

As she watched, he threw a stick in the water again for the dog. Spring runoff was finished. The river was shallow and mellow.

The dog whined, watched it plaintively, and then went and hid behind Oliver's leg, peeking out at the stick drifting lazily down the river. She watched the stick go, thinking about currents, how you could be caught in one before you knew it. You started out drifting lazily along, and then what?

He sighed, and scratched the dog's ears. "Aw, hells bells," he said. "Maybe I am keeping him." Then he turned and looked at her, gauging something.

"My sister invited us over for dinner tomorrow. Are you game?"

She stared at him. He might be keeping the dog. His sister had invited *them* for dinner. Everything was changing and deepening in the most exciting and terrifying of ways.

"Did you tell your sister about me?" she asked, something pounding in her chest. She knew from the way he looked when he talked about Della that his sister was the most important person in his world. What would it mean if he had talked to her about Sarah?

He looked sheepish. "Nah. She saw us riding bikes along the river path. She said she nearly drove into the river she was so shocked to see me on a bike. She thinks I don't know how to have fun. What do you think of that?"

"She doesn't know you at all."

He laughed. "She doesn't know what I've become in the last little while."

His eyes rested on hers with *that* look in them. The one that made her insides feel as if they were turning to goo, the one that made her heart feel as if it was expanding mightily, the one that stirred embers within her to flame.

"I'd love to go for dinner with you at your sister's house," she said.

He nodded, looked out at the river. "That's what I was afraid of."

She knew then that he felt it, too. They were caught in something as powerful as the current of that river.

"Where do you think that stick will end up?" she asked him.

It was a dot now in the distance. She thought of it ending up in a green field a long way away, a child picking it up and throwing it again. Maybe it would make it to the ocean, drift out to sea, end up in a foreign land. The possibilities, for the stick and for her life, seemed infinite and exciting.

"Probably going to go over a waterfall," he said, "and be pulverized."

Sarah felt the smallest chill.

"I have to go," she said reluctantly. "Committee meetings. Are you coming?"

"No, I better go get ready for work."

Still, it amazed her how often he did come, it amazed her how quickly and effortlessly he won the respect of his neighbors, how he belonged.

She was aware that, more and more, they were seen as a couple and couldn't suppress the thrill it gave her.

She walked into the meeting feeling as if she was still trembling from the lingering kiss he had planted on her all-too-willing lips down there by the river before they said goodbye.

"Oooh, look who's in love," Candy teased her.

Sarah had only just discovered it herself and felt embarrassed that she was telegraphing it to the whole town.

"I'm not in love," she protested, but weakly.

Candy just laughed. "Talk about a perfect ending to the story! Drowning dog brings beautiful couple together. And then they keep the dog!"

"Oh, stop, we're nowhere near a couple."

"Look, when you go to Hombre's on a Saturday

night in Kettle Bend, and order one milkshake with two straws? That's official."

"You heard about that?" Sarah said.

"I even know what you were wearing."

"Stop it. You don't!"

"White safari-style shirt, black capris, and the whole outfit saved from being completely boring by candy-floss pink ballet-style shoes."

"Oh my God."

"That's small towns, Sarah. Everybody knows everything, usually before you know it yourself. So, you can tell me you're not in love all you want. The glow in your cheeks and the sparkle in your eyes are telling me something quite different. Have you named the dog yet?"

"No." But suddenly it felt so big, that she had to tell someone. She leaned toward Candy. "But I think he *is* going to keep him."

Candy laughed. "I never had a doubt! Like I said, the perfect happy ending."

The next night, Sarah met Della and Jonathon for the first time. Della had made spaghetti, and if Sarah was worried about awkward moments, she needn't have been.

Between Jet and Ralf chasing the dog through the house, and then making spaghetti the messiest meal ever, she was not sure she had ever laughed so hard.

Sarah was astounded by the level of comfort she felt in this house. Because Oliver had brought her, she was, no questions asked, part of an inner circle she had always longed to belong to.

Family.

Sarah marveled at the feeling of closeness. There was plenty of good-natured kidding around the table, but no put-downs. Oliver and Jonathon had an easy rapport, and he and Della obviously shared a remarkable bond.

Della asked her brother to put the kids to bed, while she and her husband did the dishes.

"You go with him, too, Sarah."

They went into the boys' bedroom together. There was a single bed on one side of the room and a crib on the other.

With the baby nuzzled against her chest, Jet propped up the pillows on his bed. Impossibly they all squeezed onto Jet's skinny little bed, she on one side of the little boy, and Oliver on the other. The dog tried to join them, and looked stubborn when Oliver told him no. Then he tried to crawl under the bed, and they all clung to the rocking surface until the dog figured out he wouldn't fit, and sulkily settled at the end of the bed instead.

Finally, everyone was settled and Jet carefully chose a book.

"This one," he said, and Oliver took the book from him.

Oliver was a great reader. With his nephew snuggled under his arm, they all listened raptly as the story unfolded. Within seconds the baby fell asleep, melting into the softness of her chest.

She stole a look at Oliver and felt a yearning so strong it was like getting caught in a current that you had no hope of fighting against.

If you had no hope of fighting against it, why not just relax and enjoy the ride?

She let his rich voice wash over her. She let the sensory experience flood into her: his dark head bent over his nephew's, his hand turning the pages.

After her relationship with Mike, she had tried to convince herself she could live without this.

Now she knew she could not. This was what she wanted.

No, it was more than that.

This was what she *needed*. This was the life she had to have for herself.

When the story was done, Oliver took the sleeping baby from her, settled him in his crib, Ralf's little rear pointed at the ceiling, his thumb in his mouth.

For a moment, they stood there, together, frozen in a moment of perfection.

Then they joined Della and Jonathon on the back deck sipping coffee and watching the stars come out.

"I never saw the stars in Detroit," Della said, and Sarah was aware of how the other woman's hand crept into her husband's.

Jonathon's leg was still in a cast, but if he had any resentment toward Della for the fact he worked so far away, it certainly didn't show. He looked like a man overjoyed to give his wife the stars. Who would drive a hundred miles a day to do it for her.

The conversation was easy.

Sarah simply loved watching Oliver with his sister. Playful, teasing, protective. This was the real Oliver, with no guards up.

Later, she and Della sat at the table, the men had moved away to the back of the yard, the tips of cigars winking against the blackness of the night.

"How come you call your brother Sullivan?" Sarah asked.

"To tell you the truth, I'm amazed he lets you call him Oliver."

"Why?"

"He's never really been called Oliver. Even in school, he was always called Sullivan, or Sully."

"Even by you?"

"Threatened to cut my pigtails off while I slept if I ever told anyone his name was Oliver."

"Why?"

"Who knows? Somebody must have teased him. The school had produced *Oliver Twist* and he was probably tired of hearing *Consider yourself at home.*"

For a moment, Sarah heard the jingle inside her head. *Consider yourself at home. Consider yourself one of the family…*

The feeling she had wanted her whole life. And had felt, for the first time, in the past few days.

"My dad always called him a nickname, Sun, *s-u-n*, not *s-o-n*. He said the day Oliver was born the sun came out in his life and never went back down. I was Rainbow, for the same reason."

Sarah felt the love of it, the closeness of this family, felt the full impact of the tragedy that had disrupted their lives.

"My mom called him Oliver," Della continued softly. "She was the only one who ever did. After she died, he seemed even more sensitive to people calling him that. I think it reminds him of all he lost that night. Which is why it surprises me that you call him that." Her voice trailed off, and she studied Sarah.

"Oh," Della said, and her eyes widened.

"Oh, what?"

"You're just good for him, that's all. I couldn't believe that was him, when I saw you guys riding your bikes by the river." Della looked out over the yard, a small, satisfied smile playing across her pretty face. Contented. "Denise wasn't good for him. Thank God they never had kids."

"Denise?" Sarah asked, startled.

Della looked surprised. "Oh! I would have thought he'd told you about his ex-wife. I'm sorry. I shouldn't have mentioned it.

Oliver had been married? And he had never told her? Sarah felt the shock of it. Oliver knew everything there was to know about her. Everything. He knew about her childhood and her father's philandering and her poor choice of a man to share her future and dreams with.

Over the past days she had told him about dead pets, disastrous dates, her senior prom and her favorite movie of all time.

How was it she felt so close to him, and yet, when she thought about it, he still had revealed relatively little about himself?

A wife in his past? Sarah felt stunned. When she had first seen him with his nephews, she had concluded he was a man who would be fiercely devoted when he decided to commit.

Getting to know him, she had concluded he would be a man who would take *forever* seriously, a man incapable of breaking a vow.

She felt the wrongness of her conclusions slide up

and down her spine, reminding her she had been wrong once before.

She had been wrong about Mike, not listening to the subtle clues he had given of his growing dissatisfaction with their relationship.

Hadn't Oliver been giving her clues, too? Not naming the dog, for one. For another, he had told her point-blank he was attachmentphobic.

Why had she chosen to ignore all that?

Charmed, obviously, by *this*. By being invited to meet his family. By long walks with the dog. By making rhubarb jam together and watching hockey.

So charmed she had deliberately not seen the truth?

Suddenly, in the quiet of the night, they heard a cell phone ring.

"I hope he doesn't answer that," his sister said.

But they both heard Oliver say hello, and Della sighed. "I'll bet it has something to do with work. And I bet he'll go." She turned and looked hard at Sarah. "How will you feel about that? Because that's what finished Denise."

Denise again.

Sarah was suddenly uncertain that it even mattered how she felt about it! But she answered, anyway, a little stiffness in her voice, "I've figured out his work isn't what he does. It's who he is."

Della didn't seem to hear the stiffness. She gave her a smile that until that moment had been reserved just for Oliver, and then she gave Sarah a quick, hard hug that renewed her longing to be part of a unit called family.

But had that very longing made her blind? Just as it had before?

CHAPTER EIGHT

SULLIVAN listened to the voice on the phone. "You heard *what*?"

From the porch, he could hear his sister and Sarah laughing, and turned his back away from the compelling sound of it.

Della adored Sarah. He could tell. Is that why he had brought her here? Obviously bringing a girl to his sister's was a big step.

Akin to posting banns at the church, now that he thought about it.

Why hadn't he thought about that before? It was unlike him not to think situations completely through. Why hadn't he thought that both his sister and Sarah were going to read things into his arrival here with her that he might not have intended?

In that moment when they had climbed into that tiny bed, on either side of Jet, Sarah with the sleepy baby cuddled into her chest, he had seen that same look on her face that he recognized from the first time she had held Ralf.

Whether she knew it or not, this is what she wanted out of life.

But what had shocked him, what had come out of

left field and whacked him up the side of his head was this thought: *it was what he wanted, too.*

Suddenly, he knew what terrible weakness had allowed him to not think things through, to bring her to his sister's.

He had fallen in love with Sarah McDougall.

It was just wrong. He had nothing to bring to a relationship. He had seen and experienced too much darkness. Not just seen it, sought it out. It had seeped into him, like drinking toxic waste. It had made him hard and cold and cynical, as ready to believe bad about his fellow man as Sarah was ready to see the good.

A girl like Sarah needed a guy like his brother-in-law, Jonathon. One of those uncomplicated, regular, reliable guys, with no dark past. Jonathon was a third-generation orthodontist. Jonathon had learned as soon as he started breathing what family was all about: safety, security, happiness, routines, traditions.

Sullivan and Della had learned those things, too. But the difference was they both knew how those things could be ripped from you.

Jonathon knew Della's history, but he didn't *feel* it.

Jonathon didn't really believe that your whole life could be shattered in the blink of an eye. He didn't carry the knowledge that a man could not really control his world. Sullivan carried that knowledge deep inside himself like a festering wound.

Jonathon naively believed that his strength and his character and his ability to provide were enough to protect his family.

And Della? His sister was courageous enough to have embraced love even knowing life made no promises, even knowing happily-ever-after was not always the outcome, not even if that's what you wanted the most.

Sullivan did not kid himself that he had anything approaching his sister's courage.

"Thanks for calling," Sullivan said, and clicked off the phone.

"Everything all right?" Jonathon asked.

"Not really," Sullivan said. He had known what had to be done before the phone call. He had known as soon as he had sat on that bed beside Sarah, reading stories to his nephews. He had known as soon as he acknowledged the truth.

He had to say goodbye to her.

The phone call had just given him a way to do it. Bradley Moore had found out Sullivan was keeping the dog.

Only one person in the world had known that. One.

His anger was real. But this was the part he couldn't let her see.

He wasn't really angry at her. No, Sullivan was angry with himself. For letting this little slip of a woman slide by his defenses. For letting things develop between them when he had absolutely no right to do that, when he had nothing to bring to the table. He'd buried his parents and failed at one marriage already. In his final case as a homicide detective he had seen—and done— things that he could not forget.

This is what he brought to the table.

An inability to trust life.

Sarah sharing a deeply personal moment of his life with Bradley Moore, using it to her advantage, only confirmed what he already knew.

He couldn't really trust anyone.

Least of all himself.

Walking up from the back of the yard, toward the light, toward the warmth and laughter of the two women on the back deck, felt like the longest walk of his life.

Sarah turned and watched him coming across the yard, something troubled in her face as he came into the circle of the backyard light. As if she knew something was shifting in him, between them.

He had come to like how Sarah looked at him, lighting up as if the sun had come up in her world. The way she was looking at him now, tentatively, as if she was trying to decide something, made him aware he was already missing that other look, the one a man could find himself living for.

But a man had to deserve that. He would have to prove himself worthy of it every day.

A man would want to protect her from anything bad ever happening.

And because of what he had dealt with every single day of his working life, Sullivan knew that was an impossible task. He could not even protect her from himself, let alone forces out of his control.

Well, yes, he could protect her from himself. By doing what needed to be done. He took a deep breath and walked up the stairs.

"Sarah, we have to go." He heard the tightness in his own voice.

So did Della. So did Sarah. He saw it register, instantly, with both of them that something was wrong. He hardened himself to the concern on their faces.

"Sorry, Della. A nice night, thank you."

He whistled for the dog, who came groggily out of the boys' room. When it looked like Sarah intended to linger over goodbyes, he cut her short, took her by the elbow and hustled her out to the car.

It occurred to Sarah that the coldness wafting off Oliver like a fast-approaching Arctic front was being directed at her. She jerked her arm away from him. She wasn't exactly feeling warm and fuzzy toward him, either.

"What is wrong with you?" she demanded.

"Get in the car." He opened the back door and the dog slid in, looking as apprehensive as she felt.

He drove silently, his mouth set in a firm line. She glanced at his face once, then looked out the window.

His expression reminded her of their first meeting. The barriers were up. *Do not cross.*

Sarah folded her arms over her chest and decided she did not have the least interest in mollifying him. Or prying the reason for his bad mood out of him! Let him stew!

Still, because his bad temper was crackling in the air around him despite his silence—or maybe because of it—her heart was racing. It felt as if the current she had been caught in was moving faster and not in a nice way. Swirling with dark secrets and things unsaid, moving them toward the rapids that could break everything apart.

Finally, he pulled up in front of her house.

His voice tight, he said, "That call I took at Della's was from Bradley Moore, the news anchor who did the follow-up story."

"I know who Bradley Moore is," she said.

"Of course you do," he said silkily.

"What does that mean?" she exclaimed.

"He said with Summer Fest just around the corner, how would I like to do one more interview?"

"That's good, isn't it?"

"No, it isn't. He wants to talk to me about my decision to adopt the dog. I've only told one person in the whole world I was thinking of taking that dog," he said quietly. "You couldn't wait to turn that to your advantage, could you? Your stupid festival meant more to you than protecting my privacy."

"How could you even say that?" Sarah asked, stunned. She hardly knew what to address first, she felt so bewildered by the change in him.

Her stupid festival?

"The facts speak for themselves. You were the only one who knew and now Bradley Moore knows."

It was his detective's voice, hard, cool, filled with deductive reasoning that she found hateful since it was finding *her* guilty without a trial.

Candy had told Bradley, Sarah thought, sickly. But how dare this man think the worst of her? After all the times they had spent together, he had to know her better than that! He had to.

But obviously, he, who guarded his own secrets so carefully, didn't have a clue who she really was. Any more than she had a clue who *he* really was!

Bewilderment and shock were fueling her own sense of betrayal and anger.

"The facts do speak for themselves," she said, tightly. "And I've been mulling over a discovery of my own.

Like the fact you have an ex-wife. When did you plan on telling me that?"

If she had expected shock in his features, she was disappointed. He looked cold and uncaring, his features closed to her.

"I didn't see any reason for you to know that," he shot back. "I don't really like wallowing in my failures."

"Is that how you saw the things I confided in you?" she asked, incensed. "Wallowing in my failures? I saw it as building trust. Apparently that was a one-way street!"

"Which was probably wise on my part, given where trusting you has gotten me! Imagine if I'd told you about my ex-wife, and the reason I left my job in Detroit. I'd probably be reading about my very worst moments in a sad story designed to bring more people to Summer Fest!" he accused.

"You are the most arrogant, pigheaded moron of a man I have ever met!"

"I already knew those things about myself. You're the only one who's surprised."

Sarah got out of the car regally. She was shaking she was so angry. She was aware they had squabbled in the past. Enjoyed lively arguments. This was different. This was their first real fight.

"Don't forget to take *your* dog with you," he said tightly.

"I can't have a dog," she said. "I have a cat."

"I'm sure they'll sort it out."

Should she read something into that? That things could get sorted out? That if creatures as opposite as a cat and a dog could work it out, so could they?

Still too angry to even cry, Sarah opened the back door and called the dog out.

"Towanda, come here."

Inwardly she begged for him to comment that he didn't like the name. That he didn't approve.

But he just sat there like a stone.

She slammed his car door with a little more force than was necessary, and watched Oliver drive away.

Only when he was completely out of sight, did she finally burst into tears. The dog whined, and licked her hand, then got up and pulled hard on the leash, trying pathetically, heartbreakingly, to do exactly what she wanted to do.

To follow Oliver down whatever road he took her on.

"Have some pride, girl," she told herself fiercely.

He would figure it out. That it wasn't her who had told Bradley. He would come around. He would tell her about his ex-wife, and why he had left his job in Detroit.

Sarah tried to convince herself it was an important part of their developing relationship to have a real disagreement, to see how they worked through things.

Soon she would know if they could pop out the other side of the rapids and float back onto a more peaceful stretch of water. He would apologize for jumping to conclusions about who had leaked his secret to Bradley. He would open up about his life before her, confide in her and tell her about his previous marriage, tell her about what had made him leave his job.

Failures, he had called them.

She hated the sympathy that tugged at her breast when she thought of him using those words.

He was a man who would not like to fail. At all. At anything.

She was sure he would feel better once he confided in her. She was also sure that something deep and real had happened between them and that he would not be able to resist coming to her.

But as days turned to a week, Sarah began to face the possibility that while she was waiting for them to come through the rapids, he was seeing them as already over the falls.

Pulverized.

There was plenty of proof in her house that things did not always work out. That opposites could not always find common ground. The dog and cat hated each other. If Sarah had contemplated that she might keep the puppy herself, a reminder of those sunshiny days of early summer with Oliver, a house full of destroyed furniture and broken glass from dog-chase-cat fracases was convincing her it was not a good idea.

Maybe remembering Oliver wasn't going to be such a good idea, either. There was no explaining the depth of her anguish when she would go to bed at night, contemplating that one more day had passed. He had not phoned. He was not going to phone.

Or bump into her by accident.

Or show up at her door with flowers and an apology.

It was over.

Sarah did the only thing she knew how to do to dull the sharp edges of the emptiness he had left in her life.

She buried herself in work, in relentless activity. She walked the dog six times a day, carefully avoiding places she and Oliver had taken him. If she hoped it would drain off the puppy's energy so he would give up on tormenting the cat, she was wrong.

She began to produce jam like a maniac, trying to ignore the fact that her kitchen had become a painful place, memories of them running around the island, snapping towels at each other crowded into every corner.

She attended every committee meeting, monitoring the progress of every function. She was helping build floats and stands for the marketplace. She was putting up colorful banners on the parade route and picking up programs from the printer.

Despite the smile she pasted to her face, she felt sure everyone knew something was wrong, and everyone, thankfully, was too kind to say anything.

After spending the days trying to exhaust herself, every night with jars of freshly canned jam lining her cupboard, and the exhausted dog snoozing at her feet, Sarah sorted through the mountains of new requests delivered to her house from Kettle Bend City Hall.

It seemed all the world had watched the clip of Oliver rescuing that dog, and at least half the world his follow-up interview where he said the dog had not yet been claimed.

Now everybody wanted to adopt the dog. How was it that sorting through all these requests had fallen on *her*?

"Possession is nine tenths of the law," the city hall clerk had said, dropping off a sack of mail.

Some of it was addressed only to Kettle Bend, Wisconsin. Feeling responsible for finding the perfect home for the dog, since she could not keep him, Sarah forced herself to read every single letter, even though it was ultimately as heartbreaking as the fact she had not heard from Oliver.

She, who was trying desperately to regain her cynicism about dreams coming true, seemed to be having the reality of her dream shoved in her face routinely. These perfect, loving families were everywhere.

They were in small towns and in big cities, on farms and on ranches and living beside lakes or in the mountains.

Photos fell out of some the letters. One sent a photo of the dog who had died and they missed so terribly. She read heart-wrenching letters from children saying how much they wanted that dog. She looked at crayon drawings of dogs. A dog bone fell out of one fat envelope.

She had to make a decision, for the dog's own good. He wasn't getting any younger. He was in his formative stage. He needed a good home. One without a cat!

But in her mind, though there were obviously many homes that fit her picture of perfection, in her heart he was Oliver's dog. She couldn't even stick with calling him Towanda, not just because it didn't really suit him, and not just because it would not be fair to name the dog in a burst of mean-spiritedness.

She could not name the dog, because in her heart it was Oliver's job to name him.

But she also knew she could not keep the dog from the family it deserved for much longer.

When Barry Bushnell called, frantic because the parade was days away and they still had not agreed on a grand marshal for the parade, Sarah gave up on her dream that Oliver would come around.

She had always, in the back of her mind, thought she could convince him to be the parade marshal.

She had always, in the back of her mind, felt she could convince him to love her.

What kind of love was that? Where you had to convince someone to love you?

To Barry, she said, "Let's make the dog the grand marshal of the parade. He's the one who got us all the publicity. Visitors would love to see him. And," she steeled herself, "on the final day of the festival, right after the fireworks, we'll announce what family the dog is going to."

"Brilliant," Barry breathed with satisfaction. "Absolutely brilliant."

But if it was so brilliant, Sarah wondered, why did she feel so bereft?

In fact, going into the final frenzy of activity before the parade, Sarah was aware that Summer Fest was going to succeed beyond her wildest dreams. Accommodations in the town were booked solid. The crowd was arriving along the parade route in record numbers.

With all this growing evidence of her success, she was all too aware that she was plagued by a sense of emptiness.

On parade morning, the committee begged her to ride on the town float. But she didn't want to. Instead, she managed to lose herself in the crowd along the parade route and watched, emotionless, as the opening band came through, followed by a troop of clowns on motorcycles.

It was a perfect, cloudless day, not too hot yet. The streets had been cleaned to sparkling. Fresh flower baskets hung from light posts. Stores had decorated their windows.

Kettle Bend had never looked better.

She looked at the people crowding the parade route around her. It was just as she had planned it. Families together, children shrieking their delight at the antics of the clowns, grandmothers tapping their toes in time to the music of the passing bands. Candy apples and cotton candy—both Summer Fest fundraisers—were selling by the ton.

But as she looked at the Kettle Bend float, Sarah was aware of fighting a desire to weep. All the people she had worked with to make this day a reality were on that float, smiling, waving. She had become so close to these people. How was it she felt so sad?

The truth hit her. You could not make a town your family.

She had learned that at Della's house. *That* was what a family felt like. There was simply no replacement for it. Love had perils. Love hurt.

And in the end, wasn't it worth it? Didn't it make you become everything you were ever meant to be?

Sarah felt the hair on the back of her neck rise, and she sought out the reason.

Standing behind her, and a little to the left, she saw Oliver. She was pretty sure he had not seen her.

Like her, he had chosen to blend into the crowd. He

was not in uniform, he had a ball cap pulled low over his eyes, and sunglasses on.

He did not want to be recognized.

He did not want to play the role of hero.

He had never wanted to do that. She had thrust it upon him. She had thrust a whole life upon him that he had not wanted.

But maybe she had not completely thrust things on him. Why was he here today? Watching a parade did not seem an activity he would choose for himself.

Was it possible he missed the sense of belonging he'd felt when he'd joined her in the committee rooms? Was it possible he had read in the paper the dog would be the parade marshal? Was it possible he was reluctantly curious to see how it had all turned out?

Was it possible he wanted to see how it had turned out for her?

Of course, that would imply he cared, and the silence of her telephone implied something else.

Still, she could not tear her eyes away from him.

When a great shout of approval went up from the crowd around her, followed by thunderous applause, she glanced only briefly back at the parade route.

The dog was happily ensconced in the backseat of a white convertible, tongue lolling and tail flapping. The mayor was beside him, one arm around him, the other waving. The crowd went wild.

Then the dog spotted Oliver and jumped to his back legs, front paws over the side of the car, ready to leap. The mayor was caught by surprise, but managed to catch the dog's collar just in time. He pulled him back onto the seat beside him.

Sarah watched Oliver's face. She felt what was left of her heart break in two when she saw him watching the dog.

He took off his sunglasses and she could see the absolute truth in the darkness of his eyes. The memory of every single time they had ever spent together flashed across his face. She could see them throwing that pink Frisbee, feeding the dog popcorn that first night they had watched hockey together, and pizza the second.

In Oliver's eyes, she saw them chasing one another around the kitchen island, walking by the river, the dog cowering when he threw the stick into the water. In his eyes, she saw that last night they had spent together, saw them on the bed with his two nephews, the bed heaving up as the dog tried to get underneath it.

Oliver suddenly glanced over and saw her watching him. He held her gaze for a moment, defiant, daring her to *know* what she had seen. His expression became schooled, giving away nothing. And then he slipped the sunglasses back over his eyes, turned and disappeared into the crowd.

She stood there for a moment, frozen by what she had just seen.

The truth.

And she knew, as she had always known, that loving Oliver was going to require bravery from her. She could not hide from the potential of rejection, from the possibility of being hurt.

That day she had gone up the steps with the dog, she had found the place inside her that was brave.

She knew it was there. She was going to have to try again. Laying everything she had on the line this time.

She could not hold anything back. She could not protect herself from potential hurt, from the possibility of pain.

Real love had to go in there and get him.

But for now she had to let him go. The Market Place was opening right after the parade, and she had her booth to get ready.

Without staying to watch the rest of the parade, she, like Oliver slipped into the crowd.

The Market Place was both exhausting and rewarding. Throngs moved through it. Sarah had samples of jam for tasting on crackers, and between keeping her sample tray filled and putting sold jars of jam in bags, she could barely keep up.

A man stood in front of her. Good-looking. Well-dressed. She offered him the sample plate, turned to help another customer.

When she turned back, he pressed a card into her hand. "Call me," he said, and smiled.

Once, she would have been intrigued by that kind of invitation. Now, she just gave him a tired smile and slipped the card into her pocket.

She actually was able to laugh at herself when she took the card out of her pocket later that night.

The name Gray Hedley rose off it, finely embossed. Underneath was the well-known logo for Smackers Jam.

Misreading men again, she chided herself. *Whatever he wanted, it probably was not a date.*

It seemed like a very long time ago, a lifetime ago, that she had mistaken another man's invitation for a date.

It was time.

It was time to find out if there was anything at all in her world left to hope for. When she had seen Oliver's face this morning at the parade, she had dared to think there was.

Now, dialing his number with trembling fingers, she was just not so sure.

She knew he had call display, and so she was both astonished and pleased when he answered.

He'd known it was her, and he had answered anyway.

"Hello, Oliver."

"Sarah."

Her whole being shivered from the way her name sounded on his lips. There was no anger there, not now. Something else. Something he was trying to hide.

"Congratulations on a successful first day of Summer Fest." His voice was impersonal. Polite. But guarded.

But she knew that the fact he'd even answered the phone when he had known it was her was some kind of victory.

She felt like she had so much to tell him. She felt the terrible loneliness of not having someone to share her triumphs and truths with.

"Oliver," she said quietly, firmly. "We need to talk."

Silence.

And then, "All right." Chilly. Giving away nothing.

Yet for him, just saying "all right" was a surrender. She hung up the phone and dared to feel a flicker of hope. That flicker felt like a light winking in the distance, guiding a traveler, weary and cold, toward home.

CHAPTER NINE

SULLIVAN watched as Sarah came up his front walk. She had brought the dog with her. He wished he had thought to tell her not to bring the dog.

On the other hand, she might read into it what he least wanted her to read. It was what he had known all along.

She might know then that he had become attached and she might guess the truth.

Attachments made a man weak. Love didn't make a man strong. It made him long for what he knew the world could not give, a way to hang on to those feelings forever. There was no forever.

Not for him. Over the course of his career he had seen it way too many times. Love lying shattered.

Maybe for her, if she found the right guy, like his sister had found Jonathon, maybe there would be hope for Sarah. She could believe in love if she wanted. Yes, a nice orthodontist would be perfect for her. He should ask Jonathon to find her one.

Never mind that the thought of her with someone else made Sullivan feel sick to his stomach. That's what needed to be done.

He had always been that man. The one who did what needed to be done.

And he would do it again now.

He would send her away from him, back into the world where she belonged, where she could dream her secret dreams of wedding dresses and picket fences, babes against her breast.

The lie had not driven her away, the lie that he was angry with her about word getting out to Bradley Moore that he was going to keep the dog.

The lie had not done it. He'd thought it had. One day without her becoming another, the emptiness of his life made rawly apparent by her absence.

Then, always the brave one, she had phoned.

So he had no choice left. He had to count on the truth to do what the lie had not. He would show Sarah who he really was and it would scare her right back into her little jam-filled world.

He couldn't think, not right now, *but she doesn't like making jam.* He could not think one thing that would make him weak when he needed strength as he had never ever needed it before.

He opened the door before she knocked.

He hoped what he felt didn't show on his face. She couldn't know that he loved her little pink dress with the purple polka dots on it. She couldn't know that he wanted to smell her hair one last time. She couldn't know he had to hold back from scratching the dog behind its ears.

She could *never* know his heart welcomed her.

Sullivan took a step back from the truth that shone

naked in her face. A truth more frightening to him than any truth about himself that he could tell her.

Just in case he'd got it wrong, just in case he had misread that look on her face, she said it.

She stepped toward him, looked into his face, and he hoped his expression was cold and unyielding. But if it was, it didn't faze her.

Sarah did what he'd come to expect her to do. She did the bravest thing of all. She made herself vulnerable to him.

"I've missed you so much," she said with quiet intensity.

I've missed you, too. It has felt like my heart was cut in two. But he said nothing, hoping it would stop her.

But she plunged on, searching his face desperately for a response. "Oliver, I love you."

I love you, too. So much I am not going to do what I want to do.

Because what he wanted was to lay his weapons at her feet. Surrender to it. He wanted to gather her in his arms and kiss every inch of her uplifted face.

But loving her, really loving her, meant he had to let her go. He had to frighten her off once and for all. She deserved so much better than him.

"You'd better come in," he said and stepped back from the door, holding it open for her as she passed him. The dog was exuberant in his greeting, and that desire to lay it all down nearly collapsed him. Instead, he drew in a deep breath and followed her into the living room.

Seeing her there, on his couch, reminded him of the first time she had come in. The towel at his feet.

Accusing him of taking his decorating lessons from Al Capone. Making her blush. The day that never ended.

He contemplated what to do next. Offer her a drink? No, that was part of the weakness, prolonging the moment of truth. This was not a social call. This was an ending, and the sooner he got it over with the better for both of them.

He sat across from her in his armchair. "I need to tell you some things."

She nodded, *eagerly*, that's how damn naive she was.

"I was married. In my early twenties. It lasted about as long as a Hollywood wedding with none of the glamour. I didn't tell you, because, frankly, I didn't see the point. I might share my history with someone I planned to have a future with. Otherwise, no."

He saw a tiny victory. She flinched. Some of the bravery leached from her face, replaced with uncertainty.

"You already told me your fiancé had a mistress. Well, I had one, too. That's what destroyed my marriage."

Her mouth dropped open with disbelief. Maybe he should just let her believe that, but then he remembered his truth would be enough to scare her off. He didn't need to make anything up or embellish anything.

"My mistress wasn't a woman," he said quietly. "It was my job. The work I did was not work to me. It was a calling that was worse than a mistress. It was demanding, it took everything I had to give it, and when I thought I had nothing left, it would ask for more. I was young, my wife was young. She had a right to expect she would come first, and she didn't. The work came first.

"This was the part she didn't get. For me, it was never just another violent ending. It was never just another body. It was never just another homicide. It was never just a job.

"It was dreams shattered. It was families changed forever. It was the mother who has been waiting all night for news of her son, and the young wife, pregnant with a child, who fell to the floor howling when she found out her husband was dead.

"To me finding who did it was my life. Nothing else. That's how I honored those who had gone. I found out who did it when I could. I lived with the agony of it when I couldn't."

He gathered himself, glanced at her, frowned at what he saw. She was leaning toward him, her eyes soft on his face, obviously not getting what he was trying to tell her at all.

"But don't you think," she asked him, "that devotion to your calling was because of what happened to your parents? Wasn't every single case about finding who destroyed your family? Wasn't every single case trying to make something change that you never could?"

He stared at her. But if he looked at her too long, he would get lost in her eyes, he would forget what he wanted to do. He didn't want her insights. He didn't want her understanding. He wanted her to get that he lived in a different world than her. That she couldn't come over, and he couldn't go back.

"I've lived and breathed in a world so violent and so ugly it would steal the heart out of you."

Despite the fact she looked sympathetic, she did not look convinced that the world he had moved in could steal her heart. But that was because she was impossibly naive!

"I'm trying to tell you, each case is like a scar for me. Each one took a piece of me, and each one left something inside of me, too. Do you know how many cases I've been on?"

She shook her head, wide-eyed.

"Two hundred and twelve. That's a lot of scars, Sarah."

A mistake to say her name.

Because she took it as an invitation. She left the couch and came and sat on the arm of his chair, one hand resting on his shoulder, the other stroking his hair.

"Some people," she said slowly, "say a painting without shadows is incomplete. Maybe it's the same for a person without scars."

"I'm trying to tell you, you don't know me."

"All right," she said gently. "Tell me more, then."

Something was shifting. He wasn't scaring her off, and yet the words were fighting with each other to get out of him, like water bursting through a broken dam.

"On my last case in Detroit," he continued, relentlessly, needing to say all of it, "after thinking I knew the darkness of the human heart inside out and backward, I found out how dark my own heart was. In that last case, I came face-to-face with my own darkness."

He paused, glanced at her. All that softness. *Don't tell her*, he said to himself. *Spare her the supreme ugliness.* Just kick her out and tell her not to come back.

But he'd already tried that. From the very beginning he had tried to discourage her interest. The only weapon he had left was the truth, and he had to use it. He could not stop now. He was nearly there.

"It started like so many of them. Neighbors heard shots. Cops arrived, knew right away to call us as soon as they stepped in the door.

"You know what they found?"

She shook her head.

"A whole family, dead. The Algards wiped from the face of the earth. Mommy. Daddy. Five-year-old, three-year-old, two-year-old."

"Oh, Oliver," she said, and pressed her fist into her mouth. If he hoped she was finally starting to get it, the look in her eyes told him he was mistaken. She didn't get it! She still thought she could take some part of it, absolve him.

Why did it feel as if she was? Ah, well, she had not heard the whole sordid tale yet.

"We got it all wrong," he said softly. "We thought it was a gang war. We thought who else could do something like this? We thought they were sending a message to the whole community. Don't cross us, we run the show. Then a high-ranking gang member came to me, ridiculously young, given his status. But when I looked at that boy, I was so aware if Della hadn't saved me from that lifestyle, he would have been me.

"That kid was smart and savvy and a little cocky. Luke. Unapologetic about his affiliations. Said he'd been looking for a family all his life, a place where he could belong, and his gang was it. I can remember his exact words. *We're all just soldiers, man. Lots of kids gettin' sent over to the land of sand, killing people for less than what I kill people for.*

"And then Luke told me his gang didn't kill the Algards. He was disgusted that we would think his gang killed babies, and I had offended his sense of honor. He told me I was looking in the wrong place, and he was going to find out who did it. And you know what? He did. He had contacts and inside channels and the power to intimidate in that community that I could never have. It was humbling how fast he found the truth.

"According to Luke's information, it wasn't a gang thing at all. The perp was my adult male victim's brother. It was a family squabble gone stupidly, insanely, irrevocably wrong.

"Luke said, *I can look after it.* And that's when I found out what a thin, almost invisible line can divide good and bad. That's when I found out the darkness was in me, too. Because I wanted vengeance for that family. For those babies gunned down before they ever knew one thing good. No first day of school. No visit from the tooth fairy. No first kiss, or prom, or graduation, or wedding. I didn't want to trust the outcome to the system. Two hundred and eleven previous cases. I knew, firsthand, things did not always go the way I wanted them to.

"*Twenty-four hours*, he told me. He told me if I hadn't looked after it in twenty-four hours, he would."

"You let him," she whispered, horrified.

Oliver laughed, and it sounded ragged in his own ears. "No, I didn't. I did the right thing. I brought in the brother. Complete confession. He killed his brother in a fit of rage over an argument. And do you know why he killed the rest of them, why he shot those little babies? Because they saw him do it. That's all. Because even that two-year-old baby knew her uncle had killed her daddy."

"So, you did the right thing," she prodded him.

"I guess that depends on how you look at it. Things did not go the way I wanted them to. He walked free and I could not stop thinking of those tiny, defenseless bodies. And thinking about him out on the streets. I could not stop thinking about the opportunity I'd passed on to have things looked after. Up until that point, I'd always felt like the cowboy, always felt like I was on the side of the righteous. But suddenly everything seemed muddy. Then it got worse.

"Within hours of beating the system, the brother faced street justice and it was swift and violent. I knew exactly who killed him. So I did my job. I brought in Luke. And it twisted my world up even further when he did not walk free. He was twenty-three years old and he got life in prison.

"You know what he said to me? *Worth it. We're all just soldiers.* Well, that was the end of me. I felt turned inside out. Who was the good guy? Who was the bad guy? I felt as if I had failed at everything I ever put my hand to. I failed as a cop, I failed as a husband, I failed as a son."

"Failed? You?" She sounded incredulous, still wanting to believe the best of him even though she had now heard the worst. She was still sitting way too close to him. Why hadn't she moved? Couldn't she see he was a man who had lost his moral compass? Who had lost his faith that good could triumph over evil?

"This is what people who have never been exposed to violence don't know. You think about it all the time. You think, *What could I have done to make it different?*"

"You can't possibly believe you could have protected the whole world!"

"No," he said sadly. "You are exactly right. That is the conclusion I have come to. This is what you need to know about me, Sarah McDougall. Other people have a simple faith. They believe if you are good only good things happen to you. They find comfort in believing something bigger runs the show. But I know it's all random, and that a man has no hope against that randomness.

"And that's why I can't be with you, Sarah, why I can't accept the gift of love you have offered me, or ever love you back. Because, despite having taken a few hard knocks yourself, you're still so damned determined to find good. You're a nice girl and I've walked too long with darkness to have anything nice left in me. In time, my darkness will snuff out your light, Sarah. In time, it will."

There, he had said it all. He waited for her to move, to get up off the chair, go to the door, walk out it and not look back.

Inwardly he pleaded that she would take the dog with her.

And then he felt her hand, cool and comforting on the back of his neck. He made himself look at her. But he did not see goodbye in her face. He was nearly blinded by what he saw there.

He had tried so hard to let her go. But she wasn't

going. In her face, in the softness of her expression, in the endless compassion of her eyes, he saw what he had been looking for for such a very long time.

Rest.

Sarah stared at the ravaged face of the man she loved. Suddenly she understood the universal appeal of that video she had seen of him jumping in the river to save the dog. She understood exactly why that clip had gone viral, why so many people had watched it.

This man, the one who claimed not to believe in goodness, was the rarest of men. Here was a man willing to live his truth, a man prepared to give his life to protect someone—or something—weaker, vulnerable, in mortal danger.

She saw so clearly that ever since the death of his parents, Oliver had pitted himself against everything wrong in the world. He had given his whole life trying to protect everyone and everything.

No wonder he felt like a failure.

Could he not see that was just too big a job for one man?

With tears in her eyes, she saw another truth. Shining around him. He was willing to give up his life—any chance he had of happiness or love—to protect her from what he thought he was.

And the fact he would do that? It meant he was not what he thought he was. He was not even close.

"I have to tell you something, Oliver Sullivan," she said, and she could hear the strength and certainty in her own voice.

"What's that?"

He had folded his arms over the mightiness of his chest. He had furrowed his brows at her and frowned.

He looked like the warrior that he was.

But it was time for that warrior to come home.

"You are wrong," she said softly. "You are so damned wrong."

"About?"

"The darkness putting out the light. It's the other way around. It has always been the other way around. The light chases away the darkness. Love wins. In the end, love always wins."

"You're hopelessly naive," he snarled.

But she wasn't afraid. She was standing in the light right now. It was pouring out of her.

More importantly, it was pouring out of this good, good man who had given his whole life to trying to protect others and who had not taken one thing for himself.

Well, if it was the last thing she did, she intended to be Oliver Sullivan's one thing.

"I've lived it," he said, his voice tortured. "Sarah, I've lived it. It's not true. Love does not always win."

"Really?" she said softly. "What is this, if it's not love winning?"

She touched his neck, looked into his raised face, and then dropped off the arm of the chair right onto his lap.

"I love you," she said fiercely. "I love every thing about you and I am never, ever going to stop. I've come to get you, Oliver Sullivan. And that *is* love winning."

"You're being foolish," he said gruffly. He did not hold her, but he did not push her away, either.

"You think I would care about you less because of

what you just told me?" she laughed. "You're the fool! Oliver, I care about you *more*."

She felt his eyes on her face, searching, and she knew the instant he found truth there. His body suddenly relaxed, and he pulled her deep against him, burying his face in the curve of her neck.

She ran her fingers, tenderly, thought the thickness of his hair, touched her lips to his beautiful forehead, to each of his closed eyes.

"Let me carry it with you," she whispered. "Let me."

After the longest time, she felt him shudder against her, heard him whisper, "Okay."

And she finally let her tears of joy chase down her cheeks and mingle with his.

"Jelly," Oliver called, "Jam. Best you've ever eaten. Cures heartaches!"

"You can't say that!" Sarah chided him, but she was laughing.

He was helping her with her booth at the Market Place. It was the last day of Summer Fest. He had spent every minute since he had told her his truth with Sarah, something in him opening, like a flower after the rain.

They could not bear to say goodbye to one another.

They could not get enough of each other.

Last night, they had even fallen asleep together on her couch, words growing huskier and huskier as they had gotten more tired, finally sleeping with unspoken words on their lips. When he had woken this morning, with her head on his shoulder, her sleepy eyes on his, her hair in a wild tangle of curls, it had felt as if he was in heaven.

So Oliver Sullivan was selling jam—he'd donned an apron to get a rise out of Sarah—and he was having the time of his life. He didn't just sell jam. What was the fun of that? No, he hawked it like an old-time peddler with a magic elixir.

He moved amongst the crowd. He stood on the table. He kissed babies and old ladies.

He was alive.

How could it be that selling jam at a humble little booth set up in what was usually a school yard field could feel as if he was standing on top of a mountain? As if all the world was spread out before him, in all its magnificence, put there just for his enjoyment?

It could feel like that because she was beside him.

Sarah.

Who had listened quietly to his every secret and not been warned off. Who had set him free.

That's what he felt right now. Free.

As if aloneness had been his prison and she had broken him out. As if carrying all those burdens had been like carrying a five-hundred-pound stone around with him, and she, little Sarah, who probably weighed a hundred pounds or so, had been the one strong enough to lift it off of him.

"Excuse me, ma'am? If you'll buy a single jar of the jelly, I will show you how I can walk on my hands."

"Oliver!"

But the lady bought jam, and he walked on his hands, and Sarah laughed and applauded with everyone else. Plus, it attracted quite a crowd, and then they were sold out of jam.

"Come on, sweetheart," he said, putting the Closed

sign up on her little booth. "We probably have time to win the three-legged race."

Later, lying in a heap with her underneath him, their legs bound together, nearly choking he was laughing so hard, he wondered if this is what it felt to be a teenager, because he never really had been.

The death of his parents had cast a shadow over the part of his life when he should have been laughing with girls, and stealing kisses, and feeling his heart pound hopefully at the way a certain girl's hand felt in his.

To Oliver Sullivan, it was an unbelievable blessing that he was actually getting to experience a part of life that had been lost to him.

The falling-in-love part.

Because that's what had been happening from the minute he met Sarah. He had been falling for her.

And fighting it.

Now, to just experience it, to not fight it, made him feel on fire with life.

Somehow he and Sarah managed to find their feet, and lurched across the finish line dead last. But the crowd applauded as if they had come first when he kissed her and they did not come up for air for a long, long time!

"I think we could probably win the egg and spoon race," he decided.

"I doubt it," she said.

"Let's try anyway. I like the ending part when we lose."

"Me, too."

Laughing like young children, hands intertwined they ran to the starting line.

For supper, they bought hamburgers with heaps of fried onions and then had cotton candy for dessert. They rode the Ferris wheel, and he kissed her silly when it got stuck at the top.

Then, as the sun set, they went back to his house, briefly, and changed into warmer clothes and grabbed their blankets.

And their dog.

They joined the town on the banks of the Kettle River. People had blankets and lawn chairs set up everywhere. There were families there with little babies and young children. There were young lovers. There were giggling gaggles of girls. Young boys sipped beer from bottles, until they saw him, and then they put it away.

He and Sarah and their dog lay back on their blanket, and as the night cooled they pulled another tight around themselves.

The fireworks started.

It was exactly how he felt inside: exploding with beauty and excitement.

The dog was terrified, and had to get in the blankets with them, his warm body all quivery and slithery.

Sarah, one arm around the dog, leaning into Oliver, looked skyward, her expression one of complete enchantment. When he looked at her face, he saw her truth. He saw in her face she would always believe good things could happen if you wanted it badly enough.

And who was he to say she was wrong? She'd made this happen, hadn't she? The whole town and an unimaginable number of visitors were all sitting here on this warm night enjoying the breathtaking magic of the fireworks because of her. Because she had believed in a vision, trusted in a dream.

She had rescued him, too. Because she had believed in something it would have been so much wiser for her to let go of.

His way had not brought him one iota of happiness. Not one. Being guarded and cynical, expecting the worst? What had that brought him?

He was going to try it her way.

In fact, he knew he was going to try it her way for a very, very long time.

A firework exploded into a million fragments of light above them, and those fragments of light were doubled when they reflected on the quiet black surface of the river.

"I'm going to name the dog," he decided in a quiet place between the boom of the fireworks being set off.

She turned and looked at him, a smile tickling across those gorgeous, kissable lips.

"Moses," he decided.

"I love that. But why Moses?"

"Because I found him floating in the river. Because he led me out of the wilderness, to the promised land."

"What promised land?"

"You."

Right on cue, fireworks exploded in the sky above them, a waterfall of bright sparks of green and blue and red cascading through the sky.

She stared at him, and then she bit her lip, and her eyes sparkled with tears. She reached up and touched his face with such tenderness, such love, and he was humbled.

He knew he would not go back from this place to the place he had been before. He might be strong, but he wasn't strong enough to survive a life that did not include Sarah in it.

"Marry me," he murmured, as the sparks of the firework faded and drifted back toward earth.

Her face was lit by those dying lights.

"Yes," she whispered.

As their lips joined, the sky exploded, once again, into light and sound above them. It was the finale: shooting higher, the sky filling with a frenzy of light and sound and smoke. And as the sound died, the fireworks disintegrated into pinwheels of fiery gold that drifted down through the black sky toward the black water.

Silence followed, and then thunderous applause and cheering.

To Oliver it felt as if the whole earth celebrating this moment. This miracle.

Of the right man and the right woman coming together and having the courage to say yes to what was being offered them.

Maybe all of creation did celebrate the moment when that magnificent force that survived all else, that triumphed over all else, that force that was at the heart of everything, showed itself in the way one man and one woman looked at each other. Maybe it did.

EPILOGUE

SARAH came into the house, and smiled when she heard the sound. Banging. Cursing. More banging.

She followed the sound up the stairs to the room at the end of the hallway.

She gasped at what she saw. Where there had been worn carpet this morning, now there was hardwood.

Curtains with purple giraffes and green lions cavorting across them were hung on a only slightly bent rod.

Oliver sat on the floor, instructions spread out in front of him, tongue caught between his teeth, crib in a million pieces on the ground. Moses watched from one corner where Sushi had him trapped. She lifted her paw delicately to let the dog know who was boss, and his expression was one of long suffering as he flopped his tail at Sarah in greeting.

Oliver looked up at her. He had sawdust in his hair, and a smudge on his face. His smile did what it had been doing since the moment she said *I do.*

It turned her insides to goo.

"You know," he said, looking back at his instructions, trying to fit a round peg into a square hole, "I remember once I thought home was about rest. I was sadly mistaken. I haven't had a moment's rest since we bought this old junk heap." But he said it with such affection. And it was true. Everywhere in the house they had purchased together was his mark.

He had torn down every wall downstairs to give them a bright, open modern space that was the envy of the entire neighborhood, and especially his sister Della, who lived two doors down.

Oliver was not a natural carpenter or handyman. Sometimes he had to do things two or three times to get them right, sometimes even more. His work around the house involved much effort, cursing, pondering, trying, ripping down, rethinking and then trying again.

The fact that he loved it so, when he was quite terrible at it, made Sarah's heart feel so tender it almost hurt. This man, who had hated failure so much, had become so confident in himself—and in her unconditional love for him—that he failed regularly and shrugged it off with good humor.

That's what love had done for him. Made him so much better, so accepting of his own humanity.

She cherished that about him.

"You didn't have to start on the nursery just yet," Sarah said, and came in and ruffled his hair, flicked some of the sawdust from it. She had never tired of the way that thick hair felt under her fingertips. "We only found out we were pregnant two days ago."

"Ah, well, you know the saying. Don't put off until tomorrow what you can do today. I've been asked to consult on that case in Green Bay. You know me. Once I get going on that." He shook his head with good-humored acceptance of his tendency toward obsession.

She knew him and loved this part of him, still trying

to make all that was wrong in the world right. But there was a difference now. Now, he came back into the light after he had spent time dealing with darkness. And let her love heal him.

"What if things don't go right?" she asked, tentatively. "It's a first baby. That's why I thought maybe you should hold off—" she gestured uncertainly around the room "—on all this."

He turned and grinned at her, that smile sweeping away her fears. "Everything is going to be fine," he told her, and his voice was so steady and so confident that she believed him.

Sarah marveled at the fact that Oliver, who had once had so many problems believing life could bring good, was already committed to a good outcome. He already saw a baby in this room and he already loved it with his whole heart and soul.

"I love the curtains. Where did you find that fabric?" She went and touched it, felt teary that he could pick such a thing, that he could know it was just right. Then again, teary was the order of the day!

"Is the rod a little crooked?" he asked, cocking his head at it.

"Um, maybe just a hair."

"I'll fix it later. I got the fabric at Babyland."

"You went to Babyland?" she asked, incredulous that her husband had visited the new store on main street.

"Why so surprised?"

"It hardly seems like a place the state's most consulted expert on homicide would hang out. Or the new deputy chief. There's probably some kind of cop rule against it. You are going to be teased unmercifully."

"Just don't tell your big-mouth friend, Candy, or Bradley Moore will be calling for the inside scoop on the new deputy chief. Could you hand me that wrench?"

She wandered back over, handed it to him. "Oliver?"

"Huh?"

"Are we going to the parade tomorrow?"

"Oh, yeah. The parade, the picnic, the fireworks." He slid a look at her. "Are you disappointed by the new format?"

This year by unanimous vote, Summer Fest had been made a one-day event, all on the Fourth of July.

"No," Sarah said. "I know the four days just cost too much money, and it was too hard to get volunteers to run all the events. I know my great idea was given a fair trial, two years in a row, and it didn't even come close to saving the town, Oliver. You don't have to be gentle with me."

"Ah, Sarah, you still saved the town."

"I did not!"

But she had saved *him*. Somehow, inside herself she had found the courage to rescue Oliver Sullivan. Maybe even in a larger world, in the bigger picture, she had only thought she was rescuing the town, that thought leading her to where she really needed to be.

"I don't know," Oliver said. "When you sold out Jelly Jeans and Jammies to Smackers and they bought the old factory on Mill Street, they brought a lot of work and money to this town. Eighty employees, at last count. And you know, those articles you write for *Travel* and *Small Town Charm* do more than their fair share of mentioning Kettle Bend. No wonder we have a Babyland on the main street! No wonder Jonathon is opening an office here."

"And then," she said, "there's our most famous citizen."

Moses gazed at her adoringly, looked like he might come over, and then cast a look at the cat, and decided against it. He flopped his tail again.

Moses still got fan mail, he and Oliver were still asked to do follow-up interviews. That whole incident at the river somehow had captured people's hearts and minds and imaginations.

Why?

Sarah thought it stood for good things happening in a world where currents could take you by surprise and sweep you away. It stood for good coming from bad.

It let the world know there were still men who would sacrifice themselves for those who needed them.

And who had needed Oliver more than her?

That was the most wonderful irony in all of it. She had thought she was rescuing him.

In fact, he had rescued her.

The past two years had been beyond anything she could have ever dreamed for herself. Sarah woke in the morning with a song in her heart.

"I'm the luckiest woman in the world," Sarah said, "that you fell in love with me."

She had his full attention. He did that little thing he did. He took her hand, kissed it and then blew on where his lips had been.

"Oh, you are so wrong. I never fell in love with you, Mrs. Sullivan."

"Fine time to tell me now that you've got me knocked

up," she teased. She loved more than anything else these moments between them. Ordinary, but not ordinary. The best moments of all. When it seemed like nothing was happening, and yet everything was.

"Love isn't something you fall into," Oliver said, letting go of her hand and eyeing the instructions. He frowned at the crib panel that was definitely on upside down, and possibly backward, too.

He abandoned it suddenly, got up, swept her into his arms and kissed her until she couldn't breathe. Then, looking deep into her eyes, he said, "Love is a choice. It's a daily choice of how to live."

Live love.

He rested his hand on her stomach. There wasn't even a baby bump there yet. She touched his face, relaxed against him, and was sure she felt the new life stir within her.

There was a pure exhilaration in the simplicity of the shared moment that rose within her, and headed like an arrow into the dazzling future.

* * * * *

There was no future for Courtney with him, and she was the kind of woman who deserved futures.

She was young and beautiful and caring and came from a strong, close family.

He was past young, scarred up on the inside as well as the out, and the only family he knew—or who mattered to him—was the family of Hollins-Winword security agency.

It was a fact of life that was easy enough to remember when he was usually a continent or two away from her.

But sprawled across a bed under her *roof*?

That was an entirely different matter.

She reappeared in the doorway with a gigantic Saint Bernard at her side.

"You didn't get a dog." Mason eyed the shaggy beast. "You got a damn horse."

She grinned, bringing a surprising impishness to her oval face and tucked her long, golden hair behind her ear.

He couldn't take his eyes off her.

Dear Reader,

This year marks the thirteenth year I've been blessed to be able to share the Double-C Ranch "family" with all of you. When I started out, I had no idea what a wonderful adventure it would all turn out to be—and continues to be, every single day. Though I certainly hoped that you would welcome the family into your lives, I could never have come close to understanding how wonderful it would be knowing just what a special home these people would find with you.

Now, here we are again, with Courtney Clay, who is settling into the home and the future she wants to make. And with Mason Hyde—who has as little idea when he starts out how much he wants that home to be with him—as I did when I started out more than a decade ago.

And so their adventure begins…

Thank you for being there to share it!

Allison

COURTNEY'S
BABY PLAN

BY
ALLISON LEIGH

First published in Great Britain 2012
by Mills & Boon, an imprint of Harlequin (UK) Limited,
Eton House, 18-24 Paradise Road, Richmond, Surrey TW9 1SR

© Allison Lee Johnson 2011

ISBN: 978 0 263 89429 5
ebook ISBN: 978 1 408 97103 1

923-0512

Harlequin (UK) policy is to use papers that are natural, renewable and recyclable products and made from wood grown in sustainable forests. The logging and manufacturing processes conform to the legal environmental regulations of the country of origin.

Printed and bound in Spain
by Blackprint CPI, Barcelona

There is a saying that you can never be too rich or too thin. **Allison Leigh** doesn't believe that, but she does believe that you can *never* have enough books! When her stories find a way into the hearts—and bookshelves—of others, Allison says she feels she's done something right. Making her home in Arizona with her husband, she enjoys hearing from her readers at: Allison@allisonleigh.com or PO Box 40772, Mesa, AZ 85274-0772, USA.

For my family.

Prologue

It all started with a kiss.

A twenty-dollar kiss, to be precise.

Courtney Clay inhaled carefully and stared up at the man standing outside her apartment door. She didn't *do* this sort of thing…inviting strange men into her home during the wee hours. Or any hour, for that matter.

But then Mason Hyde wasn't entirely a stranger. He was a friend of her cousin's, after all.

And he could kiss like nobody she'd ever met.

The statement whispered through her mind, tempting.

She straightened her fingers, then curled them once more around the doorknob. "Do you want to come in?"

His eyes were deep shadows despite the porch light burning brightly above her front door. "Yes." His voice was deep. Blunt. And—as it had struck her from the first moment she'd encountered him—entrancingly melodious. That first time, when she'd heard him speaking to someone else, she'd thought how his voice didn't seem to quite match his almost dangerous-looking appearance.

The second time, just that afternoon when he'd stopped in front of her kissing booth at the town's Valentine's Day festival, plunked down a twenty for a five-dollar kiss and told her with a crooked smile that she could keep the change, she'd realized just how perfectly his voice *did* fit him.

And even though there had been a narrow table between them on which that twenty-dollar bill rested, she'd felt something curl inside her when he'd spoken. And something curl even more tightly when his eyes had stared into hers.

Her knees had felt a little shaky. Her stomach had danced a little nervously. And her voice had risen about half an octave when she'd thanked him for his generous donation on behalf of the local school that was benefiting from the funds being raised that day.

But then his lips had tilted a little crookedly, which seemed to make the thin scar that slashed down his face from his right temple to his jaw even more apparent, and he'd leaned across the table toward her and brushed his lips gently…simply…across hers.

And that's where her memory stopped dead in its tracks.

The contact of his lips on hers had simply caused every cell in her brain to short-circuit.

Which is what had led them here.

To this moment.

With him standing at her door in the wee hours of the night, exactly twenty minutes after she'd gotten off her shift at the hospital. Exactly where—and when—she'd uncharacteristically invited him, in a rushed, quiet voice, lest anyone else around the kissing booth hear her, after he'd murmured that he'd really like to see her again. Somewhere. Anywhere that didn't involve a line of ten guys—young and old—who were happy to hand over a few bucks to kiss a pretty nurse.

Now, though, despite saying that he did want to come inside, he hadn't moved so much as an inch. Instead, he was watching her intently with those eyes that she knew from the kissing booth were a startlingly pale green against his olive-toned skin.

"Are you sure you want me to come in? I'm not going to want to leave anytime soon. We could go out some- where. Have some coffee."

She hadn't expected that. Her moist hand tightened around the door handle as she continued looking up at him. She was tall. But he was a whole lot taller. A whole lot broader.

Go somewhere for coffee? Somewhere safe. Some- where innocuous. Or invite him in?

She didn't have indiscriminate encounters with near strangers. She didn't do anything in her life that wasn't well thought-out. Well planned.

But she didn't want to go to the all-night coffee shop and sit across a table from him pretending that all she wanted was conversation and coffee.

She wanted his long arms wrapped around her.

Wanted to be held against his wide, wide chest.

Wanted his warm lips on hers.

She *wanted*. Period.

More than ever before in her life.

And even though her heart bumped nervously inside her chest, she moved her bare feet, stepping back as she pulled the door fully open.

"Yes." Her voice was soft but clear. "I'm sure."

His lips slowly tilted and he stepped inside.

Without a word, he reached for her with one hand, and with the other, he pushed the door closed.

Chapter One

"No," Mason Hyde said adamantly as he stared up at his boss. And he hoped to hell he showed none of the alarm he was feeling. "You can't fire me."

"You insist on checking yourself out against medical advice and I'll have no choice." Coleman Black's voice was flat. Unmoved. "I don't need stupid agents. What I *do* need is you recovered and healthy, Mase." The gray-haired man frowned and moved across the hospital room, finally showing some emotion—even if Mason figured it was only irritation. "You just had surgery yesterday," Cole pointed out. "And two days before that, you were still in the hospital in Barcelona."

Mason grimaced and looked away. Maybe *stupid* was the perfect word to describe his desperation to get out of the hospital, but if anyone should understand why he needed to get out…get away…it should have been Cole.

Yeah, he was Mason's boss. But he was also Mason's

friend. And Mason didn't have many people in his life that he considered a friend. He had even fewer people in his life who knew his history like Cole did.

"I don't want to end up like I did before," he muttered, and hated that the admission made him feel weak.

Cole glanced at the open door to Mason's room and shook his head. "Maybe if you told the hospital what your history is, *why* you keep refusing the—"

"No." Mason cut the other man off. It had been ten years, for God's sake. But right now, lying there in a hospital bed while pain racked every corner of his body, it felt as if it were just yesterday.

Yesterday, when he'd been in another hospital—only that trip had been courtesy of an explosion rather than a deadly aimed SUV. Then, he'd been shot full of endless painkillers. Painkillers that had become the only thing he'd been able to think about and just about the only thing he'd been able to care about. He'd ended up losing everything—except his job—that really *had* mattered to him.

He'd be damned if he'd head down that road again.

And he'd be damned if he'd admit to anyone now what a hole he'd had to climb out of before. Particularly his doctors. "It has nothing to do with anything now," he muttered.

Cole raised his eyebrows and pointedly eyed the contraption that held Mason's casted left leg at a strange angle above the bed. A triangular bar was also suspended above Mason's chest, allowing the big man something to grab on to with his left hand, since his right was also in a long cast. "I believe the entire medical community would disagree," he said drily. Then he sighed, knowing that there were some arguments that never would work with Mason. The man marched to his own drummer.

The phone inside his lapel pocket was vibrating. Had been ever since he'd walked into Mason's hospital room ten minutes earlier. As the head of Hollins-Winword, he had at least fifty things that needed his immediate attention. Yet he was here, standing in a hospital room having a battle of wills with one of his most talented— and most stubborn—agents.

He stifled a sigh again. It was no coincidence, he supposed, that *talent* and *stubborn* seemed to generally go hand in hand. An agent had to have a strong will to work in the field. Cole didn't want to have anyone under his watch who *didn't* have a strong will.

But right now, that particular trait was causing him no small amount of consternation.

"Well, the doctors are up to you as long as you're inside these walls. But once you go AWOL from this place, your recuperation is up to *me*. And I'm telling you that you don't have a choice. Either you give up the notion of not needing any more medical care, or you won't *have* a job to come back to.

At the best of times, Mason's face was stoic. Cole had known the man since long before he'd acquired the thin scar that extended nearly the entire side of his face, so he knew that basic expression wasn't owed to the scar. And now, given the situation, Mason's face had all of the animation of the grim reaper.

"You can't fire me." Mason's voice was low. Gruff.

Which meant he was actually worried that Cole *would*.

And much as it pained him, that's what they both needed right now. "I can and I will," he assured flatly. Though he wasn't quite sure how. But Cole hadn't gotten to where he was without mastering the art of a bluff. Not that he was bluffing, exactly. He truly did not want to lose Mason as an agent. Whether he was profiling maniacal nuts or invisibly protecting people who weren't easy to protect, the guy had a talent that went miles beyond training. It was instinctive. As if he'd been bred into it.

But more importantly, Cole didn't want to lose Mason, period. And the damn fool was likely to kill himself at the rate he was going.

The annoyance of his buzzing cell finally drove him to pull it out of his pocket and glance at the display. More crises that, at least, had nothing to do with his business with Mason. He pocketed the phone. "Be glad you have alternatives," he continued. "I know Axel Clay has talked to you. Considering everything, getting out of Connecticut and lying low in Wyoming for a few months while you recover seems an excellent idea to me."

Mason slid him a look. Trust Cole to hedge around until he got to the crux of the matter. The older man had obviously been a spy for too damn long. How else had he known that he and Ax had spoken?

He started to reach for the bar to shift in the bed, but just thinking about lifting his arm above his shoulder sent a shock wave down his spine. Instead, he curled his good hand into a fist and breathed through the pain, reminding himself that feeling that pain was a helluva lot better than ending up addicted to painkillers again, and feeling only the uncontrollable urge for *another* numbing pill. "Bugging the hospital telephone, Cole?"

His boss didn't answer that. "His solution is pretty damn perfect, far as I'm concerned. Not only will you be under the watchful eye of a nurse without having to stay in the hospitals you detest, but you'll get some peace from the media hounds here."

"I've had enough of nurses, thanks." At any other time, Mason might—might—have found the double entendre humorous, but right then, he couldn't muster it. "I'll be bored crazy in Wyoming," he lied. Nothing had been boring the last time he'd been there over a year and a half ago.

The other man just shrugged. "Then you get yourself transferred to a twenty-four-hour care center whether you like it or not or you stay here, 'cause you're not going to your own place. I know you. You go to that box you call a home, and you'll do too much before you should and end up back here again even worse off than you are now."

If it weren't for the heavy-duty antibiotics that were being intravenously pumped into him, Mason wouldn't even have to be *in* the hospital. The collision between his body and the SUV he'd jumped in front of had happened a week ago. The most recent surgery that he'd had to finish putting Humpty Dumpty back together again was the last one he was supposed to need. And if he hadn't gotten the infection that necessitated that surgery, his doctors and his nurses would have been glad to see the last of him the minute they'd finished wrapping half his body in plaster.

"Damned if I do, damned if I don't," he muttered. The longer he stayed in the hospital, the worse he felt. But if he left on his own, Cole would cut him off from the only thing that mattered to him.

"I'll check on you tomorrow morning." Obviously unmoved, Cole headed toward the doorway of Mason's private room. "Either have a plan in place or give me your resignation." His voice was hard, and without another glance his way, the man walked out of the room.

Mason leaned his head back and let out a long, colorful oath.

Agents who pushed Cole hard got pushed back hard. And more than a few good ones had ended up walking away from the agency that had been the center of Mason's life for so many years.

He wasn't going to be one of them.

He grimaced and threw his good arm over his eyes. He could feel panic nibbling at the edges of his sanity.

And Mason wasn't a man who panicked.

Admitting it, even to himself, was damn hard.

But not as hard as it had been to kick an addiction that had ruled his life for eighteen months. And right now, ten years or not, he was craving a narcotic numbness as badly as he ever had.

"Good afternoon, Mr. Hyde. How are we feeling today?" The young nurse who came into the room on her squeaking, rubber-soled shoes greeted him in a revoltingly cheerful voice. One corner of Mason's brain had to give the kid credit for maintaining that unswerving cheer when dealing with him.

He *knew* he wasn't an easy patient.

"When you have a dozen broken bones, *we* will talk about it," he said wearily. He wasn't interested in watching her as she fussed around him—even if she was about as cute as a fresh-faced cheerleader—and closed his eyes.

She didn't reply, but he could still hear her moving around and feel her faint touch as she checked this and adjusted that. Which meant maybe the kid did have the ability to learn.

"You know, Mr. Hyde," she said after a moment,

proving that he'd overestimated, "I couldn't help but hear a little bit of your conversation with your visitor."

He opened his eyes and watched her.

She smiled tentatively, looking more than a little nervous. "I was out in the hall waiting to come in and change your IV bag. Anyway," she rushed on, "I'm supposed to help convince you that it's in your best interests to stay with us for a while longer, but I do know some really good nurses who provide home health care if you'd like some names."

He shrugged and held back a curse at the pain the movement caused. "Yeah. Sure." His voice was short. And even though he had no real intention of following up on her well-intentioned list, at least it took the nervousness out of her eyes. She could get on her way and leave him in peace.

She deftly slid the call button into the fingers that protruded below the edge of his cast. "I'll get the names for you. Be sure to call if you change your mind and want something stronger than the OTC stuff for that pain."

He'd chew off his tongue before he asked for anything stronger. He managed a relatively civil grunt in return, and her shoes carried her, squeaking, back out of the hospital room.

When he'd called Cole, he'd hoped to enlist the guy's aid to get out of the hospital. His place wasn't much, but at least he didn't have an ongoing stream of medical professionals bugging him every hour on the hour, and he wouldn't be a call button away from begging for a damn narcotic. His job kept him on the road about fifty weeks out of the year, and his apartment was more a repository for the mail that was shoved through the mail slot than it was a home.

Hell. He didn't even have dishes in his kitchen cupboards. He barely had soap and a towel in his bathroom.

The only thing he'd end up finding at his apartment was more discomfort and a barrage of phone calls from eager reporters who'd regrettably discovered he was the so-called hero who'd saved the life of an internationally known businessman's daughter.

Mason wasn't the only one who was media shy. He didn't want strangers looking into his life, poking and speculating. But he also worked for an agency that preferred operating under the radar. Their primary concern was security—personal and international—and it was beneficial for everyone concerned that their activities not be looked at too closely by an inquisitive public. Particularly since HW generally operated with the government's tacit approval. They handled the stuff that the elected boys and girls couldn't—or didn't want to—get caught up in.

Unfortunately, Donovan McDougal—or someone from his sizable camp—had opened their mouth to the wrong person about Mason's involvement in McDougal's personal security, and even though Cole had done his best to get a lid on it, the newshounds were busy sniffing out the story behind the near-tragic "accident."

He let the call button fall out of his grip and reached out for the hospital phone that was on a rolling stand beside the bed. His cell phone had been decimated by the vehicle that had hit him. He'd had no opportunity to replace it yet, but he had a good memory for numbers. He dragged the corded, heavy phone closer with his good arm so he could punch out the numbers.

Axel answered on the second ring.

"Set it up," was all Mason said. Then he let the receiver clatter back in place.

Going along with Axel's idea might keep Mason in Cole's good graces, but that didn't mean it was a good idea. Yeah, Ax's cousin was a registered nurse. Yeah, she'd recently bought a house and wanted to pick up some extra money.

From the outside, it might seem like a win-win situation. Courtney Clay padded her bank account, and Mason got Cole off his back.

But none of them knew about the night that Mason had spent in Courtney's bed over a year and a half ago. A memorable night. The kind of night that haunts a man.

But it had only been one night. He'd known that going in, he'd known it when he'd walked away the morning after and also when, during the days that followed, he'd had to fight the urge to contact her again.

Women like Courtney Clay were better off without guys like Mason Hyde in their lives.

Even she had agreed to that particular fact.

He was surprised that she'd gone along with her cousin's suggestion to not only give Mason room and board now but to also provide him with whatever nursing care he needed until he could take care of himself.

But maybe she hadn't been as haunted as he'd been by that night together. Maybe it made no difference to her one way or another who her temporary roommate was going to be. Maybe it was just about the money.

It didn't seem to fit what he knew about her. But then, what he knew most about her was what her lips tasted like. What her smooth, honey-tinted skin felt like beneath his fingertips.

She'd been the one to invite him to her place that long-ago day. He'd been in Weaver for a few days helping Axel out on a case. And though Mason had made it plain he wanted to see her again, he'd had no expectation, no plan, that it would lead to her bed.

She was too young for him, but she was an incredibly beautiful woman. Turning down that particular opportunity had even occurred to him. Until she'd whispered for him not to worry. It was just one night. She'd said those words herself.

So when she'd stared up at him in the shadowy light of her living room and began unbuttoning her blouse, he'd helped her finish the job.

He'd made the mistake of forgetting who and what he was when he'd tried to have a normal life eleven years ago. He wasn't going to do it again.

Not even when the temptation came in the form of a shapely, blonde nurse whose touch still hung in his memory.

He was in a wheelchair.

Even though Courtney had expected it, the sight of Mason sitting in the chair made her wince inside.

"Remember what you're doing this for," she whispered to herself. She needed to keep her long-term plan in the forefront of her mind. It would be the only way she could get through the short-term…awkwardness.

She gave a mental nod and drew in a quick, hard breath as she brushed her hands down the front of her pale pink scrubs. Then she pulled the door wide and stepped out onto her porch to watch her cousin push Mason's wheelchair up the long ramp that her brother had finished building just that morning over the front and back steps so that once her boarder did arrive, they'd be more easily able to get him in and out of the house.

She realized she couldn't quite look Mason in the

face and focused instead on her cousin. "Everything go okay with the flight out from Connecticut?"

"How would he know?" Mason answered before Axel could. His pale green gaze drew hers. "He wasn't the one cooped up on the plane."

A frown pulled his slashing eyebrows together over his aquiline nose. Combined with the dark shadow of beard on his jaw—evidence that he hadn't shaved in at least a few days—he looked thoroughly put out.

She lifted an eyebrow and managed a calm smile. "Feeling a little cranky, are we?"

"What is it with you nurses and the eternal *we?*"

"Ignore him," Axel advised as he pushed the wheelchair past her into the house. He pulled a fat, oversized envelope from beneath his arm and handed it to her. "He's been bitching since I picked him up in Cheyenne. Here're his meds."

Courtney took the envelope and looked inside at the various prescription bottles it contained. She'd already reviewed a copy of her new patient's medical chart. It had been faxed to her yesterday after Axel had called her out of the blue to ask if she was interested in taking on a home health care patient.

She'd done similar work before. Just not when the patient in question was living under her roof. But the money he'd said the patient would pay had been enough to get her interest, and in a hurry.

It was only after she'd agreed and had asked how he knew the patient that she'd learned *who* her new roomie was going to be.

There was no earthly way, at that point, that Courtney would have been able to back out without explaining to her cousin why. And she had no intention of sharing those particular details.

So, she'd squelched her reservations and reviewed the file when it arrived. Even though she was trained for objectivity, she'd been horrified at the injuries that Mason had sustained. She also hadn't been able to help wondering how on earth he'd been hurt, but that particular information had not been in his chart.

Which meant it was probably work related.

She was ridiculously familiar with the hush-hush aura surrounding the company that Mason worked for, because it was the same company that many of her relatives had worked for. Or still did.

Of course she wasn't supposed to know much about Hollins-Winword. But she wasn't an idiot. She had ears that worked perfectly well. The first time she'd heard the name, she'd been a schoolgirl. As she'd gotten older, she'd discerned more.

And then when Ryan went missing…

She broke off the thought. It was pointless reliving the misery of believing her big brother was dead, because he was home now. Safe and sound, miraculously enough a newlywed with a family of his own.

She followed Axel and Mason into the house and nudged the door closed behind her as she studied the labels on the prescription bottles. Various industrial-strength antibiotics and vitamins and minerals. When she got to the last bottle, though, she frowned a little.

She'd read in Mason's file that he refused to take prescription-strength pain medication, yet that's exactly what she was looking at.

There was nothing in his file about drug allergies, so—if he was anything like the men in her family—it was probably more likely some macho belief that real men didn't need anything to take the edge off their pain, even if it was only for a few days.

She dropped the narcotic back in the envelope and stepped around Mason's protruding leg cast. She set the envelope on the square dining room table near the arch separating the great room from the kitchen and turned toward the men. "Your room is at the end of the hall." Meeting Mason's gaze only made her skin want to flush, so she focused on the few stray, silver strands glimmering among the dark brown hair that sprang back thick and straight from his forehead. "The bathroom is next to it. You *are* able to manage with crutches, aren't you?"

"It's not pretty, but yeah." He sounded marginally less cranky than before, and Courtney couldn't help but feel a rush of sympathy for the man.

No matter what had transpired between them that Valentine's night, the man was recovering from several serious injuries. He had matching long, blue casts on his right arm and his left leg. She also knew that he'd suffered several bruised ribs. He was in pain and, for now, was having to depend on someone else to help him with basic functions from bathing to eating. Of course he was cranky.

Anyone would be.

She looked at her cousin. "Why don't you bring in the rest of his things, and I'll get Mason settled in bed." She could feel heat climbing her neck at that. She didn't bother waiting for Axel to respond but moved next to him and nudged his hands away from the wheelchair so she could push it herself.

Last night, before she'd gone on duty at the hospital, she'd rearranged some of the furniture in her living area to accommodate Mason. Her experience with him told her that he wasn't the least bit clumsy. But Mason was a big man and, clumsy or not, he had a cast covering one leg from foot to thigh. That, combined with the cast on his opposing arm, meant he'd need all the space he could maneuver in, whether by wheelchair or by crutches.

The wheels on the chair squeaked slightly against the reclaimed-wood, planked floor as she pushed him down the hall, hesitating only briefly when they passed the bathroom. "Tub with a shower," she told him in the most neutral nurse's voice she could muster.

"Don't tease me. Only thing I get these days is a wet washcloth."

She felt heat in her throat again as she turned his chair slightly and carefully pushed him into the spare bedroom. "Sorry. I imagine a real shower is something you're looking forward to."

He made a grunting sound in reply.

After angling the chair alongside the bed, she moved around it. She'd already pulled the covers back, and the pillows were stacked up against the wrought-iron headboard. There was also an old recliner from her parents that Ryan had muscled into one corner of the room.

She stopped in front of Mason. He was wearing a white T-shirt that strained at his shoulders and a pair of gray sweatpants with one leg split up the side to accommodate the cast. His toes below the cast were bare, and he had on a scuffed tennis shoe on his other foot.

And he still managed to make her mouth water. Which was not what a nurse should be thinking about her patient, she reminded herself. "Ready to get out of the chair?"

He looked no more enthusiastic than she felt. "You're not strong enough to lift me."

"Not if you were dead weight," she allowed. "But you're not. So which do you prefer? Bed or chair?"

He didn't look at her. "Bed."

Which he probably took as some admission of weakness. Coming from a family of strong individuals, that, too, was something with which she had plenty of familiarity. "All right." Before she could let her misgivings get in the way, she locked the wheels and removed the arm of the wheelchair. Then she bent her knees close to his and grasped him loosely around the waist, leaving room for him to brace his good leg beneath him as she lifted. "Ready?"

He gave another grunt, putting out his uninjured hand against the mattress, so he could add his own leverage. "Just do it."

She tightened her arms, lifting with her legs, and held back her own grunt as she took his weight for the brief moment before he got his leg beneath him. Then he was out of the chair, pivoting more or less smoothly until he landed on the bed, sitting.

She held on to him only long enough to be certain that he wasn't going to tip over, before she straightened. Her stomach was quivering nervously, but the sight of his pale face and tight lips took precedence. "I know," she murmured. "Not very pleasant. But it'll get better."

His expression shifted from pain to *pained*. "I don't need coddling."

She gave him the kind of stern look she'd learned from her grandmother. Gloria was retired now, but she'd been a nurse, and it was in that capacity that she'd met Courtney's grandfather, Squire Clay. And she'd had plenty of years since then to refine that stern look and pass it on to her granddaughters. "Believe me," she assured him, "you won't *get* coddling from me. Now, do you want to sit there on the side of the bed or lean back?" She didn't wait for an answer before she reached down for his casted leg.

But his hands brushed against hers as he did the same, and she had to suck down another shock of tingles that ripped through her. She moved her hand from beneath his. Feeling shaky again, she deftly tucked a wedge of foam, which she'd gotten from the hospital, beneath his leg and stepped away, while he swore and jabbed at the pillows propped behind him.

Sweat had broken out on his brow.

She curled her fingers, fighting the urge to help him as he awkwardly shifted, lest he mistake her assistance for the banned coddling. "What can I get you to make you more comfortable?"

He finally settled, his head leaning against the headboard behind him. He shoved his hand through his hair and looked up at her. "I don't suppose sex is one of the options, is it?"

Chapter Two

Courtney stared, and the heat that she'd been trying to keep at bay flooded hot and furious into her cheeks. "Excuse me?"

"You want me to repeat it?"

Her lips parted. She wanted to say something, but there just weren't any words that were coming to mind.

And then there wasn't time, because Axel came into the room and dumped a very worn leather duffel bag on the floor next to the foot of the bed. He also had a pair of metal crutches that he propped against the wall near the doorway. "I'd hang around and shoot the breeze," he told them both, "but Tara's got an appointment this afternoon and I'm on Aidan-duty. Hard to believe how much one fourteen-month-old kid can get around." He pulled a slender cell phone out of his back pocket and handed it to Mason. "Courtesy of Cole," he told him, before bumping knuckles with Mason's fist and hustling out of the room.

A second later, they heard the front door open and close.

Courtney held her tongue between her teeth and looked back at Mason. "No," she finally said, breaking the thick silence. "Sex is not an option. Obviously."

His gaze trapped hers, but she couldn't tell if he was amused or not. "Because you think I'm presently incapable, or because I didn't call you the morning after?"

She shoved her curling fists into the pockets of her scrubs. She didn't even want to entertain ideas of what Mason was capable or incapable of doing. "I didn't ask you to call me," she reminded. Not the morning after, nor during the twenty months that had passed since then. "You're here because you're recovering from an assortment of injuries. Period."

The corner of his lips lifted a fraction. "Yeah, that's what I expected but figured we might as well get it out of the way so you can stop looking worried that I'm going to bring it up."

Ordinarily, she preferred being straightforward, too. But right now, she wished she could keep up the pretense that nothing had ever occurred between them. "Number one—" she leaned over and picked up his duffel bag "—I wasn't worried. And number two, now it's out of the way. Subject done." She hefted the surprisingly heavy bag onto the empty surface of the dresser and glanced at him over her shoulder. "I'll unpack this if you don't mind?"

His lips twisted. His gaze was unblinking. "Do I have a choice?"

Her fingers let go of the zipper pull. "Yes," she said slowly and turned to face him. "Nobody is trying to run your life for you, Mason." She didn't know what was more disturbing. His presence, the taste of his name on her lips after all this time or the disturbing notion that he considered himself some sort of captive.

"You'll be the first nurse who hasn't tried."

She leaned her hip against the dresser and folded her arms over her chest. In just the one night that they'd shared, he'd learned her body better than she'd known it herself. But other than the fact that he worked for the same company that had nearly stolen her brother for good, what she really knew about Mason could have fit on the head of a pin.

"Then I'll be the first," she said quietly. "The only thing I'm doing here is making sure you continue your recovery safely and with as much comfort as possible. You're the one in control of your situation. Not me."

His eyes narrowed slightly, which just seemed to concentrate that pale green and make it even more startling against his dark lashes. "Why did you agree to all this?" He lifted his hand, taking in the room and, she presumed, the situation in general.

She chewed the inside of her lip, then went for honesty. "I didn't know you were the patient," she admitted. "Not until after I'd agreed."

He lifted his eyebrow. "Why didn't you back out?"

Now, that was trickier.

She shrugged. "I don't know." She did, but she had no intention of sharing her reasoning.

Remember what you're doing this for.

"So." She patted the duffel bag. "Do you want me to leave this for you to deal with…or…?"

He was silent for so long that she couldn't help wondering even more what was inside his head. She'd wondered a whole lot that night they'd been together, too. At least, she had during the moments when she'd been able to draw a coherent breath.

Which had been few and far between.

She swallowed down the jangling memory.

"Knock yourself out," he finally said.

Feeling ridiculously relieved to have something to keep her hands busy, she turned to the task. He had a few pairs of jeans, a half-dozen colored T-shirts and a handful of sweatpants—all one-legged like the pair he was wearing. The sum total of his clothing wasn't enough to fill even two of the six dresser drawers, and the pair of athletic shoes and scuffed cowboy boots didn't come close to filling the floor of the bedroom closet.

Aside from a small leather shaving kit, the rest of the duffel was crammed with books, which explained the weight.

Hardbacks. Paperbacks. Some that looked brand new and others that looked as if they'd seen the wear from hundreds of hands. She stacked a bunch of books on the nightstand next to the bed, where they'd be in easy reach for him. "You're a reader." And an eclectic reader, to boot. He had everything from the latest thriller topping the bestseller charts to political commentaries and biographies to classic literature.

He shifted against the pillows, and she couldn't help but see the way a thin line of white formed around his tightly held lips. "So?"

She adjusted the high stack. "Don't get defensive. It's just an observation." She left the rest of the books in a stack on the dresser. "And not that it looks like you'll run through all of these anytime soon, but I have a pretty loaded bookcase myself in the living room, too. You're welcome to help yourself. Do you prefer to get around with wheels or these?" She held up the crutches.

"Those," he said immediately. "Get rid of the chair altogether."

"All right." She propped the crutches right next to the bed, between the headboard and the nightstand. "Besides the books, feel free to help yourself to anything else around here."

He lifted his eyebrow again, giving her a long look, and she pressed her lips together. He was toying with her. "Food-wise and such," she clarified. "I'll get you set up with a meal before I have to go to the hospital for my shift and bring Plato in so you can meet him. He's gotten spoiled and used to having this bed for his own, but he's a smart boy. You just tell him to stay off and he will."

"Plato?"

She realized she was speaking so fast she was almost babbling and hated giving him any evidence that she was unsettled by his presence. "My Saint Bernard. He's out in the backyard right now."

"You didn't have a dog before."

"I didn't own a house with a yard before," she returned.

"No." His gaze felt heavy on her face. "You had that apartment."

Her throat suddenly felt dry and she swallowed, folding her arms over her chest. His gaze seemed to focus on them. Or on the achingly tight breasts that they were pressing against.

Probably her imagination.

Hopefully, just her imagination.

It was difficult enough ignoring her attraction for him, without thinking that he still carried some for her, too.

"What, um, what do you like to eat?"

His eyebrow peaked.

"For lunch," she added doggedly.

"There's nothing that I don't much like."

She moistened her lips. "You're not exactly helping me here, Mason. If I came in here with brussels sprouts, would you be loving them?"

His expression suddenly lightened, and a faint smile toyed around his surprisingly lush lower lip. "Honey, as long as I don't have to cook 'em, I'll be damn happy to eat 'em."

She exhaled and rolled her eyes. "Spoken like most men," she said wryly and headed out of the bedroom, taking the wheelchair with her.

She didn't breathe again, though, until she reached the privacy of the kitchen, and once she did, it took considerable effort not to collapse on a chair and just sit there.

But she hadn't been exaggerating to Mason. She did have to get to work soon.

Just because her bank account was going to be dancing a jig before this was all over and Mason went on his way in a few months, didn't mean that she didn't have to earn her regular wages.

She folded the chair and stowed it in a closet, then moved past the ladder-back chairs surrounding the kitchen table that was tucked into the small bay overlooking her backyard, and pulled open the refrigerator door. Until recently, she'd never made much effort at cooking for herself. She'd never had to. It was always so easy just to drop by her folks' place, or one of her other relatives', and grab a bite when she was looking for some home-cooked food.

But things were changing. Takeout and scavenged meals weren't going to do. So, after she'd moved into the house, she'd begun making an effort, and now her refrigerator was well stocked with fresh fruits and vegetables.

She had a chicken casserole that she'd made the day before, as well as sliced pot roast, and she chose the thick, sliced beef to make two sandwiches for Mason. She added a sliced apple, a glass of water and a thick wedge of peach pie that she couldn't take credit for since Ryan had brought it over.

Not giving herself a moment to dither over the meal—and dither she would, if she allowed it—she arranged everything on a sturdy wooden tray and carried it back to the bedroom, stopping only long enough to grab up the envelope with his meds and tuck it under her arm.

She breezed into the bedroom, her footsteps hesitating when she found him with his nose in a book, a pair of black-rimmed glasses perched almost incongruously on his aquiline nose.

Why she found the sight so particularly touching, she couldn't say. But she did. Which just meant that she had to push a brisk tone past the tightness in her chest. "I have soda or iced tea, if you want something to drink other than water." She tossed the envelope on the foot of the bed and grabbed the well-used folding lap table that she'd already had on hand and deftly set it over his lap, sliding the tray on top of it. "Or beer," she added, remembering that had been his preference before. "Though, you really shouldn't have alcohol right now."

She glanced at him, waiting, and found him watching her, his glasses and book set aside. "What?" she asked.

"How'd you do that without spilling the water?"

Surprised, she looked down at the lap tray and meal. "Practice," she said simply. "So…what do you want to drink besides water?"

His gaze passed her to land on the envelope lying near his foot. His lips tightened a little and he looked back at the meal. "Water's all I need." His jaw slid slightly to one side, then centered again. "Thank you. This looks good. I was half-afraid you'd be bringing in brussels sprouts."

She smiled slightly. "Behave yourself and I won't have to." She picked up the envelope and poured the bottles out into her hand. "When was your last dose of antibiotics?"

He didn't look up from the food. "Before I left Connecticut."

Which meant too many hours. She set all but two of the bottles on the nightstand, where they'd be in easy reach for him, and poured out his doses, setting them on the tray. "You missed a dose."

"I'll live."

"What's your pain like?"

He bit off a huge corner of thick-sliced bread and tender beef and shrugged.

Macho men.

"On a scale of one to five," she prodded. "Five being the worst."

"Twelve," he muttered around his mouthful.

She wasn't particularly surprised. She could practically see his discomfort oozing out of his pores. "Good thing you're eating," she said and popped the lid off his painkillers. "It'll help keep your stomach settled with this stuff."

He lifted his hand, stopping her before she could drop one on her palm. "Throw the damn things down the toilet. I don't need 'em."

She gave him a look. *"Twelve?"*

His gaze slid over hers, then away. "Fine." His voice was short. "I don't want them."

"It's not a sign of weakness to need—"

"I *said* no."

She slowly put the cap back on the bottle, sensing that this was about something other than macho posturing. And, judging by the way he was holding himself even more stiffly than before, that he didn't want her prying.

Which told her more than words could have said, anyway.

"Fair enough." She set the bottle next to the others. "But you don't have a choice about those," she said firmly. She pointed to the two pills next to his plate. "If you want your bones to heal, you've got to beat back that infection once and for all." She headed to the doorway. "I'll go get Plato."

Mason watched Courtney stride out of the room.

It was a helluva thing that he was almost more interested in the damn pill bottle within arm's reach than he was in watching the particularly enjoyable sight of her shapely form moving underneath the thin pink fabric of her scrubs.

He swallowed the last of the first sandwich, leaned his head back against the pillows and closed his eyes. Too easily, the night they'd spent together came to life in his mind.

He pinched the bridge of his nose and opened his eyes again.

Since the moment he'd thrown McDougal's daughter, Lari, to safety, he'd been in hell.

Coming to Weaver was just one more layer of it.

There was no future for Courtney with him, and she was the kind of woman who deserved futures. She was young and beautiful and caring and came from a strong, close family.

He was past young, scarred on the inside as well as

the out, and the only family he knew—or who mattered to him—was the family of Hollins-Winword.

It was a fact of life that was easy enough to remember when he was a continent or two away from her.

But sprawled across a bed under her *roof?*

That was an entirely different matter.

"Plato, come meet Mason."

He heard her voice before her footsteps and then she reappeared in the doorway with a gigantic Saint Bernard at her side.

"You didn't get a dog." Mason eyed the shaggy beast. "You got a damn horse."

She grinned, bringing a surprising impishness to her oval face, and tucked her long, golden hair behind her ear. "He's a big boy," she agreed. Her fingers scrubbed through the dog's thick coat and the beast's tongue lolled with obvious pleasure. "But he's a total marshmallow. He's four and very well behaved." She stopped next to the bed and gestured to the dog, who plopped his butt on the floor and looked across the mattress at Mason with solemn brown eyes. "Mason's a friend, Plato."

Mason stuck out his good hand and let the dog sniff him. Evidently satisfied, the dog slopped his tongue over Mason's fingers and thumped his tail a few times.

Courtney smiled, then looked at the watch around her wrist. "I've got to get to work." Her gaze skipped over Mason and around the room. She picked up the cell phone that Axel had left. "I'm adding the number at the hospital," she said as her fingers rapidly tapped. "Plus my own cell number." When she was finished, she set the phone on the nightstand. "But I'll warn you—cell service isn't always the greatest around here. There's a landline in the kitchen, though." She patted her hip. "Come on, Plato. Back outside."

"Does he always stay outside?"

Courtney shook her head. "Not always. But I don't want him disturbing you."

Mason leaned forward a little, rubbing his hand over the dog's massive head. "He'll give me someone to talk to."

She smiled slightly. "Well. He is pretty good company. I'll pop back home when I get my dinner break, but it'll be pretty late." She headed toward the doorway. "Don't hesitate to call if you need anything, though. If I can't make it over, there's always going to be someone who can." She gave a faint wave and disappeared.

Mason looked from the doorway to the pill bottles on the bedside table to the dog, who was watching him as if he could read his mind.

"Don't you worry, Plato," Mason muttered. "Soon as I get these casts off, I'll be out of here."

And away from temptation.

He looked from the prescription bottle back to the empty doorway.

Both temptations.

"It sounds like the perfect opportunity for you." Lisa Pope, the other nurse who shared the emergency room's night shift with Courtney, leaned her elbows on the counter and smiled. "Keep an eye out for a patient while he heals up *and* collect room and board at the same time."

Courtney didn't look up from the medical chart she was updating and smiled a little wryly. "It does sound perfect," she agreed. In theory.

"*Sounds* perfect," Lisa prompted. She raised her eyebrows. "What's the problem?"

Courtney shook her head. "No problem." None that she intended to share.

Lisa leaned closer over the desk. At the moment, the Weaver Hospital's emergency department was quiet. "He must not have a wife, or he wouldn't need care. So is he handsome?" Her eyes danced wickedly.

"Whether he is or not is beside the point. He's a *patient*."

Lisa sighed noisily and straightened. "Honestly, girl. You are twenty-six years old, so beautiful that other women ought to hate you, and I swear you live the life of a nun. It's practically criminal."

Courtney gave a laughing snort. "Why does it matter to you? You're besotted with your husband, and you know it." Lisa and Jay even had a darling little girl, Annie.

Lisa lifted her shoulder. "Maybe so, but that doesn't mean a little vicarious living is out of the question. So... handsome or not?"

Courtney gave a huge sigh and closed the chart. "Mason is—" She broke off, trying to find a good word to describe the man and failing entirely. "Handsome enough." She settled on the adjective, just because it was expedient. Despite the scar on his face, he was a striking man. Not handsome exactly, because he had a certain aura of...darkness around him. "More importantly, he's a *patient*."

Lisa made a face. "Well. At least tell me you're going to spend the extra money you're earning on something more interesting than fresh paint for your house trim. For nine months, all you've talked about is that house of yours."

A laugh started to bubble in the back of Courtney's throat.

Nine months.

It was almost funny.

She looked across the counter at her coworker and friend and shrugged casually, hiding the squiggle of excitement inside her. "What can I say? It's my home. I want it to be perfect."

Perfect for when it wasn't just her living there.

Then she waved her hands in a shooing motion as she turned her attention back to paperwork that needed to be completed ASAP. "Now, we'd better get back to work or the boss lady around this place will have our heads."

They both grinned, because the boss lady who ran the Weaver Hospital happened to be Courtney's mother, Dr. Rebecca Clay. But the grins didn't last long because the doors to the E.R. slid open, and Courtney's sister-in-law, Mallory, strode inside, shrugging out of her jacket as she moved. "Got a high-risk mom coming in by air," she greeted as she moved rapidly across the tiled floor past the desk where Courtney and Lisa were. "They're at least ten minutes out."

Courtney was already following her. "I'll call the team." She didn't even look back to see Lisa assume her seat at reception.

Mallory nodded and pushed through the double doors, Courtney on her heels.

The quiet evening was over, and Courtney didn't have a chance to think about much of anything until it was time for her dinner break at ten o'clock.

She drove the short distance home and let herself into the house. There was a water glass sitting on the counter in the kitchen where she hadn't left it, but that was the only indication that Mason had been moving around the house.

A light came from his room down the hall, and she headed there quietly in case he was sleeping. She stuck her head around the doorway and looked inside.

He was sprawled on the bed, more or less in the same position that she'd left him. A book was lying closed on the mattress beside him, and Plato was lying next to that.

Her dog's brow wrinkled as he looked at her, but he didn't lift his head. He looked as if he were settled for the night. Between the big dog and the big man, there was barely a spare inch of mattress left.

Courtney settled a light blanket over Mason and turned off the light. Mason still didn't stir. That was good. He needed sleep.

"Good boy," she whispered to Plato, giving his head a scratch.

She left the house again and went back to the hospital to finish her shift. The second half passed even more quickly than the first, thanks to a motorcycle accident on the highway outside of town. It was just after three o'clock when she got home again.

Mason's room was still quiet, except for the faint sound of his snoring.

She smiled a little to herself and went into her own bedroom, which was across the hall from his. She exchanged her scrubs for a pair of lightweight pajama pants and a tank and then—because she always needed to unwind for a while after getting off shift—headed out to the family room again. She'd barely sat down in front of her computer when she heard the pad of Plato's paws. He propped his head on her knee, flopping his tail against the floor.

"So, Plato. Are you ready to have a baby?"

Chapter Three

Courtney rested her chin on her palm and stared at the computer screen, her mind eagerly whisking into the future.

"A little boy or a little girl?" She didn't care which. She glanced at the dog. "Come this time next year, we'll have a smiling, gurgling little someone to cuddle. What do you think?"

Plato's warm brown eyes stared back at her. He made a low sound that she took as complete agreement.

Brilliant dog that he was.

She grinned and reached out to run her fingers through his thick, silky hair, and he grinned back at her, pushing his head harder against her palm. His long, feathered tail slapped the base of her chair. "I knew you'd like the idea, too." Plato had been around children before she'd adopted him. His previous owner had run a foster home before cancer had stricken her.

Thinking of the woman who hadn't only been Courtney's teacher in Cheyenne, but also her friend, made her
sigh.

Then she leaned over and pressed a kiss on Plato's
big head before turning back to the computer screen that
glowed in front of her. She wasn't going to end up like
Margaret, taking in other people's children when they
couldn't properly care for them. For Margaret, that had
been enough.

Not for Courtney.

She wanted a child of her own.

"Thank goodness for Axel, huh?" She didn't look
away from the computer screen. "If it weren't for him,
we'd be waiting even longer." Of course, when her
cousin had approached her about taking in Mason, he'd
had no idea of her plans and still didn't. For that matter,
nobody in her family had any idea.

She simply wasn't ready to share, yet.

She looked back at her faithful companion and
scrubbed her fingers through his thick coat again.
"You're the only one who knows," she whispered.

The four-year-old Saint Bernard gave a huge, contented sigh.

Which had pretty much been the dog's reaction ever
since she'd begun voicing her intention to add to their
small family.

She was twenty-six years old. Financially independent in a modest way. She had a good job. She—along
with the bank—owned a home that she'd spent the past
nine months remodeling.

And she wanted a baby.

So what if she didn't have a man in her life?

Weaver, Wyoming, was a small town. She'd known
all of the available men here since they'd all pretty much

been in diapers. She also knew the men who weren't available, yet liked to think they were.

She had no problem giving them *all* a pass.

The fact was, not a single man in Weaver had ever really turned her head, romantically speaking.

Well.

She grimaced slightly. Not any man who was *from* Weaver, she amended, thinking of the man sleeping right down the hall from her.

She was a modern, independent woman.

She had scads of supportive—albeit nosy—family members in the area. Everything in her life was aligned perfectly, just as she'd planned and worked for.

And now, thanks to Axel's suggestion and Mason's rent, she'd have the funds she needed even sooner than she'd planned.

If she'd learned anything in her life, it was not to wait too long to put into action the things you wanted.

Well, the waiting was done.

For months, she'd been checking out the various websites of sperm banks. Checking references. Checking reputations. And she'd finally settled on one—Big Sky Cryobank. It was located in Montana, had been around for as long as she'd been alive and came with impeccable references.

Now, given what she was earning, thanks to Mason, she would be able to bank enough extra money to pay the cryobank fees and the associated physician fees, since she knew her health insurance wasn't going to cover the process of *getting* pregnant. She'd also have enough in her savings to tide her over for a few months when the baby came, so she wouldn't have to go back to work the very second her maternity leave was used up.

"Everything is perfect," she told Plato.

The dog stared up at her as if he could read her mind.

She grimaced a little. All right. Modern, independent woman or not, she had to admit that "perfect" *would* be the husband and a wedding ring along with the baby she was desperate to have. But she wasn't willing to wait for all of that to come knocking at her door. Not when her door—save that one night with Mason all those months ago—was essentially silent. "As perfect as it's likely to get," she allowed, giving Plato a firm look.

"What's perfect?"

She jerked, her heart lurching in her chest, and spun around on her chair to peer down the darkened hallway. "Mason. What are you doing awake?"

His rubber-tipped crutches provided a slow, rhythmic clump as he moved closer.

Her heart hadn't stopped lurching, and she rose, wishing like fury that she'd thought to put on a robe over her thin knit pajamas. Thank heavens the room was lit only by a small lamp and the glow from her computer monitor. He would never be able to see the thumping in her chest, which felt so heavy it was probably visible. "I hope I didn't wake you."

He finally stopped on the other side of the dining room table. He shook his head.

She moistened her lips and pressed her palms down the sides of her drawstring pants. "Do you need anything? You were sleeping when I came by during my break, and I didn't want to disturb you then. But if you're hungry or thirsty, I'm happy to get something for you." Better to have a task to focus on, even if she did realize that she was talking too fast in the process.

He shook his head again, then jerked his chin toward the computer. "What's that? One of those computer dating websites? Searching for your perfect match?"

She barely kept herself from shutting off the computer monitor. "Sort of."

His dark gaze shifted back to her. "What're you looking for? Blond hair? Dark hair? Blue eyes? Brown?"

She laughed a little nervously. Maybe if she described him, he'd drop the subject. Or not, considering his "sex option" comment when he'd arrived.

She wasn't brave enough to find out.

Nor was she brave enough to hear what sort of comments he might have about her decision to find a daddy for her baby through a sperm bank. She pushed a few buttons on the computer keyboard, and the screen went blank, and she moved toward him. Away from the narrow desk where the computer sat. But the closer she got to him, the warmer she became.

Fortunately, there were a few working brain cells left inside her head for her to realize the heat wasn't coming from inside her, but physically radiating from him. At a temperature much higher than normal.

She reached up and pressed her palm against his forehead. He was burning up.

"Mason," she tsked. "You have a fever. Are you in pain?"

"No." He'd closed his eyes and sighed faintly when she'd laid her hand on his forehead. The kind of sigh that signaled relief.

"I don't believe you," she murmured, but left her hand on his forehead a moment longer than necessary before she tucked herself between his casted arm and his side. She slid the crutch out of her way and leaned it against the table.

The feel of his torso against hers was blazing hot.

"Come on. You shouldn't be on your feet." She

wrapped her arm behind his back for support and gently nudged him in the direction of the hallway.

"I don't want to go back to bed. I'm sick of beds at the moment."

"Okay." She shifted slightly. "How about the couch?"

He gave a faint grunt and, with most of his weight on his remaining crutch, headed toward it. By the time he'd managed to half hop and half crutch his way around until he could pretty much collapse on the smooth leather cushions, she was glad she'd rearranged the furniture. She was also out of breath, and she didn't consider herself exactly out of shape. Not with the running that she did.

She propped her hands on her hips and blew out a breath. "Now stay there."

"Funny girl." He finally let go of the crutch that he was still clutching, and it slid to the floor. "I hate this," he muttered.

A fresh wave of sympathy plowed over her. "I can only imagine." She gently shushed Plato out of the way when he tried tucking his big head on the couch next to Mason, then grabbed one of the soft throw pillows from the opposite end of the couch and deftly tucked it behind his head. "Just take a few deep breaths. I'll be right back." The dog trotted after her as she hurried into Mason's bedroom. He gave her a faint woof, then leapt up onto the bed, turned around a few times and lay down.

Courtney left him there, retrieved the wedge cushion, as well as Mason's antibiotics, grabbed a bottled water from the refrigerator in her kitchen and wet down a clean washcloth.

She went back to him and folded the damp cloth over his forehead.

He lifted his hand to it. "I don't need that."

She pushed it right back into place. "This is not coddling," she assured drily.

"Feels like it."

"Stop complaining." She rattled the antibiotics bottle. "Did you take a dose before you went to sleep?"

"Yes, Nurse Ratched."

She couldn't help but grin. The big, tall, dangerous-looking man sounded as cranky as an overtired five-year-old. "Mason, you have no idea," she warned lightly. "I work the night shift in an emergency room. I can order the meanest sons of guns around."

"I'm shaking in my boots."

"You're not wearing any," she reminded him, then went to her own medicine cabinet in her bathroom to retrieve a bottle of acetaminophen as well as her ear thermometer.

Back in the living room, she spotted the wet cloth clutched in his fist and not on his forehead.

Stubborn.

But then, so was she.

She shook out a few of the pills, opened the bottle of water and tugged the damp cloth of out his grip, then handed them to him.

"What are they?"

"Good old Tylenol. For fever and maybe to help dull the pain a little." She didn't think now was the best time to broach the subject of his prescribed painkillers. He'd already said he refused to take them, and that was his right.

He swallowed the pills and drank down half the bottle of water, then leaned his head back again against the square pillow. She folded the cloth once more over his forehead. "Leave it." She touched his chin lightly and tried to ignore the tantalizing feel of that raspy chin. "Turn your head a little."

"Why?" His voice dripped with suspicion.

"So I can torture you some more, of course." She held up her thermometer. "I need your ear for a moment."

He grimaced and turned his head slightly.

"Take comfort in the fact that it could be worse." She quickly took his temp and then sat back on her heels. "Well, it's not as high as I thought it might be, but if it's not back down to normal by morning, I'm going to have my mother come by."

He pulled the cloth off his face and gave her a look. "Your mother."

"She's a doctor."

He shook his head slightly. "Right. I should have remembered that."

She tugged the cloth out of his hand yet again and replaced it on his forehead. "Should? Why?"

"I met her once," he said, sounding annoyed. "Because I remember stuff. I'm supposed to remember stuff."

She didn't know why she was unnerved to think that he'd met her mother. He'd spent a few weeks in Weaver around the time that they'd been…uninvolved. It wasn't unnatural to think he might have met more of her family than just *her,* particularly since he'd been working with Axel. "Stuff…about cases?"

He lifted the cloth enough to give her a baleful look from beneath it. "Cases of what?"

Fortunately, she had a lifetime of experience dealing with men who thought they could control a situation with just such a look. "Cases for the agency, naturally."

Mason felt only slightly better than roadkill, yet he

still was shocked by the words that Courtney uttered so blithely. "What do you know about the agency?"

"More than I ever wanted to," she assured evenly. "We nearly lost my brother because of Hollins-Winword. You work for them, too." Her gaze drifted over him.

Maybe he did have a fever, because it felt like everywhere that amber gaze landed, a fire started to burn. "I never told you about my work." He damn sure had never mentioned the name of the agency.

"So you *don't* work for them? And I'll bet the fact that you're laid up like this has nothing to do with them, either." She was still crouched on the floor beside the couch. It was a physical effort to drag his eyes away from the warm, golden glow of her.

So much skin, and so much on display, thanks to the thin shirt that she wore.

His fingers twitched, and he pushed around the cloth on his forehead just to keep them busy. "Right now I'm not working for anybody." It was true enough in a sense. But since he was more or less toeing the line that Cole had drawn in the sand, it was only a temporary truth. "And I'm laid up because I wasn't moving fast enough when I needed to."

"Mmm." She didn't look convinced.

He wasn't in the mood to argue about it. For one thing, it wouldn't serve any good purpose.

All he needed to remember was that she was his landlady for the time being. A landlady nurse.

Who smelled like something soft and powdery and gently alluring.

She moved and her hand nudged his, slipping the cloth away. "I'll get this wet again for you."

He didn't argue that, either, and watched her straighten and move across the living area, around the small dining table that shared the space with her computer and through an arch that led to the kitchen.

Her long hair swayed against her slender back that was faithfully outlined by her thin blue tank top. And then there was the womanly flare of her hips and the long, long legs....

Watching her was like watching a fantasy unroll in his head.

Only, the night that they'd spent together had been indelibly real, and he knew good and well that the reality was eons better than any fantasy.

He heard the sound of water and then she was walking back toward him, and the front view was equally as magnificent as the rear view had been.

He wondered who had been living the fantasy with her lately and grimaced over the acid taste that thought put in his mouth. "Why *are* you trolling the internet for matches?"

Her smooth, stupefyingly feminine walk halted. She blinked once, then shrugged casually. "Why does anyone? Because they're curious? Bored?" She crossed the last few steps to the couch and lowered the blessedly cool cloth to his forehead again. "Lonely? Hopeful?"

"I'm not asking about anyone." A yawn suddenly split his face. "Sorry," he muttered and tried to shift, but the cast on his leg made it awkward, and the sharp pain in his back made it impossible. He bit back an oath. "I'm asking about *you*."

She was watching him with that sympathetic, "poor baby" look in her eyes. "I guess you could put me in the hopeful camp," she said after a moment.

"So you're trying to find yourself a husband. On the damn internet. Don't you know the dangers there are in—"

"Don't you know that I'm a grown woman and am

more than capable of handling any supposed dangers out there? How's it any worse than meeting a stranger in a bar? Or a Valentine's Day kissing booth?" she added with pointed amusement. "And just to be clear, I am *not* looking for a husband."

"Just to be clear," he returned, "I know you're a grown woman. My memory's not impaired about that, at all."

She cleared her throat, her amusement seeming to dissipate in the blink of an eye. "I think it would be better if we just pretended that never happened."

His head was throbbing. His toes sticking out from the bottom of his cast were throbbing. And every spot in between was throbbing. He felt like he was burning from the inside out, and not all of it was because of some stupid temperature.

The fever he had for her was ninety percent of his problem.

"You brought it up first," he reminded. "But if you can pretend, go for it. I can't."

"Why *not?*" For the first time, he heard frustration in her voice. "It was just one night."

"Yeah, it was one night. But there wasn't anything *just* about it."

She shook her head. It only made the long, thick strands of gold hair slide across her gold shoulder and curl over the full jut of her breast, which was clearly— thank you, Lord, for torturing him with that incredible sight—delineated by the thin fabric of her shirt.

"It's only going to make things…awkward," she insisted.

"Then things will be awkward," he said flatly. "'Cause I can't forget about it." Nor did he want to.

The night they'd spent together was as much a perfect memory as it was a very necessary reminder.

Making love with her had been the most indescribable thing he'd ever experienced. And he needed to remember that it had been *temporary*.

Short-lived by necessity.

And by choice.

He pressed the damp, not-so-cool cloth down over his eyes. "Just make sure you're careful about it." His voice sounded as dark as he felt inside. "Meeting up with whatever *hopeful* suitors you find. There're a lot of crazies out there. And guys who'll take advantage of you the second you let down your guard."

"So…you don't have any problem with the idea of me finding a, um, a date like this." Her voice went so smooth that warning bells jangled in the back of his mind.

She sounded miffed.

If he were honest, he could have told her, hell yeah, he had a problem with it.

He had a problem with the notion of her going out with any other guy, no matter where or how she met the man.

He had a problem thinking about anyone touching her. Physically. Emotionally.

But that sort of honesty wouldn't get them anywhere.

"Like you said. You're a grown woman. It would be unusual if you didn't want to date." To marry. Have children. "Though, I'd have thought you'd have plenty of pickings at the hospital and wouldn't have to *resort* to meeting strangers in a bar. Or aren't there any eligible doctors there?"

She was silent just long enough that his curiosity started nagging at him and he peered at her from beneath the cloth again. She was chewing at the inside of her lip, her eyes narrowed. But after a moment, all she said was, "You should be in bed."

"No."

He was almost surprised when she didn't argue.

"All right. But if you need to get up or anything, just call my name. I'll hear you."

The last damn thing he wanted to do was call her name so she could help his sorry butt off the couch just so he could take a leak. That was the only thing he could think of at the moment that would make him willing enough to bring on a fresh set of agony by moving around.

Unless it was to go to *her* bed.

Which would be a joke right now.

The mind and some parts of his body were definitely willing, but the rest of him—the injured, aching part of him—just sat back with a snide, cruel laugh at the very idea of it.

"I'll yell," he said, having no intentions of it at all. "G'night."

She hesitated a moment longer, still looking strangely indecisive. But then she did turn on her heel and head down the hall. A moment later, he heard the sound of a door closing softly. Then water running.

His fertile mind took off like a shot, and again, the part of him that was in control got a damn good laugh.

His head hurt. His ribs and his back hurt. He had an itch beneath the cast on his arm that was driving him batty. It was hours before he finally dozed off. The sky that he could see through a kitchen window was beginning to lighten. And when he did sleep, his dreams were a jumbled mess.

Cole was behind the wheel of the SUV aiming for little Lari McDougal. Mason watched it all unfold, his dream-state legs refusing to run fast enough, knowing he wasn't going to make it. Wasn't going to be able to save the child.

Only, Lari wasn't a child, he realized as he forced his legs to move through the sludgelike paralysis that was holding him in place. It was Courtney.

Beautiful, young Courtney.

The SUV was speeding closer. Mason could see the whites of Coleman Black's eyes.

He yelled out to Lari. To Courtney.

Knew it was too late. He was too late....

He jerked and barely caught himself from rolling off the couch. His heart was pounding in his chest, his breath coming fast and hard.

But at least he knew where he was.

In Courtney's house. Sleeping on a surprisingly uncomfortable leather couch while cool sunshine streamed through the plentiful windows.

The washcloth was still damp but annoyingly so, considering it was caught under his neck.

Grabbing the back of the couch with his good hand, he managed to pull himself up until he was sitting, and then he worked on getting his bulky, casted leg out of his way long enough so he could get his butt up and off the couch.

There was no sound from the bedrooms, and he was glad to think that she was still sleeping, since he didn't relish the idea of Courtney witnessing his fumbling struggles just to get onto his feet.

She'd left his crutches propped against the chair and, balancing on his good leg, he leaned over to grab them. Only, as he did so, something in his back grabbed with talon sharpness and before he knew it, he was off balance and crashing face-first on the floor.

"Dammit!" Pain ricocheted through every corner, and he rolled onto his back, staring up at the ceiling.

It was crisscrossed with rough-hewn beams.

"Mason?" He heard her running, and then she was in the room with him, her knees grazing his good arm as she knelt down, her hands fluttering over him. She pressed her palm to his forehead. "Fever's gone. What on earth were you doing?"

She smelled warm. Bed warm. Sweet warm.

And his hankering for that sweetness was heading straight off the charts.

Which was not a helpful thing at the moment.

She peered into his face. "Are you hurt?"

"Besides my pride?" He tried using his hands to push himself up, only to swear and fall back on the floor at the searing pain that shot through his arm. His teeth came together as he swore again.

"Don't try to move anymore." Now she was leaning over him, and every centimeter of him—despite the nagging pain in his back—homed in on the soft push of her full breasts against his chest. Only when she was slipping her arm beneath his shoulder and neck did he realize she'd been reaching for the throw pillow.

Which she tucked beneath his head.

Then she pushed to her feet and stepped right over his body, jogging into the kitchen. She was back in seconds, with a phone at her ear.

"I'm *not* going back to the hospital," he warned flatly.

Even if it meant he was going to shrivel up and rot right there on her living room floor, he wasn't moving.

"You *are,*" she returned just as flatly. "Your cast looks like it's cracked."

He automatically started to raise his arm to look for himself, but a sharp pang warned him to stop.

He muttered another oath.

"Thanks. We'll be waiting," Courtney was saying into the phone before she set it down on the table.

"Waiting for who?"

"Not an ambulance," she said, "so you can stop worrying about that."

Getting carted away in an ambulance wasn't the worst of his worries, but it wasn't something he necessarily wanted. "Then, again, waiting for whom?"

"Axel. I want some help before I get you off the floor. Plus, you'll be able to ride much more comfortably in the front seat of his steroid-size pickup truck than you would in my little economy job." She stood near his bare feet, her hands propped on her hips. Her hair was sleep tousled and tangled around her shoulders, and the pajamas that had looked thin in the middle of the night looked even thinner during the cold light of morning.

He wished he could lie there and just look at her for a long, long while.

"I'm not going to *stay* at the hospital," he warned. "They can fix the cast. But I'm not going to stay."

She tilted her head slightly and a thick lock of long blond hair curled alongside the jut of her breast. "What is it with you and hospitals? Just dislike on general principle, or are you afraid you won't be in control there, and you'll end up with some of these in your system?" She pulled something out of the hidden pocket in her thin pants and held it up.

It was the bottle of pain pills that he'd dumped in the trash while she'd been at work.

He had actually opened the bottle and poured two pills out on his shaking palm before his better sense had forced him to return them to the bottle and pitch it in the trash.

Chapter Four

Courtney knew she was skirting close to the truth when Mason's gaze flickered.

Then he narrowed his eyes, and his expression became unreadable. "Wouldn't have pegged you for someone who likes to dig in the trash."

"Since you didn't work very hard to get rid of it, it wasn't hard to find." The bottle had been the only thing lying at the bottom of the small, decorative waste bin in the hallway bathroom. It would have been pretty hard *not* to notice it. She also noticed that he hadn't emptied the bottle's contents down the drain, which told her that he didn't want them around but wasn't quite ready to make it a reality.

If she could pluck the bottle out of the waste bin—narcotic contents no worse for the wear—then so could he.

She set the pills on the table next to the telephone. If Axel was true to his word, he'd be there any second, and she needed to get some real clothes on—or at least a fresh pair of scrubs—before they went to the hospital. She didn't really want to parade around in front of her coworkers in her jammies.

Nevertheless, she pulled out one of the dining room table chairs, turned it around and sat where Mason could see her with no effort. She folded her arms across her knees and leaned forward. "I'm guessing you had a dependency problem?"

His expression went even more blank.

"You don't have to tell me all the details. Or any of them, unless you choose to. But it would be helpful where your *care* is concerned to know if it's something recent or not."

His scar, where it traveled over his temple, looked white. Whiter, even, than the line around his thinly compressed lips. "Not." The word was snapped off.

It was more of an answer than she'd expected to get.

The woman inside had a million questions that she had to squelch. The nurse, though, had only a few. "Would it be better for you if I really did flush 'em?"

"No, because I could get more if I wanted."

She knew that was true enough. "Are you going to want to?"

His lashes lifted. The green of his eyes was pale. Sharp. "That remains to be seen, doesn't it?"

His honesty felt brutal. During her nursing training in Cheyenne, she'd volunteered at a detoxification and rehabilitation unit. She'd worked with patients of all ages, both sexes, those who came from money and those who were living on the streets. Some were there by choice and some weren't. She'd heard every story, every excuse, every reason for how and why they were there in the first place, every reason and every goal for how and why they wouldn't be back.

Some made it through. Some didn't.

Those who were the most successful were the ones who were honest—with themselves, at least—through every step they took.

"Well." Her voice sounded husky, even to her own ears. "Try to remember that it isn't a crime to ask for help when you need it. And that's what I'm here for. To help you until you're back on your feet."

"The only help I need at the moment is for you to sit up, so I can't see straight down that excuse of a shirt you're wearing right to the little pink jewel stud in your navel."

She sat bolt upright. She hadn't had her navel pierced when they'd slept together. Getting their navels pierced was one of the last things she and Margaret had done together.

"Sorry." Even as she said the word, she felt heat fill her cheeks.

"I'm not. Most entertaining thing that's happened to me since I planted my face on your floor."

"Which you wouldn't have done," she reminded him, "if you'd asked for assistance." She turned on her bare heel and hurried back to her bedroom, stopping only long enough to put the dog out in the backyard with fresh food and water.

By the time she'd thrown her hair up in a clip and pulled on a long-sleeved T-shirt, a pair of cargo pants, and shoved her feet into sandals, Axel—and her brother, Ryan—had arrived.

"I stopped and picked up reinforcements," Axel told her when she stopped in surprise at the sight of her brother.

Between the two men, they had gotten Mason off the floor and onto his crutches.

"Hey, there." Courtney smiled at her brother. He'd been back in their lives now for over a year, but it still felt like a miracle every time she saw him. "How're the beautiful women in your life?"

"Beautiful." Ryan's lips tilted. "Mallory got called out early this morning on another emergency. Two in one night. I dropped Chloe off at school on my way here. When we left the house, Kathleen was trying to decide whether she wants to go out tonight with Fred Beeman—who is ten years younger than she is and can keep up with her during bowling, but lives with his daughter and granddaughter, thus cramping his style—or with Sam Driscoll, who is the same age as she is but still has all his own teeth, lives on his own and—honest to God, her words, not mine—has no need for that little blue pill." Ryan's blue gaze shifted to Mason. "Kathleen's my eighty-year-old grandmother-in-law," he told him and shook his head. "God help us all."

Courtney laughed. "We should all be so lucky to be filled with life the way Kathleen is." Goodness knew the woman had more romance in her life than Courtney did.

She realized her gaze had strayed to Mason at the thought and shook herself. "Glad they got you on your feet." She wasn't going to suggest she get the wheelchair that she'd folded up and stored in the closet. She'd told him where it was and, if he'd wanted to use it, she had no doubt that he would be sitting in it right now instead of standing there stiffly with his crutches, looking painfully uncomfortable. "Let's get that cast taken care of."

He didn't look enthusiastic, but he turned and slowly

crutched his way out of the house. When he got outside, she waited silently while he hesitated at the steps.

"For God's sake, Mase," Axel complained with the ease of friendship. "This would take half the time if you'd just plant your ass in that wheelchair you had."

Mason told Axel what he could do with his comment. Ryan rolled his eyes.

Courtney remained quiet. She might agree with the other men in theory, but Mason needed to feel like he had some control, even if it was just over the matter of trying to get out of her house.

He chose the stairs over the ramp and, even though it made her nearly bite off her tongue to keep from pointing out the pitfalls, she still said nothing. Instead, she walked down the ramp, leaving the men behind.

Between the two of them, her brother and Axel were more than capable of lending Mason some assistance if it became necessary, and she figured his pride would be better able to take it if she weren't watching.

So she climbed into the backseat of Axel's oversized pickup truck and watched the minute hand on her watch slowly tick along until finally, *finally,* Mason was inside the truck.

"The wheelchair would have been easier," he said under his breath, while Axel went around the front to the driver's side.

"Your choice," Courtney reminded.

Axel climbed behind the wheel, and Ryan drove off in his own truck, lightly tooting his horn as he went. "How the hell'd you end up on your butt, anyway?" Axel asked as he put the truck in motion, following Ryan down the quiet street.

"Trying to do too much," Courtney couldn't help answering with her own observation.

Mason just turned his head and stared out the side window, ignoring them both.

Fortunately, it took only a few minutes to reach the hospital. Axel pulled up right outside the emergency room entrance so that Mason wouldn't have to move far.

Courtney hopped out of the truck and went inside. She smiled at Wyatt Mead and Greer Weston, who were her counterparts on the day shift, while she grabbed one of the wheelchairs. "Call Richie in imaging and tell him to put down his book of Sudoku puzzles. Probably going to need him for a few minutes. And see if Dr. Jackman is around." He was the orthopedist on staff, and she'd copied him with Mason's records before he'd arrived in town.

"Jackman's not, but I saw Pierce Flannery on the floor a few minutes ago. Do you want me to flag him down before he leaves?"

She'd only met Dr. Flannery once. He had a private practice in Braden, with privileges at Weaver's hospital. After they'd met, she'd sidestepped his calls a few times, much to Lisa Pope's chagrin, who'd figured Courtney couldn't do much better than accept a date with the eligible doctor.

She would have preferred Dr. Jackman to look at Mason, but knew there was nothing wrong with Dr. Flannery except for the plain interest he'd shown in her. And her purpose there today was for Mason, anyway. So, she just nodded as she pushed the chair outside through the automatic sliding doors.

With Axel's help, Mason managed to move from the truck to the chair. "I'll come back and play taxi when you need me to, as long as it's not too late," Axel offered. "Tara and I are going down to Cheyenne for dinner tonight."

Courtney gave her cousin a quick look. "Cheyenne?"

He shrugged. "She wants to go to that bead store she likes to get some supplies for the jewelry she makes at the shop. Figured we might as well make an evening out of the drive. Right now, I've gotta run out to Tristan's office for a few minutes."

Tristan was Tristan Clay, one of their uncles, who owned CeeVid, a popular gaming company that was located in Weaver. Courtney didn't have proof, but she was pretty certain that CeeVid was also a cover for Hollins-Winword.

"I'll call when he's ready to get home," she told her cousin as she moved around the wheelchair. "Thanks."

"No prob," Axel assured as he headed around his truck again.

Courtney quickly adjusted the chair's footrest to support Mason's heavy cast and then pushed him inside. Scooping up the clipboard and forms that Wyatt was holding out, she deftly wheeled Mason around to roll backward through the swinging double doors that separated the waiting area from the exam area.

She knew it was a quiet morning by virtue of the empty beds in the exam area, and she positioned Mason's chair in the first "room"—which was really only an area that could be separated from the next bed by the long curtains that hung from U-shaped ceiling tracks. She retrieved a pen and handed it, along with the clipboard, to him.

He eyed the forms and exhaled roughly. "I don't have my reading glasses with me."

Remorse quickened. "I should have thought of them." If she didn't continually feel off balance around him, maybe she would have. "I'll fill it out for you." She took the board and the pen from him and commandeered one of the low, rolling stools for herself. She knew his first and last name, obviously, but that was pretty well it.

"Birthday?"

He told her and she filled in the squares, unable to hide her surprise. "Your birthday is February 15? The day after Valentine's Day?"

"So?"

She tucked her tongue in the roof of her mouth for a moment. "So...no reason." Just that they'd spent Valentine's night together in her bed. She guessed it was pretty plain why he hadn't thought to mention that it was his birthday the next day—because she hadn't mattered enough for him to share that fact. "I wouldn't have thought you were thirty-nine, though."

"Since I feel like I'm about sixty, I'm not sure how to take that."

She couldn't help but smile faintly. "You don't look older than your age," she assured mildly. In fact, despite his hard, scarred face and the few silver strands sprinkled in his dark hair, she thought he looked younger.

Thoughts which were not helping to get the necessary paperwork completed.

He gave her his home address in Connecticut, and when it came to his emergency contact, he shrugged. "None."

"Mason." She gave him a look. "You must have family. Someone."

"Coleman Black," he finally said with a sigh. "Close enough."

She'd met Coleman Black on more than one occasion. Not because she knew he was deeply involved in the agency that she was not supposed to know about, but because he was Brody Paine's father and Brody was married to her cousin Angeline.

Angeline, as far as Courtney had been able to discern, was much fonder of her father-in-law than Brody was.

"So you *are* with the agency," she murmured. He just gave her a stony look and she shook her head a little. "I don't see what the big secret is. Half my family has been involved with it or still are." She clicked the pen a few times. "Do you have his phone number?"

He rattled off an 800 number.

She dutifully filled it in, then turned the clipboard around for him to sign the bottom of the form. His scribble was firm, slanted and barely legible.

She flipped the form over and started on the profile on the back. "Height? Six-four, six-five?" she guessed.

"Five. Two-forty."

And not an ounce of fat to spare, she knew from experience. She wrote down his weight.

"No drug allergies." She glanced at him. "Right?" She remembered it from his medical chart from Connecticut.

"Right."

She quickly dashed down the items. "Previous surgeries?"

He gave her a dry look. "It would take more than the back of that sheet of paper to list them all."

"Any history of heart disease? Stroke? Diabetes? On your mother's side or your father's?"

"No idea. They died when I was a kid."

Her fingers tightened around her pen. "I'm sorry."

He shrugged as if it didn't matter.

"Who took care of you?"

One of his eyebrows peaked. "That on the form, too?"

"Obviously not." She studied him. Everything about

him now screamed *capable. Loner.* But he hadn't always been. At one time in his life, he'd been young. A child.

A parentless child.

If he'd had relatives who'd taken him in, they were either gone or he didn't consider them close any longer, since he'd provided Coleman Black's name as his emergency contact.

"Hey, Courtney." Richie, the acne-skinned imaging tech came around the corner, and she tamped down a swell of irritation at the interruption. "What's up?"

Getting Mason's cast repaired, and making certain he hadn't done any harm to his arm beneath, was a lot more important than peeling away the plethora of onion-skin layers surrounding Mason Hyde's life. She showed Richie the crack on Mason's dark blue cast. "Wyatt is going to try to flag down Dr. Flannery to take a look."

Richie nodded. "He'll need films?"

"That's what I'm figuring."

"I'll get the mobile unit."

Richie had barely moved out of sight, when Pierce Flannery strode into the room, his long white doctor's coat flapping behind his long legs. "Courtney," he greeted, his brown gaze warm. "It's nice to see you again."

"Doctor." Courtney smiled and gestured toward Mason, whose eyes had narrowed on the young doctor's face. "This is Mason Hyde. I'm providing his home health care and—" she touched Mason's cast "—unfortunately didn't do a good enough job. His cast is cracked."

"Well." Flannery lifted Mason's arm a few inches and studied it from every angle. "Get a film and we'll see if we need to start from scratch or if we can just patch it up." He looked at Mason, taking him in fully. "What ran over you? A train?"

"A Hummer," Mason said. "Felt like a train when I was bouncing off it onto the side of the road, though."

Courtney blinked a little.

Given his injuries, she'd assumed there'd been some sort of collision involved. But she'd also assumed that he'd been inside a vehicle of his own, at least.

Not that he'd been struck down by one.

"You were on foot?"

"Yeah." He didn't look at her, but at the doctor. "How long's this gonna take?"

"Shouldn't be long, even if we have to take off the cast and put on a new one." The doctor's gaze traveled to Courtney over Mason's head. He smiled. "Though I'll freely admit that if it takes a while, it'll be no hardship, considering the company."

He was flirting with her and obviously didn't care who witnessed it. She kept her smile in place, but made certain not to let it look too friendly. She had no interest in encouraging the doctor. "I'll see what's holding up Richie," she said and headed in the direction the tech had taken.

"So. You a friend of our lovely Nurse Clay?" Once Courtney was gone, the doctor's gaze fixed on Mason.

"Not exactly." Mason could read the younger man well enough. Even if he'd said he *was* a friend—and all that could be implied by that sometimes nebulous term—the doctor would still be interested in Courtney.

Who could blame him?

Courtney was an exceptionally beautiful woman with a smile and friendliness that would have garnered attention even if she hadn't been tall, long-legged and this side of voluptuous.

"But I am concerned with her best interests," he added with a warning edge.

"Good for you," the doctor said, and he seemed to be sincere.

When it came to his work, Mason had a knack for sizing up a person's character. He just didn't seem able to get a bead on this guy. Because he wasn't a subject that Mason was investigating? Or because he obviously had his eye on Courtney?

Either way, it irritated the hell out of Mason.

He didn't like things being cloudy.

"The portable unit is out of commission." Courtney's voice preceded her appearance by a half a second. She moved behind his wheelchair, bringing with her that soft scent of hers. "I'll have to take you over to imaging."

Flannery glanced at his watch, then nodded. "Let me know when you have the films. I've got some calls to take care of and a few patients to see." He looked over Mason at Courtney and smiled.

Just for her.

Mason's casted leg twitched with the urge to sweep the guy off his well-shod feet.

His chair began moving. "I'll make sure you're paged," Courtney told the doctor before rolling Mason out of the exam area.

He felt a grin pushing at his lips.

Unfortunately, it was still there when they reached the imaging department, and she gave him a suspicious look. "What are you looking so pleased about?"

"Nothing. I'll just be glad to get out of here again. Why are you resorting to the online things when you've got a perfectly good specimen in the doc back there?"

Her eyebrows shot up. "I beg your pardon?"

"He's interested in you."

For a moment, she looked lost for words. "That doesn't mean I'm interested in him."

"Why not? Is he a closet nerd or something?"

She laughed a little. "I have no idea. Why do you care?" Her eyes narrowed. "How did you end up getting hit by an SUV, anyway?"

"By getting in its way. Is he married?"

"No, he's not married. And *clearly* you got in the way. I figured that out for my own brilliant self. But… how? Was the driver drunk or something?"

"Or something. Doctors are supposed to be good catches, aren't they?"

She huffed. "I'm not playing catch! And that's all you're going to say? *Or something,*" she deadpanned his flat answer.

"That's all."

She hesitated for a moment. "Were you impaired?"

He frowned. "What?" Given everything, maybe he shouldn't have been shocked by the question, but he was.

And then, considering the concern in her amber-colored eyes, it was just impatience that rolled through him. "Hell. *No.*" He shook his head. "Believe me, honey. Until I became *impaired* by these damn injuries, I haven't even been tempted. Not once in a decade."

She studied him. "Actually, I believe you. Maybe it wasn't even an accident at all. Was he aiming for you?"

Mason let out a noisy breath. "You're not going to leave this alone, are you?"

"If you didn't want me to be curious, then you shouldn't have said anything about it at all when Dr. Flannery asked."

The fact that she was right didn't help him any.

He looked around the empty waiting room. "No. He

wasn't aiming for *me*. How long's this X-ray going to take, anyway?"

"As long as it takes," she returned smoothly. Then she made a face. "I don't know." She walked across the waiting area and disappeared through an open doorway, returning a few minutes later. "You'll be up next, after they finish with the patient already back there."

She sat on the edge of a molded plastic chair and plucked the clip out of her hair. She closed her eyes as the long blond strands tumbled around her shoulders and raked her fingers through them before twirling it back up into the fat clip. Then she opened her eyes again.

She looked tired.

"Would you still be sleeping if we weren't here?"

Her fine, level brows pulled together. "It doesn't matter."

It mattered to him. "You don't have to stay. I don't need a babysitter. Go track down Flannery. He'll probably ask you out on a date."

"Considering that you somehow put a crack in your cast, I'm not so sure you *don't* need a babysitter. But I wouldn't go back to sleep, even if I went home, so quit using that as an excuse to get rid of me and my curiosity. And if I wanted a date with Dr. Flannery, I'd get one. So drop it." She pushed to her feet. "I'll be back." She pointed at him. "Don't move."

"Funny girl."

She smiled faintly as she went through the doorway once more.

She was gone a little longer this time.

Long enough for a tired-looking woman to walk in carrying a brown-haired little girl with a heavily bandaged wrist. The woman gave Mason a wary look and took one of the chairs in the far corner of the room.

He'd had similar reactions from strangers before, just not when he was obviously laid up with injuries. He knew he looked like some version of scary hell, particularly as unshaven and unkempt as he was now.

He gave her a nod and a smile, but she didn't look comforted by it, and he stifled a sigh.

Mason wished Courtney would return. Playing verbal games with her was a helluva lot better than just sitting here inside the hospital. Scaring perfectly innocent people with the way he looked wasn't anything he particularly relished.

Fortunately, a girl in a white lab coat appeared and gestured to the woman. They disappeared through the same doorway Courtney had, and Mason waited alone a little longer until the waiting was wearing down his last nerve.

He shifted awkwardly in the chair and tried to ignore the itch on his calf beneath the cast by even more awkwardly trying to wheel the chair through the doorway after her. He'd made it far enough to get wedged between the protrusion of his leg and the angle of the chair, when Courtney reappeared.

She stopped at the sight of him and crossed her arms, tilting her head to one side. "Looks like you're almost stuck between a rock and a hard place."

It was truer than she knew.

Her eyes glinted when he said nothing. "Would you like some help?"

"Would you like to cut the sarcasm?"

"Maybe if you weren't so thickheaded and could possibly, just possibly, do what you are asked—"

"Told, you mean."

"—then I might be able to cut the sarcasm."

"Just move the damn chair, would you?"

She tsked and, reaching around him, pushed the chair back several inches until his cast was no longer jammed in the doorway.

Her head was inches from his. "I'm going to take you back there," she said softly and so sweetly that it made his teeth hurt. "But you're going to have to wait for Richie for about five minutes. He's still with someone else. Think you can be a good boy for that long?"

Maybe it was the ironic glint in her amber eyes.

Maybe it was the proximity of her head to his.

Maybe it was just for the hell of it.

He hooked his left hand around her neck and watched her pupils flare. "I'm no boy," he murmured. "And we both know I can be good."

Then he tugged her forward a few inches and caught her mouth with his.

Chapter Five

Before her common sense took over, Courtney felt herself sinking oh-so-dangerously into his kiss. Her heart bumped unevenly inside her chest, and her hands found his shoulders, her fingers pressing through his T-shirt to the warmth beneath.

"Ahem." The sound vaguely registered. And when it was repeated—who knew how many times—it finally penetrated.

She straightened like a shot.

Her gaze skittered over Mason's face and landed on Wyatt Mead's. The tall, lanky male nurse had a grin visible above his short goatee and a twinkle in his gray eyes.

Her lips tingled, but she stared down her coworker as she slipped behind Mason's chair and somehow managed to wrap her nerveless hands around the handles. "Is Richie ready?"

Wyatt looked even more amused. "Not as ready as you two, but yeah."

Courtney ignored the comment and pushed Mason into the first of the three imaging suites, where Richie was waiting near the X-ray table. Courtney positioned Mason's chair next to him and, when the technician took over arranging Mason's arm where he needed, avoided Mason's gaze as she practically fled from the room.

Wyatt was waiting in the corridor outside, his eyebrows raised. "Well, well, well," he teased. "The elusive and untouchable Ms. Clay does like a touch now and then."

"Shut up, Wyatt." She brushed past him, only to turn and give him a pointed glare, complete with pointed finger. "If this gets around, I'll know exactly who to blame."

"Who, me?" He pressed his hand against his chest and tried to look innocent. "All I was doing was coming back to let you know that Rodney will be here soon." He was the hospital's on-call orthopedic technician. Whether Mason's cast needed to be repaired or replaced, Rodney Stewart would be the one to do it.

"Thank you. But I mean it, Wyatt. Keep your mouth shut, or I'll make certain that you'll never get a date with an available girl in this town again." It wasn't that Wyatt wasn't a perfectly good-looking guy. But he was an R.N. and, sad to say, in Weaver, male nurses were still an oddity. Some of the locals were slow to get past it, which is why Courtney had set the guy up on more than one date with a few of her friends. He was shy until you got to know him, and the reports she'd gotten back were that he was fun and interesting, but so far the right match hadn't been made.

Which was sad, too, because Wyatt was one of those

rare breeds of men who *wanted* a commitment. He wanted a wife and kids and the whole shebang.

Now, he was just tsking at Courtney as if her threat was beneath her.

"I don't gossip," he said.

She snorted. "Everyone in this town gossips," she returned. Next to ranching, it seemed to be the preferred occupation. Even among her own family, the tendency thrived.

She had no desire for people to start wagging their tongues about her kissing anyone, and even less desire for word of that to reach her family. Considering her mother ran the hospital, it could reach *her* ears even quicker than most. "I'm just asking you—in this one instance—to forget what you saw."

"Get me a date with Dee Crowder."

Dee was an elementary school teacher who worked with Courtney's cousin Sarah Scalise. "Are you trying coercion?"

"Is it working?"

"Ask her out yourself, Wyatt. For heaven's sake, you see her every morning over at Ruby's when you're both stopping in for coffee before work."

"She's always flirting with people."

"She'd probably flirt with you, too, if you managed to give her a smile instead of just staring into your coffee and mumbling good morning." From inside the suite, she could hear Richie talking to Mason and knew that he'd be finished soon. "I'll put a bug in Dee's ear, okay? But—" she pointed her finger into Wyatt's face "—not unless you promise."

He smiled and crossed his fingers over his heart.

She exhaled noisily and rolled her eyes heavenward.

"You're a great guy, Wyatt. I wish you'd have a little more confidence in yourself. You're not shy with me."

"Yeah, but you make it easy." He gave her a wink and walked away.

"Seems to me you've got plenty of guys around here interested in you."

She turned and looked at Mason.

Richie was obviously done with him.

"Wyatt is not interested in me." She moved behind Mason to take control of his wheelchair and push him back to the emergency room.

"Every guy who isn't related to you is interested." His voice was dry.

She wasn't interested in "every" guy. Just one. And even if she hadn't already known it herself, he'd made it perfectly plain all those months ago that he wasn't interested in anything permanent.

Just remember what you're doing this for, she reminded herself.

She wasn't taking care of Mason out of any hope that something lasting would develop between them. She was taking care of him so that she'd have something lasting. Period.

A child.

"No comment?" Mason asked. "Because you know I'm right?"

Just to suit herself, she made a face at the back of his head. "No," she assured witheringly. "Because there's no point in responding to such ridiculousness."

"Courtney. I heard you were here this morning."

She nearly jumped out of her skin at her mother's voice and came to a stop with the chair, waiting for her lab-coated mother to reach them. "My patient had a little accident," Courtney greeted.

But her mom was already smiling with warmth into Mason's face as she took his good hand in both of hers. "Mr. Hyde," she greeted. The pale brown eyes that she'd passed on to Courtney were warm and sparkling. "It's been over a year since you've been to town. It's good to see you again. I'd ask how you're doing, but that seems a bit unnecessary under the circumstances."

Feeling strangely on edge, Courtney shifted. She'd almost forgotten that Mason had met her parents, too, when he'd been in Weaver. "Mason accidentally cracked his cast. We're here to get it fixed."

Her mother gave her a mild look. "It happens." She turned back to Mason. "If you're feeling up to it, you must come have dinner with us. I know Sawyer would enjoy seeing you again."

"My social calendar is pretty tight these days, but I'll do what I can."

Rebecca laughed, and her still-dark hair bounced around her shoulders. "You're frustrated with the in-activity." She patted his hand. "I have some experience with men like you." She glanced at Courtney. "Bring him by the house before you go on shift tonight. We'll have dinner, and we'll get him back to your place when he gets tired of us old fogies."

"Dr. Clay," Mason drawled, "if you're considered an old fogy, then getting older suddenly has a lot more appeal."

Rebecca laughed again, then shook her head when her name was paged. "Duty calls. See you both later." She hurried off in the direction she'd come from.

Courtney let out a careful breath. She wasn't nec-essarily surprised at her mother's hospitality toward Mason.

But she still felt a little awkward about it.

She'd never taken a former one-night stand home to have dinner with the folks.

"We going to just sit here in the corridor?" Mason finally asked. "Or do you want me to do this under my own steam?"

Flushing, she quickly pushed his chair the rest of the way to the emergency room. "I've seen the results of your steam," she reminded. "It ended up with you on the floor at my house and also wedged in a doorway. Your steam needs to chill for a while."

"Your father used to be the sheriff, didn't he?"

His conversational leap threw her.

But then, most everything about Mason threw her.

She turned into the emergency room. One of the curtained areas was now occupied. "He used to be. Now Max Scalise is. He's married to my cousin Sarah."

"Lot of family around here."

"Yup." She grinned. "I could give you a rundown on the family tree, but it would take the rest of the afternoon." She locked his wheels next to an empty exam table and, with a swift yank, pulled the long curtain around the area until they were fully enclosed. "Do you feel like stretching out, or do you want to stay seated?"

"Seated," he said immediately. "I've spent enough time flat on my ass."

"Since you were so mysteriously hit by an SUV," she concluded.

He shrugged.

Realizing she was staring a little too hard at the darkening beard on his face, she grabbed his chart and flipped it open. Then she opened one of the drawers in the stainless steel cabinet and pulled out a digital thermometer similar to the one she had at home, as well as a spare stethoscope.

"What are you doing?" He leaned his head back in avoidance when she fitted a clean sleeve on the thermometer and turned toward him.

"Making use of the time." Before he could make some sort of issue about it, she tucked the thermometer in his ear long enough to get a reading. Then she popped the sleeve in the trash, noted his temp—only a few degrees high and much better than it had been during the night—and set the thermometer back in the drawer before turning toward him with the stethoscope.

But Mason caught her wrist in his hand before she reached him. "Stop."

"I'm just—"

He gave her a hard look. "Courtney, if you put your hands on me again, I'm going to kiss you. Again. Are you ready for that?"

A nervous frisson chased down her spine and her fingers curled into her palm. For a moment long enough to shock her, she was tempted. Sorely tempted.

He was her *patient*.

She wasn't supposed to be more interested in tasting his seductive kiss than she was in maintaining some semblance of professionalism.

With a quick twist, she jerked her wrist free and caught his in hers instead. She had just enough time to enjoy the sight of *his* surprise before his hand was free from hers. "Where'd you learn how to do that?"

"My father was the sheriff," she reminded. She leaned closer and lowered her voice. "And I've been surrounded by people like *you* all of my life. They all made sure I know how to protect myself."

The slide of the curtain had her straightening with a jerk, just in time for Dr. Flannery to appear.

"Fortunately, the X-ray didn't show any fresh damage to the bones," he said without preamble.

"Good. The sooner I get out of here, the better."

"Can't say I blame you," Dr. Flannery told him, though his smile was aimed at Courtney. "Although I think the scenery here is better than it is in most places."

Mason caught Courtney's gaze before she could turn away. She wasn't sure if he looked amused or challenging. Maybe both.

"The crack in the cast is significant, though. Rather than chance its integrity, I'd like it replaced entirely. Once that's done, you are free to go," the doctor told Mason as he scribbled on the medical chart. When he was done, he left it sitting on the steel counter next to the sink. "Feel free to call if you have any questions or concerns. Courtney has my number."

As he watched the doctor walk away, Mason figured he'd chew off his own casts if he had to, before he'd call this guy about anything.

Courtney was crouched in front of the steel cabinet, fussing with something in the bottom of it. The back of her T-shirt rode up the small of her back a few inches, taunting him with the sight of her warm, creamy skin above the slight gape of her pants. His fingertips curled down against the vaguely rough texture of his fiberglass cast.

He knew her skin there was smooth. As smooth as his cast was not.

Dammit.

He'd been in Weaver for less than twenty-four hours and already the memories that he'd worked hard to lock away were back with a vengeance. Filling his head. Filling his gut.

He shoved his fingers through his hair, grimacing. He

hadn't had a decent shower since the accident, though the nurses at the hospital in Connecticut had given him sponge baths and washed his hair a few times.

What he wouldn't give for just five minutes under a steaming-hot spray of water.

His gaze drifted back to the enticing curve of Courtney's hips.

Five minutes under a freezing-cold spray of water would probably do him more good.

"What are you doing down there?"

She glanced at him over her shoulder. The action only succeeded in pulling that shirt a half an inch higher.

He felt sweat breaking out at the base of his spine.

"I'm checking the supplies for your cast. Making sure Rodney has everything he needs." She put her hands on her thighs and pushed to her feet. "The only kits I've got here are hot pink or light pink." She smiled a little wickedly. "Interested in either one?"

"I don't have anything against pink," he murmured. "You were wearing pink that night. Liked it real fine, then."

Her cheeks went rosy. Proof positive that she knew exactly what "that" night was. "I told you to forget about that."

"Pink scrubs." Knowing he was tormenting himself wasn't enough to stop him from needling her. "Pink bra. And matching pink panties with that thin, little ribbon stretching over your hips." He'd taken great pleasure in untying that particular ribbon. Taking his sweet time while she'd breathed his name and pleaded for him to go faster....

Her lips parted. "Mason." Her voice was low. Hoarse. "You're not making this any easier."

Like a switch being thrown, regret replaced desire.

He'd pushed at her because he was a slug. Because he knew he wanted her, still, and his ego didn't like feeling alone.

So now his ego was fed.

She wanted him, too.

It was plain on her face. In the drowsy, melting caramel of her eyes and the soft, parted pout of her full lips.

Which got them exactly where?

Nothing had changed since that Valentine's Day.

She was still who she was.

More importantly, he was still who he was.

A former drug addict with a face that scared most people and a career no woman should get remotely near.

He cleared his throat. "I don't care what color the cast is."

Something in her eyes flickered. She hesitated for a moment as if she wanted to say something. But then she nodded. "I know somewhere we have the same blue as what you've already got. I'll go find it." She stepped beyond the curtain enclosing the exam area.

From somewhere nearby, a baby started wailing.

Mason pinched his eyes closed. Just then, he figured things would've been better if he'd stayed at the hospital in Connecticut. Maybe he'd have been able to handle it. Maybe he wouldn't.

But at least there, he wouldn't have been continually confronted by the one woman even his good sense couldn't seem to resist.

It took another few hours, but finally—possessing a new cast that looked identical to the one that had been cut off—Axel dropped off Mason and Courtney again at her place.

It was nearly noon.

"I'll get you some lunch," she said once they were inside.

"You don't have to wait on me."

She raised her brows and gave him a look. "That's one of the things you're paying me for, remember?" She didn't wait for an answer but headed into the kitchen. A moment later, he heard the back door, and then Plato was trotting into the house, coming straight for him.

The dog sniffed at Mason's casts, then turned tail and trotted back into the kitchen to his mistress.

Factually, what Courtney had said about payment was accurate. Truthfully, however, it made him feel like some sort of weak weasel, even though he logically knew that in his present condition, he was more of a hindrance than any sort of help.

He was sitting on the couch, and his crutches, including the one he'd fallen over trying to reach, were still lying next to it. He grabbed them and, with steady determination, managed to get himself on his feet without crashing over again.

Her telephone was still sitting on the dining room table. Next to it were his pain pills.

He eyed them for a long moment. Then he snatched up the bottle and carried it down the hall and into the bathroom.

He managed to pry the lid off and poured the pills out into the palm of his right hand. The little round pills looked even whiter next to the dark blue of his cast.

He exhaled and let them fall into the toilet. Then he flushed and watched them swirl away for good.

Inside, he felt a little lighter.

Which left him with only one remaining dangerous temptation. One he could do nothing about.

Courtney.

The other temptation facing him was the shower, and he eyed the tub with admitted want. He shouldn't have Courtney, but he would have that. He couldn't get his cast wet, and getting in and out would be a challenge with one leg immobilized, but desperate times made for creativity. Sooner or later, he would have to figure it out, or he'd be enlisting Courtney to hose him off in the backyard like she was giving a bath to Plato.

Then he looked in the mirror. His reflection was enough to make him wince. And he was used to the sight.

He fumbled with his shaving kit, managing to get it unzipped. He was right-handed, so shaving with his left didn't come easy, but he did it anyway since he didn't want to chance getting the fresh cast wet. Last thing he needed was another half day spent whiling away the hours at the hospital—where every male above drinking age seemed to be infatuated with Courtney—because he'd done something else damaging to the cast.

Once his jaw was more or less shaved—save a few nicks—he tossed enough water over his head to shove his hair back and out of his face. Then he brushed his teeth and, feeling somewhat more human, hobbled back out to the living area.

He could hear her still moving around in the kitchen. He raised his voice. "Mind if I use your computer?"

"Help yourself."

Balancing on the crutch and his good leg, he hooked the desk chair and pulled it out enough to sit sideways. His leg cast bumped the desk, and a dull throb took up residence in his knee.

He ignored it and covered the computer mouse with his right hand. His arm was immobilized from his biceps to his wrist, but his fingers were free and working perfectly well. He clicked the button, and the swirling screen saver on her computer monitor disappeared.

The website she'd been looking at the night before came into view.

His lips tightened. With one click he could have closed the website. But he hesitated.

Hair color? Any.

Eye color? Any.

He frowned at the next search option. Blood type?

"Oh, wait." Courtney's rushed voice came from behind him. "I forgot something. Let me just—"

He glanced back at her. She was holding a butter knife in one hand and a piece of bread in the other. "*Specimen* type? What the hell kind of matchmaking site is this?"

Her lips pressed together for a moment. "It's not that kind of website," she finally said. Then she sighed noisily, her hands gesturing with the knife and slice of bread. "You can see for yourself what it is."

He looked back at the glowing computer screen. "Yeah. I can see." Some place called Big Sky Cryobank. "Question is, why are you looking at sperm donors?"

Despite the rise of color in her cheeks, her chin lifted slightly. "For heaven's sake, Mason. Why do you think?"

He didn't like the suspicion curling through him. It was the kind of suspicion that made a person feel nervous. Sick. "Someone wants a baby."

"Not someone. *Me.*" She moistened her lips. Her gaze was steady. Almost defiant. "*I* want to have a baby."

Confirmation didn't make his gut settle down any. *"Why?"*

She huffed. "Why not?"

His brain felt like it had been scrambled. "You're young! You've got plenty of time to find a husband." He had to force out the words now even though he'd spent the past year and a half reminding himself of that very fact. "And *then* have a family."

She started to fold her arms over her chest, then seemed to remember the bread and knife she was holding and stopped. "You're sounding very old-fashioned. I don't want a husband," she said distinctly. "I want a baby."

He hadn't thought he was particularly old-fashioned, but maybe he was when it came to some things.

Or some people.

"Borrow someone else's baby for an afternoon," he suggested rapidly. "God knows that family you're in seems to pop 'em out regularly."

She looked heavenward and shook her head. "I'm not going to debate this with you." She went back into the kitchen. "Do you want mustard on your ham sandwich?" she called out a moment later.

He didn't give a flip about mustard or the lack of it.

He looked back at the computer screen and scrolled up to the top of the webpage, then to the bottom.

Her criteria for the donor were broad.

She didn't seem to care about ethnic origins or ancestry or religious backgrounds. She didn't care about physical characteristics. The only thing she had selected was that the donor have *some* college.

Some.

Not even a degree.

The father could be any mug off the street who needed to make a few bucks by donating his genetic cocktail to a sperm bank.

He grimaced.

There was nothing about the situation that he liked. Nothing.

"What does your family think about all this?"

He heard the clink of a dish. Then she came into the living room and set a plate containing an enormous sandwich next to him on the desk. "They don't know yet. I'll get your antibiotics. You can take it after you eat that."

Impatience with his casts rolled through him when she turned and walked away and he wasn't able to stop her. "Why haven't you told them?"

She didn't answer until she returned with his antibiotics in one hand and a bottle of water in the other. "Because there was no reason to, yet. Do you need Tylenol?"

"What do you plan to do? Wait until they can see you're pregnant for themselves?"

"No," she said witheringly. "I saw no point in telling them until I had the means to even do it. I know my family. They know me. They'll be supportive, just like they always are. Not that this is any of your business, anyway." She set the pills and the water next to the plate and pulled the Tylenol bottle out of her pocket and tossed it on his lap. "Eat the sandwich and take the pills." She turned on her heel again, only to stop. She pointed at the table. "What'd you do with the pain pills that were sitting there?"

"Afraid I'm taking them?"

She gave him a steady look. "Are you?"

"I flushed them," he said flatly. "And no. I don't plan to get more."

She probably had no idea the way her eyes could soften.

But he did.

"Good for you." Then she blinked and was all back-to-business. "I still need a shower before I take you to visit my parents. If you want to change clothes before we go, let me know."

He exhaled, watching her walk away. Again.

Impatience rolled through him. Just because she clearly considered this baby business a closed subject didn't mean he did. When he heard the slam of her bedroom door, he turned back to the computer.

He didn't live under a rock.

He knew there were lots of reasons—some very good reasons—why individuals chose the services of a sperm donor.

But Courtney?

It just didn't go with his vision of her and the wholly perfect life she was supposed to have someday.

With someone else.

Someone deserving. Someone good enough for her.

He shoved half the sandwich in his mouth, even though it tasted like sawdust, and choked it down with water. He swallowed the pills.

He could hear the faint sound of water running.

He shook his head and grabbed the crutches. His back twanged warningly when he moved too fast, but he didn't slow.

He reached her bedroom and knocked. When she didn't answer, he pushed open the door.

Plato was lying on the floor next to her bed, and he lifted his head, giving Mason a steady glare.

Mason ignored him. The door to her en suite bathroom was ajar, steam rolling out near the floor, and he walked past the dog to it. "What do you mean, *means?*" he said loudly through the opening.

He heard her squeak of alarm, followed immediately by a low sound from the dog behind him. "Don't you dare come in here!"

He hadn't been planning on it, but Courtney's warning sure did make him want to. He pressed his forehead against the white-painted door frame and reminded himself that he wasn't a complete bastard. "What means?" he asked again.

The rush of water cut off. He heard the rattle of a shower curtain being drawn, and for half a second, his brain took a short circuit along the path of her nude, wet body.

Then the door was yanked open, and she stood there, covered from neck to red-painted toes in a thick pink robe. Her hair was a tangled mass streaming down her back. Her face was shiny clean, her amber eyes sparkling between water-spiked eyelashes. Heat streaked through him.

"Financial means," she said crisply. "Thanks to *you*, I can now afford to get pregnant. And sooner rather than later!"

Then she shut the door right in his face, the click of the door lock sounding loud and final.

Chapter Six

Courtney's Friday night shift, Mason learned later that day, ran from 7:00 p.m. to 7:00 a.m.

Practically the only words she'd exchanged with him, once she'd finally come out of her bedroom, were whether or not he wanted to get out of the invitation her mother had extended.

The fact that she'd obviously hoped he did want to get out of it was the only reason he'd said he didn't.

And they said that women were the contrary creatures.

Which was why he found himself awkwardly positioned in the backseat of her little car after enduring the humbling activity of having to enlist her aid just to put on a cut-up pair of jeans.

She hadn't seemed the least bit fazed by any of it. Thank God he'd been able to manage the shirt on his own.

"How soon?" he asked to the back of her head as she drove through town.

"Until we get to my parents' house? Not long."

"How soon until you plan to knock yourself up?"

"Lovely phrase," she said drily.

"Isn't it accurate?"

He saw her shoulders shrug. "I have to see an OB first. My sister-in-law, Mallory, is one, so I'll see if she's willing to sign off on my paperwork with the cryobank and perform the procedure. Hopefully, I'll be pregnant by the end of the year."

He could see the smile on her face through the rear-view mirror. "I can see the future now. Little Johnny or Mary comes to Mommy and asks where they come from. And she says…from a *procedure.*"

"I cannot believe you're so bothered by this."

"I'm not bothered," he denied. "Just…playing devil's advocate. You've figured out how to get pregnant without out a man around. But what about after that? Raising a child is an expensive proposition. It isn't just the cost of having a baby. Or in your case, buying some guy's—"

"I get it," she cut him off. "And I'm well aware of the cost. From conception to college." Her gaze met his in the rearview mirror. "Fortunately, this little gig with you while you recuperate is going to get me at least through the conception part. It's not exactly covered by my health insurance."

He grimaced. Her words didn't sit well. Not when every cell he possessed—even the ones still broken and bruised—tripped over themselves wanting to do a little baby-making the old-fashioned way. With no baby as the end result, of course.

He nearly got a rash just thinking about it.

"Okay. So forget the cost. Bringing up a baby on your own isn't going to be an easy task."

"I have a very involved, very loving family," she returned, her voice beyond patient. "I'm never alone."

"You know what I mean. Statistics show that two parents are better than one."

"I'm not interested in your statistics, Mason." Her voice turned cool. "Please drop it. And please keep your thoughts to yourself about this when we get to my parents'. I hardly want to break the news to them while you're there, glowering."

"Thought you said they would jump for joy at the news. And I'm not glowering."

She snorted. "What I said was that they'd be supportive when the time comes. And you most certainly *have* been glowering. Ever since you saw the website on my computer. I get it, all right? You don't approve."

"I think there are better ways."

She pulled up to a stoplight, one of the few that the small town possessed.

She looked over her seat at him. "Like what? Getting pregnant by a man I have no intention of becoming involved with?"

"Isn't that what you're planning to do with one of those spermsicles?"

She rolled her eyes and turned back to the road in front of her. "That's a horrible term."

"Stuff comes frozen, doesn't it?"

The light turned green, and she started through the intersection with a jerk. "What did you do? Read the frequently asked questions section on the website? Or do you just happen to have a lot of knowledge about the subject?"

He had read the FAQ section…mostly with a fair amount of morbid interest.

"You're young and beautiful. You should have the

world by the tail. Why the hell do you want to order this stuff off the internet?"

She turned off the main road onto a narrower, curving one. "Because it's convenient." Her voice was crisp. "There doesn't happen to be a sperm bank in Weaver, in case you hadn't noticed, and I can't exactly be running off to Montana every week to browse through their catalog until I decide who I want to father my baby!" Her voice had risen.

"How do you know it's even legit?"

She made a groaning sound and pulled up in front of a sprawling house surrounded by enough pine trees to populate a Christmas tree lot. "Grant me some credit, would you please? I'm not a fool. I've done my homework. The cryobank I've chosen is very well regarded. It's not like they allow people to put orders in like you would for a book! You have to be under a doctor's care, remember?" She shoved the car into Park so abruptly that he rocked against the seat in front of him. She looked back at him. "Sorry. Now, can we drop the subject before we go inside?"

She didn't wait for an answer but pushed open her car door and got out. Then she opened the passenger door, pulled out his crutches, which were lying across the floor, and gestured. "Come on. Give me your hand."

He looked across at her. "When're you going to order up your frozen future?"

Her lips pressed together, but then she shook her head and let out a laugh. "Oh, my God. Would you please *stop?*"

He realized he had a faint smile on his face, too. Dammit.

He stretched his good arm toward her, and her palm slid against his until her long fingers wrapped securely around his forearm. Her other hand went beneath his leg cast to help guide it. Using his good leg for leverage, they managed to slide him far enough along the seat so that he could plant his shoe on the ground and finish extricating himself from the car.

She handed him the crutches and then helped him stand.

Whether he liked it or not, she was good at what she did. She gave as much assistance as he needed, until he could power himself under his own steam, and managed not to hover.

Too bad every time she touched him, his nerves danced a damn annoying jig.

"We'll head around to the side door." She gestured toward the house, which was fronted by a walkway formed of several sets of shallow brick steps. "No stairs." She didn't ask him if he needed help, which he appreciated, as she began walking off toward one side of the house.

He planted the crutches and slowly followed. Knowing that he was watching her hind view didn't get him to stop, even when the bottom of his cast caught on an uneven piece of brick.

He'd already landed on his face because of his clumsiness. At least if he landed on his face this time, it'd be because he was admiring a human work of art.

She reached the side door and turned to wait. "Sure can tell it's going to be October in a few days," she said conversationally. "It's getting downright chilly."

He schooled his gaze on her face.

She raised an eyebrow as if she knew perfectly well where his thoughts were.

She probably did. Women who looked like her grew up with men's stares. In that regard, he was no better than anyone else. Maybe he was worse, because he knew exactly what he was doing.

"I suppose I should warn you," she said, "that it's not just going to be my folks here." She jerked her chin. "That's my grandfather's truck parked back there. And if I'm not mistaken, those are a few of my uncles driving up right now, too."

He followed her gaze. A big black pickup was turning toward the house. Almost on its heels was a low-slung sports car.

When he looked back at Courtney, she gave him an almost pitying smile. "Don't worry. They're all harmless. Mostly."

In the course of his work with Coleman Black, Mason had had plenty of opportunity to become acquainted with several members of Courtney's extended family. Some of them had their own history with Cole. Some didn't.

Harmless wasn't one of the words he would have used for any of them.

He exhaled and crutched the rest of the way. "Let's get on with it, then."

She pulled open the wooden screen door and stepped out of his way. The second he went inside the house, they seemed surrounded by people.

Not just Courtney's parents, Sawyer and Rebecca. And her grandparents, Squire and Gloria, and her aunts and uncles. But also cousins. And cousins' spouses.

And children.

He'd seen the Clay family en masse before, so it wasn't seeing them now that seemed a particular shock. But that first time—save the notable night he'd spent in Courtney's bed—he'd been in Weaver on an assignment to help protect Axel's now wife. He'd seen the family through the eyes of a Hollins-Winword agent. He didn't have that particular benefit this time around.

He wasn't sure why it made a difference, but it did.

Now, being around all of these people—these *family* members—made him itchy. On edge.

As if they were all looking at him, wondering what the hell kind of business he had staying under their precious Courtney's roof.

"Here." The woman in question appeared next to where he was sitting—feeling like the elephant in the room—in the center of an oversized leather couch, with his cast propped on an ottoman. She was holding a plate loaded with an immense helping of steaming lasagna and crispy garlic bread. She also was holding a plate with salad on it. "Mom doesn't believe in small helpings, so I hope you're hungry. Which one do you want to start off with?"

"I'm not exactly working off a lot of food these days," he said wryly, as he took the lasagna.

There were so many people there that nobody attempted to crowd around the long table in the window-lined dining room, but instead used every other available seat, including the floor.

"It's no fun being laid up." A petite, slender blonde sank gracefully to the floor next to the couch, her legs folded beneath her. "Even less fun feeling like you've lost your independence as a result. I'm Lucy Buchanan. Courtney's coz." She smiled at him, her aquamarine eyes twinkling. "I'd shake your hand, but mine are presently full of food."

It was an excuse, he knew, because his was stuck in a cast, making a handshake awkward. "You're new," he told her. He was good with people's faces and their names. She hadn't been in Weaver when he'd been there before.

Courtney laughed. She'd kicked off her rubbery clogs that she wore at the hospital, and sat cross-legged on the couch beside him. Her shoulder brushed against his, but she didn't seem to notice as she tucked her fork into the salad. "Luce just moved back home from New York," she told him. "She got engaged a few weeks ago. Speaking of…where are Beck and Shelby?"

"I'm here." A lanky man about Mason's age, bearing a plate as loaded as Mason's, sauntered into the room. "Shelby's spending the night at her friend's." He didn't have the quick tact of his fiancée and stuck out his hand to Mason. He made a wry face when Mason lifted his hand, cast and all. "Ah. Casts suck." Instead of shaking what was visible of his fingers, Beck bumped his knuckles against Mason's. "Beck Ventura."

"Mason Hyde. And yeah. They do," he agreed. "Who's Shelby?"

"Beck's daughter," Courtney said. "She's six."

Mason could practically see the gleam in Courtney's eyes. He figured she was imagining her own future six-year-old daughter.

Rebecca walked into the room. "As you can see, Mr. Hyde, our get-together got a little out of hand." She was wearing jeans and a sweatshirt and was holding a baby on her hip, looking as different as she could get from the white-coated doctor he'd met earlier that day. "That tends to happen around the Clays." She tucked her dark hair behind her ear and grinned.

Courtney had her eyes, he realized. And her grin. "Make it Mason, please."

At the sight of her mother and the baby, Courtney

promptly set aside her partially eaten salad and held out her hands. "Gimme."

Rebecca surrendered the tot, who was wearing a green-footed thing, giving Mason no clue whether it was a boy or a girl. Courtney snuggled the baby close, kissing the child's round little cheek.

"This," she told him, after she came up for air, "is Aidan."

Mason gave the baby a closer look. "Axel's kid?"

"Mmm-hmm." She looked up at her mother. "How'd you get drawn for babysitting duty?"

"She didn't." Another woman wandered into the room. She, too, had long brown hair and was holding a plate of food. Mason recognized her as Axel's mother, Emily. "Aidan's spending the night with Jefferson and me."

She turned her pansy-brown gaze on Mason and smiled. "But we heard *you* were coming for dinner and crashed." She leaned over and brushed her cheek against Mason's. "So good to see you again. I wish it were under better circumstances for you." As if they were old friends, instead of bare acquaintances through his association with her son, she sat next to him on the arm of the couch. "You're letting that lasagna get cold, darling, and you can't heal if you don't eat. Eat."

"Just easier to listen to her," a tall man drawled in a quiet voice as he pulled a chair from the dining room table closer. "That's what I've learned after all these years."

"Jefferson," Mason greeted. The older man was a legend in the murky world of Hollins-Winword, even though he'd gotten out of the business decades earlier. "How's the horse-breeding business?"

"Not as interesting as the cow business," answered a

steel-haired man as he stomped into the room with his cane. "Try telling my son that, though." He gave Jefferson an annoyed look even as he grabbed a chair and planted himself next to him.

Well aware that her grandfather's ornery tones hid a heart as wide as Wyoming, Courtney grinned. "My grandfather," she told Mason. "Squire Clay, this is Mason Hyde. He's the patient renting my spare bedroom."

Squire lifted a hand. "I remember, missy. Not senile yet. We met when Axel was chasing after Tara…and thinking we didn't know what was up." He fixed his sharp, blue gaze on Mason. "He was staying under her roof and getting up to mischief. You gonna do that with my granddaughter?"

"Squire!" Courtney nearly choked.

"Stay out of this, girl." Her grandfather didn't even spare her a look.

"Sir, if you'll pardon my saying so, I'm lucky if I can get up to take a leak," Mason drawled. "Mischief's pretty much out of my immediate future."

Squire let out a bark of laughter and tapped the end of his cane on the floor. "Always like a man who speaks the truth. So. Hear you managed to save that little girl in the process of getting all broke up."

Courtney jerked. She looked at Mason. The vaguely good-natured smile on his face had disappeared. "Little girl? What little girl?"

"McDonohue. McDouglas." Emily shook her head. "Name's something like that, anyway. I saw an article on the internet about it a few days ago."

"Pushed the little filly right out of the way of a truck," Squire interjected. "Saved her life, so they say. Seems to me, it's a wonder you didn't end up getting killed."

Absently jiggling Aidan on her lap, Courtney watched Mason. He was jabbing at his lasagna and clearly didn't want to pursue the subject. "Who was she? Did you know her?"

"Just a kid who didn't have the sense not to walk in the street." He shoved the last bite of lasagna in his mouth and pushed the plate at her. "Mind if I have more?"

Perfectly aware that he'd pretty much dodged her question, she took the plate and rose, taking the baby—who'd tightly twined his little fists in her loose hair—with her. Mason could be as closemouthed as he wanted. She would just hunt around on the internet and find the article her aunt had referred to, and she would know the story, soon enough.

Even if a part of her did wish that he'd tell her himself.

In the kitchen, she handed Aidan off to her mother, who was talking with a few more of Courtney's aunts, worked her hair free and added another helping from one of the multiple pans on the counter.

"So." Her aunt Jaimie tilted her auburn head and stepped right in Courtney's way before she could go back to the living room. "What's this I hear about you kissing your patient at the hospital today?"

Courtney's jaw loosened. "What?" She shot her mother a look. Rebecca just seemed amused as Aidan batted his palms against her hand. "I don't know what you're talking about," she lied.

The first chance she got, she was going to skin Wyatt Mead.

"Lip-locking," Jaimie enunciated, laughter crinkling the skin around her vivid green eyes. "With Mr. Hyde.

And I'm pretty sure that's a term that translates even to you young people."

"I can't imagine where you get your information," Courtney insisted. "You know what gossip is like in this town."

Maggie, yet another one of Courtney's aunts, laughed outright. "Sadly, that gossip is almost always founded on some kernel of truth."

"Where there's smoke, and all that," Jaimie agreed.

Courtney's cheeks felt like they were on fire, and there was no chance whatsoever that the women surrounding her couldn't see the flush. Or correctly interpret its cause. "I'm going to kill Wyatt," she muttered through her teeth.

Rebecca smiled faintly. "Fortunately, you weren't on duty, so it's not as if you were breaking any sort of hospital rule that I'd have to write up."

"Of course, if your grandfather hears about it," Courtney's grandmother, Gloria, warned humorously, "who knows what will happen. You know how protective he is of all his girls."

Emily had wandered into the crowded kitchen, and she rolled her eyes. "Fortunately, Squire has mellowed a little over the years since he kicked Jefferson out of his own home for having his eye on me when *I* was young." Perfectly at home in her sister-in-law's house, she found a mug and poured coffee into it.

"Grandchildren and great-grandchildren—" Jaimie tickled Aidan under the chin "—have mellowed Squire." She wryly corrected Emily. "The years that have passed have been purely incidental."

Whether Squire had mellowed any or not was moot as far as Courtney was concerned. She didn't want people gossiping about her. Not even her own family, whether it was good-natured or not. "I'm taking this plate back in to Mason and I don't want to hear another word about—" she waved her hand at the older women "—any of that." As she left the kitchen, she caught the surprised looks on their faces in the half breath before they all broke into laughter.

Her molars ground together. Wyatt was dead meat.

She hurried over to Mason and handed him his plate, even as she nudged her feet into her shoes. "I need to get to the hospital." She looked around the room, her gaze finally landing on her father. He was standing near the windows that overlooked the rear of their property, talking to Daniel and Matthew, who were married to Maggie and Jaimie. "You'll get Mason—" she barely prevented herself from saying *home* "—back to my place later?"

Her dad nodded.

She hadn't really doubted that he'd agree, but she was more than a little nervous about what kind of conversations might ensue in her absence.

Fortunately, Mason was looking as if he weren't in the mood to talk, and she was hoping that meant he wouldn't decide to take the initiative and start talking *spermsicles* with her family.

She stopped next to him, pulled his bottle of antibiotics out of her pocket and handed them to him. "Don't forget."

"Yes, ma'am." His voice was arid.

"I'll see you in the morning, then. Try not to break anything else before then."

His lips twisted in a sort of smile. His scar was standing out more than usual, and she suspected he was wishing that he was anywhere else other than here.

Refusing to feel sorry for him, since she'd done her best to talk him out of going to her folks' in the first place, she went over to her grandfather and kissed his cheek. "Behave," she whispered in his ear.

He grunted. "Where's the fun in that?"

She gave him a pointed look. "That's what I'm afraid of."

Then, because she really did need to leave or chance being late for her shift, she quickly gave a general good-bye and hurried out to her car.

Her mother was leaning against the hood.

Courtney swallowed a jolt of nervousness and picked up her pace again until she reached the car. "Did I forget something?"

"How well do you know Mason?"

Courtney hesitated. She wasn't sure what she'd expected, but it wasn't that. "Not well. We met, you know, in passing. When he was here a few years ago working with Axel to protect Tara. Well, it wasn't quite that long ago, but—"

"You're rambling, honey."

Courtney's lips slammed shut. She swallowed again. "I know Axel trusts him, or he wouldn't have suggested any of this," she finally said. "He's a job. Mason doesn't want to be dependent on me for any longer than necessary. His arm should be out of the cast in a month or so. And hopefully, his leg not too long after that. He'll be gone the second he can go."

"Mmm." Her mother pushed away from the car. "Just…be careful, all right?"

That was easy. "I'm always careful," Courtney reminded. "Remember?"

"I do." Her mom followed her around to the driver's side and held the door while Courtney climbed behind the wheel. "I was careful, too, when I first met your father."

Courtney raised her eyebrows. "Not exactly a cautionary comment, Mom. You and Dad have been married for a long time now." Close to thirty years, in fact.

"But it took us a long time to get to that point," she reminded gently. "Your dad and I did a lot of things wrong—spent a lot of years on it, in fact—before we managed to get it right. I'm just saying…be careful."

"I know exactly what I want out of life," Courtney assured her with more blitheness than she felt. "Mason is not going to get in the way of my plans."

Unfortunately, as her mother shut the door and moved back from the car, she didn't look quite convinced. "Drive carefully," was all she said.

Courtney couldn't help but grin at that, considering the hospital was less than five miles away. "Thanks for entertaining him," she said, before she drove off.

The first thing she did when she got to the hospital was corner Wyatt, who was just getting off his shift. "Guess you don't want that date with Dee Crowder that badly," she told him.

He gave her a surprised look. "What are you talking about?"

"About *you* talking!"

"I didn't." He defended himself. "I didn't say a word to anyone!"

"Not *any*one?"

"Well, Greer. But she wouldn't say anything."

Courtney groaned. "That's exactly how things get out. We trust someone not to say anything to anyone, and then they do, and they trust that person not to say anything, and then *they* do." She threw up her hands and walked to the nurse's lounge to store her purse in her locker. "I'll be lucky if this town doesn't have us married and pregnant by morning," she muttered.

"Who's pregnant?" Carrying an enormous cup of coffee, Lisa Pope walked into the lounge.

"Nobody."

Her coworker's gaze turned crafty. "Any practicing to *get* that way going on?"

Courtney groaned and walked out of the lounge.

It was going to be a long shift.

Chapter Seven

She was over an hour late getting off shift the next morning, but when she quietly let herself into her house, Courtney was still surprised to see Mason up.

He was sitting at her computer desk, and at first she feared he was poking around on the cryobank site again. He wouldn't find it difficult to locate since she had all of her favorite sites clearly saved.

"You're up early," she greeted as she walked across the living room, kicking off her shoes as she went. When she was closer, her nerves relaxed a little.

He was on some network news site.

"And you're off work late," he returned. He gave her a narrow-eyed look. "You look like hell."

"Well—" she smiled tiredly "—don't feel like you need to sugarcoat it or anything."

He swiveled—more or less, considering his cumbersome casts—to face her. "What happened?"

She shook her head as she walked past him into the kitchen. "Just a long night. What's your stand on eggs and toast?" She glanced outside the back door and saw Plato sleeping contentedly in a sunbeam. "You let the dog out. Thanks."

"No prob. And you don't have to cook for me."

"Part of the deal," she reminded. Her eyes felt glazed as she turned her attention to the maple cupboards in front of her. "But it's Saturday morning. How about pancakes?"

She heard the scrape-thump of his crutches and cast and knew he was coming into the kitchen. She realized she was just standing there, staring at nothing, and quickly opened the cupboard door to pull out a loaf of bread. "Or maybe French toast."

His hand closed over her shoulder, and she jumped an inch. He tugged the bread out of her lax fingers and set it on the counter. "Maybe some sleep."

"I told you, I need to decompress a little after a shift." She picked up the bread again. "And you need to eat."

"I already did." He took the bread and reached past her head to slide it on top of the refrigerator. "I had leftover lasagna that your mother sent back with me last night."

Courtney looked around the kitchen. There wasn't a sign that he'd been in here at all.

"What'd you do? Eat it cold?" She grabbed his day-old cast and ran her fingers along the bottom edge. It was dry. If he'd washed the dishes he'd used, he hadn't gotten the cast wet.

He deliberately moved his arm away. "Yes. And off the paper plate that it was sitting on. And before you ask, I took the damn antibiotics. *Go* get some sleep before you fall over."

Somehow, she found herself being turned out of the kitchen, which was a trick since she was much more agile than he was in his present condition. "I looked you up on the internet," she said, thinking that would stop him.

It didn't. "Figured you would."

"Why? Because you think I'm nosy?" Better that he think that than believe she was insatiably curious where he was concerned.

"I'd go for…inquisitive."

"That's another word for nosy." They passed the dining room table and the computer. The screen was a swirling dervish of colors now. "You didn't say that the girl you saved was Donovan McDougal's daughter. He's famous, for heaven's sake." The European businessman who seemed to dabble in everything from real estate to entertainment was often in the news.

"He's also got a big mouth." Mason's voice was low behind her. Intimate.

Despite herself, her footsteps hesitated. She had to physically draw a breath and ride herd on her imagination.

Intimate?

Hardly. The guy was practically frog-marching her down the hallway.

Mason's chest was a warm wall behind her. His crutches were on either side of her, and the cast on his leg was nudging against her backside. He was wearing the same jeans he'd been wearing the night before. She wondered if he'd slept in them, because she seriously doubted that he'd have been able to pull them back on, even though he could get them off.

She planted her bare feet as much as they could be planted on the wood floor. "Well, according to what the big mouth said, that accident was not an accident at all. You were in Barcelona protecting him because someone was threatening his life. But instead, the person went after his daughter. You were the only one who realized what was happening before it was too late." According to the reports she'd read, Mason had knowingly risked his life for the little girl, tossing her to safety before the vehicle had struck him and plowed uncontrollably into a ravine. Mason had survived with a host of injuries. The deadly driver had not.

"Since you seem to have all the details now, there's nothing else to be inquisitive about. So it's my turn. How do you plan to take care of a baby when you work a night shift like this? Or are you going to be one of those parents who stick their kid in day care all day?"

"There's nothing wrong with proper day care," she said irritably. "And I'll switch to a day shift when the time comes."

"You can just decide to do that? Doesn't a shift have to be available first, or do you figure that you can have your mom arrange things to suit you?"

She slapped her hands out, catching the door frame of her bedroom to halt their momentum, then spun around to look at him.

Her nose was practically buried in the T-shirt covering his chest. The shirt that yesterday he'd insisted he could put on with no assistance.

She carefully stepped back a few inches, pulling her eyes away from the dark swirl of chest hair that was visible in the stretched out V-neck. Her fingertips were suddenly tingling as if they remembered the soft-crisp feel of it, and she pressed them together. "First of all, my mom would never play favorites like that. And you obviously don't know me at all if you think I would even ask! Fortunately for me, there are plenty of nursing jobs in the area. If I can't find a schedule that is more suitable at the hospital, then I'll find one somewhere else." Her spurt of energy dissipated, and she turned away from him again. "Maybe I'll become a school nurse, where the biggest emergencies I'll have to deal with are bloody noses and the occasional case of head lice." At least it wouldn't be likely that she'd have the kind of case they'd had at the hospital that morning.

She pulled off the top of her scrubs, leaving behind the long-sleeved T-shirt she wore underneath.

Somehow, the giant on crutches managed to beat her to the bed. He pulled back her quilt with one tug.

"You're not supposed to do that," she grumbled.

He silently raised an eyebrow.

"Move faster than me."

The corner of his lips curved. "Honey, you're not moving real fast," he pointed out. "Did you become a nurse so you could deal with bloody noses and the occasional bug?"

Now that she was within a foot of her bed, she felt a little like a horse that scented its barn, and she aimed straight for it. "Of course not." Her knee hit the mattress and she went facedown, tugging her pillow against her cheek. "I wanted to help people," she murmured. "My grandmother—Gloria. She was a nurse."

"Yeah. Last night, I heard all about how she and Squire met when she was taking care of him after he had a heart attack."

"Sort of like us." The words drizzled out of her lips without thinking, and as soon as she heard what she'd said, her eyes flew open. "I didn't mean... I was just saying that she was—"

"I know what you were saying." He reached down

and nudged her head onto the pillow. "Close your eyes, Courtney. You're making *me* feel exhausted."

The pillow did feel wonderful. But no less wonderful, she figured, than the sound of her name on his lips.

She closed her eyes, reminding herself that she'd been running on only a few hours of sleep for two days. If she was at the top of her form, she wouldn't be thinking such silly things. "*You're* not supposed to be taking care of *me*," she returned.

"I won't tell anyone."

She felt his hand plucking at the back of her head, and then her ponytail slid free. His fingertips rubbed against her scalp and she couldn't help but sigh. "Mason?"

His rubbing stopped.

She peeled open her heavy lids and looked up at him through her eyelashes. "Do you see a lot of violence working for Hollins-Winword?"

He watched her, unblinking, for a long moment. "Yes."

Her chest went tight. Maybe because he'd given her a straight-out answer. Maybe because she was feeling wrung out from her shift. Maybe because just then, there wasn't a cell in her body that didn't want her to ask him to lie down, casts and all, right beside her. "How do you sleep at night?"

His fingers threaded through her hair once more. "Sometimes I don't."

Now, her throat ached, too. "We had a woman brought in around two this morning. Her husband had been beating her. She had a toddler with her." She felt his sudden stillness.

"What happened?"

"She had massive internal injuries. The husband followed her, evidently intent on finishing the job. It took two deputy sheriffs to contain him."

"Do you know them?"

"No." She rolled onto her back, and his hand fell away from her hair, returning to the grip of his crutch tucked under his arm. "They lived on the other side of Braden. She was trying to get away with the child, but she ran off the road, and the officer on the scene had her brought in. We'd barely gotten her into surgery, when the husband got there."

"And?"

"She didn't survive." She blew out a long breath. "The husband's been charged, and the baby got carted away by social services."

"No other family to take the kid?"

"No. How old were you when you lost your parents?"

"Four."

Her heart ached a little more. "What happened?"

"At the time, the story was a car accident."

"Excuse me?"

"He caught her cheating on him and shot her." His voice was matter-of-fact. "I looked into their deaths when I was an adult."

"Good Lord, Mason." Appalled, she sat up, curling her feet underneath her. "I'm so sorry."

He lifted a shoulder. "I don't remember them."

"You still haven't said who took care of you."

"There's nothing to say. I was in foster care. Too many homes to even remember. Some good. Some not so good. By the time I was fifteen, I was living on my own."

She frowned. "How does a fifteen-year-old boy support himself?"

His lips twisted. "Not very well. But I was a big kid

and I lied well. People believed that I was older. I worked odd jobs when I could."

"And school?"

"That didn't put bread in my mouth. Why are we talking about this? It's old news." He jerked his chin toward the pillows and swung his crutches away from the bedside. "Lie down again. Go to sleep."

"It's not old news to me," she said quietly. "And I'm interested, okay? Maybe I want to know that the little toddler from this morning—who has essentially lost both of his parents—has a chance in life that's better than the doom and gloom of the statistics. You're an honest-to-goodness hero, Mason. You grew up with no parents of your own to become a man who goes out and saves other people's lives. You've battled an addiction and won."

He grimaced. "I'm no hero."

She unwound her legs and climbed off the bed. "Donovan McDougal and his family wouldn't agree. And neither would I."

"You don't know anything about me."

"I know Axel trusts you, or you wouldn't be staying under my roof."

"We've worked together."

"I know you put your life in danger to save someone's child." She gestured at him. "And I'll say it again—or you wouldn't be staying under my roof." Before he could counter with another denial, she stepped closer. "I know you've overcome a lot, not just from your childhood, but as an adult." She touched the scar running down his face. "And I know that, even though you try to hide it, you have a great gentleness in you."

He grabbed her hand and pulled it away from his face. But he didn't let go. "I finished school from jail."

His voice was hard. "After being picked up for breaking and entering. Not so heroic."

He had a firm grip on her hand, but far from punishing.

"Breaking and entering what?"

His brows pulled together. "What the hell difference does it make?"

"I'm just…inquisitive."

"I'm beginning to feel like I'm in the inquisition." He set her hand away from him. "There's nothing admirable about my life. All I've done is survive. I broke into the store one of my former foster parents owned so I could steal the till before it was deposited in the bank. Obviously, I wasn't a very good thief, because I spent a few years behind bars, as a result. I ended up working for Cole soon after, because he's always hunting the dregs of society for…creative souls. I was good at reading people. Good at manipulating situations to my advantage. But not good enough, because the people I was supposed to be protecting nearly ended up dead, and I ended up with this." He waved at his scarred face. "After that, I let myself get hooked on painkillers for too damn long. I lost my wife and I nearly lost my job."

He'd been married? She didn't know why that stunned her, but it did. "What, uh, what did you need the money for?"

"God in heaven, woman! Aren't you listening to anything I'm saying?"

"I'm listening," she returned tartly. "But what I'm trying to do is *understand.*"

"I wanted to buy a bus ticket for the foster kid living with that old family of mine so he could get the hell away from them. God knows nobody in charge of the system believed that the churchgoing souls were abusive freaks."

"Oh, Mason."

"Don't get sympathetic. I was a thief. A bad one."

"What happened to the other foster child?"

"How the hell should I know? I was in jail."

"You never tried to find out?"

His lips thinned. "He aged out," he finally said. "Graduated high school and disappeared." He gave her a narrow-eyed stare. "Don't try to understand me anymore. There's no point. Where you're concerned, the only reason I'm here is so you can afford your baby plans. Where I'm concerned, the only reason I'm here is so that Cole doesn't fire my ass."

Her head snapped back. She blinked, almost swaying from the sting. "I, um…right. You're right. This is just a simple business deal." Why couldn't she remember that? She cleared her throat and forced a wry smile that she didn't feel at all. "Blame it on lack of sleep." She snatched up the band that he'd pulled off her ponytail and yanked her hair back once more.

She would *not* think about the feel of his fingers moving through her hair. She would *not* think about a fifteen-year-old boy who'd been desperate enough to break and enter in order to try to help someone else.

She waved her hand toward the door. "Don't close the door all the way. I want to be able to hear if you need something."

He looked at her as if she'd grown a second head. "You're serious."

She was exhausted. She was still saddened about the events at the hospital. And logical or not, she was stinging from his unsubtle reminder that her only purpose for him was born of necessity. Not choice. "Yes." Her voice was flat, and she turned back toward her bed. "That's my job."

Mason bit back an oath. In her place, he'd be telling himself to go to hell. That's what he deserved.

Feeling like the proverbial bull in a china shop, he managed to work his way out of her pretty, unabashedly feminine bedroom without doing any physical damage to her things.

The only damage he'd caused had been emotional.

He turned to look back at her when he reached the doorway.

She was lying on her side, facing away from him. She'd ruthlessly pulled her shining hair into another ponytail, and she'd hooked her arm around a pillow.

"I told you that I'm no hero," he said.

"I believe I was listening when you said it." Her voice was muffled but clear.

He'd wanted to put some distance back between them. Well. He'd succeeded.

He exhaled and pulled the door all the way closed. He'd already been the cause of one day with hardly any sleep for her. He wasn't going to add to it, even if he had to sit on his thumbs for the next eight hours to make sure she had some peace and quiet.

He crutched back to his bedroom. But the books there held no interest for him. As stealthily as he could, he went out to the living area.

He sat at the computer for a while, feeling only a little guilty for browsing all of the sites she'd left open on her screen.

Every single one of them was baby related.

The cryobank site, of course.

But then there was the all-about-baby site that seemed

to have information on everything from the moment after birth to preparing your kid for kindergarten.

And then the home-and-garden site with every decorating and safety tip known to man for making your house baby ready.

She'd even looked at a baby boutique site and added an expensive, engravable silver rattle to something called her "wish list."

He scrubbed his hand down his face and turned off the computer screen.

"Remember what you're doing here, Hyde," he muttered to himself. It wasn't supposed to have anything to do with getting involved in Courtney Clay's life, and it would be better for both of them if he could manage to remember that fact.

He laboriously managed to get onto his feet again and limped his way back to his bedroom.

Before he turned into the room, though, he noticed that Courtney's bedroom door—which he had quietly shut—was ajar.

So she could hear him if he needed her.

He eyed that wedge of open space for a long while.

Then he went into his bedroom and closed the door.

It was the smart thing to do. He knew it.

He still felt like hell.

It was the sound of running water that woke her.

Courtney rolled onto her back and rubbed her eyes. The clock on her nightstand told her she'd slept a solid eight hours, and the late-afternoon sun streaming across her bed confirmed it.

She might have slept, but she didn't feel particularly rested. Not considering the way things had ended with Mason.

Water was still running.

Frowning, she sat up and listened harder.

And then she realized *what* she was hearing, and she bounded off the bed and out into the hallway. The door to Mason's bathroom was shut, but a very fine wisp of steam was coming out from beneath it.

She knocked on the door. "Mason? What are you doing?"

He didn't answer.

She knew he was chomping at the bit for a shower. But surely he wouldn't have attempted such a thing with his casts. Would he?

It was much too easy to believe that he would.

She knocked on the door again. Harder this time. "Mason!"

Still no answer.

Visions of him knocking himself out on the cast-iron tub quickly filled her mind, and she turned the knob. The door swung open, and a thick waft of steam rolled out.

It also rolled above and around the edges of the shower curtain that was pulled around the deep, old-fashioned tub that she'd bought at an auction and had refinished at a restoration place in Cheyenne.

She grabbed the edge of the curtain, her worry far exceeding her discretion, and she pulled it back.

She got a glimpse of tight, male backside, a scarred back and slick water-darkened hair as the man—half covered in plastic bags, she realized—jerked around to face her, swearing vividly. "Dammit, Court!" He grabbed the shower curtain with almost amusing modesty and pulled it against him. "What the hell?"

She was a nurse, for pity's sake. She was not going

to blush over the sight of a plastic-wrapped, casted-up naked man.

Even *this* naked man.

"That should be my line," she said tartly and reached around him to shut off the water, unintentionally brushing her arm against a warm, wet thigh in her way. They both seemed to jump a little, though Mason couldn't do much, considering he was standing one-footed in the tub while his garbage-bag-shrouded leg was propped on the opposite side of the tub. "If you get either one of those casts wet, you'll be spending even more time at the hospital."

She snatched a thick brown towel off the towel rack. "You're worse than a child," she muttered. "Turn my back for a minute and look what you get up to." She ran the towel over his chest and shoulder, down to the edge of the plastic that he'd taped—with duct tape, yet— around his arm, above the edge of the fiberglass cast. She dried the plastic, hoping furiously that water hadn't leaked beneath it.

"I'm not a freaking child," he snapped and grabbed the towel with his free hand.

Considering that she was facing down all six-five of his bare flesh, she was reminded with excruciating clarity of that particular fact.

And even though they'd slept together, the sight of him took her breath away. Not just because of the mass of perfectly formed sinew and muscle or the remains of bruising that outlined his ribs and extended all the way over his corrugated abdomen, but because of the network of faint scars that webbed across his shoulders and back.

She hadn't seen them before.

The night they'd spent together was indelibly etched

in her mind. Also etched was the fact that they'd spent that night in her bedroom. Her darkened bedroom.

She'd never turned on a light, and he hadn't asked her to.

Given the glare on his face, she had a suspicion that she now knew why.

She forced herself to focus on the most immediate concern—that of his casts remaining dry. Her quickness kept him off guard and allowed her to grab the towel back from him and whip it around his hips. "Hold it there if you want to preserve your dignity."

He grabbed the towel at his hip. "What dignity?" His teeth snapped off the words.

She didn't look at him as she grabbed a second towel from the rack and ran it down the garbage bag taped around his thigh. "If you were so desperate for a shower, you could have asked me for help."

"I don't *want* help," he reminded.

"Just mine, or anyone's?" She didn't wait for an answer as she leaned over the side of the deep tub to reach his plastic-encased foot. "How long have you been in here, anyway?" It had to have been a while to build up as much steam as there'd been. Steam that was now dissipating but had still managed to make her T-shirt feel like it was clinging moistly to her torso.

It was also a miracle he hadn't lost his balance, standing virtually one-footed the way he was.

She straightened and managed by sheer grit not to let her gaze linger on him along the way. Instead, she focused on his face and the cool fury of his green eyes. "Since you managed to get yourself in there, I suppose you can manage to get yourself out." She glanced at the pile of clothes heaped on the floor. He'd obviously been more successful at getting out of his jeans on his own than he'd been in getting into them.

Without letting herself think about it, she scooped them up and carried them out of the bathroom. In his room—no, it was her future baby's room, she reminded herself, only on loan to Mason for the moment—she dropped the clothes in the basket she'd placed in his closet to use as a hamper and then yanked open the dresser drawers and randomly snatched out a set of clean items. She laid them on the side of the bed and sat down beside them to wait.

It took a solid ten minutes.

Ten minutes that crept by with painful slowness while she fought the urge to go and offer him assistance. Her ears were attuned for the slightest sound that he was struggling.

But all she heard was an occasional barely muffled oath, the closing of the bathroom door, which she'd left open, and the rush of water again. Not the shower, though. She could tell.

So she waited. And waited some more.

When he finally appeared, the towel was tucked tightly around his hips, though it separated over the bulge of his plastic-encased cast when he swung on his crutches through the doorway.

His gaze went from her to the clothes and she could see his lips tighten.

"I know you hate needing my help," she said bluntly. "But for now, you're just going to have to live with it." She took a breath. "Or find someone else to help you with your care that you *can* tolerate."

His brows pulled together. "I never said I couldn't tolerate you. Do you want me to leave? Money not worth the hassle, after all?"

"No!" She cleared her throat and reminded herself to be calm. Patient. "I'm not saying that at all. Mason, it's going to be a month before you'll get that cast off your arm, and another few weeks after that before there's even any hope for removing the one on your leg. If this is going to work, I need you to stop fighting me every step of the way, or that time is going to be a nightmare." She rubbed her damp palms down the sides of her cotton pants and pushed to her feet. "It's partly my fault, I know. Nobody likes people prying into their lives, and for that I'm sorry. Your business is your business, and from now on, you have my word that I'll respect that. We need to work together, and that's just as much my responsibility as it is yours."

He exhaled noisily, raising his casted arm, which would have looked comical in its silver duct tape and dark green garbage bag, if she'd been feeling at all humorous. "Stop. Just stop."

Her lips pressed together.

"I don't need you apologizing because I'm a bastard."

"I never said that!"

"I said it." His voice was flat. "I need your help. I don't want to need your help. Or anyone's help. With you it's a double-edged sword, though. And don't bother pretending that you don't understand why."

A wary nervousness jabbed through her insides. "Because we…slept together."

"We didn't sleep." His gaze flicked to the bed beside her. "We crawled inside each other's skin that night."

The nervous jab turned warm and slippery.

"I told you, I wasn't going to be able to forget. To pretend it never happened. It did."

Her breath ran short. She felt as if he were pulling her into the intensity of his gaze.

"The problem is…" His voice was low. Deep. "I can't make myself stop wanting it to happen again."

Her knees actually felt wobbly.

"But you have your future planned out—baby and all. And I've got a career to get back to. So you and I… we're not going there again. It's a bad idea, no matter which way you turn it."

"Oh?" She shook herself a little. "Right. You're right. We're not. Going there." She moistened her lips. "Bad idea. Bad. Bad idea."

"Then let's just stick to the necessities." His lips twisted. "And I'll try to be the least pain in your neck that I can be."

"You're not a pain in the neck. Or," she added swiftly when she saw his expression, "anywhere else. We'll just agree to both remember what we're doing this for."

He gave a short nod.

She let out a quick breath. "Okay. So I have just one more question."

His brows pulled together. "What?"

"Did you use up all the duct tape and garbage bags I had in the garage?"

He looked vaguely startled. Then his lips tilted a little. "There's some tape left on the roll. But you'll be needing more bags."

"Good to know." She picked up his gray soft-knit boxers. "Ready?"

He grimaced, but he moved over to the side of the bed and awkwardly sat down. "As ready as I'm ever going to be, I guess."

Chapter Eight

"**W**ell?" Lisa Pope plopped down onto the chair next to Courtney's. "How are things going with your Mr. Hyde?"

Courtney eyed her coworker. "The same way they've been going in the month since he arrived," she said blithely.

She didn't feel blithe, though.

Since the morning four weeks earlier when he'd insisted he was no hero, they'd both been very careful not to forget the rules of their arrangement.

In one sense, it was working admirably. They'd fallen into a fairly comfortable routine that had involved no more disasters like broken casts. When she got off shift in the morning, they shared breakfast together. Then she'd help him shower, when he was insistent about it—fortunately, his garbage-bag-and-duct-tape method had been effective enough to repeat—and dress, and then she'd catch her "night's" sleep while he entertained himself and often Plato, too.

Her dog had become thoroughly enamored of Mason. Probably because Mason had the patience to sit on her back deck for hours on end, throwing a tennis ball for the big dog to chase around and retrieve.

Then she'd slip in running a couple miles, come back to shower and fix them another meal, and take herself off to work again.

As simple and straightforward as they could keep it.

On the other hand, she felt ready to climb right out of her skin at what was feeling decidedly...domestic. Not even the prospect of having a baby was enough to keep her sane.

She'd finally settled on a donor.

Number 37892.

And she had an appointment set in a few weeks with her sister-in-law, Mallory, when she intended to ask if she was willing to be Courtney's obstetrician and help bring her plan to reality.

So far, Mason was still the only other person who knew her plans.

And *they* certainly weren't discussing it these days.

Not when their conversations remained strictly centered around the practical matters of his physical care and living under the same roof.

"Come on," Lisa wheedled, drawing Courtney out of her thoughts. It was nearly five in the morning and their wholly uneventful shift would be ending soon. "Isn't there even a *little* bit of...flirting? He's single. You're single. You're living together and everyone in the hospital knows that you were kissing outside the imaging suite after he first got to town."

Courtney smiled tightly. "That was a month ago," she

reminded Lisa. Wanting to ignore that particular event had proven to be fruitless when everyone in the hospital, and beyond, seemed to be in the know.

She'd hoped that it would die down, when there'd been no additional fuel added to the fire, but that was evidently a futile hope.

"Well, then what *do* you do while you're spending all those hours together?"

Courtney could have laughed. "We don't spend hours together, exactly." Then she shrugged. "He reads a lot. And I know Axel comes around pretty often when I'm not there." She had even begun suspecting that the two men were talking business, but she hadn't asked. Mason's recovery was continuing fairly smoothly, and that's the only thing she let herself focus on.

She looked at her watch, but the hands still seemed to be crawling around the numbers. "I'll be bringing him in to see Dr. Jackman in a few days to get the cast on his arm removed." Assuming that Mason could manage to wait that long, since she wouldn't put it past him to saw the thing off himself. If he were more dexterous with his left hand, she'd have been seriously worried he'd try to do just that.

As it was, she had no tools in her garage that he could use to that end, and she'd made Axel promise not to provide any if he were asked.

"That'll be good," Lisa was saying. "He'll be able to do a lot more for himself then."

Courtney stared at the duty schedule in front of her. "Mmm-hmm."

And when Mason was able to do more for himself, she couldn't help wondering if he'd decide to leave even before his leg cast came off. He'd still have difficulty managing some tasks, considering the unwieldiness of the cast, but at least he'd have both his arms usable again.

"Something wrong with the schedule?"

"What?" She glanced at Lisa. "Oh. No. Why?"

"You were frowning at it."

"Was I?" She pushed away from the desk and went around it to stare out the sliding doors. "I wonder if it'll snow soon."

"Hope it doesn't before Halloween," Lisa remarked. "Annie's going to be annoyed if her horse costume is covered up too much by a coat."

Courtney smiled. Lisa's six-year-old, Annie, was positively horse crazy. "Even if it is, there's always the fall festival the day before." The community event that included games and costumes, dinner and dancing was held every year in the high school gymnasium.

"Are you going?"

Courtney was scheduled to work the night of Halloween, but not the evening of the festival. "Hadn't thought about it," she lied.

The truth was, she'd thought about it a lot. Had thought about whether or not she should mention it to Mason. And now, with less than a week remaining before it was to be held, it loomed over her larger than ever.

She wished she'd just brought it up to him a few weeks ago. Then it would have seemed a casual mention. Something for him to do if he were interested, to break the monotony of the days. And if he wasn't interested, no big deal. She'd go herself, anyway, because she'd promised her niece Chloe that she'd make an appearance at some point.

"Hey." Wyatt walked through the doors and gave her a curious look as he began pulling off his jacket. "Why're you just standing there?"

"She's mooning over Mason," Lisa said.

Courtney whirled. "I am not!"

Her coworker just grinned wickedly. "You're sure sounding defensive."

It was true, but Courtney rolled her eyes anyway. "You guys need more things to do," she said. "Your imaginations obviously don't have enough occupying them." She nodded toward Wyatt. "Maybe you'd do better asking him how his date with Dee went."

Lisa's eyebrows shot up and she immediately looked at the other nurse. "Well, well. When did this happen and why didn't I know about it? Where'd you go? What'd you do? Are you taking her out again?"

Happy that the other woman's attention was so easily diverted, Courtney went back to the nurse's lounge and signed out. She collected her jacket and purse and quickly left before Lisa could waylay her with more questions.

It was still dark outside, and the air was cold and biting as she climbed into her car. The drive to her house was short—never giving the vehicle's heater a chance to catch up.

The light over her front door was burning. Mason always turned it on before she got home.

Now that the weather was turning colder, she parked her car in the separate garage located next to her backyard, instead of parking in the driveway close to the front door, and went in through the rear kitchen door.

Plato was sitting on the other side of the door, waiting to greet her.

She dumped her purse and jacket on the table and crouched down next to the dog, rubbing his head. She knew once he'd had a few pats from her, he'd trot right on back to Mason's room. He'd considered the bed in there his before Mason had arrived, and nothing since then had changed. If anything, her dog seemed to be more interested in attention from Mason than from her. "You're a good boy," she whispered to the dog, and straightened.

A roll of duct tape was sitting on the counter.

She smiled a little. Mason's unspoken code that he wasn't going to wait another day to be allowed another shower.

When it came to that process, they'd worked out a system there, too, though mostly it involved her sitting outside the shower curtain, pouring shampoo into his hand when he needed it, trying not to offer too much assistance and hiding the fact that the entire event kept her nerves honed to a painfully fine edge.

Just thinking about it made her edgy now, too, and she picked up the plastic-wrapped sandwich that sat on the counter next to the tape and unwrapped it as she padded into the dining room. She sat down in front of the computer and navigated to the cryobank website as she chewed the sandwich. Peanut butter and strawberry jam.

Mason had taken to leaving her sandwiches. He said it was just to prove to her that he wasn't incapable of feeding himself.

Maybe it was true.

The website loaded, and by force of habit, she pulled up the anonymous donor she'd chosen. "Hello, 37892," she whispered. "How are you this morning? We're going to make a baby soon."

Plato, evidently satisfied that she was in for the night, padded out of the dining room and disappeared down the dark hallway.

She propped her chin on her hand and stared at the screen.

The familiar spark of excitement when she thought of her plan to have a family was there. She knew what she wanted and, in her usual way, was going to make it happen.

And if that spark wasn't quite as bright as it ordinarily was, it was simply because the fantasy of it was becoming a reality. And with reality came worries.

Mason and his "devil's advocate" comments hadn't given her anything new to think about. But the closer her plan got to fruition, the more she did think about them.

More accurately, the harder it was to remember that becoming a mother was the bottom line. Not the method in which that occurred.

Nothing had changed since she'd decided on this plan of action.

Nothing except Mason coming back into your life.

She shushed the taunting little voice. Mason wasn't back *in* her life. For that matter, he'd never been in her life.

A one-night stand didn't qualify as "in," after all.

And what they were doing now was a business arrangement. Also not "in."

Plato padded back into the room and propped his head on her knee, whining a little.

She rubbed his head. "What's the matter?"

He turned and headed down the hall, stopping midway to look back at her with another soft whine.

Frowning, she followed him, turning on the hall light as she went.

Mason's bedroom was dark, but there was enough light from behind her to see where he lay on the bed.

"Mason?" she called his name softly, not wanting to wake him if he were asleep. "You all right?"

He didn't answer, and she looked down at the dog by her side. Plato was still whining softly.

"Shh." She slipped her fingers under his collar and nudged him slightly toward her bedroom. "You can sleep with me for a while."

"Wait."

The voice was almost soundless.

Alarm exploded inside her, and she went into Mason's room. When she reached the bed, she could see that his eyes were indeed open. And that his hand was clenched in a fist. "Mason? What's wrong?"

"Back." A low oath came out of his clenched teeth. "Spasm."

She gingerly touched his shoulder. He was so tense, it was like touching a brick wall. "How long have you been like this?"

"Forever." He gave a half-groaning laugh, then just groaned. "A few hours. *Damn* it."

"Can you roll over? I can try some gentle massage. See if it helps."

"I don't think I can move," he muttered.

She had a good idea what the admission cost him. "I can turn you, but I won't if you don't want me to."

"I don't care if you hit me over the head with a sledgehammer and knock me out."

She toed off her clogs and pressed one knee against the mattress, carefully moving his bed pillows out of the way. "I'm going to move your arms above your head. Slow and easy, okay?" She situated his cast where she wanted it so that it wouldn't get in her way, and when he didn't protest that he felt more pain, she slid one hand beneath his casted thigh and worked her other beneath his shoulders. Ordinarily, she would have turned him toward her, but he was too close to the side of the bed, and there was no room for her to stand on the other side. So she rolled him slowly, gently, away from her until he was on his side. "Okay so far?"

"No worse." His voice was muffled. "This is what I get for flushing the damn pills."

She didn't have to guess which pills he meant. "They wouldn't have stopped a muscle spasm," she reminded calmly.

"But at least I wouldn't have cared when I was having one." He gave a short, rusty-sounding laugh. "That's a joke."

"I figured."

"Good." He let out a long breath, and then she felt him rolling on his own until he was facedown on the mattress. "I don't want you worrying that I'm on the edge of relapsing."

"I wasn't." She was familiar with the signs, and he didn't show any of them. He hadn't ever, really, not even when he'd first arrived and his pain had been constant. She climbed on the bed next to him, kneeling beside his hip. "Your leg comfortable enough?" The angle of the cast didn't exactly promote lying facedown.

"I'll live."

She moistened her lips. Her hands hovered over him, just above the waistband of his dark gray sweatpants. "Where's the pain?"

"Everyfreakingwhere. Either do your voodoo or shoot me in the head."

"Oh, Mason." She settled her hands gently against the small of his back. "I don't suppose you'd be willing for me to cut off your shirt." She didn't want to cause him more pain by trying to get it off over his head.

"I'm not wasting a perfectly good shirt."

"How frugal of you." It was easier to keep talking, because then she wouldn't be *thinking* so much about what she was doing.

Her fingertips lightly explored the contours of his back, searching out the areas of tenderness through the cotton knit. It was pretty easy to find the muscle that was cramping. It was hard as a rock beneath the warmth of his skin. Plus, he ground out a curse and stiffened up when she began working around it.

"This would be easier without the shirt." And with some massage lotion. "Your scars don't bother me, in case that's what you're thinking. I'm a nurse."

"So was my ex-wife. They sure as hell bothered her."

She was so surprised by the admission that her hands stopped moving for a moment. Aside from the one time that he'd mentioned he'd been married, he hadn't referred to it again. She hadn't had the nerve to ask, since it was clearly outside the bounds of their arrangement. She viciously chewed back the questions that rose in her—how'd they meet? How long were they together?

Did he still carry a torch for her?

Was that why his emotions were off-limits?

"I'm not your ex-wife," was all she said. She shifted slightly, gradually applying more pressure along his spine in response to the muscles she could feel slowly loosening under her fingers.

"So I'm learning."

She closed her eyes for a moment, not sure how to take that. "How often does your back get like this?"

She could feel him breathing carefully as she worked. "Happens if I lie around too much. Don't get enough exercise."

"What kind of exercise?"

"Chasing bad guys." His voice turned short.

She swallowed. Chasing them, or being run down by them? She decided to change the subject. "I, um, I confirmed your appointment day after tomorrow to get your arm done."

"Good."

She put a little more of her weight behind her slow, smooth strokes. "If you're getting cabin fever and want to get out a little, Weaver has a fall festival on Saturday. It's a fancy term for a Halloween carnival, but there's food and music and…stuff."

"Ax told me about it."

Of course. She didn't know why she hadn't thought her cousin would mention it. Axel's wife was one of the local business owners who helped sponsor it.

"You gonna do another kissing booth?"

She was glad his face was turned away from her. "That was just that one time. To, um, to raise money for the school."

"I remember the line around your booth. You must've raised a lot."

She had, and had earned herself a lot of ribbing from her family as a result. "The *event* did."

"But the thing this weekend isn't a fundraiser?"

"Nope. Just a community event. People dress up in costumes if they like. They've held it every year since I can remember."

"What're you dressing up as?"

"I hadn't thought about it." The only thing she'd thought about was whether or not Mason would want to go. And if he'd think she was being too *personal* by asking him.

"Think you should go as an angel," he murmured. "My back is actually starting to feel better."

She snorted softly. "That doesn't make me angel material."

"Putting up with me does."

She moistened her lips. "You're not so bad," she managed lightly. "No matter what you think." She was well aware that he hadn't said whether or not he was interested in going. Which she was smart enough to realize meant he was not.

"Why'd you invite me to your apartment that night?"

He couldn't have shocked her more if he'd tried. She stared at the back of his head. "Why'd you show up when I did?" she asked without thought.

"I'm a man." His voice was dry.

She took her cue from that. "And I'm a woman. You think men are the only ones ruled by their sex drives?"

"Generally speaking? Yeah." He turned his head, and she could feel the weight of his hooded gaze. "I know you weren't intending to get pregnant then. We used condoms."

Her face felt like it was on fire. "The last thing on my mind then was having a baby."

"Your brother was still missing then, wasn't he?"

"Mmm-hmm." She focused on his back, working a little harder.

"And then he gets back, and you suddenly decide you want a baby."

"Not exactly. But I will admit that his return helped cement my belief that a person shouldn't necessarily wait for those things in life that they really want." The cotton knit of his T-shirt kept bunching beneath her hands. And she *wanted* to tear it off, and not just because it was hindering her massage, but because her hands simply ached to touch his bare skin.

As if he could hear her thoughts and wanted to put

an end to them, he suddenly rolled onto his back, proving that, not only had she managed to tame the muscle spasm, but he'd become much more agile over the past weeks than she knew.

Which would make her even less of a necessity to him now.

"I guess you're feeling a little better." She brushed her hands together and scooted to the side of the bed, but his hand latched around her wrist, halting her.

Electricity shot through her. "What?"

Almost as soon as he'd grabbed her, he released her. "Nothing." His voice was gruff. "Just…thanks."

She chewed the inside of her lip. Pushed off the bed and felt around with her feet for her clogs. "That's what I'm here for."

"You looking forward to having your place back to yourself? Start turning this room into a nursery?"

Just nod and agree. How hard was that?

"Looking forward to the nursery? Yes. Looking forward to you leaving?" She finally found the shoes. "Surprisingly, not so much." Then, before her unwise tongue could get her into even more trouble, she hurried out of the room.

She closed herself in her bedroom and leaned back against the door. "Stupid, Courtney," she whispered. Just plain stupid.

And then she saw the box sitting on her bed.

It was small. And it was wrapped—rather unevenly—in brown paper. The same kind of paper as the bags at the grocery store where she shopped.

She went over to the box and picked it up. There was no tag. No label.

Shaking it lightly gave her no hint of what was inside and she slid her finger beneath the tape, pulling off the paper wrapping. The box it covered was plain white, also offering no hint.

Inside her chest, her heart skittered around. She lifted the lid off the box.

Her knees went loose and weak and she plopped down on the bed, staring at the silver rattle that was nestled snugly among the padding inside the box. She held it up.

It had been engraved. *Mommy's little angel*.

Her hand trembled and the rattle jingled softly.

Without thought, she left her room again and went into Mason's. Still holding the rattle, she sat down on the bed beside him.

"I don't care if it is a bad idea." Before her mind could stop what her heart wanted, she leaned over and pressed her mouth to his.

Stars might as well have exploded inside her chest for the sensation that streaked through her. She lifted her head, catching her breath, but his hand came up, sinking through her hair, pulling her back to him.

The rattle slid from her nerveless fingers when his mouth opened against hers. She felt herself sinking deeper into him and tore her mouth away. She pushed her hand against his chest, resisting even though the last thing she wanted to do was resist. "Tell me what to do about you," she whispered. "You want to keep me at a distance, and then you do this?" She jiggled the rattle and it rang musically between them. "You, who doesn't even approve of my plan?"

"You put the rattle on that wish list."

She laughed a little brokenly. "And obviously, you've been poking around on the websites I happen to visit on the internet. I ought to be angry. I would never have even realized you've been spying, except you go and announce it by putting a box on my bed! What am I supposed to make of this?"

"It's just a gift. And there's no spying involved, considering how you never seem to close a browser window."

His fingers were still threaded through her hair, and she lowered her forehead to his chin. She pulled in a long, slow breath. Let it out even more slowly. "Nothing with you is ever *just*."

"I didn't give it expecting something in return."

"Something." She lifted her head. Peered into his face. "Like me throwing myself at you again?"

"You never threw yourself at me."

"What would you call it then?"

His fingers slid along her neck. It took far more control than she possessed not to shiver. "A night of miracles," he murmured.

Her throat tightened. "Be careful," she warned, much more for her own benefit than his. "That sounded unabashedly romantic."

"That the knockout young nurse could see past a face that scares children?"

Her chest squeezed. He really meant it. "I don't think it's the scar that scares anyone." She ran her finger down the jagged mark that slashed his face. "It's the fact that you have a very fierce glower when you try." She laid her palm against his cheek. "But you smiled at me when you paid for your kiss." And she'd been sunk.

He wasn't smiling now, though. If anything, he looked…regretful.

He caught her hand in his. "You should go to bed."

She lifted her eyebrows, even though her stomach was sinking. "I'm guessing that's not an invitation." She didn't wait for the obvious answer and sat up, sliding off the bed. She lifted the rattle. "It's a beautiful gift, Mason. But it's much too extravagant." That's why she hadn't ordered it herself. Because she couldn't quite justify the cost.

"It's a gift." His words were clipped. "You're not supposed to worry about the expense."

"But—"

"I can afford it, okay? Just because I'm not currently the picture of gainful employment doesn't mean I'm broke."

"That never occurred to me." She shook her head. "I…we're getting off track." The last thing she wanted to do was offend him. She turned the rattle between her fingers. "Let me try again. Thank you, Mason, for the very thoughtful gift. I'll cherish it always."

"You mean, the baby will."

She smiled sadly. "No. I mean *I* will." And then, before she could forget herself yet again where he was concerned, she went to her bedroom and closed the door.

She held the rattle cradled against her chest and sighed.

Chapter Nine

"**M**ason looks like he's enjoying himself." Courtney's cousin-in-law Tara slipped into the folding chair beside her at one of the round tables that the family had commandeered at the fall festival. Courtney looked over to where Mason was propped on his crutches among her cousins and her brother. He had his newly cast-free hand wrapped around a beer, and a grin on his face.

"I think he's so glad to get out of one of his casts that he'd enjoy most anything." She smiled a little wryly.

Until that morning, she'd believed that Mason had no intentions of coming to the festival. But when she'd gotten off duty from the hospital, he'd been up waiting for her and had asked what time the "thing" was.

She'd been nearly stunned stupid before she'd stammered out the time.

Then, when she'd gone to her room to grab some sleep, she'd just laid there staring at the ceiling.

"Well, now that he's obviously getting out and about more, maybe you can get him to Sunday dinner."

Courtney stifled a sigh and lifted her shoulder. "Maybe." Every week, someone in the family put on a big Sunday dinner for whoever could come. Since Mason had arrived, Courtney had missed all but one, and he'd flatly refused to "intrude," even though she'd assured him he wouldn't be doing any such thing.

Mostly, she figured he'd had enough of her family en masse when they'd gone to her parents' for dinner that one night.

"D'you ever think you can figure a man out?" Realizing she'd spoken the question aloud when Tara gave her an amused look, Courtney felt her skin turn warm. "Rhetorical question," she said quickly.

Tara didn't take it rhetorically, though. She looked over at the men again. "As much as a man can figure out a woman," she said. Her gaze slid to Courtney. "It helps when you can both talk to each other about what's going on inside."

Courtney couldn't help making a face at that. "Some men are better at that than others, I'd think."

"So are some women," Tara pointed out. "My personal take? When you can allow yourself to start trusting the other person not to hurt you the way you expect... or fear...then amazing things can happen." She smiled gently. "Even coming to understand what makes that particular man tick. And understanding even better what makes you tick."

Courtney propped her chin on her hand. "I know what makes me tick," she murmured. "Family."

"A true Clay," Tara said. "Think that's pretty consistent among all of you."

"You're one of us now, too."

Tara's gaze looked past Courtney toward the men. She smiled, and there was such a contented satisfaction in that smile, Courtney felt a little envious.

"I still have to pinch myself sometimes," Tara admitted. "My parents are gone, though I have my brother, of course. But your family is particularly tight. I'm not sure if all of you realize how unique that can be since it's the way it's always been for you."

"I don't know about unique, but I do know that I can't imagine *not* having the family I have." Courtney looked at Mason. "It's one of the reasons I never wanted to move away from Weaver. I can't imagine growing up without that particular bedrock. We're lucky, I know." Then she grinned. "Even during those times when I wish—for a moment—to have just a little more privacy."

Tara laughed. "I have to admit there are a few times when I've thought the same thing." Her eyes danced. "Particularly when the boys drop by unannounced to play pool with Axel." She pushed her chair back and stood. She was wearing a floor-length, royal blue velvet gown, with a sword strapped around her hip. She looked like a petite character out of Narnia. "Come on. I haven't seen you dance once yet this evening, and you're usually the belle of the ball. Get that man you can't stop looking at out on the dance floor."

"I'm pretty sure Mason doesn't want to attempt dancing while his leg is in a cast." Or any other time. Not with her, at any rate.

If he did, he'd have asked her.

That she did know about him.

Tara lifted her brows, as if she could read exactly what was in Courtney's thoughts. "Then dance with someone else," she suggested pointedly. "It's not like you haven't been asked a dozen times already."

That was true enough. Courtney had turned down all the offers, though, because the only arms she was interested in holding her belonged to her enigmatic boarder.

"Good point." She pushed to her feet, too, and tugged down the thigh-length tunic of her orange-and-red clown costume. She glanced around, spotted a good target and made her way across the room in her long-toed red shoes. When she reached Wyatt Mead, where he was hovering against the wall near the door, she grabbed his hand. "Come and dance with me."

He looked horrified. "I don't even know how."

"You owe me," she reminded. "You can escape later."

"I wasn't planning to escape," he huffed.

"Please." She pulled him toward the dance floor. "You were just about ready to slide out the door." She turned toward him and held up her arms. "You can either put your arms around me, or we can stand here looking like idiots."

He looked even more horrified and grabbed her hand in his. He put his other hand on her waist, and they began shuffling around the crowded dance area. His only concession to a costume was the wildly colored, spinning bow tie he wore with his flannel shirt and jeans.

"Don't worry," Courtney told him in a low voice. "Dee is watching every move."

"What?"

"Why haven't you asked her to dance?"

"Because I don't know *how* to dance," he reminded.

Without any effort, she managed to guide them a little closer to Dee. Plus, she could see Mason over Wyatt's shoulder. "Seems like you're dancing well enough to me."

She could practically hear him grinding his teeth. "What do you women want, anyway?"

She almost laughed. "We want the men we're interested in to be interested back."

He frowned. "How can she not know I'm interested? We went out on a date!"

"Did you ask her for another one?"

"Well, not yet, but—"

"Why not?"

"She's been busy. They're doing all sorts of special stuff over at the school these days."

"Doesn't matter," Courtney advised. "Busy or not, she wants to know you want her. For Pete's sake, Wyatt. She's not so busy that she didn't come tonight. And as far as I can tell, she hasn't taken her eyes off you." For that matter, the other woman was presently glaring daggers at Courtney. "At least *ask*."

The fact that she was advising Wyatt to do what she herself refused to do was not lost on her.

But she'd known both Wyatt and Dee for years. Nudging them together was perfectly logical when she knew how they both felt.

Pushing herself toward Mason when she didn't have a clue what he felt was another matter entirely. And besides, what was the point of trying to engage Mason in something that would only end sooner rather than later?

She had plans.

So did he.

And those plans weren't exactly on intersecting paths.

The only thing they had that could conceivably intersect was chemistry.

Good, old-fashioned S.E.X.

She realized the song was winding down and stepped

away from Wyatt. "Go on," she insisted. "Better to ask and get shot down than not ask and never know."

She watched him only long enough to see him pull in a deep breath and take a step toward the side of the gymnasium where Dee was sitting.

Then she turned.

Her gaze collided with Mason's from across the room.

Her stomach dipped and swayed, but she set off toward him, marching her way around and through the crowd in her silly clown shoes until she stopped next to him. Her eyes were on him, though her smile included her brother and her cousin Casey, who were standing there with him. "Having fun?"

"Having fun watching you try to walk in those big ol' shoes," Casey drawled. "You're never gonna snag a man looking like that, honey."

Courtney gave her cousin a kind look. "And you're never gonna snag a woman, Casey, unless you figure out how to open your mouth without inserting your foot in it."

Ryan chuckled and slid his arm around Courtney's shoulders. "Case is just jealous," he said, "because he knows all you have to do is crook your little finger and guys come running from miles away. He, on the other hand, hasn't had a pretty girl look his way all night."

"Women are too much trouble," Casey groused, though his gray eyes were full of goading laughter. He took a pull on his beer. "Give her an inch, and she'll wanna take a mile."

"And a man like you is any different?" Courtney shook her head. Her handsome cousin was twenty-eight and showed no sign of wanting to settle down. Which was not to say that he didn't enjoy his share of female company. As long as it didn't last past a night or two.

She looked at Mason and, ignoring the dancing nerves in her stomach, gestured toward the dance floor. "Do you want to give it a try?" It was an effort, but she managed to keep her voice light. "I can be your human crutch."

His brows pulled together slightly. "Then I'll be the one looking like a clown."

Even though she'd expected him to turn her down, her disappointment didn't feel any less acute. "Never hurts to ask," she dismissed blithely. "Ryan, how about you?"

"Since my wife abandoned me to deliver a baby and my daughter prefers the company of the games over there—" he jerked his chin toward the side of the room that was set up with carnival-style games "—might as well."

Courtney rolled her eyes. "So good for my ego." But she was smiling as she headed out to the dance area and turned to her brother, because it still struck her as a miracle that he was around at all.

He smoothly swept her into a two-step. "How's it going with Hyde?"

"Fine."

He smiled faintly. "Okay. Now, how's it *really* going with Hyde?"

"Fine," she insisted.

"What about the two of you playing tonsil hockey at the hospital?"

"We most certainly weren't doing anything of the sort!"

He raised his eyebrow.

She huffed. "First of all, that was weeks ago. Second, you know what gossip is like in this town. Things get blown completely out of proportion."

"I can always tell when you're lying."

She exhaled noisily. "I'm not lying! Admittedly, he's not the perfect patient, but he's come a long way in the time he's been here."

"So, you're telling me that the only thing going on under your roof is the nurse-patient deal?"

She swallowed. "That's all." And that, sad to say, *was* the truth.

"Then why," he asked in a low voice, "did he have Axel drive him to the drugstore yesterday, where he bought a box of condoms?"

She stumbled over her own bright red clown shoes. "I have no idea," she said faintly. "Maybe you should ask him."

Her brother's eyes were narrowed, obviously unconvinced. "Maybe I will," he said.

She cleared her throat, desperate to change the subject. "So, um, when I was watching Chloe for you last weekend, she told me she's decided it's time you and her mom give her a baby brother or sister."

"She's been on that kick for a while now."

"And…? It's not like you're getting any younger, brother dear."

"No," a woman's laughing voice said from behind her, "but he just keeps getting better."

Startled, Courtney turned to see her sister-in-law ready to cut in and could have wept with relief. "How'd the delivery go?"

"False alarm." Mallory smiled. She was still dressed in pale blue scrubs. "Just some strong Braxton Hicks contractions, as Mom kept trying to convince Dad, but he was convinced that she was in true labor. Poor guy is out of his mind worrying about his wife." She raised her eyebrows. "Mind if I cut in?"

"Please," Courtney offered, as she stepped away from her brother. "He keeps stepping on my clown toes."

"Hard not to when they're about six inches too long," he defended himself as he swept his wife into a close hold.

Courtney moved away, with the sound of Mallory's soft laughter in her ears.

Mason had bought *condoms?*

She was afraid to assume that he meant to use them with her.

Everywhere she looked, she saw couples. Families.

Thoroughly agitated, she collected her purse from their unoccupied table and headed toward Mason again. Dinner was long over, and the only things left for the night were more carnival games for the children she didn't have and dancing with the partner she didn't have.

The non-partner who'd bought condoms.

She stopped next to him. "Do you want to stay longer, or are you ready to go?"

He immediately set his beer on the table behind him. He gave her a close look. "What's wrong?"

She shook her head. "Nothing. Do you want to stay or go?"

"Go."

She nodded. "Fine. I'll just say good-night to my folks and meet you by the door." She didn't wait to watch him crutch his way there but looked around to find her parents. They, too, were on the dance floor. She worked her way close enough to wave goodbye, then headed to the main gymnasium doors, where Mason was waiting.

She pushed them open and waited for him to pass through. "I'll bring up the car."

"I can make it to the car."

"Your choice." She headed across the sidewalk toward

the crowded parking lot, digging in her purse for her keys as she went. She could hear the thump-slide-thump of Mason behind her and had to fight off the urge to slow her pace and hover closer to him, lest his crutches catch on an uneven bit of pavement. She reached the car ahead of him and had the back door open and waiting by the time he got there.

Handing her the crutches, he used both—hallelujah—of his arms to lower himself onto the seat and slide across it until his cast was inside the car. Without a word, she handed him the crutches to lay on the floor behind the seats and closed the door, then went around to the driver's side.

In minutes, she was driving out of the parking lot.

"What's bugging you?"

She glanced in the rearview mirror, but the only thing she could make out were the headlights of the car behind her. "Nothing."

"Yeah, right."

She cleared her throat with a soft cough. "Just some gossip I heard."

"About?"

She pulled the car off to the side of the street, shoved it into Park and looked over the seat at him. "About you. Buying condoms!"

"And that has you pissed off?"

Her hands tightened around the steering wheel. "Why do you need to be out buying condoms?"

"Because I couldn't find any in your house."

She gaped. "You've been *looking?*"

"Yes."

His answer was so calm and immediate that she blinked. "What do you plan on doing with them?"

Even in the dim light, she could see his eyebrow

lift. "*If* I plan on doing something, it won't be making X-rated balloons out of them." His voice was mild.

She pressed her fingertips hard against her temples. "*Who* are you planning to use them with?" She dropped her hands. "Maybe you need me to take you to Colbys, so you can pick up some women, too?"

"Don't be stupid."

She stared at him. "Well, what am I supposed to think, Mason? You're practically hands-off for weeks, and you wouldn't even try to dance with me. I get it that you didn't want to dance. Pretty hard to do, with the cast and all, but—"

He leaned forward until his hand could catch behind her neck. "I bought them because of you," he said evenly. "Because I'm not sure how much more my self-control can take." Then, before she could wrap her mind around that, he let go of her and was sitting back again. "How did you even find out, anyway? Axel just dropped me off in front of the store. He doesn't know what the hell I bought."

"This is Weaver," she said faintly. "You can't do anything in this town without somebody taking notice and spreading the word along."

He grimaced. "Nice."

"You said it was a bad idea for us to go down that path."

"And people go down paths they shouldn't all the time. If I'm no better, then I at least want to be prepared. Oh, hell. This is great," he muttered. He'd turned to look out the back window.

Her mouth was dry. A million thoughts were racing through her head, but nothing was coming out of her lips. He was still looking out the back, and her gaze followed his to the flashing red-and-blue lights, but for a moment, even they didn't make sense to her.

And then, when a police officer knocked on the window beside her head, they did.

She groaned and rolled down the window. "Hey there, Dave."

The deputy sheriff cocked his head, eyeing her. "Everything okay, Courtney? You're in a no-parking zone."

"Sorry. I'll move on."

The man nodded, though he gave Mason a long look. "Drive safe," he said and thumped his hand on the top of the car before walking back to his patrol vehicle.

Courtney rolled up her window and put the car in Drive. "I can't believe you bought condoms." She shakily pulled back onto the street.

"Better to be prepared," he said dismissively.

Except she didn't want the subject dismissed. "Because I want a baby, and you want to make sure it's not yours?"

"That's not what I said."

Her hands twisted on the steering wheel. "But it's true, isn't it?"

She heard him sigh. "I can't believe everyone in this freaking town knows everyone else's business," he muttered.

It wasn't a direct response, but it didn't have to be.

She knew the answer.

"Maybe I've changed my mind, too. Maybe I don't want to sleep with you again."

"Then you won't."

How easily he said it. As if it hardly mattered to him one way or the other. Maybe that particular intersection was more in her mind than in reality, after all.

A lump lodged in her throat, and she continued the

drive home in silence. She let him out next to the house and drove back to park in the garage. He'd gone inside by the time she went in through the back door.

There was no sign of Plato. Her dog had fully defected to the enemy.

She toed off the silly clown shoes in the kitchen and padded in her stocking feet through the dining room, then down the hall.

Mason was waiting. There was no mistaking that particular fact. Not with him leaning against the wall, one crutch propped under his arm to help support him.

Plato sat next to him, leaning his big, fluffy body against Mason's cast.

Her heart charged unevenly inside her chest. Because it felt safer, she looked down at her dog and held out her hand. "Have you forgotten who buys your dog food?"

Plato rolled to his feet and came forward, his tail wagging as he sloppily dragged his tongue over her hand. She crouched next to him and rubbed her hands over his coat. His tail flopped harder, and his soft brown eyes looked hearteningly ecstatic. "Yes, you're a handsome boy, even if you do prefer someone else over me."

"He hasn't lost his loyalty to you," Mason assured her. "He just tolerates me 'cause I've tossed him the tennis ball a few times."

"Hmm." The dog sprawled on the floor and rolled over, waiting for his belly to be rubbed. She couldn't help but smile a little at the blatant invitation and complied. "I don't think *tolerate* is quite the word." She pushed to her feet. "He's going to miss you when you leave."

"That sounds more like a reminder to us both that I will be leaving."

"I don't need to remind myself," she said. "I'm aware

of it every…single…day. Just as I am aware that you purchasing a box of condoms doesn't change that." She lifted her chin. "Maybe I don't want anything to change. Maybe I like the fact that you'll be leaving. No strings and all that. It works both ways."

The corner of his lip curled. "I'd bet my last dollar that it doesn't work that way for you."

It didn't, but he didn't have to know that he was right. She did have *some* pride. "I told you before that I wasn't looking for a husband." She spread her hands. "I'm not even looking for a baby-daddy. As you well know, I've got that angle covered with number 37892."

His brows yanked together. "What?"

"Number 37892," she repeated blithely. "That's the donor I've chosen."

"I can't believe you're still going through with this."

"If you thought I wouldn't, why'd you buy that keep-sake rattle?"

"Let me rephrase. I can't believe you still want to have a baby via spermsicle."

She propped her hands on her hips. "We're back to that now? Why shouldn't I?" She waved her hands. "I'm reasonably responsible. I can afford to raise a child if I'm careful, and I have a fabulous family around me for support! I'd rather do this on my own than depend on a man to be with me who doesn't even want to be there in the first place!"

His eyes narrowed. "Are you speaking generally or specifically?"

She huffed. "Neither. For heaven's sake, Mason. Stop worrying. I decided I wanted a baby long before you came back into the picture. Don't want to bash your ego, but you really had nothing whatsoever to do with it. I just realized that for those things you really, *really* want in life, you shouldn't wait. Because you never know what might happen." She gestured at him. "You're a perfect example," she said. "You could have been killed by that SUV. Wasn't there anything in your life that you would have regretted *not* doing, if you hadn't been as lucky as you were?" She made a face. "Oh, that's right. I'm sorry. You're the emotional-island guy. You don't let yourself care about anything else besides your job."

"My job was—is—the only thing that I'm good at." His voice was flat, the scar on his face standing out whitely. "I didn't fail it. And it hasn't failed me."

"Who'd you fail, Mason? Your ex-wife? The one who didn't like your scars? Who didn't hang around to see you conquer your painkiller addiction?"

"Don't waste time analyzing me."

"And don't you waste time thinking that I should wait around for some guy to sweep me off my feet and make my every dream come true," she said swiftly. "I live in Weaver, Mason. I know nearly every guy in this town. If there was someone around who made my bells ring, then I'd be out there ringing 'em, but there's not."

"Weaver's not the only place in the world."

"You think I don't know that? I lived in Cheyenne while I was studying nursing. I've traveled with my parents around the United States. I've traveled abroad with friends. I *choose* Weaver. It's where I grew up, and it's where I want my child to grow up. Everywhere I turn, I am surrounded by family and friends who've found their partners in life. Who've got their metaphorical white picket fence, with babies and all." She lowered her hands finally. "Well, I'm not waiting for a white picket fence that may never come. Maybe you and I aren't so different, after all. You know who and what you are. And

I know who and what I am. They're just on completely different planes."

She took a step back, waiting for her pounding heart to climb down out of her throat. Waiting, too, for him to say something. Anything.

But all he did was stand there, his fist clenched around the handgrip of his crutch, a muscle ticking in his jaw.

Her heart did climb out of her throat then. It slowly sank, heading right for her toes.

"It's late," she finally said huskily. "I'm going to bed." She knew better than to ask if he needed anything before she went.

Because even if he did, he wouldn't ask.

Chapter Ten

She went out on a date.

With Dr. Flannery.

Despite all her claims that she wasn't interested in finding a man, she'd gone out with one.

Mason still couldn't believe it. Not even after he'd watched Courtney—wearing a dress that gave new meaning to little and black—climb into Flannery's low-slung car, parked at the curb.

Mason was inside the house, watching from the window, and *he'd* seen the length of sleek, shapely leg that was exposed when she'd climbed into the sports car. He was pretty damn certain that Pierce Flannery—orthopedic guy that he was—had been studying that perfect limb, too.

And now, they'd been gone for over four hours.

It was nearly midnight, and Mason was about ready to climb out of his skin. What the hell were they doing that it took four hours?

He knew what he'd want to be doing. Same thing he'd been wanting to do from the day he'd seen Courtney again. Same thing that had driven him to buy condoms. Just in case.

The damnable thing was that he'd *had* opportunities. After that rattle business. He'd held her in his arms. She'd even kissed him before he'd pushed her away. And the day of the Halloween shindig. Before she'd found out about his not-so-anonymous purchase and his "just in case" theory had flown out the window.

He should have danced with her.

Even if he'd made an ass out of himself trying, he should have danced.

He shoved his fingers through his hair. It felt odd without the cast, which had been removed the week before, but he was mighty glad to have the thing off even if his arm—paler than the rest of him—looked like some sort of alien thing.

If she hadn't found out about the condoms, would she have still decided to go out with the doctor from Braden?

He grimaced and looked over at Plato, who was taking up nearly as much of the couch cushions as Mason was. "Where the hell are they?"

Plato sighed noisily and flopped his tail twice. His eyebrows seemed to twitch as his gaze went from side to side.

"I know," Mason muttered. "It's none of my damn business. At least that's what *she* would tell me." Grabbing his crutches, he managed to pull himself off the couch. He headed toward the kitchen but stopped at the computer desk in the dining room.

He slid the mouse around, and the swirl of stars on the screen disappeared. Number 37892 stared back at him. Or at least the webpage describing 37892's attributes stared back at him.

Six foot one. 190 pounds. Straight brown hair. Green eyes. A lawyer.

"Probably an ambulance chaser," he muttered and kept moving into the kitchen.

Courtney had left him a plate of food that was ready to go. All he had to do was punch a few numbers on the microwave.

She took the whole room-and-board thing pretty seriously, even if she had come to the realization that he was an ass. And if—*when*—she got home from her date with Dr. Feelgood, she'd expect that plate to be empty or worry why.

So even though his appetite was just as nonexistent as it had been after she'd left, he heated the plate and ate the chicken and rice concoction while standing at the counter. It was easier than trying to carry the plate over to the table and sit down.

When he was finished, he rinsed the plate in the sink, set it in the dishwasher and crutched his way back to the living room. He sat down next to Plato again, where he had a view out the front window through the wide-open plantation shutters.

"Guess we're waiting, Plato."

The dog circled a few times before settling with his head on Mason's knee. The dog sighed hugely.

So did Mason.

"Are you sure I can't talk you into a nightcap?"

Courtney smiled at Pierce and shook her head. She knew the guy was angling for an invitation inside, and she just couldn't make herself pretend she was interested.

Not that the evening had been unpleasant.

Pierce Flannery was an attractive, intelligent and relatively engaging companion. They even had similar interests, not to mention their complementary professions. They'd driven to Gillette for dinner simply because Courtney had happened to mention that she enjoyed Thai food and that was the closest place for it.

By all rights, she should have thoroughly enjoyed herself and been more than happy to extend the evening a little longer.

But encouraging the man wasn't fair.

For that matter, accepting his invitation to dinner hadn't been exactly fair.

Not when she'd agreed only because she wanted to get Mason out from beneath her skin.

Or maybe get underneath Mason's skin, a fact that didn't make her feel any less guilty.

Mason was still burrowed right where he always had been—maybe even further—and if he was bothered in the least by her unexpected date with the eligible doctor, he'd certainly hidden it well.

And now she had managed to encourage a perfectly nice man in whom she had absolutely no interest.

All in all, she felt like the worst sort of slug.

"I'm sure," she told Pierce. "I have an early morning." They were parked at the curb in front of the house, and thanks to the lamp burning in her living room, she could easily see Mason through the front window, sitting on the couch. Despite the late hour, he was up.

Waiting?

Trying hard to ignore that fact, she leaned over the console and quickly kissed Pierce's cheek. "Thank you for dinner. It was very nice."

"I'll call you again."

She sighed a little. Oh, she hated this. "Pierce, you're a really nice man. But I'm just…well, I'm not in a place right now where I'm ready to—"

"Not even for a simple dinner?" His smile was rueful as he looked past her toward the house. He could see Mason just as easily as she had. "Well, it never hurts to ask."

Before she could stop him, he climbed out of the car and came around to her door to open it.

Feeling even worse, she got out, too. "I did have a good time, Pierce."

"But I'm not the right man to be having a good time with," he surmised. He smiled slightly and caught her hand, lifting it to his lips. "Don't look so upset. You know where I am if you change your mind."

She knew she wouldn't, but she still appreciated his kindness. "I do." She stepped back from the curb and watched him walk around his car once more. She tugged her coat more closely around her. "Drive safe."

He sketched a wave and drove away.

She let out a long breath and slowly turned on her heel to face the house. Mason had moved from the couch and was waiting with the front door open. He was barefoot, wearing his cast-altered jeans and a short-sleeved gray T-shirt, and if he was bothered by the definite chill in the November air, he didn't show it.

And just looking at him made something inside her stomach dip and sway.

A part of her wished that would go away.

A larger part of her wished that the sensation would never end.

And wasn't that a fine thing?

Steeling herself, she marched up the walk. "This is your fault," she told him as she stomped past him. She peeled out of her coat and tossed it on a chair. "That was a perfectly nice guy. One I wouldn't have even gone out with if you hadn't driven me to it." Reaching around him, she shut the door with perhaps a little more force than she'd intended.

"If he's such a nice guy, why are you pissed off?"

"Because I don't *want* a nice guy!" Her voice rose. "Foolish me, I just want *you*." Annoyed with herself for admitting it just as much as she was annoyed with him for…well…everything, she kicked off her pumps. They went sailing across the living room, and Plato launched off the couch, catching one of them in his mouth. He brought it back to Courtney, dropping it at her feet. Courtney barely noticed. She hadn't taken her eyes off of Mason. "You went out and bought those darned condoms, but if we end up using any, you're going to hate yourself. And as much as I want you, I don't want to be one more reason for you to do that. Not when it seems you already have enough to beat yourself up over."

He looked pained. "You deserve more than I can give you."

Her annoyance suddenly wavered, which was not a good thing. Because in its place something far more dangerous began taking root. The same thing that had been trying to take root for weeks. The kind of thing that made her forget all the good, logical reasons why his staying with her *was* temporary.

"I'm an adult," she said with as much starch as she could maintain. "And as I have tried to make plain before, I get to decide for myself what I deserve. What I want." She stepped closer, deliberately invading his space. "Or have you forgotten that I am a grown woman?"

The pale green of his eyes seemed to sharpen. "Not

likely. And be careful how hard you poke that stick, Courtney. You might get more than you bargained for."

The fact that she could goad him at all sent sharp-edged excitement skittering through her. She took another step closer. The toes of her bare feet brushed his. "If you weren't concerned about that, why concern yourself with being *prepared?* Why take that little trip to the drugstore?"

"Because I'm a practical man," he said flatly. "And I'm used to covering all the bases. The fact is, I can't be around you for long without wanting to make love to you. Doesn't matter that common sense tells me we're better off not going there."

It was hardly a romantic response.

But it was honest.

And she knew deep in her heart that she'd rather have Mason's honesty than pretty romance from someone else any day of the week.

She tilted her head back, looking up at him. She moistened her lips, but her mouth still felt dry. "Do you want to make love to me now?"

His jaw flexed. If she moved her head an inch, she'd be able to brush her lips against it.

"Don't ask stupid questions."

She inhaled carefully, ruthlessly containing her leaping nerves. "*Will* you make love to me?" She waited a beat. "Now?"

"Courtney—" His hands lifted, then clenched into fists, not touching her. "You're killing me."

"*Will* you?"

"Somebody should have taught you when you were a kid not to play with fire." And then he muttered an oath and pulled her to him.

His mouth covered hers and her senses leapt. She

pressed closer. Her arm knocked into his crutch and it clattered against the wall behind them. His stance wavered and he tore his mouth from hers, swearing again. "This is an accident waiting to happen."

She handed him his crutch again and leaned up to brush her lips over his. "Only while we're standing."

And then she went back down on her bare heels and took a few steps away. She gave him a steady look, even though there was not a single cell inside of her that felt steady. "I know how to solve that." Without giving herself a chance to think about the wisdom of what she was doing, she turned and headed down the hallway.

After a breathless moment, she finally heard the distinct sound of him following.

The relief she felt was nearly crippling. But she went blindly into her bedroom and hadn't even had a chance to pull back the quilt on her bed, when he came in the room. He didn't stop until he stood behind her.

His crutches dropped to the floor, and she started to turn, but his hands closed over her shoulders, staying her. Shivers danced down her spine when he brushed her hair over her shoulder and kissed the back of her neck.

He slid one arm around her waist, his long fingers splaying flat against her belly.

Breathing normally suddenly became a challenge. Because she couldn't help herself, her hand closed over his as if she were afraid he'd let go of her before she was ready.

If she ever was ready.

"You're better at balancing on one foot than I thought."

He made a faint sound. His mouth moved from the nape of her neck along her shoulder, left bare by the boatneck of her dress. "Nearly six weeks of practice."

She didn't want to think about how long it had been. She threaded her fingers through his at her waist and turned within the circle of his arm.

Her breasts brushed against his hard chest, and his body heat seemed to singe through the fabric between them. She wasn't sure if it was her pounding heart or his that vibrated between them. Without thought, her hands moved to his arms. Up over his shoulders to his neck. Her fingers slipped through the unruly length of his dark hair, tugging his head toward hers. *Kiss me.* The demand swirled through her mind, and whether he read her thoughts or understood the urgency behind her grasping hands, his mouth covered hers.

His hands clasped her hips, and he dragged her into him.

And the world whirled.

As if no time had passed at all since that other time when he'd turned her inside out.

One tiny part of her mind scrambled toward sensibility. Toward reason. As much as she wanted him, she couldn't lose herself to him again.

Not completely.

The first time had been difficult enough to recover from. Now...

"Wait." She tore her mouth away from his. Her lips tingled and her voice was raw. Focus on something practical, she thought with near desperation. Focus, and remember that this is only about sex. "The condoms. Are they in your room?"

His hand moved away from her. And then like a magician pulling a coin from out of thin air, he held a square little packet between his fingers. He'd had it in his pocket.

He tossed it on the nightstand, where it landed next to

the base of the lamp that she'd left lit, and put his hands on her again. "What are you wearing under this dress?"

Her brain felt like it was operating in gelatin. "What?"

His lips curved faintly. "Under the dress," he murmured again. He pressed his mouth to her shoulder, and she felt the zipper at the back of her dress suddenly loosen under his nimble fingers. With no effort at all, he nudged the wide collar off her shoulders and down her arms. With no other impediment, the narrow black sheath slipped to the floor at her feet, leaving her clad only in her panties, a strapless bra and the pink jewel in her navel.

"Pink," he murmured. "I keep thinking about you in pink."

She shivered again. For every moment when she felt in control, two more came on its heels when she felt it slipping out of her grasp. She twisted in his arms and stepped out of the dress, kicking it aside. Then she put her hands on the hem of his shirt and dragged it upward. "Off," she said huskily when he tried to stop her—as she'd known he would. "Or you're not going to see anything beneath the pink panties and bra." She met his gaze. "I've seen the scars, remember?"

His eyes narrowed a little. "You've seen everything. More than once," he corrected, "since you won't let a man take a shower in peace. A distinct inequity, if you ask me." Between his dark lashes, his pale eyes seemed to gleam. Then quick as a flash, his hand went behind her, and she felt the clasp of her bra come loose.

Her nipples pulled together even more tightly.

Her chin lifted. She let the bra fall away and was gratified by the slight glazing that seemed to come over his eyes. "When you get your cast off, you can shower in peace all you want," she purred.

Of course, at that point, he wouldn't need her at all.

She kept pulling on the shirt, and finally, he lifted his arms and yanked it off his head. His balance wavered a little, and her arms shot around him.

The contact was blistering and she gasped. Her fingertips curled into the warm, satiny skin stretching up his spine. She only realized that they'd dipped lower, sliding beneath the waist of his jeans, when he gave a laughing curse and grabbed her arms, pushing her gently until her legs hit the mattress.

She tumbled backward, and then he stood over her, balanced again on his good leg. His eyes ran over her like a physical caress that left her quaking.

And just that easily, she didn't care about maintaining the upper hand. Couldn't even remember why it had seemed important.

She lifted her arms toward him and the bed dipped under his weight as he joined her. His hands slid around her back, rolling her toward him even as his mouth found hers again. "I don't want to crush you," he said against her lips.

"You won't." She pushed him even further until his shoulders were flat against the quilt, and she slid her leg across his hips until she was straddling him. She leaned over his chest, kissing his chin. His temple. His mouth. His hands were flexing against her waist, and she pulled them to her breasts.

He made a low sound in his throat that thrilled her to her core. The denim of his jeans felt rough beneath her, needlessly reminding her that there was so much more to come, and she slid away from him just enough to unfasten his straining fly.

And then, when she succeeded and for some unfathomable reason hesitated, he lifted an eyebrow and smiled faintly. "You gonna stop now?"

Her lips firmed. She'd helped him dress dozens and dozens of times by now.

She grasped the jeans and pulled them—as well as the boxers beneath—down his narrow hips, over cast and leg.

And then there was simply no amount of nurses' training or experience that could lessen the impact of Mason lying on her bed. For her.

Her heart pounded dizzily as her greedy gaze took him—all of him—in.

"Courtney."

"What?" She could barely form the simple word, and he gave that faint smile again.

"Take off your panties." His deep voice whispered over her nerve endings.

She moistened her lips, slipped the scanty bikini off her hips and stepped out of them.

He let out a long, audible breath. And then he held out his hand.

Shaking inside, she took it. He tugged and she mindlessly knelt on the mattress, then settled over him.

His hands caught her hips, pressing her harder against him, and a vague portion of her mind feared she'd actually begun purring. And then his hands slid up her spine, urging her torso toward him, and his mouth caught one breast, then the other.

She could have wept for the perfection in his touch. Almost of their own accord, her hips moved against his, maddening them both with the slide of her against him.

And then, despite his weighty, cumbersome cast, despite her own not inconsiderable height, he lifted her just enough to sink to the very depths of her.

She cried out and he went abruptly still. "Did I hurt you?"

Foolish tears were burning at the backs of her eyes. She shook her head, leaning against him to find his mouth. "No," she promised. She slowly rocked against him. He would never hurt her.

Not making love.

When he left, then she'd be hurt.

And even knowing that couldn't stop them now.

Not when he filled her so deeply, so completely. Not when she couldn't tell where his hard flesh stopped and her soft flesh began. And not when his hands tightened on her, urging himself deeper. And not when she felt him growing impossibly thicker, harder, and not when she felt herself flying into a million bits of ecstasy while he groaned her name and flew with her.

It was only later...much later...when she could draw normal breath again, when she could manage to unlock their fused hips and slip off of him, that they both recognized one important thing.

The condom was still sitting untouched on the nightstand.

Silently calling himself every vile name he could think of, Mason looked at the packet. He—ever prepared, ever safe—had forgotten the damn thing, even when it was sitting within arm's reach.

Courtney's long, curvaceously lithe body beside him suddenly moved. She pushed her hand through her tousled hair. Her amber gaze skittered over him, then away. "I suppose you think I did this deliberately."

"I wasn't thinking anything of the sort." His voice was flat with blame. Self-blame.

Her lovely throat worked. She scooted off the bed

and disappeared into her walk-in closet. When she came out, she had a thin black robe wrapped tightly around her that did nothing to help disguise the mind-boggling curves beneath. "Well, whatever you're thinking, you don't have to worry. It's totally the wrong time of month for me to conceive."

His jaw felt tight. "Wouldn't want anything to get in the way of 37892?" He rolled over to the side of the bed and managed to scoop up his boxers and work them on but not without some struggle. "Damn cast." He had two more weeks before they'd even entertain the idea of removing it, and he was going to be out of his tree by then.

She was chewing her lip. Her cheeks were pale. "Mason—"

He lifted his hand. "Don't. This is my fault. I knew better, and I still let myself get carried away."

Color suddenly filled her drawn face. "You think you're the only one responsible? Maybe it escaped your attention, Mason, but I started it."

He gave a bark of humorless laughter. "Believe me, honey. I noticed." He'd noticed so damn well that he hadn't thought of another single thing, least of all protecting her. Whether she wanted to be protected or not.

A pain set up residence between his eyes.

If he'd taken his chances with Connecticut and the doctors and the reporters there, all of this could have been avoided.

Courtney wouldn't have had the funds to invest in good ol' 37892 yet...and maybe she would have changed her mind with more time to think about it. She might have dated Dr. Feelgood on her own, and maybe she'd be looking at the whole white-picket-fence deal with him that she claimed she didn't want.

And they wouldn't have ended up burning the sheets again, only this time with the additional wrinkle of his failure to exercise even a semblance of caution.

"I don't care what the timing is," he said. "Good or bad. If you're pregnant, then—"

"I won't be," she interrupted emphatically. "So there's no point in even discuss—"

"Then I'll do what's right," he finished.

Her eyes widened. "And in your mind, that would be…what?"

"It won't involve me abandoning you. Pretending I'm not the father. No kid of mine will grow up not knowing where he comes from, the way I did."

"And that's all this theoretical child would be to you? A responsibility." It wasn't quite a question.

The nape of his neck felt itchy. "A child *is* a responsibility. That's what I've been telling you ever since I learned about your baby plan."

She pressed her lips together for a long moment. The high color faded from her face. The storm in her amber eyes calmed. "Well. I can assure you that your responsible nature won't be called into play," she said coolly. "The timing's wrong." The corners of her lips lifted, but there was no humor in her smile, either. "And that's something that I have been paying close attention to. Getting ready for number 37892, after all."

Then she turned and walked through the door to her bathroom, shutting it behind her.

She didn't come out.

Mason knew that she wouldn't. Not until she was sure he'd left her room.

He retrieved the crutches from the floor, as well as his jeans, which had fallen on top of them, and levered to his feet. At the bedroom doorway, he looked back.

The bathroom door was still closed. Her quilt-covered bed was tousled.

Something inside his chest ached, and he rubbed his hand against it.

Then, with a sigh, he left Courtney's bedroom and went into his own.

Plato stood in the hallway, looking in at him. Then the dog turned and padded into Courtney's room.

He didn't blame the dog.

If he didn't have to endure his own company, he wouldn't, either.

Chapter Eleven

"How's the leg coming?"

Mason sat on a chair on Courtney's back deck, watching Plato romp around in the snow that had fallen overnight.

She'd gone to church that morning. Probably to pray that their folly during the middle of the night wouldn't result in a pregnancy that would come with more complications than she wanted.

Namely...*him.*

"Mase?"

He focused on Cole's voice, coming from the cell phone he held to his ear. "Bad connection," he lied. "Leg's doing fine. Gonna be out of the cast in a few weeks." He wasn't going to entertain the notion that his leg wouldn't be ready, even if Courtney had cautioned that it might not be.

"Then you'll be ready to go back active after Thanksgiving," Cole was saying, and at the word *active,* Mason tuned in more carefully.

"Yeah. If not before." The cast was supposed to come off a few days before the holiday. "I could be back in Connecticut by then." He should have felt more enthusiasm at the prospect. His inactivity over the past weeks had driven him buggy. Not even going over some case files with Axel had been enough to alleviate that.

"No need to rush," Cole said. "I'll be in Wyoming for the holiday, anyway." Mason could hear a faint smile in his boss's voice. "My daughter-in-law invited me. Expect it'll drive Brody nuts, but driving him nuts is one of my remaining pleasures in life."

Mason still found it hard to believe that his boss had a son, even one he was estranged from more often than not.

But it just went to prove that—for men like them—families and work weren't a combination destined for success.

"We'll talk when I'm there," Cole finished. "And I can see for myself that you're not trying to get back before you're ready."

Mason's molars ground together. Yeah, he'd had a rocky start to his recovery. But since that first week here with Courtney, he'd been a model—okay, *nearly* model—patient.

At least he hadn't managed to crack his casts after that first episode.

The rest of the time, he'd alternated between grumpy and grumpier. It was still astonishing that she'd tolerated as much as she had.

"Fine," he told Cole. "Thanksgiving. But after that I'm back to work. Even if I have to ride a desk for a few days, I'm back to work."

Cole snorted. "Don't blow that smoke around, Mase. I know you've been meeting regularly with Ax."

He shifted in his chair. Plato was sniffing around the back edge of the property like he'd found something interesting. "All I did was work up a few profiles for some cases."

"And you haven't done any profiling since the bombing," Cole countered. "You had me put you in security, despite everything I said at the time. If I'd known all it would take to get you back to where your real talents lie was to break your arms and legs, I'd have done it years ago."

Mason politely told his boss what he could do with his comment. Cole responded with a rusty laugh before he hung up.

Mason shoved the phone in the pocket of the jacket that Axel had loaned him. It was too tight in the shoulders, but it was serviceable enough. He whistled to Plato, but the dog was still digging around in the corner of the yard, showing no signs of stopping.

He pushed to his feet and swung down the steps. He took the crutches only because he didn't want to have to put up with the stink of a wet cast on top of the inconvenience of the thing in the first place. "Plato, whatcha hunting, eh?" He reached the dog, and balancing on one crutch and holding his cast aloft over the snow, he leaned over and nudged the dog's big head aside.

A wet, bedraggled kitten was lying still in the snow.

Mason grimaced. "You had to find a dead kitten?"

Plato whined and pawed at the snow around the kitten. Afraid the dog would decide to use it as a toy, he leaned over and scooped it up in his hand.

The body was still warm. Still alive.

He found himself chuckling and realized his laugh sounded just as rusty as Cole's laughter had. He rubbed his thumb over the minuscule head, and the kitten's skinny, wet tail curled. The kitten couldn't have been more than a few weeks old. Mason tucked the little animal inside his shirt and looked at Plato. "Any more?"

But the dog had turned to face the house again. He wagged his tail and gave a soft bark.

"Good dog." Mason started for the house, and the dog trotted ahead of him. Inside, he shrugged out of his borrowed jacket and left the crutches propped against the table. He fished the kitten out from inside his shirt.

His eyes, or hers—Mason couldn't tell at this point—were open. He grabbed a clean dish towel and wrapped it around the cat. Then, even though he wasn't supposed to put weight on his cast, he limped over to the refrigerator without his crutches and poured a small amount of milk in a coffee mug.

With the cat in one hand and the milk in the other, he sat down at the kitchen table, where he'd earlier left the newspaper and his reading glasses. He slipped on the glasses and peered more closely at the cat, rubbing it with the towel until the short gray fur dried and stuck out at all angles and he could hear the faint rumble of a small purr. Then he dipped his finger in the milk and rubbed it over the kitten's tiny snout. "Come on, tiger," he murmured. "Show a little life so I've got a reason to find your mama." And the other kittens that had to be around, since he didn't think any cat could ever have just one kitten in a litter.

Watching silently from the back doorway, Courtney pressed her hand to her stomach. Plato lifted his head and noisily flopped his tail, apparently breaking Mason's intense concentration on the kitten, so small it was easily eclipsed by his big hand.

He looked up at Courtney over the rims of his narrow glasses, and her stomach took its usual free-falling tumble.

"I didn't hear you come in."

Spurred into motion by his voice, she finished closing the door behind her. "I figured." She unwound the plaid scarf she'd tossed around the shoulders of her coat and folded it over the back of the chair next to Mason.

Since she'd locked herself in her bathroom the night before—well, it had been the wee hours of the morning, really—she hadn't spoken two words to him.

Like the coward that she was, while he'd been in the bathroom, she'd left him only a written note telling him that she'd gone to church before she'd snuck out.

She'd heard the shower running, but since he hadn't left out the duct tape for her to see, she'd taken her cue that he wasn't interested in performing their usual shower ritual anymore.

Considering everything, she couldn't really blame him.

Now, she deliberately pushed aside the tangle of emotions inside her and finished pulling off her coat as she eyed Mason and the tiny kitten. "I'm doubting that you've been to a pet store at this hour on a Sunday morning. So, what gives?"

"Plato found him. Or her." His attention was firmly back on the little kitten as he coaxed it to lick another drop of milk off the tip of his finger. "Buried in the snow by the back fence."

Courtney looked through the window. There was a house under construction on the other side of the back fence, but it wasn't occupied. Her neighbors to the right had a cat, but she knew for a fact that she was at least twelve years old. Hardly a likely candidate for whelping a litter of kittens. And the couple that lived on the left had only two little dogs. "No sign of more kittens?"

He shook his head. "Didn't look. I went off Plato's lead."

"I doubt he'd lead you astray," she said. "And I'm glad to hear you weren't tramping around in the snow. I'll check in the corners of the garage after I change clothes." But it was hard to tear her eyes away from Mason.

She'd known he got along well with Plato. But then everyone did. Even self-proclaimed non-dog-lovers. But she hadn't given any thought to whether or not Mason was, in general, an animal person.

Despite the hours and days she'd spent in his company, living under the same roof, struggling not to get too sucked in to the alluring aura of domesticity, she realized yet again just how much she *didn't* know about him.

Unfortunately, when she witnessed something new— like now—it didn't do anything to lessen his appeal.

How could she ever imagine the sight of his big body, hunched over such a tiny little creature, would make something inside her ache in a way that had nothing to do with passion?

Her throat felt tight. She quickly escaped to her room to change out of the dress she'd worn to church and into a pair of jeans and a thick sweater. In the bathroom, she pulled her hair back in her usual ponytail and stared at herself in the mirror. "Nothing has changed," she told her reflection.

Unfortunately, the woman staring back at her with the pitying expression told her that everything had changed. It had been changing since the moment Mason had rolled into her house, and that slow, downhill slide had gone into free fall when he'd given her that incredibly beautiful baby rattle.

She truly believed that she couldn't possibly have conceived a child last night. She hadn't exaggerated. The timing was wrong.

"But you wish the timing was right," she whispered to her reflection. Not because she wanted a baby, period.

But because, from the moment she'd realized they'd both forgotten to use that darn condom, it had become startlingly clear that the baby she wanted was *his*.

Only his.

Nothing had changed. Mason was still going to leave.

And everything had changed.

The woman in her mirror gave her a sad smile, and she turned away.

He was still in the kitchen with the kitten. Only now, Plato had managed to perch his big, oversized body on a kitchen chair next to Mason and was resting his head on the table, his nose only inches away from the minuscule feline.

Afraid the burning behind her eyes would get out of control, she hurried past both the males in her household and went outside.

The cold was mercifully bracing as she tramped around the perimeter of her yard, pushing through the small drifts of snow for any sign of more kittens, even though she didn't expect to find any. Plato would have discovered them first, if there were any. So after her yard was bordered by her footprints, as well as Plato's, she gave up, went into the garage and used a flashlight to search out all the shadowy corners.

Again, no kittens. No mama cat.

The cold air was penetrating her sweater, and she

went back inside, rubbing her hands together as she nudged the door closed with her hip.

"Should have worn a coat," Mason said.

She shrugged. "When I was a kid, I used to run around in the wintertime wearing shorts. Drove my folks nuts." She peered around his shoulder at the kitten that was now curled into a ball, seemingly content in its bed of bright red kitchen towel. "We could take it to Evan. My cousin's husband? He's the vet around here."

"Dump it off on him?" Mason looked at her over the rim of his glasses, a frown on his face.

No." She shook her head. "I mean to have him—her—whatever it is—looked over."

"He can't have been in the snow for long," Mason said. "I don't think he would have survived."

Courtney couldn't disagree with that. She reached past Mason to run her finger gently over the sleeping kitten's fur. "Do you have pets?"

"I had a cat once." His expression closed, and he nudged Plato off the chair. "Never seen a dog that big sit on a chair like that."

"He knew lots of tricks already when I adopted him. A good friend of mine had raised him from a pup. When she died, I took him in."

He gave her a quick look. "What happened?"

"To Margaret, you mean?" She crossed her arms and leaned against the counter. "Pancreatic cancer." She looked at him. "She was one of my instructors from nursing school in Cheyenne. She was a foster mother, too. For the human variety, not just the canine. What happened to the cat you had?"

His brows yanked together. "My ex-wife took her."

The ex-wife again.

Courtney studied her thumbnail. "How long were you married?"

"What is this? Twenty questions again?"

"Just being inquisitive." She smiled coolly. "Do you still love her? Is that why you don't want to talk about it?"

He sighed noisily. "Do *you* like talking about your failures?"

He had a point. "Sorry." She nodded toward the kitten. "So, do you want Evan to look the kitten over?"

He grimaced. "Yeah. And no. I'm not still in love with Greta."

There should be no earthly reason for her to be relieved hearing it. But she was. Mostly because she knew Mason wasn't lying. If he didn't want to tell someone the truth, he simply didn't say anything at all.

That was something that she did know about him.

"Well, Sunday dinner is at my uncle Dan's today. You can bring the kitten. I'm sure Leandra and Evan will be there as usual."

"Dinner," he nearly barked. "I thought you meant taking the cat to his office or something. *You* can take the cat."

"You're the one who rescued it." She tilted her head slightly. "What is so horrifying to you about attending a simple dinner? You've been over to my folks'. What's so different about this?"

"It's Sunday dinner! That stuff's for family."

"That stuff is for whoever is welcomed," she corrected him mildly. "And when I saw my aunt and uncle at church this morning, they specifically mentioned they hoped you'd come."

His eyes narrowed slightly. "You mean they hope that

you go since you've been giving the whole Sunday deal a miss since I got here."

She shrugged. "Don't take it personally. Sunday afternoons are also when I have a chance to play catch-up around here. Laundry and housecleaning don't happen on their own. Everyone in my family is used to my hits and misses."

He didn't look entirely convinced. "Fine. Just so the cat can get looked over."

She hid a smile. "We'll need to leave in an hour or so."

He nodded grumpily and picked up the nearly empty mug he'd been finger-dipping from, and with one long arm, reached over to set it in the sink. Then he grabbed his crutches, pulled to his feet and headed out of the room.

But before he made it, he turned back around to scoop the kitten out of the towel and tuck it neatly inside his shirt pocket. "Body warmth," he muttered.

Then he crutched out of the kitchen.

Courtney looked down at Plato. The dog was staring after Mason, his dark brown eyes soft.

She rubbed his head between his ears. "I know," she murmured. "I love him, too."

Then she went through the arch to the dining room, stopping next to the computer on its narrow desk. She slowly sat down and moved the mouse.

The screen saver cleared.

Number 37892 came into view.

She stared at the computer screen for a moment. And then with the flick of a finger, she turned off the computer.

"She looks fine to me," Evan said later that afternoon after he'd gone to his truck to get the vet bag that went

everywhere with him. He held up the kitten in his hand
and tickled her little belly, which had grown round with
all the milk she'd consumed. "A little too young to be
weaned, but Mason's obviously got that covered."

He looked over at where Courtney and Mason were
sitting, in the kitchen of her aunt and uncle's house, surrounded by several children who were all anxious to see
the new kitten.

Everyone else who'd come to dinner was in the family
room, loudly watching a football game. Loud, because
half the room was rooting for one team and half for the
other.

"It is strange that the mother cat wasn't nearby." Evan
handed the kitten to Courtney. "She might have gotten
trapped in a garage or something."

"I checked with both of my neighbors before we got
here," she said. She cradled the cat so that Shelby and
Chloe—the two oldest children—could stroke its fur.
"Be gentle," she reminded them and looked back at
Evan. "They haven't seen a stray cat around at all, ei-
ther."

Evan sighed a little. "Well, if she doesn't turn up in
the next day or so…" He shook his head, his gaze going
to the children.

"Wouldn't there be other kittens?" Mason asked.

Evan lifted his shoulder. "Not necessarily, if the
mother was particularly young herself. A first litter.
Without being able to examine the cat, it's all specula-
tion." He smiled and rose from the table, scooping up
his three-year-old son, Lucas, as he did. The boy chor-
tled and reached for the kitten, then smiled widely when
the kitten snatched its tail out of his fingers. "Looks to
me like you've got yourselves another family member,"
Evan commented. "Come on, Luke." He hefted his son

up to his face. "Let's find your mom and Katie, and you can play with the kitties at home."

"Katie don't play," Lucas complained.

"Katie is one year old," Evan reminded him with a patient grin. "Soon enough, there will come a time when you'll wish you could get her to stop playing with you. I know, 'cause I had a little sister, too."

"Uh-huh," Lucas said emphatically. He peered over his father's shoulder as they left the kitchen, his little hand opening and closing in a wave.

"What are you gonna name her, Auntie Court?" Chloe and her soon-to-be cousin, Shelby, leaned shoulder to shoulder against the table.

"She's Mason's cat." Courtney ignored the sidelong look she earned from the man at that. "It's up to him."

"She's not my cat," he said.

"You found her."

"Plato found her. Guess that makes her Plato's."

The girls giggled wildly at that particular notion.

Courtney smiled, too, even though she knew that Mason wasn't entirely joking.

"Well." She handed the nameless kitten to him and rose. "I'm going to tell everyone goodbye so we can head out. Uncle Matt said he smells more snow coming, and I want to get home before it hits."

Mason had to either take the kitten or let her fall onto the table. The two little girls—one belonging to Ryan and one to Beck, the guy engaged to marry Lucy—had been stuck like glue to him and Courtney since they'd produced the kitten from the basket they'd brought her in.

"Plato can't name her," Shelby said seriously. "He's a *dog*."

Chloe giggled. "He would only name her *woof*."

"Woof the cat." Despite himself, Mason grinned. "Think I like it."

Chloe beamed at him. "Are you gonna marry Auntie Court?"

His grin suddenly felt strangled. "What?"

"No," Courtney said, sailing back into the kitchen. She swept her niece up in her arms from behind and kissed the back of Chloe's neck, making her laugh even harder, before setting her back on her feet. "Nobody is marrying Auntie Court." She treated Shelby to the same upswing and kiss. "Mr. Hyde's just a friend, remember?"

Chloe wrinkled her nose and eyed Mason. She touched his cast with gingerly fingertips. "Does your leg hurt?"

"Not anymore."

"Does your face hurt?" Shelby stared up at him, innocence personified.

He saw the way Courtney caught her lip in her teeth as her startled gaze turned toward him. "Not anymore."

"How'd you get it hurt?"

The kitten was curled on his arm, purring. He could feel its faint vibration, even though it was too soft to hear. "My leg or my face?"

"Your face," Shelby replied immediately. "Lucy already told me you got your leg broke from a truck. You're not supposed to get in front of trucks that are moving."

"You're right about that," he agreed ruefully.

Courtney reached for his crutches, propped out of the way near the door, and held them out to him. "We should get going."

Strangely enough, he ignored the bailout.

Shelby was still watching him curiously. There was

no fear in her face. No horror. Just a child's simple curiosity.

"I got hit with a lot of broken glass," he told her with huge understatement. "It was a long time ago in another accident."

Chloe's face crunched up even more. "My dad broke a glass in our kitchen and he got a piece stuck in his toe. He was *mad,*" she added. "But my mom picked it out and put a bandage on it. You must have had a *lot* of bandages."

He nodded. "Yup. I did."

Evidently satisfied, Shelby touched his cast. "Can we sign your cast? Jenny Tanner's brother at school had a cast on his arm, and everyone in his class signed their name on it."

Chloe nodded. "But you don't have any on yours. Can we?"

"Girls—" Courtney started.

"You'd have to find a pen." Mason cut her off. Her amber eyes widened a little. Then they turned all soft and dangerous again, and he wished he would have just taken the crutches and bailed like she'd obviously expected.

The girls ran out of the kitchen.

"Glass?" Courtney asked.

"And metal and whatever else was part of the building that exploded," he said in a low tone that wouldn't carry.

She held the crutches against her. "What happened?"

"I didn't stop a psychotic bomber quick enough. He liked targeting Canadian day care centers."

She looked horrified. "Did you catch him?"

"Once I'd gotten all of the kids and staff out of the building. Yeah." He waited a beat. "I killed him before the bomb blew." He'd known he hadn't enough time left to get out of the building after making sure everyone else was away, but he'd been damn certain that the other guy wouldn't, either.

Her lips pressed together. "I think I'm glad," she said after a moment.

"It was just a job."

The corners of her lips turned upward. "Right."

The girls came running back into the kitchen, both bearing black markers. And then they were bent over his cast for long enough that he stopped wondering what Courtney was really thinking to worry about just what the little girls *were* writing.

Turned out that six- and seven-year-old girls didn't just sign their names. They had to draw flowers and hearts around them, too.

"Thanks," he said when they were finally finished.

Courtney wasn't even trying to hide her smile.

"You sign it, too," Chloe demanded, holding the pen up to her.

Without looking at him, Courtney leaned over the cast, near his ankle, and wrote. He tried to see what it said, but the angle was impossible.

By then, Mallory had come into the kitchen. And she, too, needed to sign the cast.

And then Mason found himself sitting there while everyone in the whole damn house signed the cast.

By the time they were done, and he and Courtney were finally making an escape—and it *did* feel like an escape—there was writing over ninety percent of the thing, and Courtney was smiling like the cat who'd stolen the cream.

She waited while he pulled himself into her backseat, as usual with his leg stretched across the seat, then handed him his crutches as well as the basket containing Woof. "That wasn't so terrible, was it?"

He eyed the doodles and the names and the comments that littered his cast. "I thought you planned to get home before the snow started," he said.

Her smile didn't dim. She looked up at the sky, where snowflakes had begun drifting down. "Oh, well. Plans change. We'll get home, anyway." Then she closed the car door and went around to the driver's side.

Mason looked down at the kitten he held.

If he could have, he'd have blamed the hollow ache inside him on cat claws.

But the kitten just lay there curled against his chest, silently purring.

Chapter Twelve

"**S**o you're positive?" Mason eyed Courtney's face closely.

If she lied, he'd know it. He'd see it in her eyes.

"Yes," she assured. "I'm positively *not* pregnant." It was six days since the night they'd made love. She set the plate containing a meat loaf sandwich in front of him and turned back to the sink. "I told you the timing was wrong, and turns out, I was right."

He eyed her back. She was wearing a long-sleeved black running top and matching body-skimming running pants. Her hair was tied back in a ponytail, and she had a red winter scarf wrapped around her neck.

He could see that she was telling the truth.

But he couldn't tell if she was relieved or not.

"Then nothing can get in the way of number 37892 anymore," he said.

"Right." Her voice was chipper. She dried her hands

on a towel and picked up the gloves that she'd left sitting on the counter. "I'll be back in plenty of time to drive you to the hospital. Do you need anything else before I go?"

He needed plenty.

But he wasn't going to ask and she knew it.

He shook his head. "Thanks for the sandwich."

She just smiled and headed for the door, stopping only long enough to pet Plato where he was lying by the door, his big body curled protectively around tiny little Woof.

And then she was pulling on the gloves and slipping out the back door. Through the window, Mason could see her begin the routine of stretches she religiously performed before she went on her runs. Didn't matter that there was still a thin layer of snow on the ground or that the air was cold enough to send rings around her head when she breathed.

His appetite gone, Mason pushed aside the plate and limped into the dining room. He was having his leg x-rayed that afternoon to see if his cast would be coming off the following week as scheduled or if he would only be graduating to a smaller, more walking-friendly cast.

Either way, there would be no more reason for him to stay with Courtney. He could head back to his anemic apartment and get back to work.

That fact should have filled him with relief.

He made a face, sat down at her computer and turned it on, then sent an email to Cole using a convoluted path of servers.

And then he just sat there in front of the computer, looking at nothing in particular.

He needed to remember that he and Courtney had dodged a bullet.

No baby.

Not one of his, at any rate.

Courtney would be gone for at least an hour on her run, so he pushed away from the computer desk and half jumped, half limped down the hall to his bedroom. He'd already read all of the books he'd brought with him. And he'd read all of the ones on Courtney's bookshelf that he didn't already have.

Turned out they had similar tastes.

He looked around the bedroom, trying to envision it as a baby's nursery.

The vision came much too quickly, and he blamed it on the fact that he'd seen Courtney's choices for furniture and such on the damn computer.

When his cell phone rang, he nearly jumped out of his skin. Shaking his head at himself, he pulled it out of his pocket. "Hyde."

"Clay," Axel said with laughter in his voice. "You busy?"

Making himself crazy? Definitely. "Not at the moment."

"Courtney out?"

His eyes narrowed. "Why do I have the feeling that you already know?"

"Because we just saw her running past us. Be there in a sec." The line went dead.

Mason exhaled and headed out to the living room just in time to see Axel's truck pulling into the driveway.

The "we" part was quickly explained when he saw Tristan Clay, Axel's uncle, climb out of the truck, too.

Mason sat down in one of the chairs and waited. As he'd expected, Axel didn't stand on ceremony. He just walked right on in. "Hey."

Mason looked from the younger man to the older. "What's going on?"

Tristan smiled faintly and held up the thin file folder that he was carrying. "Axel showed me these profiles you've worked up."

Mason eyed Axel. "Helped work up," he corrected. "And you've got a big mouth." Cole had known about Mason's help pulling together a few profiles on some cases Axel had on his plate. And now Tristan did, too.

"I want you to come and work for me," Tristan said.

Mason raised his brows. "I already work for HW."

Tristan nodded once. "On Cole's side of the operation. All international." He sat on the arm of the couch and tapped the file against his thigh. "We've got needs on the domestic side, too. One in particular that I believe you can fill."

"Cole know you're poaching on his side of the fence?"

The other man smiled, looking unperturbed. "I'm not worried about Cole."

Neither was Mason when it came right down to it. "I got out of profiling a long time ago."

"After the Canadian day care incident." Tristan nodded. "I know."

Mason figured that Tristan probably knew what had followed, as well, since he was as close to being the number two man in the agency as it was possible to get. What he didn't know was how much his nephew Axel knew about his past.

Despite working together on numerous cases, Mason had never discussed it with him.

"But these—" Tristan tapped the file folder again "—clearly prove that you haven't lost the gift. There has already been some action on two of the cases where the feds were previously stuck against a brick wall." He smiled faintly. "'Course, you'd be working mostly out of Weaver, which—as you've probably discovered—doesn't offer quite the conveniences as Cole's shop does."

Mason was shaking his head before Tristan even stopped talking. "No. I'm not moving to Weaver."

"You'd be well compensated."

It wasn't the money. He was already well compensated for the work he did. If he wanted to, he could retire right now. "Thanks, but no thanks."

"Stubborn. Cole warned me."

Mason almost smiled. "I appreciate the offer. But Weaver's not for me."

"Too bad." Tristan slanted a look at his nephew, then pushed to his feet and went to the door. "I think you'd be a good addition around here. If you change your mind, let me know. I can always put a guy like you to good use." He pulled open the door and stepped outside.

Axel followed him. "Just give it some time to roll around in your head," he advised, hanging back. "No harm. No foul."

"I can't stay here."

"Because of Court?"

Mason grimaced. "What makes you think that?"

Axel gave him a look. "This is Weaver, man. You were kissing in public. Unless you like having water-balloon fights with condoms or something, you're obviously sleeping with her. And besides all that, anyone with decent vision—and mine is perfectly fine—can see the sparks flying in the air when you're with each other."

Mason muttered an oath. He shoved out of the chair and started to pace, but there wasn't a lot of satisfaction in it when he had to hop on one foot to do it. "Nothing's private in this town." Except the fact that they hadn't used a condom at all. Except the fact that he hadn't gotten her pregnant, anyway.

He knew for certain that Courtney wouldn't have shared those details with anyone. And he sure as hell hadn't.

"There are a few things a person can keep a lid on if they try." Axel shrugged. "Tara's pregnant again, and we've managed to keep it quiet for the past month and a half."

Mason stared.

"We wanted to wait until she was further along before we shared it. She had a miscarriage a while back that only we and her OB know about, too."

"She's okay?"

Axel nodded. "Perfect. And as of this week, she's a solid four months along, with no indication that anything'll go wrong."

Mason shoved his hand through his hair. "How do you do it?" Yeah, Axel was younger than he was. He hadn't been with the agency as long. But he'd still seen his share of action. He knew how things could turn bad in the blink of an eye. "Act like you've got a normal life?"

"Because it *is* a normal life," Axel returned.

"Tara knows what you really do." She had to, since Axel had been assigned to protect her when her twin brother, Sloan, had come to the agency for help. "She knows you don't—" he air-quoted "—breed horses."

"I do—" Axel air-quoted "—breed horses. Real horses. But she knows I also work for Tris. It's normal for us, because we make it that way. Because being together is what is important."

"And if you don't come walking in the door some

weekday afternoon at five o'clock because you ended up on the wrong side of a weapon, that's gonna be normal?" Mason shook his head. "I don't believe it."

"Cops get married," Axel returned. "Anyone who's a first responder gets married. They have lives."

"And a damn high divorce rate," he muttered. And statistically speaking, he knew the success of marriages for HW operatives was even rarer.

"Anyone who gets married takes that chance." Axel glanced out the doorway. "Just because Greta couldn't take it doesn't mean Courtney can't."

Mason stiffened. "Who the hell said anything about *that?*"

Axel just shook his head. "Dude. You have got it bad."

"She's too young, anyway. I've got thirteen years on her, for God's sake."

At that, Axel laughed. "Twenty-six years on earth, a hundred and six years in her soul. Tara said something like that once about her. Called her an old soul. Said it's one of the things that makes her such a good nurse. That ability she's got to let people just be who they are. If you haven't noticed that about her by now—" he shook his head "—then maybe I do need my vision checked. As far as I'm concerned, age differences—one way or the other—only become an issue if you make them one."

"She's your cousin. I'd think you'd want to protect her a little more."

"From the likes of you?" Axel rolled his eyes and walked toward the door. "That is one of the most asinine things I've ever heard come out of your mouth." He lifted his hand. "Think about Tristan's offer. Profiling instead of direct security? Would get you out of the way of flying objects more often. It's not quite a banker's nine-to-five, but in our business it's as close as you're ever likely to get."

Mason didn't reply.

He watched Axel stride to his truck, where his uncle was waiting, and drive away.

He slowly pushed the door closed.

Plato and his new sidekick had padded into the living room. Even as Mason watched, the dog picked the kitten up in his mouth and set her on the couch. Then he jumped up beside her, circled a few times and settled down with a harrumphing sigh.

"Talk about the odd couple."

Plato just wagged his tail a few times. If the dog understood, or agreed, it was pretty obvious that he didn't care.

"Healing nicely." Dr. Jackman was peering at the computerized X-ray of Mason's leg. He tapped the end of his pen against the screen. "There. And there." He tapped again. "And there. Those are the sites of the fractures." He tapped once again. "That's where the first pin became infected." He nodded and slid his pen into his lapel pocket as he turned to face Mason. They were sitting in his office at the hospital. "It all looks good." The gray-haired doctor smiled at Courtney. "Nice job, Nurse Clay."

Courtney shook off the praise. "All I did was give him a few meals and make sure he took his meds on time."

She'd done a helluva lot more, Mason figured, but that was none of the orthopedist's business. "Good enough to cut me out of this thing early?"

Courtney suddenly pushed out of her chair. Mason eyed her. She didn't look at him, though. Her eyes were trained solely on the doctor.

"Actually—" Dr. Jackman considered for a moment "—yes. You'll need to follow up with a few weeks of physical therapy to strengthen the muscles again. But yes."

The answer took a moment to sink in. Then Mason leaned forward in his chair. "Seriously." He knocked on the cast. "You're gonna let me out of this place without the fiberglass monster."

Dr. Jackman nodded. "I'll call down and arrange it with my technician."

"I can," Courtney offered abruptly. "I saw Rodney down in Emergency when we got here."

The doctor nodded. He scribbled on Mason's medical chart and handed it to her, then stuck out his hand. "Congratulations, Mr. Hyde. Try to avoid getting in front of moving vehicles for a while."

Mason shook the man's hand, then pushed to his feet. "I will." He grabbed his crutches and followed Courtney out into the corridor.

"Congratulations, indeed," she told him with a whisper of a smile. "In a few more minutes, you'll be a free man again." She walked briskly along the tile corridor. She was already wearing her nurse's getup. The blue scrubs were as unfitted and loose as her running gear had been formfitting, and he found her just as mesmerizing either way. "Now you have something else to celebrate."

Else?

He caught her by the back of her shirt, halting her midstep. "I'm not celebrating the fact that you're not pregnant," he said.

"Shh!" She looked around them. "Keep your voice down, would you please?"

"I will when you stop spouting bologna like that."

She jerked her shoulders, and her shirt slid out of his grasp. "Don't pretend that you're sorry about it." She took off again along the wide hallway.

The hospital wasn't particularly huge.

But Mason knew if he didn't keep up with her, he'd still end up in a maze, because there wasn't a hospital he'd ever been in that hadn't been constructed that way. Not in the United States or elsewhere.

He followed, moving fast on the crutches until he caught up to her. "You're the one who should be celebrating," he said in a low voice. "Now you can have your baby with no complications to mess it up. Your plan can proceed just the way you want it to."

She whirled on her rubber-soled heel so fast he nearly ran into her. "The only thing about any of this that has gone as planned is *you*. You've healed well." She lifted her hand and smiled humorlessly. "So, voilà. Now you can get back to your life. I know that's the only thing that you want." She turned again and strode away, soon turning a corner and disappearing from view.

He hurried after her, his crutches thumping the tile. He caught up with her just as she reached the emergency department.

Which was, for the first time in his experience, full of people. All of the beds were curtained off, and people in scrubs and lab coats were moving quickly around.

Courtney didn't look as surprised as he felt, though. She just continued out into the waiting room, holding open one side of the swinging doors for him. "You'll have to wait out there." She nodded toward the molded plastic chairs. Most of them, too, were full. "I'll see how quickly Rodney can get to you."

He wanted to stop. To tell her…something. But what? Their business was all but complete. She'd made it plain that she was organizing her life exactly the way she'd wanted, and he could get back even earlier than he'd hoped to what he knew.

Work.

His crutches cleared the doorway, and she stepped back, letting the door swing closed.

It nearly hit him on the butt.

Wyatt—the only guy he'd seen her dance with at the Halloween thing other than her brother—was sitting at the reception desk, giving him a sympathetic look.

Mason ignored it and aimed for one of the chairs— the only one that wasn't surrounded by sneezing kids. He sat down and rested the crutches on the empty chair beside him.

He stared at his cast, stretched out in front of him. The black writing all over the blue surface seemed to leap out at him. His finger traced one of the hearts that little Chloe had drawn. He angled his head, but he still couldn't read what Courtney had written around his ankle.

"Looks like you have a lot of family and friends." The old man across from him was looking at Mason's cast, too.

"I don't have any family," Mason returned, hoping the guy would go back to his wheezing and keep his comments to himself. He folded his arms over his chest and closed his eyes.

"Then you got a lot of friends." Obviously, his hint hadn't been received.

Mason sighed. He opened his eyes. "What're you here for?"

"Emphysema," the guy wheezed. "Lifelong smoker." He patted the narrow oxygen tank that was sitting in a wheeled contraption next to him. "Now this is my lifelong friend."

At that moment, Mason was glad he'd never taken up the habit of cigarettes.

"You're not from around here," the guy continued. He was nodding his bald head. "Can't breathe for nothing anymore, but the memory's still good."

"Connecticut," he said.

The guy's thin eyebrows rose. "You're the one staying with the Clay girl, then."

He wasn't even surprised anymore at the well-developed grapevine that Weaver seemed to possess. "Guess I am."

"Heard you're a real live hero."

Mason grimaced. He'd never particularly felt like one. He'd just tried to do what was right. Live up to what he'd been paid to do.

He wasn't getting paid a thing here in Weaver. Not with Courtney. And he damn sure wasn't feeling heroic when it came to her.

He eyed the old man. "Anybody here with you?"

The man coughed into his plaid handkerchief and shook his head. "Ain't got no one. Never seemed to find the time." He coughed some more, then took a drag on his oxygen line. Judging by the attachment at the end, Mason figured he was supposed to have it leading into his nose all the time and not hanging around his neck like some necklace. "Live over in Braden, but gotta come here to Weaver for the fancy doctors."

"Mason?" He looked up when he heard Courtney's voice. She was standing at the double doors again. "You can come on back."

He grabbed his crutches—for the last time, he figured—and stood. He stuck his hand out to the old guy. "Good luck."

The man's lips stretched into a smile. His hand trembled, but his handshake was still firm. "G'luck to you, too, young man." His gaze slanted toward Courtney. "She's a catch. The kind to make time for."

"That she is." He was glad, though, that she was standing far enough away that she was unable to hear them. He swung around on the crutches and headed toward Courtney.

She didn't meet his gaze as she waited for him to pass through. She pointed. "The last bed on the right."

Mason held back. "That guy with the emphysema out there needs attention more than I do."

Her amber gaze slid to him, then away again. "Different issues," she said. "Mr. Martin will be seen as soon as one of the doctors is available. You've already seen Dr. Jackman. Now all you need is for Rodney to remove your cast." She held out her hand toward the far bed. "And clear the exam area again as quickly as possible," she added pointedly.

He headed toward the last bed. She followed him and set his medical chart on the stainless steel counter, then gave the curtain a tug. It swung smoothly into place. "Rodney will be with you in a few minutes."

"Wait a minute. Where are you going?"

She still didn't look at him. "They're so slammed, they asked me to clock in early."

"*They?* Or are you just looking for an excuse to get away from me?" Not that he had any reason to blame her for that.

Her lips twisted a little. "I'm just trying to do my job," she said. "Of all people, you should understand that. Don't worry, though. I talked to Ax. He'll come and get you when you're finished. He said just give him a call when you're done." She ducked out from behind the curtain.

He sat on the edge of the examining table and stared down at his cast. After two months of it, he wanted the thing off so badly he could taste it.

There was also a part of him that wished it had to stay in place.

Because then *he* could have a reason to stay, too.

Courtney managed a friendly smile as she coaxed a feverish little Bethany Jones onto the exam table two beds down from Mason. She could hear the distinctive pitch of the saw that Rodney was using to cut off Mason's cast.

Inside, it felt like *she* was being cut in two.

"What's that noise?" Bethany gave her mom a worried look.

"Someone's getting a cast taken off," Courtney soothed. "Nothing to worry about."

Bethany's mother sat on the table beside her daughter. "Remember when Daddy had a cast on his arm? That's what it sounded like when he got it off, too." She smoothed her daughter's hair back from her face and looked at Courtney. "Will the doctor be very long?"

"Not long." She knew that the on-call doctor had been called in to help with the unexpected load. She took Bethany's vitals and noted in the chart all the information the doctor would need, then tucked the chart in its holder and excused herself.

The sound of the saw stopped.

Which meant Mason's cast was now a thing of the past.

Which meant that his time in Weaver was a thing of the past, too.

She swallowed the knot in her throat. What she wanted to do was find a private room somewhere and cry her heart out.

Instead, she forced herself to wash her hands and did what she was trained to do.

She moved on to the next patient.

It took four hours for the waiting room to get cleared. By then, the time for Courtney's usual shift had already begun. She worked straight through until morning and tried to tell herself that she wasn't really waiting for Mason to try to call her. To talk to her.

Just as she'd arranged, her cousin had driven him home when he'd finished with the cast removal. If Mason hadn't gotten a clue by now, it was because he didn't want to. So really, what was there left to talk about?

She wasn't going to beg the man to stay with her, when he was clearly anxious to leave.

It was snowing lightly when she drove home from the hospital, and the tension inside her had relaxed a little by the time she got there.

The porch light was on. And beyond the plantation shutters in the front window, she could see a warm glow.

As usual, Mason had left the light on for her.

He hadn't left, after all.

She parked in the driveway and nearly ran into the house. Plato and Woof were sleeping on the floor by the door. Her dog lifted his head and stood. He pushed his head into her hand even before she had a chance to set down her car keys and purse.

Her heart sank all over again.

"He's gone, isn't he?"

Plato just stood by her side. His tail didn't wag.

She sucked her lip between her teeth and made herself

walk through the house. When she reached Mason's bedroom, she could only stand in the doorway.

His bed was made with military precision. The stacks of books were gone from the nightstand.

The only thing out of place was an envelope sitting on the dresser.

A part of her—the part that ached because he could so easily walk away—wanted to rip it in two.

She inhaled deeply and pulled out the contents.

Just two items. A folded piece of paper surrounding a check. She barely glanced at the check. He was just paying the last of the agreed-upon room and board. She looked at the paper, though.

"Raising a family gets expensive," he'd written. "What with a child and a dog and a cat."

Her chest tightened and her knees felt shaky.

She sank down on the foot of his bed, glanced at the check he'd made payable to her and went stock-still.

The exorbitant amount jumped out at her. She could have opened an entire orphanage with the amount he'd written.

Her fingers closed jerkily around the check. "Oh, Mason." How could he try to give her this when all she wanted was him?

Plato padded into the room, carrying Woof in his gentle jaws. He smoothly leapt up onto the mattress beside her and deposited the kitten in her lap.

Courtney lowered her head over them both and cried.

Chapter Thirteen

"I'm sorry, sir, but you can't take that on the plane with you."

Mason gritted his teeth.

It had taken him all night just to get from Weaver to the airport in Cheyenne. Now if he could only get *on* the damn plane.

He eyed the security agent and held up the thick, black plastic bag that contained his cast. It was cut into several separate pieces, but they were still bulky. "It's a fiberglass cast," he said for about the hundredth time. "Run it through your machines or whatever you need to do, but it's going on the plane with me. I'm not having it crushed in a pile of luggage." He wished to hell that he'd just waited long enough to arrange a private flight through HW. But no, he'd been in too much of a damn hurry to get away from Weaver.

"I'm sorry," the kid was saying. His gaze was glued

to Mason's face, and his Adam's apple bobbled in his throat as if he was afraid that Mason was going to resort to violence.

He wasn't. He just wanted—needed—to get on the plane and get home so he could get back to work. Get back to what he was good at.

There'd be no Plato. No Woof.

No Courtney.

He'd left the cat behind, because it was the sensible thing to do. He couldn't take care of a kitten, even though it would grow into an independent cat. For that matter, he couldn't take care of a cat.

Not with his lifestyle.

He realized the kid was eyeing him with increasing alarm. The last thing Mason wanted was to get hauled into the security office because he looked like a suspicious traveler. "Fine." He grabbed his duffel bag off the conveyor belt, and with the unwieldy bag in his other hand, he moved out of the security line.

He could feel anxious eyes boring into his back as he made his way back through the airport.

It still felt strange walking with two shoes and no cast after two months, and as much as he hated to admit it, his leg was aching and tired. He could have sat in any number of chairs that he passed, but he was well aware that two uniformed officers were following him at a not-very-discreet distance.

Being irritated with them didn't accomplish anything. They were just trying to do their job the best they could, too, and he wasn't exactly the picture of a harmless tourist. Not with his face. Not with his jeans that had one leg split up to the thigh. And definitely not with the bulky bag he refused to surrender.

He finally exited the terminal and climbed into the

first taxi that came available. He asked for the closest hotel, then leaned his head back against the seat and sighed. He'd regroup and arrange a charter, once and for all.

"Going home for the holiday?" the taxi driver asked.

"Something like that." It took no effort at all to imagine the get-together that the Clays would put on for Thanksgiving. It would be crowded and noisy, full of opinions and laughter and chasing children and crying babies.

He pinched his eyes closed. Courtney had been home from the hospital for several hours.

She'd seen the check he'd left.

He rubbed his hand against the hollow in his chest and looked down at the garbage bag beside him.

He still didn't know what stupid sentimentality had made him keep the thing. Just because it had been scribbled on by a bunch of people? But when Rodney had started to pitch the pieces he'd cut away into the trash, Mason had stopped him. And instead, the technician had dropped them in the black bag. When he was finished, he'd tied the top closed and handed it to Mason. "Sentimental value, eh?"

Mason had just taken the bag and, wearing a paper bootie on his bare foot, he'd left the hospital before he could find Courtney and tell her to hell with plans....

And once he'd started moving, he hadn't let himself stop. He'd tied up his loose ends at the house, threw the ball for Plato a few times and let Woof claw her way all around his shoulders. And when midnight struck with no word from Courtney, he'd called the only cab in town and paid him a fortune to drive him to Cheyenne.

If he had just pitched the bag in the trash at airport security, he could have been on his way back to

Connecticut, once and for all. And from there, it would have been a quick matter to get Cole to assign him to a security detail—anything, even if it meant piggybacking on someone else's case—as long as it was out of the U.S. of A., the country of Courtney Clay.

The cab pulled up in front of the airport hotel. "Need help with your stuff?"

Mason's lips twisted. "I got it." He paid the fare, added a tip and climbed out.

In minutes, he was inside a bland, sterile hotel room.

He dropped his stuff on the bed and moved across to the window, pulling open the drapes to display the grand view of a crowded parking lot. The sight of a woman with long blond hair crossing between the cars jolted him.

But after that first glance, he looked away. Not Courtney.

She wouldn't know he was in Cheyenne for one thing. And for another, even if she did, she wouldn't follow him. Why would she?

He turned on the television to drown out the sound of his own thoughts and flipped open the refrigerated minibar to find something to drown out the rest.

He extracted a beer. "It's five o'clock somewhere," he muttered and popped it open, then threw himself down on the hard mattress. He set the beer aside and dragged the bag close enough to untie it.

He hadn't looked inside it after Rodney had dropped the pieces in the bag. Now, he slowly pulled the fiberglass pieces out, fitting them together like a puzzle.

He wanted the part that had been around his ankle.

The part that Courtney had signed that he hadn't been able to read, not even when he'd tried using a hand mirror one night when she'd been at work.

The part, he realized after he'd pulled all of the pieces out of the bag, that Rodney had cut neatly in half.

Sighing, he tried to ignore the shaking of his hands as he fit the two pieces together.

And then all he could do was stare at the sawed edges of her writing.

"Even the best plans can change," she'd written, "when you find something better than 37892."

He closed his eyes as pain—worse than anything he'd ever felt—ripped through him. Pain of his own making because he was too damn stubborn to see what had been in front of him all along.

And then, doing the smartest thing he'd done in the past twelve hours, he pulled out his phone and he called Cole.

Courtney saw the truck as soon as she rounded the corner on her street. It was parked directly in front of her house.

She had a stitch in her side from running too hard and too fast for too long. But no amount of running had been able to get the pain out of her chest.

Shaking her head at her own foolishness, she pressed a hand to her side and slowed to a walk as she finished crossing the distance to her house.

She gave the truck—a delivery truck, she realized as she got closer—another glance as she passed it. One of her neighbors must have purchased some building supplies from one of the big-box places in Gillette. Two men were unloading a shrink-wrapped pallet onto the sidewalk, and they gave her a nod. "Afternoon."

"Afternoon." She turned up the walkway, which she'd shoveled clean of snow that morning when she couldn't sleep, and wondered how long it would be before she would be able to sleep again.

She supposed that depended on how long it took a broken heart to heal.

She pulled off her gloves and went up the front steps, trying hard not to look at the wooden ramp that was still in place.

She'd call Ryan before she went to work and ask him to pull it off. The one over the back steps, too. The sooner she got rid of the evidence that Mason had been there, the sooner she could start pretending she could forget him.

She walked in through the front door and stopped dead in her tracks.

Mason was sitting at her computer desk, Plato and Woof lying by his feet. "You ran longer than I expected," he greeted.

She actually felt dizzy.

"What are you doing here?" Her voice sounded breathless, and her pride hoped he'd attribute it to her running.

Her heart, though, didn't care about anything except the sight of him. He was clean shaven and he'd had a haircut. The thick hair that had grown unruly and over-long was now short and brushed away from his hard-hewn face. He was wearing a white button-down shirt tucked into black jeans. Jeans that hadn't been cut up to accommodate a cast. "You, uh, you left," she reminded him needlessly.

"Yeah. You going to close the door, or do you plan on kicking me out of it?"

She realized that the door was still open behind her, and she pushed it closed against the cold air. "That depends on whether you deserve to be kicked out."

His brows pulled together in a frown. "It's not about what I deserve."

She crossed her arms tightly, hoping to hold in her shaking. "Mason, what are you doing here?"

He glanced at her computer. "It was off," he murmured. "I noticed it before but didn't take note of it until it was too late."

"So?" She lifted her chin a notch. "Turning it off saves electricity."

"You quit looking at the cryobank's website," he said. "The last time you looked at it was the day Plato found Woof."

It was better that her hackles rose, because she could concentrate on them, rather than the aching inside her. "More spying?"

He didn't deny it. "Why?

She swallowed the knot in her throat and looked at him, not answering.

"What did you find that's better than 37892?" His pale green eyes stared back at her. "I finally read what you wrote on my cast."

"It's not like it was a secret," she reminded him. "It's been there for the past week!"

"Yeah, well, for the past week, I couldn't *see* behind my ankle, which is pretty much where you wrote it."

"Don't act irritated with me," she retorted. "If you wanted to know what it said, you could have asked anyone. Even me."

His lips thinned. "I didn't come here to argue about things that don't even matter."

She took an involuntary step forward. "Then what *are* you here for?"

"For you." His answer was quiet. Simple.

And it stopped her in her tracks.

She trembled harder than ever, afraid to let herself believe he could possibly mean what her heart was begging him to say. "Why? Because you feel badly now that you know I've changed my mind about using the cryobank? You can have your check back, by the way." She gestured with one arm, only to quickly rewrap it around herself. "It's in that envelope on the table. I was going to mail it back to you this afternoon."

"If I hadn't wanted you to have it, I wouldn't have left it."

She forced her chin up. "And as you now realize, I don't *need* it. I can support myself," she reminded him, less tartly than she would have preferred. "I can even afford to take care of Plato and Woof—" she waved her hand toward the two animals, who were watching their exchange "—since you abandoned her, too."

His lips tightened. "Would you rather have had me take her back to an apartment that I'm never at? Break Plato's heart?" He shook his head and clawed his fingers through his hair. "This is not going how I planned."

"Well." Her jaws felt clenched together. "Plans change, don't they?"

Her blood pounded heavily inside her head when he started crossing the room toward her. He didn't stop until he was only a few feet away. "What'd you find that's better than 37892?"

His eyes were searching hers, seeming to look straight through to her soul. And the only thing she had left was the truth. "Not what." Her voice sounded raw. *"Who."*

His scar was standing out whitely. "You want my baby."

She blinked hard, but the tears burning behind her eyes wouldn't go away. "I want everything," she whispered. "You. Our baby. The whole deal. But the only thing I *need* is you."

"You can do better than me." His voice turned husky.

She shook her head. "No. I really don't think so." She swiped a tear from her cheek. Took a bracing breath. "But I don't want you here unless this is where *you* want to be. I don't need you throwing yourself in front of this particular bus to save me from being hurt, Mason. I can take most anything but that."

He closed his eyes for a long moment. When he opened them again, they were bloodshot. And damp. "Then save me."

She pressed her hands to her chest. "Oh, Mason."

"There aren't many things I've loved in my life," he said gruffly. "And everything that I had, I've lost. It's always been safer not to let myself feel anything. And then I met you. Doling out kisses for five bucks a pop. I don't want to end up like that guy at the hospital, old and alone because he didn't stop to make time for what mattered. *You* are what matters, Courtney. If I'm not too late."

She couldn't bear another moment.

She reached out and wrapped her arms around him, stretching her cheek up toward his. "You haven't lost me."

His arms came around her, nearly lifting her off her feet. "Not yet."

"Not ever," she vowed. She pulled back to look into his eyes. "That's the thing about us Clays." She smiled shakily. "We're stubborn. And when we find what we want, we don't budge."

He lowered his forehead to hers. She could feel the charge of his heart against hers. "It might take some stubbornness. I'm told I'm thickheaded."

She gave a tearful laugh. "Well, you are. And I love you anyway."

His arms tightened around her. "I'm thirteen years older than you," he reminded her. "I'm not getting any younger. And my job isn't going to go away. I'll do what I can to stay in Weaver. Tristan's got some ideas about that—"

She caught his face in her hands. "See? Thickheaded. I love you, Mason. Just as you are. I couldn't care less how old—"

He covered her mouth with his. And when the words died on her lips and her knees had gone to gelatin, he let her up for air. "I'm not getting any younger," he repeated softly. "Which means I don't want to waste any time."

"I can't think straight when you kiss me like that," she complained.

His lips tilted crookedly. "I'll have to remember that. It might come in handy in the future."

Butterflies flew around inside her stomach. "Future?"

He grasped her ponytail and gently tugged her head back until her eyes met his. "I want you. For now. For always."

Her vision turned watery, all over again. "You promise?"

His expression went soft. His thumbs brushed over her wet cheeks. "I promise." He kissed her gently. Slowly. And so sweetly that if her heart hadn't already been his, it would have fallen into his hands right then and there. "I even brought proof."

"What's that?"

He pulled her hands from his hair and kissed her knuckles. Then he tugged her toward the front door and threw it open. Wholly bemused, she looked out into the yard.

The two men she'd seen before were still standing outside the delivery truck. Mason waved at them. "You can start," he called.

"Will do, Mr. Hyde." The first guy swept a knife over the pallet and lifted something off the top.

Her lips parted as she realized what it was.

A white picket fence panel.

Mason turned her toward him. "I love you, Courtney Clay. Will you take my picket fence and all that goes with it?"

"I will." She threw her arms around him and laughed through her tears. "For the rest of our lives, I will."

Epilogue

They were married in the candlelit living room of her parents' house on Christmas Eve.

Courtney wore a simple white gown with her hair pulled back in a ponytail and looked like his own personal angel. Mason wore a dark blue suit and managed not to pull off his silvery tie, even though he wanted to.

Plato was too dignified to wear a ring of flowers around his neck, though both Chloe and Shelby gave it their best efforts to keep it on him. He was also kept pretty occupied during the ceremony, corralling Woof so she wouldn't run up the gold-and-silver-decorated Christmas tree that filled part of the room.

The entire family was there, and Coleman Black, too, who'd stood up as Mason's best man.

It was crowded and cozy, and even though Mason had worried that Courtney was only going along with the small, quickly planned ceremony to keep him happy, all he had to do was look at the glowing face of his bride after they'd slid their rings on each other's fingers to know that their wedding had been everything she'd wanted it to be.

And she was everything he'd ever wanted.

"Come here." The vows were said and Sawyer and Rebecca were busy handing out flutes of sparkling champagne. Taking advantage of everyone's distraction, Mason tugged Courtney toward the French doors that opened onto the deck overlooking the back of the property.

Her palm slid against his, and she gave him a knowing look. "It's cold out there. How do you intend to keep me warm, Mr. Hyde?"

He nudged her through the door and wrapped his arm around her. "I have a few ways, Mrs. Hyde."

She shivered and snuggled close into his chest. Her hands slipped beneath his jacket and her sparkling eyes met his. "And I do love those ways," she admitted throatily. "Have I told you today how much I love you?"

Desire was ripping through him. But there would be time for that. Plenty of time. "Agreeing to wear this—" he grabbed her hand and kissed her finger where the narrow platinum wedding band rested "—tells me a lot."

Her smile softened. "Agreeing to wear this—" she returned, finding his hand with hers and rubbing the ring on his finger "—tells me everything." She leaned into him again. "I wonder how quickly we can escape our own wedding without looking rude," she whispered.

He laughed softly. This woman was either going to keep him young or make him die a very old, very satisfied man. He took off his jacket and slid it around her shoulders before pulling a ring-sized box out of the lapel pocket. "I wanted to give you this."

Her lips parted. "Mason, I don't have my gift for you. It's back at the house. I should wait until you can open yours, too."

He just shook his head. "This *is* a gift for me. Open it now."

She nudged her finger against the thin, white satin ribbon that surrounded the box. "Is this by any chance an engagement ring?"

The box *had* contained the diamond ring she'd insisted she didn't need, telling him the only ring she cared about was a wedding band. And while he believed her, he still wanted her to have the diamonds that went with it.

He wanted her to have everything.

Which was why the ring was not actually in the box but in his pocket to give to her later.

"Open it and see."

"You're spoiling me," she told him wryly. But she pressed open the box anyway and gave a surprised "oh." She laughed a little, pulling out one of the familiar condom wrappers that he'd tucked inside in place of the ring. "It's empty." She pulled out another. She lifted her eyebrows. "They're *all* empty."

"I know." He lowered his head to whisper in her ear. "The only gift you need to give me now is that baby."

Her lips parted. She pulled back her head to stare into his eyes. "Are you sure?"

"Never more."

Her eyes glowed. She tucked the wrappers back in the box, closed it, then slid it back into its place inside his jacket. "Poor 37892. He never even knew he didn't have a chance against you."

"Good grief." Squire's distinctive drawl came through the door, making them both jump. "What're you doing out in the cold? Gonna turn into Popsicles if you're not careful." He jerked his head. "Get in here and drink some champagne so *I* can have some cake." Then he grinned and turned back into the house.

Courtney and Mason looked at each other.

He smiled. She giggled.

And hand in hand, they went inside.

* * * * *

A sneaky peek at next month...

Cherish™

ROMANCE TO MELT THE HEART EVERY TIME

My wish list for next month's titles...

In stores from 18th May 2012:

❏ A Cold Creek Reunion – RaeAnne Thayne

& A Weaver Proposal – Allison Leigh

❏ The Nanny and the Boss's Twins & The Nanny
  Who Kissed Her Boss – Barbara McMahon

In stores from 1st June 2012:

❏ The SEAL's Promise & The Marshal's Prize
  – Rebecca Winters

❏ Mendoza's Return – Susan Crosby

& Fortune's Just Desserts – Marie Ferrarella

Available at WHSmith, Tesco, Asda, Eason, Amazon and Apple

Just can't wait?

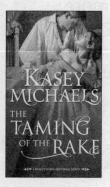
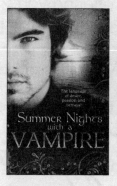
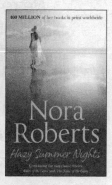